THIMBLES

Thimbles
by
Paul Anthony

The right of Paul Anthony to be identified as the author of this
work has been asserted by him in accordance with
the Copyright, Designs and Patents Act of 1988

~

This is a work of fiction.
The names, characters, businesses, places, events, and
incidents contained in this novel are either the products of the
author's imagination or used in a fictitious manner.
Any resemblance to actual persons, living or dead,
or actual events is purely coincidental.

~

First Published 2020
Copyright © Paul Anthony
All Rights Reserved.
Cover Image © Margaret Scougal & Linda Moth

Published by
Paul Anthony Associates UK
http://paul-anthony.org/

By the same author

~

The 'Boyd' Crime Thriller Series…
The Fragile Peace
Bushfire
The Legacy of the Ninth
Bell, Book and Candle
Threat Level One
White Eagle
The Sultan and the Crucifix
Thimbles

~

The 'Davies King' Crime Thriller Series…
The Conchenta Conundrum.
Moonlight Shadows
Behead the Serpent
Breakwater

~

In the Thriller and Suspense Series…
Nebulous
Septimus

~

In Autobiography and nonfiction…
Strike! Strike! Strike!
Scougal
Authorship Demystified

~

In Poetry and Anthologies…
Sunset
Scribbles with Chocolate
Uncuffed
Coptales
Chiari Warriors

~

In Children's book (with Meg Johnston) …
Monsters, Gnomes and Fairies (In My Garden)

~

To Margaret - Thank you, for never doubting me.
To Paul, Barrie and Vikki - You only get one chance at life.
Live it well, live it in peace, and live it with love for one another.
To my special friends - Thank you, you are special.
~

With thanks to Margaret Scougal, Pauline Livingstone and Pat Henderson for editing, consulting and advising on my various works over many years….
Paul Anthony

~

Dedicated to the memory of
ORPHEUS

Thimbles.

A thimble is a small, hard, pitted cup worn to protect the finger that pushes a needle in the craft of sewing. They are invariably made of metal and, euphemistically, are 'as hard as nails.'

Usually, thimbles with a closed top are used by dressmakers and those who join, fasten, or repair material by making stitches with a needle and thread or a sewing machine. However, special thimbles with an opening at the end are used by tailors since this allows them to manipulate the cloth more easily.

When a thimble pushes a needle to the extremity, regularly, and with bitter unrivalled determination, the job gets done much quicker than you might otherwise imagine.

However, one should always be wary of a callous thimble that exerts pressure to the limit. A rogue thimble, for example, can be aggressive, cold-hearted, lethally dangerous to mankind, and have no equal.

If the needle is the 'spy' who complies with instructions from the leader, then the thimble is the one who pushes the needle and is, therefore, the 'Spymaster'.

Herewith the story of 'Thimbles'… The Spymasters…

The Good, the Bad, and the Rogue…

… Paul Anthony

INTRODUCTION

The grey Mercedes moved into the fast lane and continued to gain speed as the vehicle climbed a long, enduring ascent and the southbound carriageway of the motorway became clogged with heavy goods vehicles in the other two lanes.

Gradually, traffic reached the summit and headed downhill as the road ahead meandered slightly and a panoramic view of the Midlands lay before them. Soft music played from the Mercedes radio as the needle on the speedometer edged towards one hundred miles per hour and the driver gently tapped his fingers on the leather-bound steering wheel.

He checked his mirror, knew he enjoyed diplomatic immunity from all road traffic offences and criminality in the UK and squeezed the accelerator pedal further to the floor.

Oh yes, he thought. Any such misdemeanour might result in me being expelled from the country, but we'll cross that bridge when we come to it.

Stretching his left arm out, he turned the volume up as a thirty-two-tonne articulated wagon edged into the fast lane partially blocking the Mercedes. There was a flash of headlights and a blast on the Mercedes horn as the car driver ploughed on relentlessly.

The wagon driver moved further into the fast lane causing the driver of the Mercedes to stand on the brakes and swerve violently into a crash barrier to avoid contact with the vehicle.

Crash!

There was the scrape of metal upon concrete when the front offside wing of the Mercedes collided harshly with the crash barrier in the central reservation. The articulated wagon continued unabated down the fast lane of the carriageway; its driver unaware of the motorway mayhem developing to its rear.

The Mercedes driver wrestled with the steering wheel when the car rebounded from the central carriageway and spun dangerously into the southbound carriageway.

As the driver of the Mercedes looked to his offside, a white Transit van careering down the middle lane ploughed into the offside of the grey car and spun it around again. A look of total horror filled the Mercedes driver's face when he whirled around the carriageway having completely lost control. Another wagon, this time in the slow lane, smashed into the rear of the Mercedes causing it to roll over onto its roof.

Like a rag doll, the driver lay upside down hanging from his seat belt as the Mercedes rolled over and over in the centre of the southbound carriageway.

Eventually, the grey Mercedes came to a standstill. Steam blew from its engine block, the windscreen and rear window exploded into a thousand pieces of tiny glass, and the bodywork mangled into a twisted, bizarre ruin.

Finally, when an austere silence dominated the scene, the rear diplomatic number plate clattered to the ground. A loose screw that had once secured the plate bounced on the tarmac and rolled relentlessly towards the hard shoulder.

In the aftermath of the tragedy, police attended the scene, closed the motorway, and began an investigation into the fatal collision. Hours later, alerted by the senior officer on site, an unmarked helicopter landed unceremoniously on the carriageway and several plainclothes personnel made their way to the rear of a police vehicle where the body of the Mercedes driver had been laid out.

'Mikhail Korobov,' replied Antonia Harston-Browne, the red-headed lady from MI5, Britain's Security Service.

'You know him then?' remarked Boyd, Commander of the nation's Special Crime Unit.

'Not in a casual or private capacity,' replied Antonia. 'However, I have endured a long-held interest in the deceased.'

'Why?' questioned Boyd.

'Because he works out of the Russian Embassy and he has long been suspected of being a member of the Russian Intelligence Service.'

'His brief?' quizzed Boyd.

'How long have you got?' queried Antonia.

'I need to know,' replied Boyd. 'Everything!'

'Mikhail Korobov is the son of Sergei Korobov. Sergei is the Head of the Second Chief Directorate in Moscow,' explained Antonia. 'The department is responsible for counter-intelligence and it's where we believe the deceased initially began his career in the Russian Intelligence Service.'

'Yes, I know what they do. Go on.'

'Mikhail was eventually transferred to the First Chief Directorate where he monitored foreigners and consular officials in Leningrad. He then progressed to Moscow for further training at the Yuri Andropov Red Banner Institute. He has reappeared in various parts of Europe as an administrator, a translator, and a trade envoy.'

'Tell me he got four GCSEs at school and did all his homework on time,' chuckled Boyd.

'Better than that, Boyd,' revealed Antonia. 'As a youngster, he went to Volgograd State University and took part in the 'Capture the Flag' competition at school.'

'What the hell is that?' queried Boyd.

'A computer hacking competition for kids from all over Russia.'

'You're joking?'

'I wish I was,' sighed Antonia.

'Our girls still play netball at school. How far behind are we?'

'Miles ahead if you want to bring up kids to enjoy life and be healthy, happy, and social. A hundred miles behind if you want them to be cybertechnology experts in their early teens.'

'Choices!' exclaimed Boyd, shaking his head.

'Tea or coffee?' replied the redhead with an enquiring smile.

'Computer hacking!' remarked Boyd. 'How advanced are they at that State University you mentioned?'

'One school team defends its computer server whilst another school team attacks it. When the defenders deny all the competitors, they attack the other servers and dominate the computer world, the internet, social media, and every online thing you can imagine that those servers look after. Of course, it's only a school project so that world is fairly small.'

'But if you transferred that teaching to the real world?' suggested Boyd.

'You'd potentially end up with a global cyberwar and total carnage,' admitted Antonia.

'And an ability to destroy the western world without ever firing a bullet or launching a missile in anger?' ventured Boyd.

'Precisely!' remarked Antonia, her red hair swishing across the shoulders of her elegant trouser suit and slim body. 'Mikhail was one of the most important spies ever to work in the United Kingdom.'

'Well, you can end that investigation,' suggested Boyd. 'Case closed!'

'Possibly,' remarked Antonia. 'I'm the case officer for the individual in question. The file will remain open until I close it.'

'How long will that take?' probed Boyd.

'Who knows?' replied Antonia. 'We'll need to inform the Russian Embassy. There'll be a coroner's court, diplomatic questions and answers at ministerial level, who knows? A couple of years at least, probably longer. You see, in the world of espionage, it's necessary to acknowledge the capability of your enemies and Mikhail Korobov was one of their best. Sadly, he died in a truly tragic manner. Practically, and politically, the Russians might take the stance that we deliberately killed him and are publicly looking for the driver of a heavy goods vehicle that never existed. Someone sitting around that oval walnut table in the Kremlin might construe that it wasn't a real road accident and that we – the Brits – deliberately murdered one of theirs. Historically, it's what they've done to some of our people in MI6. They'll think we've retaliated and made it look that way. If that's what they conclude, it might just agitate a retaliation of some kind from them. Anything might happen.'

'And that might depend on whether the man in charge is popular or unpopular at the present moment,' suggested Boyd. 'Politicians sometimes react to an apparent attack in the hope that they might get more votes than doing nothing. I suppose such matters are open to interpretation and how the State might twist the actuality of the event to their advantage.'

'We call it 'spin',' replied Antonia. 'I think 'advanced spin' might be a better term.'

'Enforced delusion?' queried Boyd.

'Possibly!'

'It's the espionage world that the public does not recognise and has no practical understanding of,' suggested Boyd.

'A good way to put it,' responded Antonia.

'Time will tell,' suggested Boyd. 'We need to search the body and the car before we formally recover the corpse and inform the Russian Embassy. I'll do all the paperwork. You know the protocols. Can we activate them before the media learn about the helicopter and arrive in a minibus?'

'Yes, agreed! Let's activate the agreed protocols!'

With veiled respect for tragedy and death and a discreet admission of intelligence gathering, the team began their mission.

Just a collision on a motorway. They happen every day.

But tomorrow. What of tomorrow?

~

1

Tomorrow
Carlisle, Cumbria

Drumsticks announced the beginning of the torchlight procession.

Initially, there was just one lone drummer but as the seconds ticked by and the sky darkened to leave twilight behind, another drummer joined in, and then another. Within minutes, perfect timing saw the entire Regimental Corps of Drummers dominate proceedings as the ensemble set off at the head of the parade.

Line abreast and row by row the drummers marched down the street to the cheers and applause of the flag-waving public.

As the Corps moved off the rest of the procession filtered in behind and into their allotted positions. It would take two hours before the last of the entertainers reached the starting line. It was going to be a long night for all concerned.

The city's roads were clogged with floats, marching bands, school choirs, and dancing troupes as the parade meandered its noisy way through the historic streets of Carlisle. The drummers led a band of buglers who were followed by dancing girls and male acrobats, poi spinners and jugglers, and baton twirling entertainers bringing joy and laughter to the huge crowd lining the streets.

Police, paramedics, and ambulance service personnel were present in appropriate numbers as the hot dog stands, pop-up bars, and takeaways vied for business on one of the busiest nights of the year.

The parade was escorted on either side by torchbearers who lit up the sky as twilight faltered and night eventually enveloped proceedings. As if by magic, a succession of bare-chested fire-eating performers jumped from the rear of one of the floats and began an awe-inspiring demonstration that seized the audience and held their attention.

Meanwhile, the drummers kept on drumming and the buglers continued to bugle in a tumultuous frenzy of fun and frivolity.

'Best night we've had for years,' remarked Boyd above the noise.

'One of the few nights you've been home long enough to enjoy,' laughed Meg.

'Yes, but I wanted to do well in my career for us,' countered Boyd. 'It wasn't easy being away so much.'

'You're the Head of the Special Crime Unit now, Chief Superintendent,' chuckled Meg. 'Or should I say Commander? 'It's all you ever wanted, isn't it?'

'Of course!' revelled Boyd as he swirled his wife around before picking up their two children and attempting to smother them all with love and affection. 'I'm walking on water according to the Commissioner. I went from Chief Inspector to Chief Superintendent in six weeks and it was all because I netted a corrupt Chief Constable, a Russian spy, and a crazy terrorist.'

'And not for the first time,' laughed Meg. 'Enjoy it! You deserve it.'

'Ice cream, Izzy, James?' suggested Boyd.

'Yes,' they yelled.

'Me too,' shouted Meg. 'With chocolate, please. I mean, you can afford to treat us now you know.'

'Well, only if you do well at school,' frowned Boyd to the children.

'We will, we will,' they promised.

'Give them a chance, Billy,' remarked Meg. 'They've only just started, it's their first year or have you forgotten that already.'

'Who me?' joked Boyd. 'I never forget things.'

'Then don't forget the chocolate flakes in the ice-cream,' scolded Meg with a smile. 'Spend some of that money you've made.'

Heading towards an ice-cream stall, Boyd - tall, athletic, with broad shoulders and a finely-honed body to match - disappeared into the throng as the procession gradually meandered through the city centre accompanied by the skirl of the pipes, the drums pounding, and a hundred fiery torches lighting up the sky.

Elsewhere, but close by, John Dillion was the lone policeman who had been assigned to patrol the back streets, lanes and byways in the environs of the colourful parade. Annoyed that he could hear the music and sense the atmosphere but could not see the performers and be part of the action, he shone his torch on the wall of the building opposite and began to make pointless circles of light on the façade.

Bored, thought John Six months service to my credit and Sergeant Riley gives me a dead-end job. Everyone else gets the front street where the disorder is likely to break out when the drink begins to flow, but I get dozens of streets filled with parked cars and closed shops. What did I do to deserve this? This is my second night shift and They've put me in the same place again. How will I ever learn anything if they keep doing this to me?

Twenty years of age, six feet tall, as a thin as a rake and sporting a thin whispered growth of hair on the end of his chin, Police Constable John Dillon turned into the municipal car park and made his way through row upon row of parked cars towards the lane that ran parallel to the main street and the torchlight procession. Above the roofs of the shops, an orange glow from the torches began to battle for supremacy with the dark of the night.

Reaching the entrance to a long lane, Dillon paused, listened to the music, and settled his back against the wall. Casually, he delved into his trouser pocket and withdrew a tube of sweets.

The eerie silence in the lane was broken only by the slick unwrapping of a sweet paper before Dillon began chewing a toffee.

I wonder what's happening on the front street, thought John.

At the parade on the front street, Boyd returned with huge ice-creams and shouted, 'Here we go!'

'You remembered,' replied Meg. 'Chocolate too.'

'Of course, one for you, one for Izzy, and one for James.'

The twins seized upon their treats and relished the cold ice-cream when it trickled across their lips.

'What's that smell?' queried Meg.

'Paraffin!' replied Boyd. 'It's what the fire-eaters use in their act.'

'Really,' reacted Meg with a look of surprise. 'I thought it was capsules that they broke in their mouth.'

'No, definitely not,' replied Boyd. 'Pure Paraffin. Look out!'

One of the fire-eaters momentarily lost control and watched his fiery torch crash onto the highway.

'Missed me by a mile,' laughed Meg. 'Come on! Let's walk along the pavement and keep up with the fire-eaters. They are marvellous.'

Decision made, Billy Boyd – newly appointed Commander of the nation's Special Crime Unit – guided his family along the pavement as they enjoyed a rare evening in each other's company.

'More paraffin?' ventured Boyd. 'It's just a strong brandy really.'

'I'll stick with the ice-cream,' chuckled Meg. 'The smell of paraffin is more than enough, thank you and, by the way, drinking that stuff is likely to destroy your innards. They say it can be good for dry skin if you don't use too much but it's dangerous and poisonous.'

'Yes, I know,' laughed Boyd.

'It will leak out of your bum if you drink it,' continued Meg, and may well cause you to die.'

'Thank you, Nurse Boyd. I'll remember that.'

'It's Sister Boyd! Stick to your ice-cream, Billy.'

Elsewhere, the self-styled paraffin man was at work.

A shadowy figure splashed a trace of paraffin onto his hands and then smoothed the liquid into the dry skin before raising his fingers to his nose and sniffing the paraffin to his satisfaction. Breathing heavily now, virtually addicted to the substance, he gradually splashed the contents of the paraffin tin until it covered the front door of an old wooden building.

The dark clothed individual stood back, listened, set down the tin, and studied the sky above. A trillion stars twinkled silently down on the solitary figure standing in the grounds of an ageing bowling club.

Distanced from the torchlight procession, the man heard only the faint sound of faraway traffic and a soft unexpected rattle when he reached into his pocket to feel for a box of matches. Lost in his mind, detached from the city centre entertainment and his fellow man, he shuddered when the rattle of the matches disturbed the quietness of the occasion and alarmed him.

Stepping back quickly into the bushes, he squatted down in the foliage and listened to the thunder of his heartbeat.

A rocket exploded in the sky and a score of coloured remnants fell gradually to the ground. Someone somewhere was adding fireworks to the occasion, and he was loving it.

The paraffin man exhaled and crept towards the closest window. Peering inside the bowling club, he saw only his reflection before his eyes eventually focused on a row of amusement machines lined up next to a bar. Squinting, he moved on splashing more paraffin on the wooden decking that encircled the building.

Nightfall hid the dark circles of despair surrounding his eyes. Almost bizarre, weird to those who might have seen him in the flesh, it was as if these circles were a heavenly halo sent to glorify his addiction and inspire him onwards. With a sallow, sickly complexion, he sported dry skin that wrinkled his forehead and gave him the appearance of being in his fifties. Yet he was slightly over twenty years of age. He scratched his crotch in an agitated manner before removing a pewter hipflask from his back pocket and taking a swig of cheap vodka.

Deep inside his tormented mind, the paraffin man watched the dying embers of the rocket fall towards the ground. Anger invaded his soul when the last ember extinguished itself and left only the black of the sky where the incendiary had been. Nothing followed. It was over. It was as if he had lost part of himself in a dark void that moments earlier had been ablaze with fire.

There was a slight glug in the hipflask when he knocked back another mouthful and began rubbing himself in the groin. Fire! It was his everything, his reason for living, his best friend, secret lover, and closet supporter.

Unscrewing the top of the tin, he peered in and checked the level of the fuel he had concocted. It was a mix of petrol, paraffin and white spirit. The smell would repel many. To the paraffin man, it was the scent of roses.

Pocketing the hipflask, he donned a pair of leather gloves and finally removed the box of matches. He stood back and struck a match. It was his time, his moment, his reason for being. He was the undisputed ruler of his very own secret kingdom.

With an unwavering glare, he threw the lighted match onto the paraffin and followed its flight.

There was a gratuitous flash when the paraffin mixture exploded allowing the flames to reach out and burn the decking and front entrance of Carlisle's Bowling Club.

Sexually excited now, the fireraiser stepped back into the bushes once more. Rivetted by the growing inferno before him, he embraced it, followed its short violent destructive path, and watched as the flames rushed along the length of the decking lighting the paraffin on its long journey around the building.

Within minutes, the old wooden building was well alight. Unzipping himself, the fireraiser reached inside his jeans and achieved a sexual climax that he had not imagined was possible. The flames seemed to reach out towards him, extended, burnt, destroyed, and sat conspiratorially beneath a curl of black smoke that spiralled upwards into the heavens.

Sweating from the flames and heat, spent by his physical exertion, but still totally absorbed by the hell hole he had created, the mentally disturbed paraffin man gulped down another mouthful of vodka and deliberately threw the empty paraffin tin onto the blaze.

Meanwhile, in the back streets of the city centre, Police Constable 2257 John Dillon was quietly muttering, 'Five weeks of lone patrol, unsupervised, my second night shift, and I find myself in a dead-end street. I'm virtually a veteran by now.' He chuckled as he scuffed his boots on the edge of the pavement and continued, 'In a world of advanced technologies that activate police response to criminality why am I still walking on an old-fashioned beat? I'm a response cop, for God's sake.'

A burglar alarm sounded. Its shrill screaming voice penetrated the policeman's mind and shook him into reality.

Flashing his torch, he scanned the nearest roof before sweeping the full length of the dark lane ahead of him. Nothing.

'2257!' burst from his radio. 'Alarm sounding Maxwell's jewellers, Botchergate! Attend?'

'Roger! Wilco!' fumbled Dillon. 'I'm there I think.'

'All units, south city central attend Maxwell's jewellers, Botchergate,' from Control.

'Will do,' radioed Dillon as he broke into a run down the lane.

'What do you mean, you're there?' radioed Control. 'Sitrep?'

Dillon fought to control the adrenalin running through his body before steadying himself and replying, 'I'm in back Botchergate Lane checking the property. Stand by!'

'First unit to the front, second unit to the rear to assist 2257,' ordered a voice on Dillon's radio.

On the front street, at the parade, a flurry of uniformed police officers ran past Boyd and his family as the last of the ice-cream trickled down a throat and an acrobat began doing backward somersaults to the applause of the crowd.

'Where are they going?' asked Meg.

'I'll be back in a minute,' replied Boyd.

'Billy!' chided Meg as Boyd set off following the uniforms as they attended Maxwell's burglar alarm. 'Billy! For God's sake, you're off duty! You don't need to get involved.'

A hundred yards along the street, the first responders shone their torches into the jeweller's shop to see a pair of legs dangling from the ceiling.

Simultaneously, at the rear of Maxwell's, John Dillon flashed his torch onto the roof and saw the top half of a darkly clothed male who was struggling to get out of the premises.

Or was he struggling to get into the building, thought Dillon? He's neither in nor out.

There was the swift clatter of a jemmy hitting the ground when the burglar realised he was in the policeman's torch beam and the alarm was sounding louder than anything he had ever heard in his life. Kicking his legs, pushing upwards from the rooftop, the burglar began his escape bid.

Boyd arrived at the front of Maxwell's shop and flashed his warrant card with the words, 'Police! Boyd! Special Crime Unit. What's going on?'

An officer turned, paid brief attention to Boyd's credentials, and replied, 'You tell me. Is he dropping in or on his way out?'

Pushing himself forward, Boyd saw a pair of legs waggling from the ceiling of the building as the alarm continued to scream and the Corps of Drummers pounded their way down the street followed closely by three tumbling acrobats, a pipe band, a dozen fire-eaters, a hundred ice-creams, a score of candy floss, and a two-mile stretch of floats.

Some two miles away, a key turned in a lock and the paraffin man slunk into his one-bedroomed apartment. Throwing his gloves to the floor, he unwound a thick grey scarf from his neck, disowned a dark blue anorak, and removed the hip flask from his jeans pocket. He took a long swig and finished the bottle before flopping onto an old leather armchair.

Checking his mobile 'phone, the paraffin man selected an icon and sat back. On the screen, a video he had taken of the fire at the bowling club began its five-minute journey before stalling at the end. A finger tapped the screen and the video started again. It was as if the paraffin man had never left the scene of the fire. His mind was still there, settled into the action of fire-raising. He was master of all he surveyed.

Arson, they called it. Or was it something else? Another academic term he had no knowledge or understanding of. Such terms were irrelevant to the insensitive paraffin man.

Tapping the screen on his mobile phone, he recapped the previous three fires he had been responsible for in the city of Carlisle. Later, when his battery was failing, he moved to an area above his bedside and touched the newspaper cut-outs that he had pinned to the wall. Each cutting portrayed a recent fire in the city, but one included an article with the headline, 'Unknown arsonist destroys six buildings in six months.'

But the paraffin man was not interested in such mediocrity. It was the flames he was reliant upon. Turmoil ripped open his brain, discarded the contents, and threw them into total disarray when his fingers reached out and touched the very images that he adored, worshipped, and idolised. It was his reason for living.

In the city centre, a unique opportunity arose when the fire dancers formed a static line to demonstrate their skills whilst simultaneously illuminating the inside of Maxwell's, the jeweller's shop.

'Stay there, guys. We can see now,' shouted Sergeant Riley. 'Just right there!' Then, turning to Boyd, he asked, 'Are you the one they call Boyd?'

'Yes! Why?'

'Oh, no particular reason,' replied Sergeant Riley. 'Other than the fact that I have a shift of young bobbies who idolise you. Did you know you are the subject of hero worship?'

'No, I think they need a dose of reality,' suggested Boyd. 'They watch too much television.'

'If you say so, Commander,' replied the Sergeant.

An astonished Boyd, and a hero-worshipping Sergeant, peered in to see that their torches had unwittingly lit up the interior of the jeweller's shop. A pair of legs were still dangling dangerously from the ceiling but the ceiling itself was sagging towards the floor where the weight of the intruder risked bringing the entire structure crashing to the ground. Here and there, a display case had been smashed and the contents rifled. Items of jewellery lay strewn across the floor, but they were surrounded by broken glass from the cabinets. Shards of glass lay next to diamonds, emeralds and rubies galore.

From the trouser pocket of the intruder, Boyd watched a bag of jewels fall to the ground.

Then he was gone. With a sudden heave, the burglar was out of sight with the last glimpse of ankle slightly ahead of part of the ceiling that tumbled to the floor and caused a minor explosion.

A cloud of dust and debris billowed towards the shop's front window and momentarily clouded the audience's view.

The burglar was out of the shop and onto the roof, in a kneeling position, as he weighed up his chances of survival.

John Dillon closed with the culprit and shone his torch into the crook's face.

Feet first, the shop-breaker leapt from the roof, propelled himself through the air, and landed on Dillon's chest. Then he rolled over and was up on his feet and sprinting down the lane like a man possessed with the policeman's torch rolling in the gutter and a beam of light flashing on a cat that had seen too much.

The cat leapt onto the nearest dustbin and then catapulted itself onto a low rooftop. The burglar did likewise at the end of the lane when he used his skill and strength to scale a perimeter wall.

Boyd led the charge down Botchergate, swung left into the back lane, and watched helplessly as the young crook bounded over the perimeter fence and headed into a built-up area often known as bedsit land.

Leaping over the fence, Boyd and Sergeant Riley chased the offender but all they could see was a pair of skinny ankles burning up the footpath at a colossal speed.

'He's not wearing socks!' yelled Boyd. 'No socks!'

'He's a bloody whippet!' screamed Sergeant Riley through gritted teeth.

Reaching a gable end, Boyd came to a standstill, collapsed into a nearby doorway, and filled his lungs with fresh air.

'Too old for this,' he spluttered as Sergeant Riley and three uniforms sprinted past him still in pursuit. 'It's a kid. He's a greyhound, and I'm past my best.'

Moments later, with Boyd still gasping for breath and the police still chasing the wanted man, John Dillon broke into a canter, reached Boyd, and asked, 'Which way did he go?'

'Who?' seethed Boyd. 'The Sergeant or the flash of lightning that no-one can catch?'

'The radio,' shouted PC Dillon. 'They want the Sergeant to attend another incident?'

'Such as?' enquired Boyd.

'The club at the bowling green has been burnt down. It's all happening tonight.'

Boyd felt the ice-cream in his stomach suddenly rebel. A wave of sickness threatened his very being when he stepped away, gulped for air, and reluctantly replied, 'It certainly is.'

At Heathrow airport, London, an Airbus A330 touched down. Air traffic controllers had monitored its arrival from Sheremetyevo International Airport, one of four airports serving Moscow.

The aircraft taxied to its stand and a short time later the passengers began to disembark. A man and a woman walked down the steps both carrying hand luggage. He was dressed casually in dark trousers and a jacket. She wore a dark blue trouser suit. They were both in their late twenties and neither stood out particularly when they strolled through the arrivals lounge towards Passport Control.

Twenty minutes later, the couple were in a taxi heading towards central London and by late evening they were in a hotel reception area engaged in the booking-in procedure as they waited for their room keys.

The hotel overlooked the prestigious area of Saint Katherine Docks Marina, near the Tower of London, and was teeming with tourists from across the globe. Many of the travellers had decided to relax in the lounge and have an evening meal as they viewed the activity in the marina.

A yacht cast away from her moorings and moved astern as another smaller vessel politely surrendered water and waited to fill the docking area.

Watching proceedings from a seat in the lounge, a lady of gathering years set down her cup, replenished it with tea from an attractive ceramic teapot and turned her head slightly towards the new arrivals standing at the reception desk waiting for their room keys. Casually, the grey-haired lady allowed her head to swivel slowly towards the revolving doors that controlled the entrance to the hotel. They were motionless, securing the downstairs of the building from the weather and other undesirables. The lady scoured the café and seated area close by and then reached into a shoulder bag which lay at her feet.

A hand reached out across the reception desk and received a folded paper wallet containing a plastic key. There was a polite handshake and a shuffle of feet as the newly arrived holidaymakers from Moscow moved away and took a lift to the sixth floor.

Removing a quilt from a bag, the lady took a needle and thread and began to quietly work the textile as she watched the couple take the lift carrying their hand luggage. The quilter's hand passed the needle and thread through all the layers of material before she brought the needle back up. Smiling, she expressed satisfaction that the padded material would be stronger and more resilient when she had finished the work.

Glancing at the lift, the electronic display showed that it had stopped on the sixth floor.

The lady with the quilt took a sip of tea, tidied her thin grey hair, and watched for those who might rush to take the next lift to follow the young couple. Then she turned her attention to the multi-layered textile in her lap. Traditionally composed of three layers of fibre, a woven cloth top, and a layer of wadding, the quilt was an intricate mix of colourful flowers with a unique border that was being decorated with a silver thread.

Taking a porcelain thimble from her bag, she put it on her finger before pushing a needle carrying a silver thread upon its journey. Alone, settled, ignoring the rest of the world, the maker of fine quilts pushed her favourite thimble, guided her silver thread, and watched the comings and goings of those who clustered in the reception area of the grand hotel.

Fifteen minutes later, the lady glanced up at the man who walked out of the lift and towards the revolving doors. She recognised him as the male of the recently arrived couple and, head down, she continued to tend her quilt. Only occasionally did she look up and capture the movements of those around her and of those who ventured in pursuit of the man who walked through the revolving doors into the street outside.

He stood for a moment, braced himself in the moonlight, and waited to see if anyone might follow him out of the hotel and collide with him. No-one followed. Lighting a cigarette, he inhaled deeply and deliberately turned to his left and right so that anyone in the area might see the end of his glowing cigarette. He began a walk around the environs of the building, and as he did so, he cupped the cigarette inside his hand.

Pausing at the corner, he allowed the cigarette to be seen again so that his presence could be detected by its glow and anyone following him would see where he was standing. Then he took a step around the corner, stopped with his back against the wall, and waited. No one followed. He stubbed the cigarette out on the wall and no longer carried the light that gave testimony to his presence. The man then casually moved on courting the shadows caused by the odd buttress of the building and its contemporary design. He moved between the shadows, inside the shadows, and wove his body into the confines they offered as he 'dry-cleaned' himself from those who may be watching, waiting to follow him, planning to continue their surveillance upon him.

Cleverly, he used the reflections of a window to see who might be behind him and then turned another corner. He walked along the side of the dock, scanned the yachts and vessels moored there overnight, and then casually glanced at the vehicles parked close to the hotel. It was the way he had been trained. One of many ways.

A check of his wristwatch revealed his walk had taken over fifteen minutes so far.

A black cab came into view and motored slowly by. The London taxi drew up at a side entrance and a male passenger alighted from the vehicle, paid the driver, and entered the hotel by the side door.

The hotel guest from the Moscow flight memorised the taxi number as it drove away and then strolled to the side door only to read a sign indicating it was a private staff entrance. The man walked on as if he were checking that all around him was safe, that no-one was watching, that he was alone in his endeavours.

When he had carried out the procedures that he had been taught, the man returned to the hotel an hour later, took the stairs to the sixth floor, and used a plastic key to enter his room.

In the lounge cafe, a porcelain thimble pushed a needle that carried a silver thread around the border of a quilt. The grey-haired lady of gathering years paused, took another sip of tea, and continued her work.

In the City of Carlisle, to the north, the fire at the bowling green had reached its peak.

A huge crowd gathered, watched in awe of the flames, and pondered at the fate of the firefighters charged with dousing the raging inferno.

The shadowy figure of an arsonist hugged the shrubbery and watched the emergency services at the scene. Excited by the arrival of the Fire Service, the paraffin man was vibrant, pulsating, alive with the pure thrill of it all. It was his second visit to the location that night. For him, skirting the shrubbery and foliage was merely returning to the scene of his heinous crime to deliberately celebrate his criminality and prove to himself that life was worth living. He knew he was invincible: A God of Fire, an Emperor of the Firestorm, the Lord of the Blaze. In the deep privacy of his mind, a complex disjointed brain gloried in its actions in the sure and certain knowledge that it could never be inspected or interpreted by others because such people did not realise the paraffin man lived in a false world of his own making. At the moment of his supreme ecstasy, his brain shot off at a tangent from normality in its never-ending battle to ease the stress within him.

Two police cars and a police van arrived at the scene of the incident. A police officer with stripes on the arm of his uniform jacket took over the scene and the paraffin man quietly slunk back to his home for the second time that night. To his rear, a succession of circling blue lights competed with the orange-red flames from the bowling club.

By morning, only the charred corner uprights of the building would remain.

In a hotel in London, the lady placed the quilt in her bag, took the lift to the sixth floor, and strolled along the corridor until she reached her destination.

Tapping three times, she stood back slightly when the door opened and the man's jaw dropped in surprise before he exclaimed, 'Colonel! Is that you, Colonel?'

Immediately, she walked directly into the room pushing him backwards and closing the door behind her.

'Nadia!' remarked the man. 'We have a visitor. It's the Colonel!'

Dominating the space, the Colonel – a grey-haired lady of gathering years - chided, 'At least you remembered who I am but are you completely stupid? You know better than to refer to me as Colonel in a place like this.'

'Sorry! We weren't expecting you. I am Major Viktor Petrov, and this is Senior Lieutenant Nadia Koshkin. We are from…'

'Yes, I know who you are,' snapped the Colonel. Circling the duo with an unwelcome glare and penetrating eyes, she added, 'Indeed, I know all about you and why you are here.'

'What can we do for you, Colonel?' asked Major Petrov nervously. 'Do you know that we are on assignment to Mikhail Korobov?'

'You were,' explained the Colonel with a hint of sadness in her voice. 'Now you are reassigned to me by order of the Supreme Commander-in-Chief.'

'You mean...'

'Yes, the President himself, the Supreme Commander-in-Chief of the Russian Armed Forces,' confirmed the Colonel. 'You are mine now.'

'But what of Lieutenant Colonel Korobov?' queried Major Petrov.

'He was killed in a road accident very recently,' revealed the Colonel with a hint of grief.

'Killed!' remarked Lieutenant Nadia Koshkin. 'I'm so very sorry to hear that, Colonel. I am truly sorry for your loss. We did not know. That's terrible. Was it an accident or did the British murder him?'

'Diplomatically speaking,' offered the Colonel. 'Mikhail was the victim of a tragic road accident on a British motorway. He crashed into a wagon according to police reports. On the other hand, how would we know the truth? The British are masters at faking the news to their own accord. But now they have me to contend with. As far as I am concerned, he was murdered by the British Establishment and no-one will convince me otherwise.'

'And you are the master of disguise,' beamed Major Petrov. 'The chief of our spymasters! A legend in your lifetime! I remember you showing us that disguise some years ago when we were...'

'Enough!' barked the Colonel. 'I remember you from the training school too but don't think for one minute that I asked for you on this operation. Moscow wants something doing urgently but despite my protestations, they gave me you two because you were already assigned to Mikhail and were on route to the UK.'

'We are proud to be your servants,' expressed Major Petrov. 'Aren't we, Nadia?'

'Yes! Yes, of course,' the Lieutenant confirmed. 'There is none better than yourself, Colonel.'

'You're slipping. Both of you!' growled the Colonel placing her bag on the table. 'You both walked right past me in the arrivals lounge in Heathrow and again in the foyer downstairs in this hotel. Neither of you had any idea that I was watching you. Where is your surveillance training?

You both acted like you were on an afternoon picnic at a family Dacha in the Motherland. Are you both stupid? I think I should send you both back on the next flight.'

Slowly, gradually, the Colonel removed her grey wig, unbuttoned the collar of her blouse, and peeled a prosthetic nose away from her face. As the mask detached itself, it also removed a thin film of plastic that had served to distort her forehead and give the appearance of an older woman. In a second, the wrinkles on her forehead had been folded neatly into her bag.

'Sadly, it is not a trick of the light, my friends. I really am halfway into my sixties now. The disguise changes my appearance slightly and perhaps persuades some that I am closer to eighty than seventy but, alas, my bones grow old and I am not getting any younger.'

'You are still a legend in the Motherland,' replied the Lieutenant. 'I've heard people compare you with Eli Cohen.'

'Who?' queried the Colonel.

'Israel's greatest ever spy,' explained the Lieutenant. 'The Mossad spy who penetrated the Syrian government to such an extent that he became chief advisor to the defence minister. He feigned sympathy for the soldiers exposed to the sun on the Golan Heights and had trees planted so that they enjoyed the shade. He then reported that information to his spymasters. He told Israel to use the trees as targeting markers to bombard the Syrian line.'

'Well, well, well,' chuckled the Colonel. 'You were obviously awake when I gave that lecture. Actually, Nadia, I prefer to compare myself with the famous Anna Vasilyevna Chapman. She was part of our Illegals Program spy ring in the United States in the early part of this millennium. We had over a dozen sleeper agents carrying out long-term, deep-cover assignments in America.'

'What did they do?'

'Nothing for a few years then they were activated and gradually got close to people who were scientists, politicians, and military. Anyone with access to intelligence that we might be interested in. Sadness is that in 2010, it all fell apart and they were eventually arrested. Mind you, a handful got back to Russia unscathed and undetected.'

'What happened to Chapman and why did she have an English sounding name?' enquired Nadia.

'She married an Englishman in England in order to become a British citizen and get a British passport. That was part of the operation so you can see how long it lasted. She was charged with espionage but swopped later that year for a bunch of American prisoners. The British stripped her of her citizenship and excluded her from the country.'

'But you are still the best we know, Colonel.'

'Kind of you to say so, Nadia. Just remember, we're not here to plant trees like that Israeli, we're here for something else entirely.'

'Tell us, Colonel. What did we do wrong?' asked Major Petrov softly.

'Well, at least you recognised my theatrical make-up. I rather hoped you would remember that disguise and I was right. You realised it was me a moment or so after I knocked on the door. The problem is, I watched you arrive,' explained the Colonel. 'I should have put my furry Cossack hat on. That would have given you a clue as to my presence so that you would be on your toes from the very start. I was wrong. As I said before, you walked past me in the arrivals lounge in Heathrow and again in the foyer downstairs. You didn't see me in either of those places because you weren't even looking. You were not on your guard.'

'We were tired after the flight,' suggested Major Petrov.

'Really?' commented the Colonel. 'Tired after the flight? It's not good enough. I know you can do so much better. You must remember that the British are hostile to us. They are our enemy and they are all over the airports with their security windows and hidden cameras watching out for people like us. This is a hostile enemy state, my friends. Expect anything and everything and stay alert. It's time to switch on.'

'I did dry clean the hotel,' remarked Major Petrov. 'I circled the hotel looking for people that might have followed us from the airport.'

'I know!' nodded the Colonel. 'I watched you go and come back from my seat in the lounge. Had I been a member of British intelligence I would have quietly remained in the same place waiting for you to return to the hotel in the knowledge that, had you caught a taxi, my colleagues outside would have been on your tail right away. Why on earth didn't you check the lounge area first? Any more mistakes like that and you'll be gone. Understand?'

'Yes! Yes!' replied Viktor anxiously.

'Basics! Remember the basics, Viktor and never forget I am authorised to terminate associations. Do you know what that means?'

'Yes,' whispered Nadia Koshkin nervously. 'We do.'

'We will not let you down, Colonel,' responded Major Petrov. 'I don't think either of us plans to be terminated on foreign soil, or anywhere else for that matter.'

Nodding, more approvingly, the Colonel relaxed and advised them both, 'You are highly trained professionals who have got off on the wrong foot with me because I expected better. Maybe I was wrong and need a rest from this madcap game we play every day.'

'We recently ended a covert operation in Lisbon,' replied Major Petrov. 'Once this one is over, we'll take a rest on the shores of the Black Sea.'

'Whereabouts?' probed the Colonel.

'Sochi!' revealed Lieutenant Koshkin.

'Yes, I know it well, Nadia,' replied the Colonel. 'It has a lovely beach and is a good choice if I may say so.'

'There is a health resort on the outskirts of the town, Colonel. We have been there before. Peace and tranquillity are a byword,' suggested the Lieutenant.

'Good! But now you must do things the way I know you are capable of. Spend time just getting to know the area. Take a counter-surveillance route every day to ascertain if you are under surveillance. Leave nothing to chance. Watch the English people, read their newspapers, listen to their speech so that you can melt seamlessly into their ways in a restaurant, a bar, a bus queue, or whatever. In fact, go to a pub, have a drink in the hotel bar, take a burger from a hot dog stand.'

'Understood,' replied the Major. 'We can do these things. It's what we are trained in. You know that.'

'I do,' replied the Colonel. 'And I will tell you now that I told you a lie before. I asked Moscow for you because you both look bland. You are neither tall nor short. Your hair is neither black nor white and your dress sense is such that you don't stand out in a crowd. You both look pretty average and that's just the way I want you to stay so don't go buying any colourful clothes in Harrods. Resist such temptations. Whilst you have the ability and looks to blend quietly and unremarkably into the woodwork, you are also supremely capable of counter-surveillance and, when it becomes necessary, anti-surveillance. There may be times when you will be required to carry out operations whilst you know you are being watched. That is where our anti-surveillance techniques will come in handy. Be aware, specialised equipment has been drawn from the office in Khoroshyovsky forty-eight hours ago. It will be in our possession in due course. Meanwhile, use this mobile phone to contact me. It's clean. Here…'

The Colonel handed over what appeared to be a carton of cigarettes typical of what one might buy in an airport duty-free shop. Inside the package lay an unused mobile 'phone.

'What do you want us to do?' enquired Major Petrov.

'A safe house has been acquired and you will move to it on your fourth day here if there are no problems. Live as man and wife on holiday. I want you to remember that British Intelligence has probably already noted your arrival at the airport and expressed an interest in why you are here. Let them find you if need be. Don't panic that they are onto you. You're not doing anything illegal at the moment so don't worry. It's what they do and what we do in Russia. Just relax and do nothing. If they decide to put surveillance onto you then just let them get bored with you. You are tourists but I want you to meet Pavel and Talisha who have travelled here from Berlin. They arrived this morning. I know you have worked with them before. Viktor, you outrank them and therefore I require you to ensure they maintain the standards that I require. Understood?'

'Yes, I understand,' nodded Major Petrov.

'Standards, Viktor. You will strive to meet my standards at all times no matter what that involves. Understood?'

'Yes,' snapped Major Petrov.

'Pavel and Talisha have been fully briefed on the operation and have relocated as instructed,' continued the Colonel. 'You will receive regular calls from me and when we have assessed that the time is right a hire a car will be made available. You will drive to a location that I will inform you of in due course. You will be completely clean of British surveillance by then. Stay a few days but always remember that the British are not fools. If they suspect you, they will chase the passport you use, the credit cards, bank cards, anything that links you to the digital electronic system or the extensive CCTV system that dominates their town centres. Use some of those basic tricks of the trade I taught you if need be. Don't be surprised if the British put a team onto you. There are false passports in the document bag for use only in an emergency and you will need to adopt the disguises that have been accredited to you should circumstances dictate that you need to leave the country at the earliest opportunity. Okay?'

'Spot on!' replied Major Petrov.

'Mmm... You have found your English vocabulary, Major,' remarked the Colonel.

'I try,' smiled the Major.

The Colonel delved into her bag and handed over a document folder and a tablet computer.

'Am I right in thinking that there are four of us on this operation?' queried Lieutenant Koshkin. 'Are we split into two teams?'

'At the beginning, yes. That is correct,' revealed the Colonel. 'There is a security team with us. They are busy hiring vehicles and renting hotel rooms that will be used in the operation as well as planning our escape route. There is no need for you to know of them at this stage. As you might expect, I work on a need to know basis and, at the moment, you don't need to know. If all goes well, and I expect things to go very well, you will eventually meet the rest of the team.'

'What is the brief?' probed Major Petrov.

'It's all on the secure tablet,' replied the Colonel. 'Use the agreed codeword to access the tablet and click into the holiday folder on the desktop. You will find all the instructions there. Please note, you will get an email soon. It will tell you where and when you may pick up various hire vehicles that have been acquired for your use. Change the vehicles regularly. It's what the British expect. Don't disappoint them. Make it harder for them to keep tabs on you.'

Major Petrov ripped open the seal of the document bag, located the tablet, and then began to browse the highly classified contents.

'Your brief is to destroy the individual,' ordered the Colonel. 'The subject is a threat Moscow can no longer tolerate.'

Half an hour later, the Colonel from Russian Intelligence left the hotel room with her bag, her disguises, and her thimbles and quilts. She took a taxi to a safe house in North London.

Major Viktor Petrov glanced at Nadia and said, 'Poor woman! How she must feel having lost Mikhail, we'll never know.'

'Determined is how she will feel,' suggested Nadia. 'Now tell me who the target is.'

Viktor Petrov viewed the tablet screen before him and began a slideshow of photographs. He paused the computerised procedure and pointed to one particular image saying, 'This one, Nadia. This one.'

On the dark windswept streets of London, Sasha Morozova walked along the footpath. A black taxi drew up alongside the young woman. The rear nearside door opened allowing Sasha to bend low and step into the rear passenger compartment.

Removing a scarf from her hair, Sasha allowed her dark locks to billow out across her shoulders, and offered, 'Sorry! I'm late. It was a busy day at work. My father! Any news?'

'Jump in!' replied Antonia Harston-Browne. 'And I'll update you, but it's not going to be at all easy.'

The door closed behind Sasha and the taxi drove off into the busy streets of the nation's capital.

~

2

Seven days later
The Special Crime Unit
London.

'And this is my deputy, Detective Inspector Anthea Adams,' remarked Boyd.

The Mayor of London smiled politely and extended a handshake to the auburn-haired detective saying, 'I am pleased to meet you, at last, Inspector Adams. Indeed, ladies and gentlemen, I feel quite honoured to be here today. I have heard so much about the unit that I could not miss out on the opportunity to visit you when the Commissioner extended his invitation. Now tell me from the beginning, Commander Boyd, what is the unit about?'

'The unit is a hand-picked team of detectives drawn from Counter Terrorist Command, formerly the anti-terrorist branch, together with some top detectives from all over the British Isles and some hand-picked individuals from MI5 and MI6 as well as other national agencies appropriate to our remit,' replied Boyd. 'They are all experts in some field or other and serve between three and five years, in some cases longer. We select only the best of the best and will settle for nothing less than total loyalty to the unit. The unit's remit is 'to police and defend the freedom of the nation and its people.'

'An excellent assignment if I may say so,' offered the Mayor. 'And quite a few medals on the route, I understand?'

'Sergeant Janice Burns, Inspector Bannerman, Anthea, and I, have all been awarded the Queen's Gallantry Medal recently,' revealed Boyd. 'But that doesn't necessarily make us heroes. It just gives us more kudos when we book our seats on Charlie Tango Charlie.'

'What on earth is that?' enquired the Mayor, a stout middle-aged man who was stooped over slightly with a long-term back injury.

'It's our response helicopter,' replied Boyd. 'Callsign Charlie Tango Charlie. An Agusta 109 with a maximum speed of 180mph.'

'I see,' nodded the Mayor. 'May I presume that when there is a need to whisk me away to a place of safety, Charlie Tango Charlie will be on hand to do just that?' asked the Mayor.

'Well, you just never know,' chuckled Boyd.

Bannerman walked into the office, smiled, and said, 'Sorry, I'm late. The traffic is horrendous.'

'Not to worry,' replied Boyd. 'I'd like you to meet the Mayor of London, Bannerman. I think you are aware that you have been assigned to his protection team for the foreseeable future?'

'Yes, indeed,' beamed Bannerman reaching out to shake the Mayor's hand. 'Delighted to meet you, sir. I just hope that your visit here today will put your mind at rest somewhat and if you don't mind me saying, wouldn't a walking stick help your back at all?'

'Yes! It does,' replied the Mayor. 'But there are times when I make myself do without it. I need to strengthen my back and it's too easy to rely completely on a stick.'

'Well, I'll bow to your personal experience,' nodded Bannerman. 'But I must say that it can't be easy for you having received those death threats. I presume that unnerved you more than having a bad back?'

'Just a little, yes,' confirmed the Mayor. 'I didn't expect to be appointed Mayor of London and then receive so many death threats from the very people I'm supposed to be serving.'

'I expect that's what becomes of being London's first Jewish Mayor,' offered Boyd.

'That's the problem, Commander. With a name like Benjamin Epstein, people presume I'm Jewish. I'm not.'

'I understand that's the case,' remarked Boyd. 'But if you don't mind me asking, why the Jewish name if you're not a Jew?'

'I'm not Jewish,' confirmed the Mayor. 'My parents were Jewish, and they gifted me with the name tags before they died in a train crash in France when I was a youngster. I survived and was brought up initially in an orphanage in Paris before moving to the UK as a young adult. Thinking back, I should probably have changed my name by deed poll, but it didn't occur to me at the time. Anyway, would you like to know of my parents, Commander? It may help you understand the threats against me.'

'It's your floor, sir. Do tell,' encouraged Boyd.

'They were Haredi Jews which is a branch of Judaism that regard themselves as the most religiously authentic group of Jews in the world.'

'Extremists in the religious sense?'

'You could say that, Commander.'

'Then I must apologise because although I am familiar with the Torah, I am not familiar with the term Haredi,' revealed Boyd. 'And that troubles me because if the 'phone rings in the next half hour I could end up speaking to a terrorist or someone who is offering information against a terrorist group. Knowing about extremism is of personal importance to me as a professional.'

'Surely they teach you such things,' queried the Mayor.

'Actually, they don't,' declared Boyd. 'They teach you the law on the subject and how to shoot. The rest you pick up yourself. Either way, I choose to have an excellent knowledge of all such religious groups, their beliefs, and aspirations.'

'Haredi Judaism is merely a term that describes the extremism of orthodox Judaism, revealed the Mayor. 'It is founded on a reaction to how society changes and requires steadfast adherence to Jewish Law. My parents chose to segregate themselves from modern society since they did not believe that the way people lived their lives was a good way. They wanted perfection and did not find it.'

'I don't think it exists,' replied Boyd. 'Permit me, sir, but are you telling me your parents kept themselves to themselves and had strong beliefs in their faith?' probed Boyd.

'Correct!' replied the Mayor. 'I think someone like you might associate it with the extremities of Islam that can be found in the Salafi movement of the Muslims. The difference is that Salafi wants to take us back fourteen hundred years. The Haredi just want us to be normal and not stupid.'

'Never going to happen,' chuckled Anthea nearby. 'Neither!'

'Interestingly,' continued the Mayor. 'The estimated global population of Haredi Jews is growing rapidly from a base of two million. There is a virtual absence of interfaith marriage and a high birth rate that has caused the increase.'

'I sense you decided some time ago to break free from the shackles of your parents and make your way in life regardless of them?' quizzed Bannerman.

'Yes, indeed! My mistake was getting involved in politics. Now my life is in danger.'

Chuckling, Bannerman replied, 'We all make mistakes, sir. I got involved in the police and I can't remember why. It's so long ago.'

'It seems you have all done well,' replied the Mayor with a friendly smile.

'Why is it that the majority of people think you are Jewish when you're not?' probed Boyd.

'I've no problem with the Jewish community, Commander,' explained the Mayor. 'But try as I might there are many who choose to see me the way they want to see me and not as I am. They often try to liken me to a Haredi Jew without actually knowing what such a person would look like. They usually wear a black suit and a white shirt with either a black fedora or a black Homburg hat. Such people wear black skull caps under their hat and often sport long beards or long locks in their hair. I usually wear a mixture of variously coloured suits, shirts and ties and I think that upsets the critics who are all too keen to put one over on me. Plus, of course, displacing the previous Muslim Mayor has put me out of favour with many. I was elected on a different ticket to the previous incumbent. Lots of different policies that need not be discussed now. The electorate took to me and voted me in and this surprised many because it is known that I am quite a wealthy man living in a not so affluent part of London. When you are rich, Commander, not everyone is pleased for you. Many are simply jealous of such self-generated prosperity. The sadness is that consequently I now have a stack of enemies that I could do without. I could stand on a stack of bibles outside County Hall and swear aloud that I'm a Christian, but it would go in one ear and out the other for many because they have convinced themselves that I am a Jew. Commander, I think I'm closer to becoming an atheist than anything else.'

'That's your choice to make,' sir,' remarked Boyd.

'Put simply,' replied the Mayor. 'There are those who just prefer to see me as of Jewish extraction because it suits their own personal or political agenda.'

'Sadly, that's quite usual these days,' explained Boyd. 'But I hope your visit here will enlighten you and reveal that we are just a small cog in a big wheel.'

'I'm told this cog is most likely to pick up on any intelligence that confirms I am on a hit list, Commander,' argued the Mayor. 'And that is the main reason I accepted the Commissioner's invitation to visit you. My protection team tell me there is intelligence to suggest that my life is in danger because my political decisions upset some sections of the community.'

'For example, your opponents, and elements of the non-Jewish community who would prefer someone else,' suggested Boyd.

'Apparently, your unit is most likely to be on the case if things start to go wrong, Commander. Is that the truth?'

'Probably,' confirmed Boyd. 'It would depend on how the circumstances unfolded. However, let me tell you this. The unit has one Commander – that's me - and four wings each supervised by a Detective Inspector with two Sergeants and ten detectives. The various wings can either work independently of each other on their own targets or if needed, they all come together to work on one specific target.'

'Fluid Flexibility?' queried the Mayor.

'Precisely,' admitted Boyd. 'We have one vacancy and that is at the level of Detective Chief Inspector. I'm hoping to fill that shortly. With administrative civilian support, the total operational strength of the unit varies between sixty and seventy relevant to illness and availability. I can assure you that if intelligence comes to light concerning your safety then the threat level against you will be heightened still further and everything possible we can do will be done to protect you from those who would wish you harm. Inspector Bannerman is on temporary secondment with us from the Special Escort Group of the Met's Royalty and Protection Squad. We're hoping to secure his services full time when a vacancy on one of the wings occurs.'

'Thank you,' replied the Mayor. 'It's good to know that I have an expert of some standing looking after me.'

Bannerman shuffled his feet nervously.

The feet wore size ten shoes and he stood six feet five inches inside them. Broad across the shoulders, he was quite muscular despite a slight paunch around his midriff. A chiselled square chin gave him the appearance of a man older than he was whilst a crop of microscopic ginger hair sprouted from a rounded skull and crept dangerously towards his ears. From a distance, he looked almost bald. Up close, no one told him so. His friends called him the big man, but enemies called him the screaming skull.

'Do you have a first name, Mister Bannerman?' probed the Mayor.

'No! Everyone calls me Bannerman and that's fine by me.'

'I see,' smiled the Mayor. 'Bannerman it is then.'

'If you don't mind, sir,' remarked Boyd. 'I'm going to leave you with Anthea and Bannerman. They can show you around and explain things in more detail. I have some urgent business in hand but suggest we touch base for coffee after your tour.'

'Of course,' replied the Mayor. 'I'll look forward to it and for the information of your people, my name is Benjamin, Commander. And that is how I would like to be addressed if you don't mind.'

'Of course, Benjamin,' smiled Boyd. 'As you say, Benjamin, it is.'

As Anthea took over the Mayor's visit, Boyd stepped back, turned, and headed into a secure room. The four walls protected a million pound plus cyber package called the Ticker Intelligence system. The system was linked securely to a score of law enforcement agencies around the world as well as hundreds of criminal records, intelligence reports and analysis some of which originated from the sharp end of global warfare as well as the global cyberwar. The system was such that it was the envy of many.

Antonia Harston-Browne QGM sat at the computer screen tinkling the black and white tiles on the keyboard.

Antonia's long red hair flowed down her back covering her shoulder blades. Tall and slim, with an hour-glass figure, she wore a dark blue, two-piece, executive-style suit set off with a silver brooch worn on the lapel. The neatly tailored skirt stopped short just above the knee. She called it her office uniform and wore it well. Antonia was one of those individuals who just didn't age. Every inch a lady, she was articulate, sophisticated, cultured, educated well above the national standard, and of upper-middle-class bearing. Indeed, Antonia carried a highly polished professional demeanour wherever she went enjoying two honours degrees and playing a merciless game of squash. At the quintessential exclusive country club, she was in her element with the so-called 'county set'. Whilst in the oak-panelled corridors of Whitehall and the highfalutin financial offices of the City, she could wheel and deal with the sharpest of kids on the block. In the City, she wined and dined at expensive restaurants and wore long, flowing gowns that vitalised her sophisticated charms and discarded the facade of her other life. She was privileged, virtually blue-blooded, the daughter of parents since departed: parents who had left her a financial legacy that revealed her to be of comfortable private means. In the City, in the country club, she had no enemies, save those who bitched at her pretentiousness. Moreover, Antonia had connections in every corner of society that one might imagine: the good, the bad, and the ugly. As a Senior Intelligence Officer, she was a leading member of the controversial Special Crime Unit – and was in love with Phillip Nesbitt, Director-General of the security service.

'I've had to allocate Bannerman to the Mayor's protection team,' revealed Boyd as he approached Antonia. 'To be honest, I can do with Bannerman here with us, but that's the way it is. Tell me you have something on Ticker about the threats to the Mayor? Somebody has told him we're his life-savers.'

'Probably the Commissioner,' suggested Antonia. 'It's the way people pass the problem to you without actually contacting you to tell them the problem is on its way. That way they get rid of the problem. Congratulations! You caught the ball. The problem is now yours.'

'Ahh! You're in a bad mood. I can tell,' replied Boyd. 'Anything of interest on the Ticker system?'

'Nothing new on the Mayor's case,' responded the redhead. 'Analysis suggests extremist Muslims might be behind the recent spate of death threat letters and 'phone calls but more interestingly for you, there's this. I thought it might update you.'

'Go on,' demanded Boyd.

'There's been another fire in Carlisle. Arson again. Plus, the jewellery burglary you told us about is reported at £100,000 worth of diamond rings.'

'He dropped one bag at the scene. It fell out of his pocket.'

'And got clean away with another bag by the looks of it,' delivered Antonia.

'This is Carlisle, Cumbria, Antonia, not Amsterdam. If the jeweller had £200,000 worth of diamonds in their shop for sale – plus other jewellery that wasn't touched – then they must have a turnover that doesn't quite equate to a small city centre shop in the backwoods of the North West. That needs checking. I wonder if the insurance claim is genuine?'

'I can't help you there, Boyd.'

'Any suspects yet?'

'No,' smiled Antonia. 'That little whippet of a kid you chased seems to have got away with it this time. As for the arsons, well, the reports here indicate six fires now and the damage is estimated at close to six million pounds and rising.'

'Really! That much?' barked Boyd. 'A million pounds a fire. That will break the bank in Cumbria. Any analysis or intelligence in the pipeline?'

Tapping the black and whites, Antonia paused for a moment, read the screen, and replied, 'No! The real problem you need to recognise, of course, is that offences of arson aren't really on the Ticker system. But it gets worse and perhaps more interesting when you read these papers.'

'Such as?' probed Boyd.

'According to my research, statistically, there are about three thousand arson attacks every week in the UK. Very few are detected let alone formally investigated.'

'Do you mean deliberate fires or arson attacks, Antonia,' quizzed Boyd. 'I'm sure the Fire Service put out lots of bonfires throughout the year. These aren't necessarily criminal offences.'

'It doesn't say,' offered Antonia. 'Either way, there's a lot of arsons that seem to be getting under the wire without being snagged.'

'Yeah, I'd agree,' nodded Boyd. 'No intelligence to offer then?'

'Not on Ticker, I'm afraid,' revealed Antonia. 'It may be a multi-million-pound global state of the art intelligence system that's the envy of many, but if people aren't putting 'suspect arsons' into the system, then there are no records or circumstances to analyse. It's about as simple as that.'

'Brilliant! Not a good start,' noted Boyd. 'How about socks?'

'Socks!' declared Antonia. 'Look if you need new socks, take a break and go and treat yourself at Marks and Sparks. Better still, Harrods! Don't get me involved in your socks.'

'No,' chuckled Boyd. 'Ticker! The burglar wasn't wearing any socks. Can you work that into the system and see if anything comes out?'

'No!' growled Antonia. 'It's trendy, Boyd. It's a modern fad to be barefoot and not at all an indication that sockless people are criminals. It's like wearing shorts. It's cool!'

'Cool? Fashion is it?' murmured Boyd. 'Is that what the fashion police are for?'

'No such thing,' sniped Antonia.

'Well, can you tie socks into scenes of crime? Who has been arrested, convicted or suspected of carrying out crimes in their bare feet?'

'Jesus of Nazareth!' suggested Antonia.

'No, he walked on water,' replied Boyd.

'Mmm… I'll think about it,' smirked Antonia. 'I might even have to write a new programme for the computer.'

'Antonia, just do it … Please,' begged Boyd.

'Cost you a glass of Bollinger on Friday night.'

'Oh my,' laughed Boyd. 'A glass of bollies! Still, that's cheaper than a bottle. Crack on then.'

'Just at the moment, Boyd,' snapped Antonia. 'Threats against the Mayor of London are a damn sight more important than fire-raisers in Cumbria and barefoot whippets that old men can't catch anymore.'

'Ouch! You certainly know how to hurt people, don't you?' retaliated Boyd.

The black and whites tinkled lightly as the redhead from MI5 interrogated the Ticker system and Boyd reached for a coffee pot.

Antonia glanced at Boyd and instructed, 'Black, no sugar, and I should have demanded a bottle of Bollinger, not a glass.'

Elsewhere, a black BMW saloon car cruised along the main road, paused in the traffic, and then safely turned into a country lane where a small hamlet of detached houses was situated.

Major Viktor Petrov held the car in second gear, glanced at Nadia in the passenger seat, and advised, 'We're here. Which one is it?'

Nadia Koshkin denied an answer, checked an address on a piece of paper lying on her lap, and said, 'Keep it slow. It must be one of these.'

Viktor glimpsed in the rear-view mirror, maintained a low speed, and eventually pointed at a large detached bungalow standing in about half an acre of land. As his hand rested on the gear stick, he offered, 'Rich! Successful! Powerful in their line of work. I'll put a donkey on that one.'

'You mean a pony,' replied Nadia. A pony is cockney slang for twenty-five pounds. A donkey is an ass like yourself.'

'I'll never make a Londoner,' chuckled Viktor.

Checking her notes again, Nadia declared, 'Yes, that's the target's address. Nice house and look it has UPVC doors and windows at the front. I think it's a porch prior to entry into the main building.'

'Good!' smiled Viktor. 'That's a big help. Take some photos so that I can study the layout later.'

Pointing a device, the size of a small matchbox, Nadia activated the covert camera and took a succession of photographs of the target premises.

'Slow and steady please.'

Viktor obeyed and reduced speed further.

'Got them. Looks like a standard UPVC front door with associated porch,' remarked Nadia. 'A locking system bolts the door into the frame and secures it at multiple points at the turn of a key. I think you could manage that one without much problem.'

'Agreed,' replied Viktor squeezing the accelerator slightly. 'Nice to see it's not locked up as well as a bank. It's hardly Fort Knox. The door will be fitted with a common pin tumbler cylinder lock.'

'It's the target's home. What did you expect?' queried Nadia. 'The Crown Jewels?'

'I'd no idea,' replied Viktor. 'But they are still quite security conscious. Look at the trees. Tell me what you see.'

Nadia swivelled her head to the offside and realised they were in range of a system of covert cameras that were hidden in the lower branches of the tree-lined lane.

'Nice one as they say,' replied Nadia. 'Well-hidden unless you know precisely what you're looking for. It also means they've got us on camera. Don't stop.'

Viktor nodded and replied, 'I know what I'm doing. Just act naturally and make the call. We are under surveillance as we speak. The Colonel told us this might happen. You have my permission to speak to Colonel Korobov.'

Removing a mobile from her handbag, Nadia replied, 'How kind! I'll do as I am told, oh noble leader.'

'Just do it,' scowled Viktor.

Nadia hit the digits and waited. A voice on the other end answered and Nadia remarked, 'We've located the lair.'

Listening, nodding, Nadia eventually closed the phone, and stated, 'We're on.'

Viktor smiled and cruised smoothly away from the isolated area.

At Carlisle police station a keyboard controlled by the unwilling fingers of Police Constable 2257 John Dillon churned out the second page of a typed statement.

Dillon read the checklist provided by Sergeant Riley:

Describe the burglar! Male or female! Age! Clothing! How long did you have the burglar in your view? Was he carrying anything? How far did you chase him? Did you chase him? Did you run after him and if so, why didn't you catch him? Report please - When the burglar alarm first went off, you said you were already at the scene. Is that factually correct? Submit a statement and then discuss forward progression.

Forward progression? thought PC Dillon as he sent the document to the printer nearby. What the hell does that mean? He got away because I wasn't quick enough, and he's done it before. How do I write that in a report for a Sergeant who wants to be rid of me?

John Dillon snatched the paper from the printer tray, screwed it into a little ball, and then fired it towards a bin in the corner of the room.

The bundle missed the bin and landed forlornly next to the skirting board.

Holding his head in his hands, Dillon closed his eyes and counted to ten. Reluctantly, he returned to the keyboard.

'Again!' he said aloud. 'Should I title it the one that got away? That's what they are thinking, isn't it?'

In an adjoining office, thoughts of the one that got away were a mile away from Sergeant Riley's mind as he sat opposite DI Stan Holland and listened to an update on the recent blaze at the bowling club.

The meeting didn't last long. Without any positive leads, there wasn't much to discuss.

~

3

Carlisle
That night.
Shortly after midnight

Constable John Dillon had taken enough jibes and criticism to last a lifetime. He couldn't take much more. The situation had continued relentlessly since that memorable night when he'd allowed the jewellery burglar to escape. They'd told him that he wasn't fast enough, couldn't catch a rabbit with a limp, and needed to get fit, and carrots!

Carrots!

They'd told him he should eat more carrots because there was a library of photographs of local criminals in the local intelligence office and he couldn't identify the burglar he'd seen face to face for that split second. It was on the night of the Torchlight Procession when the so-called Whippet Kid had looked him in the eye and then legged it down the lane at a breakneck speed never to be seen again.

Carrots improve eyesight, they'd told him. The shift had no room for losers, second place, or 'also ran'. Step up to the mark, they'd said.

'It was a kid that did it,' he'd replied. 'Probably not old enough to have a criminal record that necessitated a photograph in an album.'

They refused to listen to his argument.

'Bastards!' he'd shouted in anger not seen before.

Halfway through his meal break, Dillon threw his toys out of the pram and decided he hated Sergeant Riley and everyone else on the shift.

Grabbing his torch and radio, he propelled himself through the rear door of Carlisle police station and headed into the streets of the city. The town hall clock showed one in the morning and there was no way he was going to sit in the canteen and take any more criticism.

As PC Dillon strode furiously up the main street, Sergeant Riley casually poured more tea into his mug from a flask, smiled at the gathering enjoying their break, and offered, 'He's a lovely lad but we need to make him or break him. No room for passengers anymore.'

'Hear! Hear!' from one corner.

'Cruel!' from another.

Outside, John Dillon began patrolling the darkened streets thinking back to those quite horrible people in the canteen, the face of a youngster he'd like to meet again, and a job he was beginning to tire of.

Elsewhere in the city, the rear door of the paraffin man's house was pulled tight as the bizarre mentality of a disturbed young man, in his early twenties, guided him into the black of the night.

Pausing in the lane at the side of his house, the paraffin man held leather gloves to his nose, deeply inhaled the scent of the fuel he adored and donned his gloves. He pulled tight the strings of a black hoodie that closed around his face, protected it, hid the features from others, and fostered the security of his private persona.

Boldly, he stepped into the night.

A box of matches rattled in the pocket of his dark blue denim jeans as his footsteps guided him towards his destiny.

Somewhere in that turbulent maelstrom of a mind, a set of cognitive signals were pushing him forward, encouraging him to find another target and to destroy an individual or a commercial business. But there was much more to it than that and he knew deep inside that his desire to create mayhem for no apparent reason veiled a profoundly personal wish to relieve the stress growing within him as well as simultaneously provide a bizarre form of sexual stimulation.

Closing his eyes for a moment, the paraffin man's intellect spun into a whirlpool of malcontent that unbalanced his brain and gradually crushed it beyond repair. Yet the problem he faced at that precise moment was beyond his grasp, out of reach of the current state of his mind and those who might strive to understand his fractured personality. Put simply, it wasn't that he had run out of paraffin or had lost all his sexual desires. He had no target, and lacking a tangible objective unmercifully added to the stress falsifying his understanding of the world around him.

The paraffin man began his quest as he walked beside the wooden fence that bordered his garden.

Allowing his hand to drop onto the fence, his brain kickstarted when he realised the structure was made of wood.

'Wood! Timber! Planks!' he muttered as he walked beneath a lamp standard. 'Where will I find you? You burn so easy. Where are you? Where? Oh, where?'

A long shadow cast upon the footpath as the malfunctioning creature gradually limped into the night.

In a street off the main A10 trunk road in Stamford Hill, Hackney, two figures wearing dark clothing crept along the hedgerow that bordered an area where about twenty detached houses were part of the landscape.

Using only the streetlights to guide them, they moved quickly towards their target before embedding themselves on the gravel driveway near a grey Volvo saloon car.

Moments later, a light from one of the bedrooms came on briefly before the area plunged into darkness once more.

Nodding, one of the intruders whispered, 'Now! Let's do it. Quickly!'

'In my time,' snapped an accomplice.

There was an audible scrub from a pair of black trainers on the gravel, a slight tear in a pair of denim jeans, and then a sudden wheeze when one of the trespassers slid beneath the grey saloon. A parcel was removed from inside their clothing.

'Going right under,' whispered the invader.

'Good! Make it count!' came the reply.

The man lay on his back and gradually edged further under the car. There was a gentle clunk when he fixed the package to the car and the magnetic field eventually married the underside of the vehicle.

Shuffling out into the open air, he concluded, 'Done! Let's go.'

A bathroom light shone. The two figures froze. A toilet flushed. The light went out.

Creeping low along the side of the hedgerow, the intruders made good their escape as they brushed away gravel clinging to their clothes and the loose green foliage of Hackney borough that had adhered to their garments.

Minutes later, they unlocked their vehicle and drove away into the night unaware of developments in the north of England.

On his way into the heart of Carlisle, it was just the slightest twist of a crowbar wrenching a wooden door frame that Police Constable John Dillon heard when he wandered past the entrance to a lane.

Pausing, he listened again to the noise of a crowbar splintering wood, and then took a step back.

A jemmy, he thought and then quietly radioed his location whilst also stating, 'Burglary in progress. Assistance required!'

Hearing a loud thud when a door unhinged itself from the framework of the building, Dillon knew the jemmy had finally forced entry and the culprit was ripe for arrest.

Spinning quickly on his heel, the young policeman impulsively shone his torch into the dark void that was the lane which led to the rear of a popular bookmakers.

'Oy!' he shouted.

The short crowbar fell to the ground dropped by a burglar surprised in the act of his criminality.

Startled, the crook looked up, saw the dark uniform now running down the lane towards him, and realised he was in danger of being caught like a rat in a trap.

John Dillon's torch beam bounced from wall to wall when the movement of his sprinting body played havoc with the light. For a moment, only a fleeting second, the beam caught the presence of the burglar and took in his full height and what appeared to be gloved hands. Dressed in a dark blue tracksuit, which bore a flash down the side of the trouser legs, the burglar looked forlorn, uneasy with his lot, and near to capture and arrest.

Then the torch beam flashed once more and illuminated the burglar's face.

'Stand still!' screamed PC Dillon. 'I've got you this time.'

Galvanised into action, the would-be burglar turned and shinned up a drainpipe at the side of the bookmaker's shop.

Dillon reached out, grasped a training shoe as it sought purchase on the rusting drainpipe, and then watched the footwear disappear when the burglar heaved himself up onto a low roof and began to clamber away.

'Socks!' screamed PC Dillon. 'It's you again. No bloody socks. The Whippet Kid!'

There was a noisy unwelcome sound when a skylight ruptured, and the burglar's feet narrowly missed falling into the building below.

Then he was gone from sight with PC John Dillon hollering on the radio, updating everyone, arranging for the area to be surrounded, and thinking to himself, 'No! Goddam you, you bloody whippet of a barefoot kid. Not again! Please! Not again!'

'We're on our way!' from the policeman's radio. 'Just hold your ground until we surround the area and box him in. Where is he now?'

'He's up a drainpipe, Sarge,' radioed Dillon following the noise of footsteps. 'I can hear him running across the rooftops.'

Five minutes later, Sergeant Riley arrived at the scene and pronounced, 'He's got clean away again and all we have is a jemmy and your memory of a sockless kid who is some kind of superhuman enigma! Still, we might have his fingerprints on the jemmy.'

'I don't think so, Sarge,' offered Dillon.

'Why's that?'

'He was using his socks as gloves,' replied Dillon. 'His socks were around the jemmy. There are no fingerprints to find.'

Sergeant Riley nodded with, 'And no socks either. Look, that's the way it is sometimes. But you saw his face again. Can you recall enough about his looks to help an artist draw a good likeness?'

'I'll try,' replied Dillon. 'We've nothing to lose.'

'You've everything to lose, young man. You're getting a reputation for always missing out. I'll arrange an artist.'

Further north, moonlight glittered on the water's surface and witnessed only the briefest of undulations in the wave patterns that could be seen from the lounge windows of the nearby building.

Virtually motionless, the water here was at its narrowest before broadening into a massive basin of deep freshwater that dominated the serene countryside. Where the water met the land, there was a short beach that rose slightly towards the rear garden of the detached holiday let that was set in three acres of countryside. The house had been deliberately chosen due to its position which was both isolated yet close to the main arterial highways that fed the nation.

Inside one of the downstairs rooms, one wall had been transformed into a bank of computerised technology featuring stand-alone encrypted external hard drives and ultra-secure linked portable servers that did not necessarily rely entirely on the internet.

'All goes well, Nikolai?' queried the Colonel studying the complex system.

'Absolutely,' came the reply. 'The satellite is nearing its correct position and the signal is growing from weak to strong. I'm just about to load the first programme.'

'I trust my orders have been followed to the letter and it will take us back historically?' probed the Colonel.

'Yes,' replied Nikolai, the keyboard operative. 'The program is very new and has been written in a particular programming software which will give the appearance that the result is historic. Hence the ability to create unique pathways not used operationally before.'

'Good! Then we shall make it a success first time out.'

'Can you tell me how far you want me to go, Colonel?

'What do you mean, how far?'

'The destruction! I understand you want to destroy the subject.'

'Not quite. Begin with impoverishing the subject,' ordered the Colonel. 'I want the individual to squirm, Nikolai. I want them to feel our power, to cry all day and weep all night. Are you ready yet?'

'Whenever you say,' replied the computer boffin.

'Then let the destruction begin but gradually as defined in my briefing papers.'

'Gradually, yes, I have the order of things here in my notes,' remarked Nikolai.

There was a swift rattle of keystrokes followed by a blurred image on the computer screen and a cryptic message that appeared in the middle of the screen and then faded.

'I don't understand,' muttered Nikolai. 'Something has gone wrong.'

'Then you'd better learn quickly,' snapped Colonel Korobov checking her wristwatch. 'I will not countenance mistakes on my team. I have no time for such people. The satellite will not be in alignment for another three minutes. Wait until then and retry but next time get your procedures right because we have a two-hour window before the satellite is in alignment again.'

Outside, there was a sudden rush of water that invaded the shore, washed the beach, and then receded once more as the moon played hide and seek with the clouds and darkness continued to play her hand.

Seconds ticked by as Nikolai waited patiently for a low altitude Russian satellite orbiting one hundred and twenty miles above the planet to plunge into a new orbit and respond to his cryptic commands. With the Colonel standing immediately behind him, Nikolai felt her breath, knew an icy glare awaited him because of his schoolboy error, and then began to perspire heavily as she paced impatiently around the room watching him.

Notification of a strength ten satellite signal appeared in the bottom corner of the computer screen. Nikolai acknowledged the message with a mouse click as the spymaster took closer order and watched his every move.

Colonel Korobov studied the computer screen when it burst into life as Nikolai's eight fingers and two thumbs eventually danced along the keyboard sending countless digital orders into cyberspace.

'Better,' she delivered. 'Much better! Indeed, congratulations, Nikolai.'

'Thanks! Yes, thank you! I was just too keen to get started before, that's all,' spluttered Nikolai apologetically. 'I am here to serve the Motherland, Colonel.'

'Really, my nervous little computer doyen,' remarked the Colonel with an unexpected smile. 'I see you are somewhat tense due to my presence, Nikolai but that is why I am here - to drive you, to hammer the team into place, to make things happen.'

'Yes, I understand.'

'They call me the Spymaster,' revealed the Colonel. 'Do you know why?'

'No, Colonel.'

'They say I am one of the best at running spy rings because of my elaborate and extensive network of contacts across the globe. Sometimes I laugh at such people because they know not what I do. In your eyes, Nikolai, what do I do best?'

'Destroy the enemy,' suggested Nikolai. 'And frighten people like me.'

'Good!' responded the Colonel. 'By the way, I meant it when I said congratulations. Not only have you set up this elaborate mini-supercomputer framework all on your own you are the first to use the destruction module of our latest cyber weapon. Please, proceed as authorised.'

'Thank you, Colonel,' uttered the more confident Nikolai. 'Proceeding as authorised. But could I ask you one question, Colonel?'

'Of course!'

'Have I misunderstood this operation?'

'What do you mean by that?' quizzed the Colonel.

'I thought the primary reason for our visit was to secure a secret piece of enemy equipment, not mount a war on an individual.'

'Oh, did you now?' frowned the Colonel.

'Yes,' nodded Nikolai. 'Please don't think that I do not trust you or am suspicious about things it's just that this operation seems to have changed a little since we arrived in this country.'

'Well, things change, Nikolai,' proposed the Colonel. 'All you are required to do is follow my orders. Is that clear?'

Nikolai glanced at the Colonel and took in a look of deep scorn before he replied, 'Yes! Yes, of course. It's just that there is no mention of a specific piece of enemy equipment in your briefing papers. It all seems to be verbal from you and I wondered why?'

'You don't need to know,' replied the Colonel harshly. 'Just follow your orders and do as you are told.'

'The operation could have been explained to me in a better way,' suggested Nikolai. 'I have been told that you are quite brilliant at putting our agents into positions where we can gain intelligence from the enemy with regards to science, the military, people in charge of companies that we are interested in and things like that. Proper spying.'

'Yes, that is correct,' voiced the Colonel. 'It's what I do best.'

'And you are a legend, I am told.'

'Yes, so they say. Why do you ask, Nikolai?'

'Because if you are a legend then is it because you've never been caught? Surely the British have heard of you.'

'I suspect they have,' offered the Colonel. 'What are you driving at, Nikolai?'

'Why did Moscow send you on a top-secret mission to the UK if the British know about you?'

'It was Moscow's decision,' blustered Colonel Korobov.

'Then I have to tell you that I don't see any truth in this operation,' revealed Nikolai. 'Destroying someone in the way you have outlined to me doesn't seem to be an espionage activity that is widely known about or something that I have been party to previously.'

Angry now, the Colonel eyed Nikolai and blurted out, 'What don't you understand about the term 'you don't need to know'? I need you to follow my orders to the last letter. Understand?'

'Yes, of course,' replied Nikolai as he analysed the look on the Colonel's face and the assertive anger in her voice. 'I assure you your orders will be obeyed.'

'Good!' replied the Colonel resting a hand casually on Nikolai's shoulder and continuing with, 'Very good! Now get on with your job and don't ever query my orders again. I require total compliance at all times.'

Nikolai nodded and concentrated on his computer work.

Outside, the moon peeped from behind a cloud, shrouded the garden with a complex mix of enigmatic shadows, and caressed the gentle still waters of the loch as the night moved steadily into a new day.

In London, dawn was accompanied by a sad drizzle that finally disappeared at the precise moment Big Ben chimed seven fifteen in the morning. Simultaneously, a hand snatched open the door of a public telephone box situated near the City Hall and reached for the 'phone.

The emergency number was dialled before the caller revealed to the police, 'The Mayor of London, the Jew boy Epstein with the Yiddish connections in Tel Aviv, usually leaves home every morning at seven-thirty. This morning there will be a very loud bang when the bomb beneath his car explodes and blows his legs off. Death to the Kikes. No more Jews. You have been warned.'

Leaving the 'phone hanging loosely from its cradle, the caller retreated from the box, turned, and stepped into a four-wheel-drive SUV that drew up at the kerbside.

The vehicle drove casually away and crossed the River Thames at Tower Bridge.

Scribbling down a brief note, the police controller spun in her chair and delivered it to an Inspector responsible for emergency responses in the capital. Situated in an office in Scotland Yard, the Inspector nodded and ordered, 'Send the nearest three mobiles to the Mayor's address. Inform Hackney Borough Command and advise all units attending to exercise extreme caution.'

The controller flicked a radio switch and began diverting mobiles to the scene as the Inspector used technology to playback the recorded 'phone message. Assessing the tone and depth of the message content and the caller's voice, the Inspector hit the keyboard and began digitally transferring details of the incident to those listed on the computer screen who were to be informed of all such hostile intentions towards the Mayor.

Moments later, a message appeared on the main computer screen of Detective Sergeant Terry Anwhari: the duty officer in the Special Crime Unit. It was read quickly before the recipient turned to DI Anthea Adams and remarked, 'The Mayor of London again! True or false? Another hoax? It's the first of the day, Anthea.'

'Not another one,' replied DI Adams. 'That's how many this week?'

'Eight so far,' responded Terry. 'But it's the only one that mentions a bomb. Monitor and report or unit attendance?'

'Bannerman is in charge of the Mayor's protection, isn't he? Yes, monitor and report,' decided Anthea. 'Keep me informed, Terry, and add it to the list. Borough Command will be there long before us. Just keep an eye on it for now. Hopefully, Bannerman will keep us informed as the situation develops.'

'Will do!'

In Hackney, a single crewed mobile patrol, Constable Lionel Wood, arrived at the scene in time to see Benjamin Epstein and his protection officer, Detective Inspector Bannerman, walking down a gravel path towards a grey Volvo saloon car. The Mayor activated a remote-controlled wireless car key to unlock the doors as PC Wood wound the police car window down and shouted, 'Stand back! I've got a report the Mayor's car may be boobytrapped.'

Bannerman held the Mayor back with his free hand and demanded, 'Why wasn't I informed of this sooner?'

'I've no idea,' replied the response officer. 'Probably because there have been so many hoaxes concerning the Mayor that the duty officer decided not to trouble you. I was told to respond to the scene and secure the location. That's all I know. I'd guess this is another hoax, but you never know.'

'Okay!' replied Bannerman as he approached the Volvo. 'I'll take a quick look.'

The protection officer approached the Volvo.

As Mayor Benjamin Epstein retreated from the car with PC Wood, Bannerman slid an under-vehicle inspection mirror on a telescopic stick beneath the vehicle and gradually worked his way towards the front of the Volvo. Pausing for a moment, he studied an image on the mirror and then dropped to his knees to take a closer look beneath the Volvo before confirming his suspicions.

'Call bomb disposal and evacuate the immediate area,' he instructed. 'There's a box of some kind fixed to the underneath of the Mayor's Volvo and at this stage, I'd say it might be an under-car booby trap bomb.'

Shocked, the Mayor stood open-mouthed for a moment before Bannerman ushered him inside and activated the rest of the protection team who were charged with securing the Mayor's house.

'Check the CCTV system,' ordered Bannerman.

Within minutes, the radio waves were alive with transmissions as the immediate area was closed down, the road closed, and an evacuation zone created. It would be fifteen minutes before the Bomb Squad arrived and an operative used a mobile x-ray device to determine that the alleged bomb was a cardboard box that had been cleverly painted and constructed to resemble an under-car bomb. A magnet had then been added to the box to attach it to the vehicle and give the appearance of being an authentic device.

Bannerman stood beside the bomb disposal officer and PC Wood when the box was opened. He read aloud the words on a piece of paper left inside, 'Yiddish Jew... Shylock... Go back to Israel.'

'Charming,' uttered the bomb disposal officer. 'Maybe you'll get fingerprints or something from the piece of paper or the underside of the car?'

'Nothing useful from the CCTV, I'm told,' remarked Bannerman. 'But I doubt we'll get fingerprints. Anyone who has taken the trouble to make a cardboard box resemble a bomb has the patience of Job and probably sufficient intelligence to know what they are doing. That said, we'll give it a go. Someone really doesn't like the Mayor of London. The war against him is heating up. That could have been a bomb, a real one, and we need to respond!'

'What do you want me to do?' demanded PC Wood eagerly.

Bannerman checked his wristwatch and said, 'Phone the result into Control and then you can take us to the Mayor's office since the Volvo is going to be off the road. His work must go on and forensics will be all over the Mayor's car when they arrive. Meanwhile, I'm going to phone the Special Crime Unit. The situation is such that the car needs to be upgraded to incorporate TALOS.'

'What's that?' enquired PC Wood.

'An under-car bomb detector,' explained Bannerman. 'We deploy the device when the level of protection we require rises. It's an advanced system that uses state of the art microprocessor techniques. It works out noise levels, magnetic fields that detect hostile attachments and generally makes use of a network of hidden sensors to detect hostile environments. When an alarm goes off it immediately sends a text to a mobile network.'

'So,' probed PC Wood. 'If it had been a bomb today and TALOS had been fitted, you would have got a text on your mobile phone telling you the car had been tampered with?

'Yes,' admitted Bannerman. 'Something like that, and a lot more besides.'

PC Wood looked at the Volvo, the cardboard box, and Bannerman before saying, 'Lucky today then.'

In Scotland, a gentle wake unfolded behind the cabin cruiser as it journeyed along the loch. The water behind the vessel made an ever-increasing arrowhead pattern as the cruiser made its way northwards towards Drumnadrochit Bay. Eventually, the tension of the waves surrendered to the foreshore where they washed the thin strip of ground between the loch and a section of developed land.

In the vessel's cabin, the operator lectured his passengers on the history of the loch revealing, 'I've never actually seen it but some of my friends say they have. I really don't know the truth, but the story can be traced back fifteen hundred years when St Columba encountered a beast in the local river. In the 1930s, the Inverness Courier reported the first modern sighting.'

'Oh dear,' drawled an American tourist. 'Are we all going to be killed?'

'I doubt it,' replied the helmsman. 'I'm not aware of any story suggesting the monster has ever killed anyone. If there is a monster, it's a friendly one.'

'I see,' nodded the tourist as she looked out across the water towards the area between the village of Foyers and Easter Boleskine. 'I don't think I want to be eaten alive.'

'You won't be,' stated the helmsman.

In the distance, the lady saw a grey building rising from the land overlooking Loch Ness and resting quietly in the glorious splendour of the Highlands of Scotland.

In the building espied by the American, a computer geek was at work.

'Have you established a security blockade?' enquired the Colonel.

'Do you mean firewalls and anti-hacking protocols?' replied Nikolai.

'No,' snapped the Colonel. 'Even my run-of-the-mill knowledge of computers allows me to detect such facilities. No, I mean a passive infrared detection system that deploys sensors to detect motion at the perimeter of our enterprise and is connected to our computer system.'

'I've not had time yet,' replied Nikolai. 'So much to do.'

'This is supposed to be our Operations Centre, not a school classroom for computer wannabes,' fumed the Colonel. 'Are you familiar with the manual I gave you?'

'Yes! Yes, of course,' stuttered Nikolai timidly. 'I've already told you that.'

'Then you ought to be aware of the first requirement which is to lay down perimeter security for this building,' barked the Colonel. 'All objects whose temperature is above absolute zero emit infrared radiation. The alarm system is unobtrusive and aimed at human beings infringing upon our operation. If an individual intrudes our designated area, the system picks up their radiation and warns the computer operator of an intrusion. I shouldn't need to supervise you on this matter. Drop what you are doing and secure the perimeter as previously instructed. We must secure the operation.'

'But I…'

'Now!' barked the Colonel aggressively. 'Control means control. Immediately!'

As Nikolai sheepishly recounted his steps and began the security process, Colonel Korobov tried to calm herself down. Stepping some distance out of earshot, she rang an encrypted number and waited. When her 'phone was answered, she declared, 'This is Cyclops. I need a replacement cryptologist on the next flight.'

Listening, turning to glance at Nikolai, she eventually spoke to the other party on the 'phone saying, 'I have a job to do and I want the best, not an individual who is lacking ability as well as the right attitude. With respect, I expected the best from the centre. I am disappointed in you and should not be making this call. I'm in control of a clandestine operation and want immediate security.'

The Colonel grimaced at the reply and then calmly countered, 'You seem to be unaware of my authority in this matter. This is Cyclops. I require you to comply immediately with my instructions and refer you to my mandate which was sanctioned by the office of the Supreme Commander.'

A pause in the conversation followed allowing the Colonel to glimpse a view of Nikolai bent over the computer keyboard. Eventually, she received a response and replied, 'Good! You've obviously read my credentials and operational standing. You would do well to focus on my status and range of responsibilities in this matter and ensure that my instructions are carried out to the letter. Understand?'

Nikolai looked up from his keyboard, could not hear the conversation, but offered a weak smile to the Colonel.

The Colonel returned a friendly grin, heard a positive answer on her 'phone, and closed the conversation with, 'Yes! The next flight.'

Content, the Russian spymaster satisfied the undoubted desire for power aching within her as evidence of her self-induced megalomania rose to prominence when she informed the other party, 'No! He won't be returning on that particular flight.'

Smiling now, the Colonel closed her phone and returned to Nikolai with, 'Not to worry, my friend. I'm sure we can work things out. Tell me, how far have you progressed to date?'

'These are for posting,' replied Nikolai pointing to a couple of envelopes.

'Thank you,' replied the Colonel taking possession of the letters. 'Anything else?'

'Just a few false stories on the web,' ventured Nikolai. 'Shoplifting for clothes, things like that.'

'Good!' replied the Colonel. 'I'm driving down to see our partners shortly. I'll be away overnight and trust you will be up to speed upon my return. Meanwhile, show me which department stores you have highlighted and what types of clothing were stolen.'

Further south, two secret agents were dressing up in new clothes to play a game.

'You look the part, Nadia,' offered Major Petrov. 'The long grey dress suits you.'

'Why thank you, Viktor,' replied the female spy. 'I wish the same could be said of that hat you are wearing but I'm afraid that is not the case.'

Viktor chuckled, squared away the peak of his dark brown trilby, and suggested, 'You are grey, and I am brown. Let's keep it that way. Unobtrusive and not at all memorable.'

'Until we start to knock on doors,' queried Nadia.

'An essential part of our cover for when we return,' explained Viktor. 'It is like the Colonel said. We are going to do a job whilst we are under the camera's eye. We will beat them with this clever idea.'

'I thought it was crazy myself,' responded Nadia.

'Mrs Grey, do you believe that Armageddon is upon us?' demanded Viktor Petrov with a huge grin. 'Of course, you do. Do you believe that the destruction of the present world system is imminent?'

'Of course, I do, Mister Brown,' laughed Nadia.

'And that the establishment of God's kingdom over the earth is the only solution for all problems faced by humanity?'

'Absolutely, Viktor!'

'Good! We'll take these publications with us. We know we will be captured on security cameras, but they will think we are Jehovah's Witnesses. Make sure the residents see the Watchtower and Awake magazines. They are more likely to recall the magazines as opposed to our nondescript faces and drab attire. Just act naturally and I'll do the rest when we reach the target. Okay?'

'Don't worry! I know what to do,' replied Nadia. 'But tell me, why did you pick on this to be our cover?'

'Because that religion is banned in Russia,' explained Viktor. 'If they ever latch onto us, which is doubtful at this stage, the British will be chasing local bible bashers and we'll be on the beach at Sochi enjoying our medals and promotions. MI5 will never equate Jehovah's Witnesses to spying. Are you ready, Mrs Grey?'

'Yes, I am, Mister Brown. Come on. I'll drive.'

Half an hour later, Nadia turned from the main road towards the target premises. As she approached the building, Viktor glanced at the porch area, scanned the garden, and said, 'Looks vacant. Turn around at the end of the road and we'll play the game. We'll start with the house six doors along from the target. Okay?'

'Fine,' remarked Nadia as she followed orders and eventually slid the car into a convenient parking area.

During the next twenty minutes, Nadia and Viktor knocked on doors in the area, left magazines to be read later, and engaged their audience in polite conversation about the beliefs of the Jehovah's Witnesses. Guiding the conversations their way, they soon learnt that the target address was unoccupied.

Calm, unflustered, they worked their way along the street consciously aware of the security systems that captured their every movement. It wasn't long before they realised that the various systems were static cameras taking still pictures.

'Upper middle class, fairly wealthy, not public-school types,' stated Nadia. 'And the cameras appear to be unmanned. Still photographs only if they are lucky.'

'Even those in the tree branches that are supposed to be hidden,' remarked Viktor.

'They could have been put there by bird watchers,' suggested Nadia.

'True,' admitted Viktor pulling his collar up. 'Then let them record the birds and not us. Hello! We're here.'

Nadia strolled towards the front door with Viktor by her side. She pressed the bell and then rapped the front door with her knuckles in an attempt to raise the occupants within.

There was no reply.

'No-one at home, just like the neighbours said,' delivered Viktor. 'Watch my back.'

'Are you going in?' whispered Nadia.

Viktor delved into a trouser pocket and removed a small black leather case from which he extracted two pieces of thin metal. Each one was specially designed to do a different job.

'Yes, that's the general idea,' replied Viktor as he handled the first piece of metal.

Taking the tension wrench, Viktor inserted it into the bottom of the keyhole. He applied slight pressure to the piece of metal and simultaneously inserted the other piece into the top of the lock. Whilst applying slight torque to the wrench, Viktor jiggled the top lockpick back and forward in the keyhole.

'Nearly there?' enquired Nadia.

'Shush, woman!' replied Viktor. 'My mind is inside the lock feeling the pins. Quiet please.'

Nadia turned and looked towards the street saying, 'Sorry. It's my first time.'

'Not mine,' replied Viktor. 'You just need to visualise the inside of the lock to become part of the pins you are messing about with. It's all about lining up the pins.'

There was more jiggling of the lockpick before the door opened and Viktor triumphed with, 'Not bad, less than five minutes.'

'It's done in seconds in the movies,' suggested Nadia.

'But not in real life,' remarked Viktor. 'I'm going in. Keep watch.'

As Nadia did as she was told, Viktor took a couple of steps from the porch into the hall and then stood quietly for a few moments. Only the sound of a ticking clock from somewhere in the house invaded his ears.

Viktor strode down the hallway pausing at every doorway to take a photograph of each room before locating the bedrooms. It didn't take long to find the double bedroom which was the largest in the house.

Carefully, he prized the wardrobe opened and selected a dark suit from the rail. Holding it to the light, he thought back to a briefing and a photograph of the target wearing this suit. He convinced himself of his choice, selected two more suits, left the bedroom, and hung them on the outside door handle. Then he returned to the wardrobe, removed numerous pairs of gent's trousers and placed them on the floor close to the suits he had chosen.

Removing his wristwatch, he slid the back away to reveal that the timepiece was no more than a storage compartment for more than a dozen conveniently sized listening devices. Selecting the first, he bent down and fastened it to the underside of the bedroom door before walking confidently towards another room. He opened the door to find the living room. Rather than enter the room, the secret agent bent down once more and fixed a second listening device to the underside of the living room door. Spinning around, checking his surroundings, Viktor discovered the kitchen and inserted another tiny device beneath that door. Each device was slightly smaller than a drawing pin.

'The triplets are down, Nadia. How do you receive?'

At the front door, Nadia removed a mobile 'phone from her handbag and switched it on.

'Standby! Searching! App engaged,' she replied followed by 'Located! Sending signal now.'

Nadia pressed an icon on the phone display and knew that a wireless signal was on its way to the three devices.

Checking her display, she gradually revealed, 'I'm receiving a signal from one, two and…. Yes, number three is also acknowledging. We're all set but we've nothing to upload at the moment.'

'Good! Number four going down.'

Viktor approached the phone in the hall and pinned another device to the underside before reporting, 'Leaving now.'

'Four down!' confirmed Nadia from her App. 'I'm putting them into sleep mode. They are voice activated so their presence cannot be detected electronically until they waken up and transmit.'

'Thank you,' replied Viktor.

Collecting the suit and trousers hanging from a door handle, Viktor made his way to the front door to find Nadia looking out towards the roadway.

'All clear,' she reported.

Closing the front door behind him, the interior pin system collapsed into the locked position. Viktor folded his spoils into a bag and accompanied Nadia to their vehicle. There was a burst of life from the engine before the pair drove away from the area, joined the main road, and headed to a rendezvous.

At Carlisle police station, Sergeant Riley ushered Constable John Dillon into his office, invited him to take a seat, and then said, 'John, I've some news for you. It's a golden opportunity and I'd like you to take it with both hands.'

'What? You're either sacking me, transferring me, or carrying out some heinous trick that is designed to get rid of me permanently.'

'Why should I do that?' queried the Sergeant.

'Because I'm a failure,' offered Dillon. 'I've spent my career so far chasing shadows and socks up lanes and drainpipes and never caught a thing. I'm a born loser, Sarge.'

'No, you're not,' responded Riley. 'You had a good start when you first joined us, but you've hit a bad patch early on. That's going to change as from today.'

'How?' enquired Dillon.

'The detectives have asked for you. I've agreed. You start tomorrow on day shift for one week.'

'Me, a detective? There must be some mistake,' proposed Dillon.

'No, John,' responded the Sergeant. 'The detectives have asked for you because you're the best lead to finding the Whippet Kid. You're the only one who has seen him, and it looks like they have linked him to quite a few burglaries in the area. Nine o'clock tomorrow morning, I want you to report to the CID office and ask for the DI. He'll explain things to you and introduce you to the team that's leading the enquiry. One of the first things you'll do is sit down with the artist I've arranged and try and put together a good drawing of the suspect.'

'Then what?'

'You'll be in the team dedicated to catching him. Understood?'

'Yes! I suppose so,' murmured PC Dillon nervously. 'But the detectives! They'll bin me if I don't make the grade.'

'You've read too many crime stories, John,' offered the Sergeant. 'Go home, iron a nice clean shirt and a suit, and join the jacks for a week. You've nothing to lose and everything to gain. Okay?'

'Yes, okay,' replied John Dillon. 'A detective already and I've not got six months in yet.'

'Not quite like that,' laughed Sergeant Riley. 'Just do your best. Of you go.'

John Dillon lifted his tall, lean frame from the chair and made his way out of the office. Then, pausing at the door, he turned and asked, 'Will I get a detective allowance?'

Without looking up from his desk, Sergeant Riley tended to some paperwork but offered, 'No, you'll need to buy your own beer. Good luck.'

John Dillon stepped into the corridor, closed the Sergeant's door behind him, and shrugged his shoulders.

Last chance, he thought. Last chance.

In a hotel room on the edge of Carlisle, a quilter pushed a porcelain thimble against a needle and carried on sewing as she advised her audience, 'Good work, so far. Are you both feeling confident?'

'Yes, Colonel,' admitted Viktor. 'It went well today, and we've established an acceptable cover under which to work.'

'Agreed! It is most satisfactory,' replied the Colonel as she manipulated a thimble, a piece of thread, and a needle into position. She guided the needle in and out of the hem of a jacket and continued, 'Can you complete the operation this afternoon?'

'I believe so,' responded Viktor.

'Nadia?' queried the Colonel. 'Your thoughts? Are you confident that part two can be completed?'

'Yes, of course,' replied Nadia. 'Most definitely. We've learnt the target will be vacant until later this evening. The plan is to visit more houses as we did today and then penetrate the target once we are happy to conclude the business.'

'Excellent,' smiled the Colonel. 'I wish everyone had such a positive attitude. There, I've finished. You can return them now.'

Replacing a needle, thread, and thimble in her bag, the Colonel held a suit out and smoothed away the corner hem of the jacket saying, 'The wearer will never know they are carrying a listening and location device with them.'

'I watched you do that,' nodded Nadia. 'The devices are so thin.'

'But proven to be strong enough to do the job,' remarked the Colonel. 'They won't last forever. There is a time limitation in play. It is more than enough to establish whether or not you are being discussed as suspects if they realise the house has been illegally entered. It's all down to the battery life of the devices but I've also sewn similar appliances into the trouser hems. Now listen to me. I'll be sat in the front window of this hotel drinking tea and reading. When your operation is completed, I want you to return promptly, park outside the newsagent opposite, and buy a newspaper. Stay inside the newsagents and browse the shelves. We'll do a brush contact in the shop during which time you can hand over the package. You can be on your way as soon as we are done.'

'Yes,' replied Viktor. 'Minimum contact is essential.'

'Correct!' nodded the Colonel. 'Now you must go. Time is of the essence.'

The two spooks shook hands with their Spymaster and left the hotel room as Colonel Korobov checked her thimbles, threads, and needles. She bundled them away once more and watched from the window as her accomplices returned to their vehicle.

'Is she watching us?' whispered Nadia as the two snoopers approached their vehicle.

'You can bet your life she is,' replied Viktor. 'Her codename is Cyclops for a very good reason.'

'Which is?'

'In Greek mythology,' explained Viktor. 'The Cyclops were giant one-eyed creatures from a race of wild lawless individuals who possessed neither social manners nor fear of the Gods. Apparently, they were shepherds from Sicily. Would you believe they ate human beings?'

'Sounds fearsome but they were males?' stated Nadia. 'The Cyclops were all male, weren't they? The Colonel is most definitely female.'

'Yes, but then I didn't give her the codename,' replied Viktor. 'Someone else in the organisation did. Maybe it was all about trying to fool the enemy into thinking Cyclops was a man. I don't really know but what I do know is that if she only ever had one eye then it would always be focused on one thing, and right now that's us.'

'Su-ka!' snapped Nadia.

'Keep it English, woman,' growled Viktor. 'We're not in the Motherland now.'

'Sorry! Bitch then!' barked Nadia.

'Don't look around,' ordered Viktor. 'Just get in the car. Years ago, the Colonel was a good teacher in class but now she is a legend, an enigma at times, and not a lady that you might want to cross from what I've heard.'

'Is she really a terminator?' enquired Nadia. 'I mean, I've heard she works directly to the top landing. Will she destroy us if we get things wrong?'

'I'm not intending to find out,' replied Viktor.

'Me neither. By the way, have you checked your jacket hem?' suggested Nadia.

For a second, Viktor's fingers dropped to the hem of his jacket before he quickly slid his hand in the pocket saying, 'No, she wouldn't. Would she?'

'I don't know. You tell me,' grinned Nadia. 'You're the boss.'

An hour later, in Cumbria, two people pretending to be Jehovah's Witnesses revisited the scene of their earlier crime, worked the neighbourhood doors with their polite talk and magazines, ignored the security cameras in use, and lockpicked the target house once more.

As Nadia kept watch at the door, Viktor entered the bedroom and replaced the suits and trousers he had removed earlier that day. Then he visited every room in the house before finding the family computer in the living room. He switched it on and inserted an electronic catchment stick into a port at the side. Three minutes later, the data carried by the computer had downloaded onto Viktor's device.

Returning to their car, Nadia drove to a newsagent shop situated opposite the front bay window of a hotel.

Viktor alighted from the vehicle, entered the shop, bought a newspaper, and browsed the shelves looking at magazines.

Moments later, an elderly lady entered and bought a tablet of chocolate before brushing casually against Viktor as she left the shop.

In the moment of swift unseen contact, Viktor passed the electronic catchment stick to the Colonel by hand and then continued to check out the shelves.

Two minutes later, Viktor strolled nonchalantly from the premises and joined his accomplice who selected first gear and drove off.

Later that day, at the same location, a postman walked down the gravel drive and cascaded a succession of envelopes through the letterbox. The letters mingled quietly next to an envelope containing the milkman's handwritten bill, the parish magazine, an array of junk mail, and a copy of the publication Watchtower.

Simultaneously, in a building elsewhere in the nation's capital, a hand reached out and flicked a switch that caused an electrical current to power an industrial cordless vacuum cleaner.

A young lady propelled the vacuum cleaner along a corridor and into the main office. It was what she did every evening when the offices closed for the day. Only a skeleton crew remained on duty, working through the night, manning the communications system, updating and downloading computers, as a young lady passed between them guiding her vacuum cleaner in a dedicated manner.

It was almost as if she intended not to miss anything. She would visit every nook and cranny in the offices she visited. There would be no stone left unturned. The individual was renowned for her meticulous ability to tidy things up and make sure everything was where it should be at the close of play, and that all desk and workplaces were clean and uncluttered.

Popular, attractive, yet quiet and unobtrusive, she rarely spoke to the workers. Indeed, there was a tendency on their part to ignore Sasha Morozova. She was unimportant in so many ways, just a lowly paid cleaner distantly related to someone in the organisation who lived back home. They didn't know who she was and didn't really care. Sasha was just the cleaner. It was her job to clean, not theirs.

There was an occasional grin that escaped her face, perhaps a contented nod, or a few words of gratitude when someone moved out of her way or helped in some way.

Alexei always smiled when she approached with the hoover, turned his computer screen away, removed his mobile 'phone from the desk, and smiled at her again.

His eyes caught hers. He winked. She looked away.

'Dinner?' queried Alexei. 'One night after work perhaps?'

Caught off guard for a moment, Sasha replied, 'After work? No, not possible. I'm sorry. I'm always busy after work.'

'Surely not?' replied the persistent Alexei. 'How about the weekend?'

'Very kind of you, really it is, but I think you would be better off asking one of the girls in the office. I'm just the cleaner, Alexei. Not good for your image, and I really am very busy this weekend too.'

'Image?' shrugged Alexei. 'I'm asking you because I'd like to know more about you.'

'I'm fine, honestly,' offered Sasha. 'And very busy. Now if you'll excuse me, I must get finished. There is so much to do.'

Alexei stood back as Sasha guided the hoover around him and continued her way through the office. Shaking his head, he forced a smile and watched the cleaning lady pass by, open the office door, and disappear into the corridor.

Sasha Morozova was hardly important in the scheme of things as she guided her vacuum cleaner through the office complex that was the Russian Embassy in Kensington Palace Gardens, London.

Much further north, shortly after midnight, as the waters of the loch gently washed the shoreline, a thumb plunged the thin, hollow tube of a hypodermic needle downwards until the sharp tip penetrated the skin of an incompetent suspicious cryptologist.

There was a sudden gasp of agony when he felt the force of the plunger inject a lethal substance into his body.

His hands rushed to his neck, but it was all over in seconds.

As the body slumped downwards, eager hands guided it into an oversized golf bag and forced the physique into the meagre space. It was a tight squeeze but the larger bag was made for golfers seeking to accommodate all the extras a tour player might require in their quest for fame and fortune, or a lower handicap: namely space for waterproofs, gloves, balls, tees, drivers, putters, irons, refreshments, and extra clothing. At that precise moment, the golf bag was the last home of a human being.

The sound of a high-pitched zip sliding on its journey to engage the device's teeth filled the air before the weighted-down body bag entered the water and dropped silently into the depths of the watery basin below.

4

London
Early morning

Bannerman threw himself through the air when he saw the assailant move from behind a parked car and throw something at the Mayor of London. Taking the full force of a medium-sized tin of yellow gloss paint, Bannerman crash-landed on the footpath.

Mayor Epstein stepped backwards, lost his step and tripped over, ending up flat on his back with a conveniently placed photojournalist snapping away merrily with his camera whilst the assailant screamed, 'Kike Ikey…. Kike Ikey…. You need a yellow star just like in the holocaust, Jew boy!'

As Bannerman lay on the ground, partially covered in paint, he took the aggressor down with a sudden leg sweep that connected with the antagonist's calves. An agonising scream from the attacker followed when he hurtled downwards and landed on top of Bannerman.

In the melee that ensued, Bannerman clambered to his feet and seized the reprobate before slamming him hard against the wall with the words, 'You're nicked, pal.'

'My legs! You've broken my legs!'

'Not yet! But there's always time.'

There was a quiet unforgiving sound when a cheek scraped against the rough brick of the wall and a smear of blood escaped the facial area.

As the journalist thrust his camera forward, Bannerman's fist shot out and collided with the body of the camera smashing it into a hundred pieces.

'Don't stick things in my face,' growled an angry Bannerman.

'My camera!' uttered the photojournalist.

'My face,' replied Bannerman. 'That could have been anything. Now get out of the way.'

Groaning, Mayor Epstein twisted over and then grasped his back mouthing, 'Damn it, man. My back's gone again.'

'Are you alright, sir?' asked a concerned Bannerman.

'Better than you,' replied the Mayor. 'Have you seen your suit?'

'It'll wash off,' suggested Bannerman.

'I doubt it,' responded the Mayor. 'You'll need a new one. By the way, check your firearm. Did the paint reach the trigger mechanism?'

As the reporter gathered up pieces of his camera, Inspector Bannerman withdrew a pistol from his shoulder holster and held it up to take a good look.

'No! No!' screamed the cameraman. 'It was only supposed to be a bit of fun. Don't shoot me. He told me he was going to throw feathers at you.'

'It could have been an acid attack,' responded Bannerman coldly. 'In fact, you're nicked too as you're obviously in cahoots with your mate.'

Pieces of the camera fell to the ground again when the journalist turned and began to make a run for it.

The Mayor stuck out a leg, brought the man to the ground, and proposed, 'There's two down. Anymore?'

Bannerman laughed. Using his undoubted power and stature, he secured the second prisoner of the day against the wall and used his mobile to ring for assistance.

Dripping from yellow paint, Bannerman asked, 'Are you okay? Your back? Do you need a doctor or an ambulance?'

'No, just a tot of whisky will do,' chuckled the Mayor as he straightened up. 'I'll be alright in a moment or so.'

'Are you sure?'

'You know, I think I'm getting too old for all this. It's just one thing after another. From hoax car bombs to paint attacks. What next?' declared the Mayor. 'Will it ever settle down?'

'That's why it's relentless,' suggested Bannerman. 'They're trying to grind you down until you walk away from it all.'

'That will make them happy?' enquired the Mayor.

'For a short time,' replied Bannerman. 'Then they'll find another target they dislike. They call themselves activists, but it would be rather nice if they could become active in something useful.'

'I don't think you're supposed to have a political opinion, Bannerman,' chuckled the Mayor.

'True, but I'm wondering if the two idiots we've just arrested are also connected with the hoax car bomb at your home.'

'What's your gut feeling?' queried Mayor Epstein.

One of the prisoners tried to twist away from Bannerman. The other swung his elbow backwards in an attempt to unbalance Bannerman.

'Let's ask them,' proposed Bannerman as he pounded both prisoners against the wall again whilst yelling, 'Come on! Speak up! What do you know about the bomb beneath the Mayor's car? Come on! I can't hear you.'

Benjamin Epstein winced as the face of the photojournalist clattered against the brick wall once more.

'Nothing! What car?'

'Stop it! For God's sake, stop it!'

'Then stop trying to run away!'

'We're not terrorists!'

'No, you're both terrible bloody activists,' declared Bannerman as he let go of both prisoners and allowed them to fall to the ground.

'Definitely bloody now,' muttered the Mayor. 'What do they feed you on, Bannerman?'

'Steak!'

'Rare?'

'Of course,' replied Bannerman. 'In answer to your question, I'd say it was difficult, at this stage, to connect these two to the under-car bomb incident. The hoax bomb incident needed some thought and planning whereas someone throwing a tin of paint at the Mayor outside his office isn't quite in the same league. I'm going to ring Anthea and update her. An interview and investigation into our suspects might turn something up. You never know.'

The sound of police sirens could be heard growing louder.

'Well, whatever happens,' remarked the Mayor. 'Thank you. I'm so pleased Boyd bolstered my protection with the likes of you, Mister Bannerman.'

'Why yellow paint?' probed Bannerman. 'And you're right, this suit of mine is ruined. I only bought it a month ago.'

'It could have been worse,' replied the Mayor. 'Try black chinos and a blue roll neck sweater next time.'

'Oh yes,' said Bannerman. 'You'd love it if I dressed up in scruff gear. What colour do you prefer, Mister Mayor? Yellow?'

'Not yellow! It's the colour long associated with anti-Semitism,' explained the Mayor. 'Most people particularly remember the yellow star that the Nazis made the Jews wear in the last war. If you were a Jew, you were discriminated against because they all wore the yellow star.'

'It can't be easy for you even now?' offered Bannerman.

The Mayor's reply was drowned by a police siren that filled the air. Moments later a van arrived and took the two prisoners into custody at a police station in central London.

Elsewhere, a woman in a nurse's uniform sat at the kitchen table and poured over a collection of mail that had arrived earlier in the morning. Scanning the envelopes, she quickly binned the obvious advertisement leaflets and unsolicited mail before finally ending up with three letters addressed to Mr and Mrs Wm M Boyd.

She tore the envelopes open and began reading them.

'Debts!' Megs whispered to herself. 'I didn't even know we had a credit card. What has Billy been doing? I don't understand.'

'Mum! The telephone is ringing!'

'Coming, Izzy,' replied Meg.

A telephone continued to ring in the hallway and Meg went to answer it.

Five minutes later, more worried than before, Meg switched on the kettle to make a pot of tea whilst she said aloud, 'More debts. And they've got our number. What's going on? What on earth has happened? Do I need to cancel work today or should I go in?'

Shaking her head, lost and confused, Meg engaged her mobile phone, waited for a reply, and then said, 'I'd like to speak to Commander Boyd, please…. Yes, it's his wife, Meg.'

She waited on the line before answering, 'Can you tell him I rang and would like him to ring home as soon as he can. Yes, it's... No, it's not urgent. Just make sure he gets the message, please.'

Closing the phone, Meg slumped down into the nearest seat and spread her hands across the letters that she had just read.

'Debts!' she mouthed. 'Debts that I know nothing about. What the hell has Billy been up to? All these years together and I've never had occasion not to trust him. This is so unlike him. He's not that kind of man. I don't understand what's going on.'

In the Commissioner's office in Scotland Yard, London, the Head of the Metropolitan Police set aside his pen and a pile of documents and addressed his guest with, 'Commander Boyd, I can confirm your appointment and it will be to the rank of Detective Chief Superintendent. It has to be said that the most recent enquiry you undertook in relation to a corrupt chief constable, a Russian spy, and an ISIS terrorist was such that you deserve recognition. This promotion brings you in line with my senior management team and is authorised as of today. Congratulations! It is well deserved.'

'Thank you, sir,' replied Boyd.

'I have the utmost confidence in you,' remarked the Commissioner. 'And expect you to continue to provide the very highest level of service to the nation.'

'I shall try my best, sir. Or rather, the unit will stand firm.'

'Good! That's what I wanted to hear but something most unexpected has arisen, Boyd, and I want you to deal with the matter expeditiously before I finalise these promotion papers and send them to the Home Secretary.'

'The Home Secretary?' queried Boyd.

'Details of all members of my senior management team are sent to the Home Secretary, Boyd. She likes to be kept aware of developments at the top level. Now, what shall we do about these problems I mentioned?'

'Problems?' quizzed Boyd.

The Commissioner leaned back in his leather chair, engaged Boyd directly, and probed, 'Have you any problems of a financial nature, Chief Superintendent Boyd?'

Boyd swivelled uneasily in his chair before replying, 'No! None whatsoever, sir. What makes you ask?'

A hand reached into a folder, removed a letter, and handed it to Boyd.

'Read this,' ordered the Commissioner. 'It was received here today. It's from a debt collector and it mentions you. It would appear you have missed a couple of payments on your credit card.'

'Credit card!' exclaimed Boyd. 'What do you mean, sir?'

'I carried out a credit check on you, Boyd,' revealed the Commissioner. 'It's standard practice for those who work under a veil of secrecy as you know, and you are not immune from the practices and procedures that underpin such positions. Put simply I have a letter from a debt collector stating you owe money. This is confirmed when your credit rating is checked via numerous online companies.'

'I… I don't know what to say, sir,' stumbled Boyd. 'My security clearance is undertaken every six months as well you know.'

'It's just that when I did a security check on you this morning,' explained the Commissioner. 'There was a hitch in so far as you appear to have missed some payments on your credit card. It's as simple as that and, at the present moment, that information is in my possession only. Look, Boyd, I suspect you have been so busy chasing spooks, crooks and corrupt police officers that you've not had time to sit down and tend to your finances. Do me a favour and sort this out pronto. I cannot sit on this for too long. Just sort it as quickly as you can and let me know when the payment has been made and everything balances.'

Shaking his head, Boyd removed a wallet from his jacket, opened it, and said, 'Look inside! I only have a debit card, Commissioner. I don't have a credit card. There's been a mistake somewhere along the line.'

Smiling, the Commissioner eased forward in his chair and replied, 'I'm sure that is the case, Boyd. You are one of the highest-paid officers in the entire police service. So, I don't expect you to have credit card problems. Highly paid officers are much less likely to accept bribes and be susceptible to corruption whereas badly paid officers are an obvious target for those crooks who seek to manipulate them and use the paucity of such officers to their best advantage. In my experience, Boyd, I'd perhaps have a word with your wife. I don't mean to be personal, but the answer may be there. Fix it, Boyd. Pronto! Otherwise… Well, I'm sitting on this until you do. Understood?'

'Leave it with me,' replied Boyd. 'I'll deal with it. There's been a mistake of some kind. Wrong name! Wrong address! I'll make some calls.'

Standing now, the Commissioner stepped away from his chair, sat on the corner of the desk and stated, 'Maybe this promotion has gone slightly to your head, or your wife's. You both knew it was on the cards. Believe me, Boyd, I know what it's like. Don't be embarrassed. She's booked a month's cruise up the Amazon, a fortnight in Disneyland, or two weeks in an exclusive hotel in Las Vegas or New York. It's a surprise for you. Something like that. I know what it's like. Take a break and sort her out.'

'She doesn't need sorting out, Commissioner. I'm telling you now that something is wrong, and it wasn't caused by malpractice on either my part or my wife's. We are not fools. Something has gone wrong at the bank and I need to investigate what that is. Since everyone is making their assumptions, I'll need to investigate that myself. My problem is that I need to knock on the right door and so far, Commissioner, all those doors remain closed to me. Looks like I may have to kick some down.'

'There's no need to explain, Boyd, and no need to get upset about things. You're best suited to investigating yourself, I suggest. Look take some Garden Leave! Yes, take a form of what you and I will call Garden Leave. That will give you time.'

'I'd rather carry on working, sir,' explained Boyd. 'There's the bank to sort, Benjamin Epstein, the Mayor and…'

Cutting Boyd short, the Commissioner growled, 'Bannerman has that in hand. You do trust him, don't you?'

'Yes, I do,' replied Boyd.

'You must trust the people you bequeath responsibility to, Boyd,' advised the Commissioner. 'It's part of being both a leader and a manager. Both positions are different, but both involve trusting others to do something they are instructed to do. Why don't you take a look at the arsonist job that you told me about? It's a serial criminal by the look of it.

I'm sure the Cumbrian force wouldn't mind a hand. Do you want me to ring their new chief and tell them you are offering your services?'

'No,' snapped Boyd. 'Definitely not! I had enough problems with the last one. I'll do it if you don't mind.'

'Not at all. Maybe you just need to rest. Just phone me when things are sorted.'

'Yes, I'll do that,' nodded Boyd. 'The worst-case scenario is that Meg has sold me short or planned a huge surprise for me then forgotten to pay. I can't believe that has happened. I suspect, however, that the bank has made a mistake and haven't realised it. She has her career, by the way, sir. My wife is financially secure and not dependent on me. That's why a lot of stuff at the bank just doesn't make sense at all.'

'Brilliant,' smiled the Commissioner. 'And yes, I am aware of her position. Garden Leave, Boyd, of a kind. Sort things out whatever they might be.'

'I can't think why but a short break might do us both good and the circus is in town. Meg likes a clown.'

'The circus,' laughed the Commissioner. 'Take a tip, Boyd. You've reached the pinnacle of your career. Don't let the circus change you into a clown.'

'I won't, sir, and thank you,' nodded Boyd.

The two men shook hands. Boyd left the office and the Commissioner read again the letter from a London based debt collector. There was a twist of a key when the Commissioner shook his head and placed the document in his desk drawer and locked it tight.

Boyd walked down the corridor away from the Commissioner's office. He withdrew his mobile phone, saw another missed call from his wife, and pocketed the device.

'Wait until I get home,' he muttered to himself. 'What on earth has she been up to? Debts! Credit cards! All these years! I thought I could trust her. She's never let me down since we were married. What the hell is going on? Is she up to something that I don't know about?'

Boyd found his office, slammed the door behind him, and withdrew a bottle of brandy from a filing cabinet.

The first tot fell all the way to the stomach as he looked out of the office window, studied the Thames rolling towards the estuary, and allowed his mind to direct his thoughts to that of home and a wife who seemed to have upset the balance of things.

Meanwhile, Boyd's wife - Meg – scanned another postal delivery and began adding to a pile of letters that were quite unpaid bills that had been accrued in recent months. Finally, she opened a window, took in some clean fresh air, and then broke down sobbing as she angrily scattered the letters across the kitchen floor.

'Another woman!' she cried aloud. 'Yes or no? I don't believe it. He's never been unfaithful to me.' Then, chuckling, she added, 'He never has the time for another woman anyway. But has he made time for someone else? For God's sake! I don't understand this. What's happening?'

By late afternoon, Boyd stepped from the London-Glasgow high-speed train and took a taxi to his residence on the edge of Carlisle. Arriving home, the children ran to him and he gathered them up in his arms and smothered them with love and affection.

Meg smiled wryly, scowled, walked into the kitchen, and then slammed the door behind her.

Moments later, joined by her husband, Meg pointed to a collection of letters on the table and challenged Boyd with, 'Debts, Billy! We need to talk. You can't hide behind the telephone anymore. You're here in person. Something is going on and I want to know what it is.'

'Later,' replied Boyd. 'I promised the kids we'd take them to the circus. Let's do that then we can have a chat about all this when we get back.'

'Have a chat?' probed Meg dryly. 'A dozen letters from people demanding money, half a dozen debt collection agencies, and a note from the garage indicating they are considering seizing the Porsche because of non-payment of monthly finance, and your answer to all this is we'll have a chat.'

'Meg!' snapped Boyd. 'Have you been spending money on some kind of surprise for us because of this promotion of mine?'

'Of course not,' snapped Meg. 'Where did you get that idea from?'

'Yes or no! Is it true?'

'When did I ever do that?' scolded Meg.

'Oh!' whispered Boyd. 'I thought you had. I mean you made me wonder about things. It's just that I thought…'

'I don't care what you think, Billy,' replied Meg angrily. 'I'd never spend the kind of money that's mentioned in these letters. Do I look stupid? Do I normally behave irresponsibly? No! It's you that's been reckless, isn't it? And your answer is to have a chat. No, Billy Boyd. I want the truth, the whole truth and nothing but the truth. Have you heard that one before?'

'Of course,' spluttered a confused Boyd. 'Look, if it's not you that's spent all this money and it's not me then it's pretty obvious there's been a mistake made at the bank.'

'Do you really think so?' gasped Meg, suddenly taken by surprise. 'Thank goodness for that. Are you sure?'

'Well, what else can it be?' voiced Boyd.

'I don't know. I thought it was incompetence on your part,' proposed Meg. 'I'm so confused I don't know what to think.'

'I'll go to the bank tomorrow and sort it all out,' suggested Boyd. 'It's probably a technical hitch of some kind. Leave it with me, Meg.'

'I'm not sure I believe you,' replied Meg. 'Not sure at all. Is there anyone else?'

'Of course not. How could there be? There will never be anyone else for me. I'll sort it all out tomorrow,' repeated Boyd. 'I promise.'

Unsure, equally perplexed, Meg stared at Boyd but offered no reply.

'Can we both calm down?' suggested Boyd. 'All we've achieved in the last two minutes amounts to nothing other than the potential to destroy all the years we've been together.'

'I agree,' replied Meg. 'And that's most of our adult life. What's happening to us? Why is everything upside down?'

'That's what I want to find out,' revealed Boyd. 'I love you, Meg. There's never been anyone else and never will be.'

'And I love you,' returned Meg. 'But I've never experienced anything like this before. I'm worried, confused, agitated and don't know which way to turn.'

'Into my arms would be a good start,' suggested Boyd.

'That's an easy answer. What's the real answer?'

'I'm going to the bank tomorrow to see if I can sort things out there. I have a nine o'clock meeting with Stan at the nick, then the bank. You could come to the bank with me if you want?'

Thinking it over, Meg replied, 'You're better at such things than me. I'll leave it with you provided you obtain the very latest bank statement relative to our account. I want it to cover the last twelve months. Can you do that for me?'

'Of course,' said Boyd.

'Good! In that case, I'll go to the gym in the morning. It will do me good.'

'How about eleven at the Coffee House?' ventured Boyd. 'By then, I should know where we stand and what the hell is going on. The bank has made a mistake and they probably won't know until we tell them.'

'The Coffee House on the corner by the bank?' queried Meg. 'Yes, I'll be there.'

'Good!' voiced Boyd. 'I mean it. Trust me, Meg. I won't let you down.'

'Dad! Mum! The circus!' pleaded Izzy.

'Yes, the circus,' smiled Boyd. 'Meg!'

The hostile atmosphere dividing man and wife was hurriedly modified when Meg bent down, lifted her daughter, and said, 'Yes, we'll take you to the circus and then, when we return, it's off to bed. And that goes for you too, James.'

'Great!' grinned James who then nudged Izzy before they began singing, 'We're all going to the circus. We're all going to the circus.'

The children continued to sing as they launched themselves towards the front door.

Scowling angrily at Boyd, Meg stared directly into his eyes and growled, 'And then we'll have a chat about things. Oh yes, Billy, we'll have a chat about it alright. By God, we will. Look, Billy, going to the bank or not tomorrow is fine but I'm so worried about things. Bank or no bank some of these letters need to be looked at in detail and replies sent.'

She brushed past Boyd, gathered the car keys, and led the family to the door and a circus that awaited them shouting, 'It's okay, Billy. I bought the circus tickets with cash weeks ago. Not a credit card in sight in my bag.'

'Like I said, Meg,' replied Boyd. 'Calm down! I'll sort it. I'll go to the bank tomorrow and sort it all out?'

'Make sure you do,' growled Meg. 'Or you will end up as the biggest clown in the circus. Let's go or we'll be late.'

Shaking his head, gesturing to regain control, Boyd finally capitulated and sheepishly followed Meg and the children as he closed the door behind him.

Fixed to the underside of the Boyd family kitchen door, a listening device transmitted data to a geostationary spy satellite orbiting the planet at an altitude of two hundred and twenty miles. The satellite was regularly used to capture images for the military and intelligence services of a hostile enemy state even though it purported to be sponsored by an international media enterprise.

Recent technological modifications relevant to the 'spread' and 'angle of reach' had allowed the cyber message to be routed from the satellite to a computer facility situated in a house nestling on the shores of Loch Ness. It was one of the most important reasons that the Colonel had chosen this location to mount her operation.

A message appeared on the computer screen assigned to Colonel Korobov. It read, 'CYCLOPS SECURE AUDIO ALERT'.

Calmly, setting down her quilt, her thimble and threads, the Colonel typed in a password and beamed satisfaction at what she heard.

At the circus, seated on the second row, Police Constable John Dillon sat with his girlfriend, Fiona who was also a police officer. Off duty, they enjoyed the gathering of entertainers as they watched the show. There were clowns, acrobats, beautiful horses, musicians, dancers, tightrope walkers, jugglers, magicians, unicyclists, and other stunt-oriented artists.

Candy floss and toffee apples vied with hot dogs and ice-cream as the usherettes mingled with the crowd at halftime and tried their best to boost sales.

In the front row, Boyd and his family did their best to keep the children happy as each harboured their thoughts about the other.

'Hi, there!' shouted a voice close to Boyd.

Spinning around in his seat, Boyd recognised John Dillon and offered, 'Oh yes. It's you. What a small world. How are you, young man?'

'Fine, and you, sir?'

'I'm good. Enjoy the night,' remarked Boyd.

'Oh, we will,' returned John shovelling popcorn into his mouth.

'Who's that?' whispered Meg. 'Someone we owe money to?'

'Stop getting worried over the slightest thing, Meg. He's an off-duty policeman,' replied Boyd. 'Just a guy I bumped into recently, that's all. I can't even remember his name. It will come back to me. Now, will you please stop moaning and enjoy the show.'

A cold glare escaped from Meg's eyes and penetrated Boyd.

Seconds later, with lavish pomp and circumstance, a rotund ringmaster entered the arena to the sound of blaring trumpets and tumultuous applause as the second half of the evening's entertainment got underway.

'Ladies and gentlemen,' boomed the grandiose host. 'Are we all having a great time?'

'Yes,' replied some of the audience.

'I can't hear you,' bellowed the stately master of ceremonies. 'Are we all having a great time?'

'Yes,' a little louder this time.

Then, gesturing for more noise, the ringmaster bounded around the circle shouting, 'I can't hear you. Are we all having a great time?'

The audience took the hint and returned a deafening, 'YES' before things subsided and the ringmaster took up a position in the centre circle.

'Ladies and gentlemen,' he continued. 'It gives me great pleasure to introduce you to the most daring, the most audacious, the most valiant act in the circus today. I give you the Prince of Balance, the Emperor of the Ropes, the Conqueror of Gravity, the Sultan of the Sky and the King of the High Bar. I give you the one and only Fredrik, the Flying Finn.'

There was unbridled applause when the presenter finally stepped back and pointed to the entrance of Fredrik, the Flying Finn.

Bare-chested and dressed in white skin-tight gym trousers, Fredrik bounded into the circle, took a bow, and then began climbing a rope to the trapeze bar above.

'There's no net,' remarked Boyd. 'He's either a great performer, stupid or forgetful.'

'Or all three,' replied Meg. 'Is he Finnish?'

There was a hint of a continued argument between man and wife when Boyd declared, 'How on earth would I know?'

Every few yards, as Fredrik climbed the rope, he paused, struck an awesome pose to show off his well-toned muscles, and then continued his ascent towards the very centre of the Big Top.

Beneath the climber, securing the access rope for the trapeze artist, a younger man in dark trousers and a blue silk shirt leaned backwards to take the strain as he ensured the rope remained rigid for the star performer.

A drum roll began as Fredrik neared the pinnacle of his climb and the trapeze bars came into view. One of the trapeze bars was fitted with two rings. It was motionless until the youngster in the blue shirt activated another rope and watched it begin to swing back and forward as the trapeze artist made height.

The drum roll stopped. A pair of cymbals clashed. And then it happened.

With a timely, but graceful leap, Fredrik engaged both hoops and began to swing through the air whilst simultaneously heaving himself upwards in a blatant display of raw strength.

The crowd cheered and clapped as Fredrik, the Flying Finn, began his stupendous airborne routine. He flew through the air with consummate ease, reached out and grabbed a bar, and then hunched up before hooking his legs over the bar in a death-defying show of contempt for gravity. Secured only by the knee pit - a shallow depression at the back of the knee joint - he spread out his arms to tumultuous applause.

'Awesome!' remarked Fiona. 'Incredible. I've never seen anything like it.'

'I have,' replied John Dillon. 'It's him. That's the Whippet Kid!'

Laughing, Fiona replied, 'Not tonight, it's not, John. You're off duty. Remember? Now give it a rest and enjoy yourself. This guy is going to be really good.'

'Oh, he's good alright,' snapped Dillon. 'No mistake, Fiona, and no joke. I'd recognise him anywhere. That's my burglar.'

'What! Seriously?'

'Yes! Seriously! I'm going to see Boyd. We'll need help to arrest this one.'

'I'll help you, John,' suggested Fiona. 'We can manage without anyone else.'

'Not this one,' explained Dillon. 'The Whippet Kid will outrun everyone and that will include Boyd.'

'Boyd?' queried Fiona. 'Is that the man from London?'

'Something like that. Hold on! I'll be back,' replied Dillon.

Seconds later, John Dillon clambered over a row of seats and tapped Boyd's shoulder saying, 'Mister Boyd! It's him. It's the Whippet Kid!'

Turning around, Boyd engaged Dillon and enquired, 'Who? Fredrik?'

'No! The one wearing the blue shirt.'

'Do you mean the younger looking one holding the ascent rope for the trapeze artist?'

'Yes! That's the man. He's the one. I'm sure of it. Will you give me a hand to arrest him? I think we should rush him now and take him to the ground.'

'I think you should sit down and wait until the show is over,' advised Boyd. 'All that will do is cause widespread panic amongst the audience. They don't know we are off duty police officers. Now settle down and convince me you have got the right man. How sure are you?'

'Very sure!'

'How long did you have him in your sights when you saw him committing the crime?'

'Seconds!'

'That doesn't seem very long,' suggested Boyd.

'Enough to convince me,' contended Dillon.

'Okay!' replied Boyd. 'In which case, I suggest you ring the nick and tell the DI that you've identified the Whippet Kid and intend to arrest him at the end of the show. Tell him you are with me and your lady friend. He might decide to leave it until tomorrow morning when the place isn't swarming with the public and we can talk to the circus owner.'

'According to the posters,' revealed Dillon. 'This is the last night. They move to Dumfries tomorrow morning. He could be gone by then.'

'It's only an hour up the road.'

'And then further north into Scotland after that,' continued Dillon.

'What's going on?' asked Meg interrupting the conversation.

'Nothing to get excited about,' explained Boyd. 'But I need to help this chap make an arrest.'

'Can't it wait until tomorrow?'

'Sorry! No!' delivered Boyd. 'It will have to be when the circus ends.'

'Why am I not surprised?' replied a scornful Meg. 'You don't need to do this, Billy. Any excuse to cancel our chat, it seems.'

'No, that's not the case,' argued Boyd. 'That will keep.'

'Have I upset something?' probed Dillon.

'No! Nothing that can't be sorted out later,' replied Boyd. 'Look! Go back to your seat and wait until the show is ended. We'll join up then.'

'Okay,' from Dillon who engaged his mobile 'phone. 'Meanwhile, I'll phone the DI.'

'Fine!' replied Boyd.

The performance continued with all eyes focused on Fredrik, the Flying Finn swinging gracefully and athletically from bar to bar above the circus ring.

A quarter of an hour later, it was all over, and the spectators began filing gradually out of the Big Top.

'Catch you later,' remarked Boyd to Meg and the children as he joined John Dillon and Fiona and set off to find the Whippet Kid.

Once outside, a sudden shower of rain killed the smell of fish and chips, hot dogs, and toffee apples and began to gather in pools on the downtrodden soil.

'I'm hungry,' ventured Dillon.

'That will have to wait,' insisted Boyd as he pointed to his left and ordered, 'This way. I can see some caravans in the distance. That will be where they all live. Come on. We need to find the circus owner if we can.'

'According to the posters it should be someone called Charles Dubois,' remarked Dillon.

'Sounds French,' offered Boyd.

'It is,' confirmed Fiona.

Within minutes, the trio was on the outskirts of the village of caravans where the circus performers lived. Noisy and colourful, the village displayed an abundance of circus life. It was one big family of entertainers dressed in a variety of guises, but the costumes were about to get wet as the weather took a turn for the worse and the rain began to pelt down still further.

Boyd was stopped in his tracks when a line of dominant white horses suddenly crossed his path. Led by a couple of animal carers, the Arabian horses gradually made their way towards a transporter where they would be fed and watered before the morning journey into Scotland.

'You're right, John,' said Boyd. 'They seem to be packing the animals away for a long journey. Looks like they are going tonight, not tomorrow.'

The ringmaster approached the trio with, 'I'm sorry, but you've taken the wrong turning. This is the private area of our circus. You'll have to go back towards the Big Top to find the way out.'

Smiling broadly, Boyd immediately introduced himself, produced his warrant card, and then asked the way to the caravan where the young man holding the ascent rope for Frederik could be found.

'Straight on,' replied the ringmaster. 'It's the one with the blue roof but I think you should meet Mister Dubois, the owner of the circus before you go anywhere.'

'I agree,' stated Boyd. 'I'm pushed for time and need to speak to your man as soon as possible. What do you call him?'

'Eddy!' revealed the ringmaster. 'Wait here and I'll get Mister Dubois.'

As the ringmaster walked away, Boyd raised his voice slightly and said, 'Thank you! Tell him we'll meet him at Eddy's caravan.'

Before receiving a reply, Boyd spun on his heel and directed John and Fiona towards the relevant caravan saying, 'Quickly! They're packing up and on the move. Our man might be on his way already. Let's locate the target before it's too late.'

A caravan with a blue painted roof soon came into view.

'John! You know what to say, what to do?'

'Yes! I'll be fine,' nodded Dillon.

'Here we go,' said Boyd knocking on the door.

Seconds later, a youth wearing dark trousers and a long-sleeved dark blue silk shirt opened the door and looked down on his visitors.

'Eddy?' queried Boyd.

'Who wants to know?'

'We are police officers investigating a series of burglaries in the city and we'd like to speak to you if you don't mind.'

'Why?' from Eddy.

'PC Dillon?' queried Boyd.

Seizing the moment, John Dillon stepped forward and declared, 'Yes! This is the man, Mister Boyd.'

'Then do the honours, John,' ordered Boyd.

'Can we step inside, Eddy?' enquired Dillon. 'We've met before. I'm sure you remember. I see you've got socks on tonight. Isn't that unusual?'

Caught unawares for a moment, Eddy replied, 'What's this all about? I work in the circus. I'm not a burglar.'

'Then you'll not mind if we search your caravan?' suggested Boyd.

'Not without a search warrant,' replied Eddy. 'It's not my caravan. It belongs to the boss.'

'And the boss is?' probed Boyd.

'Me!' boomed a voice approaching the gathering. 'Charles Dubois! Circus owner and entrepreneur extraordinaire. Who the hell do you think you are? Stand aside and get away from my caravan.'

'We are police officers engaged on enquiries into a criminal offence,' replied Boyd flashing his warrant card once more. 'My apologies but I see you are making ready to decamp and move on. We must speak to this man as part of our investigation and it's imperative that we do so as soon as possible, Mister Dubois. I'm sure you understand.'

'I'd rather you just left the area,' replied Dubois angrily. 'I have no time for the police. No time at all. All these caravans belong to me. You are not allowed in any of them. Now clear off and don't bother us again.'

'That's not possible,' argued Boyd. 'And I advise you not to obstruct us in the execution of our duty. My colleague is in the process of arresting one of your workers. PC Dillon!'

Moving towards Eddy, John Dillon addressed the suspect with, 'I am arresting you on suspicion of committing an act of burglary…'

Midway through the sentence, Eddy bolted for freedom and pushed Dillon out of the way before lashing out at Boyd.

Fiona reacted by withdrawing an expandable baton from her shoulder bag. She shook the baton to lengthen it but before she could use it, Eddy struck her in the face and jumped from the caravan onto the ground.

Boyd wasn't famous for his rugby skills, but he hunched low, caught the escapee in his arms, and pushed him bodily back into the caravan where he was quickly restrained.

'Leave him alone,' yelled Dubois. 'That's police brutality.'

'Search the caravan, John,' ordered Boyd. 'He's under arrest and you've got the legal right. Search it! Fiona! Call for assistance!'

As Dillon began searching the caravan, Boyd restrained the suspect whilst Fiona used her mobile phone to call for help.

A small crowd was gathering outside the caravan and the most vociferous was the circus owner, Charles Dubois, who was screaming, 'Get out of my caravan. Get out!'

'Great time to meet the anti-police brigade,' muttered Boyd as he continued to restrain and overpower the prisoner.

Two men dressed as circus clowns stepped from behind Dubois and closed on the caravan.

'Drag them out of there,' ordered Dubois. 'Get rid of them! I want them off the premises double-quick.'

The clowns moved forward but met Fiona standing in front of the caravan with her baton shouting, 'I'll use it. I'm warning you all.'

There was a sudden clatter from inside the caravan when Dillon opened a wardrobe door and a travel bag fell from a shelf to the floor. Scores of pieces of jewellery spilt from the bag onto the floor.

Diamonds! Emeralds! Rubies! Sapphires!

'Bingo!' shouted Dillon. 'That's what I'm looking for.'

Eddy headbutted Boyd, pushed him out of the way, and leapt from the caravan onto the ground.

'Run!' shouted the ringmaster. 'Run!'

'What the hell is going on?' yelled Dubois. 'Where's Eddy going?'

Boyd was up on his feet giving chase with Dillon following close behind and Fiona backing into the caravan standing over the jewellery with her baton fully extended before her.

Swinging her baton from left to right, a terrified Fiona threatened, 'I've got pepper spray too. I'm warning you. Don't come any closer.' Dropping her 'phone, Fiona held a PAVA incapacitant spray in one hand and a fully extended baton in the other before she continued, 'Who wants it first? I'm not joking.'

In a Police Operations Centre, a hand triggered a switch and a controller radioed, 'All units! Officers in need of urgent assistance Dubois Circus. All attend. I repeat Dubois Circus. All attend.'

Two clowns became four clowns as the crowd grew and the circus family realised what was happening to one of their own.

'What's going on? Who are they? What are the police doing?' from the onlookers.

'Boys, we're rumbled,' voiced the ringmaster. 'Get the jewellery and run for it! Now!'

Realising there was a gang involved, not just one individual, Fiona swung her baton wildly as the sweat poured from her skin and adrenalin peaked. Fear drove her, inspired her, and fuelled the confidence that was gradually building inside her.

The ringmaster charged forward. Fiona swung her baton at the intruder.

Ducking, the chubby overweight ringmaster slipped in the wet clart and crashed to the ground with a splatter of mud rising into the air and catching one of the nearby clowns in the face.

Consequently, the clown raised his hands to protect his eyes, lost his footing in the mud, fell over the ringmaster, and banged his skull on the caravan step as he fell to the ground. A colourful cone-shaped hat escaped his head and a shiny red plastic nose dropped to the ground when he rolled over in agony.

The crowd surged forward but only to catch a view of the melee, two muddy people, and a determined woman now holding her baton in strike position – ready and waiting.

Sirens sounded from afar and began to invade the ear of Charles Dubois who had a turn of heart when he shouted, 'Settle down! Leave the lady alone!'

The ringmaster felt a tug on his collar when Dubois, the circus owner, dragged the roly-poly man from the mud, shook him, and shouted, 'What's going on? Who does that jewellery belong to? What have you been up to?'

There was no reply.

'Do you hear me?' screamed Dubois. 'Where did the jewellery come from?'

As the ringmaster and his gang of wicked clowns realised their crooked scheme was in danger of being uncovered, Fiona grew in confidence and shouted, 'On your knees! All of you! You're all under arrest!'

Dominating the ground, Fiona held her PAVA spray high and shouted, 'On your knees! All of you!'

'Do as you're told!' ordered Dubois. 'Do as you're told until I find out what the hell you've been up to. The jewellery! Where did it come from?'

Complying, silent, found wanting, four wet and muddied clowns together with a chubby ringmaster dropped to their knees when the circus owner suddenly sided with Fiona and signalled others to join him in his quest.

Meanwhile, Eddy, the Whippet Kid, was striding out like an Olympic athlete in a bid for freedom.

Dashing between a line of white horses and a trailer loaded with circus equipment, Eddy fumbled for a set of keys in his pocket as he headed for a car park. A posse of circus horses fitted with garlands of flowers hindered him. Reducing speed, he glanced over his shoulder to see Boyd and Dillon gaining on him.

'Stop!' screamed Dillon. 'You're under arrest!'

'Then you'd better catch me,' chuckled Eddy. 'Because there's no way I'm stopping for you.'

Negotiating the animals, splashing through countless puddles in the pouring rain, Eddy showed a clean pair of heels as he pelted through the caravan village with his head down determined to escape the clutches of the law.

Dillon hit a deep puddle, wobbled, tumbled to the ground, and then got up again equally determined to recapture his prisoner.

Gritting his teeth, Boyd jumped a puddle, and then another, and focused on the body ahead of him.

Unaware of the chase taking place, a performer wearing a top hat, a union jack outfit, and walking on stilts suddenly came into view from behind two circus trailers. Taking large steps into the village, he gasped in disbelief when Eddy ducked low and ran between his legs, jumped a fence into the car park, and headed for a nearby Ford motor car.

The stilt walker twisted on high to watch Eddy's surge for freedom but in so doing, the stilts closed, denied the chaser's progression, and collapsed when Boyd slammed into one of the stilts.

There was a fearsome crash when the stilt walker lost his balance and hurtled towards the ground with Dillon raising his arms to protect himself and Boyd struggling to escape the timber falling on top of him.

Eddy found his car and dived into the driving seat. There was a throaty roar from the engine followed by the panicking crunch of first gear when Eddy drove away.

DI Stan Holland braked at the last minute, slung the steering wheel to the left, but still collided with Eddy's Ford on arriving at the scene.

Jumping from the passenger seat, DS Mark McAdam rushed to the driver's door, pulled it open, and dragged Eddy from the vehicle onto the ground.

Moments later, a breathless Boyd and Dillon arrived, secured the prisoner with handcuffs, and slammed him hard against the bonnet of Stan's squad car.

'Eddy!' voiced Stan. 'Or to be more precise, should I say Eduardo Menzies.'

'You know this man?' enquired Boyd.

'No!' replied Stan Holland as he directed more police vehicles into the heart of the camp to assist Fiona. 'But earlier today we received a call from the Dutch police telling us that one Eduardo Menzies is part of a gang wanted for smuggling stolen diamonds from Amsterdam into Estonia. They believe he's working in a circus somewhere in the north of England.'

'Is this the man?' queried Boyd.

Producing a photograph from an inside pocket, the DI showed it to Boyd, compared it to the prisoner, and delivered, 'Oh Yes! Undoubtedly! That's our man. There's a European arrest warrant in force for him. Well done!'

'Are you Eduardo Menzies?' probed Boyd turning to the prisoner.

Eddy nodded in agreement.

'The rest of the gang?' queried Dillon. 'Are they here or somewhere else?'

'Judging by the welcome we received when we searched that caravan, I think we might be closer than you think,' suggested Boyd. 'I reckon we need to tie up with Fiona, recover the jewellery, and see what we've got.'

'More prisoners!' revealed DS McAdam who was on the 'phone to Fiona. 'She's got a caravan full of jewellery, four clowns and a fat ringmaster locked up, and wants to know what to do next.'

DI Holland took control and stated, 'Get Eduardo here down to the nick double pronto. Put him in leg shackles if you need to but don't let him escape again. I'll meet up with Fiona and we'll take it from there. How many cars do we have?'

'Three so far,' replied DS McAdam. 'Another three and a van should be here soon. It was an 'all units' call. We'll need them all by the sound of it.'

'I'll leave you with it then, gentlemen,' declared Boyd. 'I don't think you need my services anymore. I'll catch you in the morning.'

'The division can sort this out, Boyd,' confirmed Stan Holland. 'Thanks for your help. Touch base in the morning.'

'Will do,' replied Boyd melting away into the background as the city took over the enquiries. 'What a great way to end the day.'

In another part of the city, the day was not over for some.

Wandering into the suburb of Morton, the paraffin man carried a plastic can full of his favourite mix. His mind was set, determined, full of hope for the immediate future as he stepped from the pathway and crossed a deserted building site. Ahead of him lay the wooden hut which was the site office for the construction project being undertaken.

A telephone wire ran from a nearby telegraph pole and filtered into the roof area of the hut. The temporary building was set on strong wooden trestles and designed to provide a centre for workers on the site. There was a gap beneath the floor of the building where oxygen was in obvious abundance. It was here that the paraffin man laced the area with his mixture of paraffin, petrol, spirit and diesel.

Glancing casually around, the paraffin man paid scant regard to anyone nearby. He was so focused on his task that thoughts of capture, or being witnessed, disappeared into an irrelevant cloud that his mind did not recognise. He did not see the CCTV camera angled towards the office from a building nearby.

In the dead of the night, with only a slight drizzle falling from the skies above, the paraffin man continued to walk around the wooden cabin. He soaked the bottom of the wood with the mixture and then tipped his canister upside down and watched the mixture gather in a pool beneath the trestle foundation.

Withdrawing slightly, he struck a match, threw it, and then felt the power of the explosion when it knocked him onto his back.

Hitting the ground hard, the paraffin man laughed with joy when he saw the flames suddenly climb into the air.

Within seconds, the wooden site office was well alight. The fuel devoured the oxygen beneath the wooden trestles, scorched the foundations, fed the fire, then lashed around the building at phenomenal speed when a line of fuel caught fire and Carlisle's latest arson burnt its way into local history.

Dancing!

The paraffin man danced with the flames, sang with the sound of burning timber, and screeched with delight when the roof collapsed and dragged the overhead telephone wire down into the burning building.

'Glory be!' he chanted. 'Glory be!'

A voice shouted, 'Oy, you!'

The paraffin man glanced around, caught sight of an older man approaching and stepped back.

'Yes, you!' shouted the voice.

Frightened now, scared stiff, the paraffin man withdrew further into the shadows when he realised the older man was wearing the dark uniform of a security guard.

Running!

Running as fast as he could, hobbling from one side to the other, striding out as best he could, the paraffin man dropped his plastic can, crossed the road, ran towards the housing estate, and melted into a plethora of alleyways and lanes that dominated suburbia.

The security guard gave chase, stopped at the first dark alleyway, and then returned to the building site where he dialled 999 and called the Fire Service.

A short time later the police also attended the scene and began yet another investigation into a case of deliberate arson.

Out of breath, nearing exhaustion, the paraffin man bolted from the concrete jungle of suburbia and made his way across the parkland towards his home.

Looking back over his shoulder, he stopped for a moment to catch a view of the flames climbing into the air. He saw the sparks, revelled in the flames, gloried in the pure disaster of it all, then turned for home, sanctuary, and a session with photographs taken on his mobile phone accompanied by a half a bottle of cheap vodka.

It was his night's work. The paraffin man had reached the epitome of his criminality. He held no true fear of being caught by either the police or anyone else. They were just people to avoid because they caused him to panic. Sometimes they shocked him to the core when they were close to him. Yet, they were not truly part of his eerie persona, his broken lifestyle, his bizarre mentality.

The door closed tight when the paraffin man arrived home, threw himself on the bed, and began to laugh with gratitude at the complexity of his damaged brain.

Unaware of the latest bout of fire-raising, Boyd arrived home, late, tired, and ready for bed. Sneaking quietly into the house, he found Meg asleep with the children. They were all in the same bed.

Shaking his head, he approached the bar in the living room and retrieved a litre bottle of Bushmills Irish whiskey. He selected an appropriate tumbler and poured three fingers of the alcoholic spirit into the tumbler. He downed it one quick session as his mind tried to blot out the turmoil that was all around him.

Reluctantly, he removed his jacket to use as a blanket, settled onto the sofa, and eventually fell asleep in the silence of the night.

~

5

Carlisle
The next day

Boyd's phone alarm sounded and encouraged him to meet the coming day head-on. He scrambled from the sofa, washed and shaved, looked in at Meg and the children, and then joined the rush hour traffic to reach the early morning meeting at Carlisle police station.

Grabbing a black coffee from the canteen, Boyd raced up the stairs into the CID office where he took a seat in the briefing room next to DI Stan Holland.

It was eight o'clock. Time for the morning crime conference.

Grey-haired and in his fifties, the time-served Stan Holland began by praising PC John Dillon for capturing Eduardo Menzies from Estonia and recovering a huge amount of jewellery that was believed to be the proceeds of crime. He then commended PC Fiona Watson, Dillon's girlfriend, for acting courageously and safeguarding the recovered jewellery before the arrival of reinforcements.

Both the officers were present and nodded their appreciation although it would be fair to say that they both felt seven feet tall.

'Where are we with this one?' probed the DI. 'John?'

It was young Dillon's first appearance at the morning crime conference. He stood up and coughed nervously before stating, 'After the arrest, we made a further search of the prisoner's caravan and recovered more jewellery hidden inside cushions and pillowcases. Some of the jewellery has been identified as having been stolen from the burglary in Botchergate. Other items appear to be identical with items reported stolen from South Cumbria and North Lancashire. We have some of the victims travelling to see us today to hopefully identify some of that property. During the search, we also recovered some jemmies, screwdrivers, gloves, socks, and plastic bags full of money. Over fifty thousand pounds in notes so far! Some of them are Euros.'

'Excellent!' replied Stan. 'Make sure the articles are forensically examined and ask that they are compared with outstanding marks from other burglaries. One of those screwdrivers or a jemmy might have been used in the other burglaries you mentioned. Check the individual numbers of the banknotes and get them tested for fingerprints if you think it will progress the investigation. Remember, the main man is from Estonia so think a little bit broader than usual. If those banknotes are stolen, they might be from anywhere in Europe. Work closely with Mac on this matter. Those banknotes have a life story. Follow it through. I will authorise the forensic examination paperwork.'

'Thanks! Will do,' replied DS McAdam.

'Just one thing,' remarked Dillon.

'Go on!'

'The amount of jewellery reported stolen from the Botchergate burglary does not correspond with what we've recovered and we don't think Eduardo and his friends have had time to pass it onto their criminal contacts otherwise we probably wouldn't have recovered any jewellery from the caravan. The paperwork the jeweller showed me at the time of the Botchergate break-in does not match what we've recovered. There's just something fishy going on. That's all.'

'What do you make of that?' enquired Stan.

'I think the jeweller is telling lies,' responded Dillon. 'Yes, he was burgled, and some property was stolen, but I think he told lies by adding items that hadn't been taken and bumping the value up.'

'Why should he do that?' asked the DI.

'So that he could claim more on the insurance,' replied Dillon.

'Precisely what crossed my mind,' admitted Stan. 'Work with Mac and bottom it out, please. Interview the owner again once you've resolved what the stock holding should be against the stock holding alleged to be stolen. If there's a fraud in action, you'll find it. When you have enough, interview our Estonian friend and let me know what the position is. DS McAdam will put a team together. I want you all to work on the clowns and ringmaster. Turn the circus upside down. No safety nets! Let's see what they've been up to.'

'So far,' interrupted Mac. 'We can tell you that the clowns, the ringmaster, and the Estonian seem to be members of the same gang. It looks like there's a crime epidemic everywhere they go. We're not sure about Dubois, the circus owner, he may well turn out to be in the clear, but we have a cellblock full of prisoners to interview. I think it will take some time, but we'll get there in the end.'

'Good,' replied the DI. 'I'm told the Dutch police want to speak to their man too so expect their arrival the day after tomorrow. I want you to concentrate on clearing up the mess, sorting out what crimes have been committed, who did what and why, and then put a file of evidence in. The legal beagles can decide who puts Eduardo on trial first. Us, the Dutch or the Estonians, we'll consider the others in due course. Just do what you can and keep me informed. Any problems, you know where to find me.'

'Will do, sir,' replied Mac.

Dillon nodded and sat down when the DI moved on with, 'Next up is another arson. This time in Morton. Mac! What's the score with this one?'

'Yet another fire to add to the toll but for the first time we have an image of the offender.'

'About time,' replied Stan Holland. 'Is the image good enough to identify the offender?'

'Blurred,' declared Mac. 'Enough to suggest it's a male wearing dark clothing and carrying a plastic fuel can to the scene. His face is well covered. The CCTV shows him approaching the office on the site but not much more. Sadly, the CCTV system has not been maintained correctly. The tapes have been used so many times they are no longer any good to anyone. We've had words with the site manager; he tells us he will improve matters. He also tells us they recently dismissed a male employee – about two weeks ago – and they have been expecting retaliation from the individual because he wasn't one little bit happy about losing his job. For what it's worth, the manager reckons the CCTV image resembles the man he sacked. If that's the case, we might be on the way to clearing up all this fire-raising that's been going on.'

'Brilliant,' replied DI Holland. 'See what forensics can do with the CCTV photograph. That could be our man. Get him arrested and follow it up. Try to connect him to the outstanding arsons if you can.'

'Will do!' replied Mac.

'I don't think so,' ventured Boyd.

'Why not?' probed an anxious Stan Holland.

'Correct me if I'm wrong,' explained Boyd. 'But you have a situation where there have been several high-value arson attacks in recent months. Despite numerous enquiries, you've got nowhere with them. Then this one comes along, and you think you're on a winner. I've studied the historic files, Stan. Sorry, what you are proposing doesn't fit my thinking.'

'In that case, Commander Boyd,' remarked DI Holland. 'What does fit your thinking?'

'All the cases of arson so far have resulted in high-value damage,' suggested Boyd. 'This one is a fairly low value. However, they each have some common factors which affect them all.'

'Such as?' probed Mac.

'All the objects damaged are, primarily, of a wooden structure,' revealed Boyd. 'The arsonist, I suggest, selected his targets because wood is easier to burn than brick, cement, iron, metal, or normal building components. Besides, the fuel used – according to Forensics – is a mix of paraffin, petrol, diesel, and alcoholic spirit. That alone is odd because if I want to start a fire, I'll use petrol or commercial firelighters, not a mix of peculiar inflammable substances that catch fire at different temperatures and in different conditions.'

'But they still work,' remarked Mac.

'Yes, they do!' replied Boyd. 'But why would you make a bizarre mix of fuel to make fire when a can of petrol will do the same job at half the price and in half the time?'

'Not sure,' replied Mac.

'I really don't know,' added the DI.

'Okay,' continued Boyd. 'The other matter I want to draw your attention to is the motive. Mac has explained that this last fire carried with it a suspect. The site manager points the finger at somcone who was sacked some weeks ago. If that person is responsible, then tell me why he has committed the offence of arson and set fire to a building where he used to work?'

'Revenge!' offered the DI. 'It's as simple as that.'

'Agreed!' added Mac.

'Fine!' replied Boyd. 'If you arrest the employee who was sacked from the building site and he admits that he set the fire, or you can prove that he did from other evidence, then you're on a winner. And he probably did it for revenge.'

'So, we're all agreed?' proposed Stan.

'That's where we are not in total agreement,' argued Boyd. 'Arson is dealt with under the Criminal Damage Act. An easy explanation is the unlawful damage of property by fire, but it is always accompanied by a motive: a reason why the act was done. Most arsons occur because the person setting the fire seeks revenge, or wants to threaten someone, or intends to make a fraudulent insurance claim, or wishes to further an act of political power, perhaps as part of an act of terrorism.'

'Understood!' remarked the DI. 'We know you are involved in counter-terrorism, Commander. 'But what are you driving at?'

'I'm suggesting you have one fire – the building site at Morton – where you may have a motive in that the employee that was sacked set fire to the office where he worked as an act of revenge. Just remember, it's made of wood and that is our fireraiser's favourite target. But if you were that person you would have known about the CCTV system. So why would you go back to a location that you knew was under surveillance to commit a crime that you might be implicated in by virtue of the sacking? Only an idiot would do that. That said, the world is full of idiots so maybe I'm wrong. I don't think you are looking for an arsonist. I suggest you are looking in the wrong direction. You should be searching for a pyromaniac.'

'A pyromaniac?' queried Mac. 'And where will we find one of those?'

'It won't be easy,' ventured Boyd. 'Pyromania is also known as 'Jomeri's Syndrome', named after a psychologist who studied and developed the first forms of treatment for the disorder. It's an impulse control disorder which makes it a mental health problem.'

'In what way?' asked Mac.

'It's a psychiatric disorder,' explained Boyd. 'We don't often come across it but when we do it's characterised by a failure on the offender's part to resist temptation. Such a person cannot resist an urge within themselves. It's like being an alcoholic or having a gambling problem except pyromania may lead to the loss of life through fire-raising. A pyromaniac will gain an intense fascination in the fire and may also experience pleasure, gratification or relief. Another long-term contributor often linked with pyromania is the build-up of stress. Think of it in another way, if you will. Why do people refuse to stop smoking? Why do others go on binge eating sessions? It's because psychologically their mind is such that they cannot refuse themselves. They've somehow lost the plot and cannot think straight. It wouldn't surprise me if we end up looking for a rather sad individual the like of which we do not encounter regularly.'

'I see,' replied Mac. 'At least, I think I understand.'

Boyd continued, 'I'm advising you that the fuel used to start these fires is unusual as well as the wrongdoer you're looking for. The structure of wood is the target, not the building itself, and there is no obvious or specific motive developing in respect of any of these fires you are investigating. Put simply, I think the whole thing is bizarre and the person responsible is a pyromaniac who has a serious mental health problem. An arsonist is a pure criminal, a crook, a wicked person. A pyromaniac is not a crook or a criminal intent on monetary gain or political power. Rather, such a person is mentally unstable. I think you're on the wrong track and looking for the wrong type of offender.'

There was a silence in the room before Stan Holland said, 'I'll buy that ticket, Boyd. We've got nowhere chasing would-be crooks, possible blackmailers, sacked employees, and revenge artists. The problem in these investigations, as you know, is that you must rule out the criminal motives before you arrive at the pyromania factor. Maybe we just took too long to get there. We have to investigate the obvious before ending up thinking out of the box to get to the centre of things.'

'I just think it might be a good thing to change tack now,' proposed Boyd.

'We'll see,' replied the DI. 'What do you suggest?'

'A broader pattern of thinking to the investigation. Perhaps a hook up with health professionals. Has the wrongdoer ever been burnt by an explosion from one of his fires? Do we have any old records relating to odd people who may have come to notice years ago because of something to do with bizarre behaviour at or near a fire? What about the mental health brigade? Can they help? I'd turn the drawers inside out and think right outside the box to sort this one out.'

'Ladies and gentlemen,' declared DI Stan Holland. 'Commander Boyd has a reputation for thinking outside the box. That's a metaphor meaning think differently, unconventionally, or from a new perspective. Not everyone likes that. Many would criticise such a course of action for a whole variety of reasons. Often, it's because they can't come up with a better line of enquiry themselves. So, we'll take that advice and move to the next phase. Mac! Follow up on the possibility of an ex-employee being responsible for setting fire to the building site office at Morton. Bottom it out and see how you go. Then take time out and write down a list of things that may seem unusual enquiries to make but might progress the investigation into the entire series of fires that are on the books.'

'Will do,' replied DS McAdam making notes.

Boyd glanced at his wristwatch and said, 'If you'll excuse me, Stan, I have an urgent appointment elsewhere. I'll catch you later today if that's okay?'

'Of course, it is,' smiled the DI. 'Drop by later for a catch-up.'

With a casual thumbs up, Boyd was on his feet, out of the door, and on the way to an appointment with his bank manager.

In Loch Ness, an underflow was at work.

An underflow is an underwater current that is found in lochs, lakes, rivers, and stretches of ample water where becks, ghylls, streams or minor tributaries enter the main body of water and cause an underflow. A waterfall is an example of how the entry of its water to the main channel causes a current of water below the surface which moves in a different direction from the surface water above. Obstructions or barriers under the surface, temperature changes in the water caused by the depth of the channel, and the geological make-up of the watercourse also contribute to an underflow. There is also the possibility of underwater holes or caves and in the landscape of Loch Ness, most of these elements are present in the deep, freshwater body of water.

Colonel Anna Korobov looked out across the loch unaware that an underflow was at work or what caused them. Moreover, she had no idea that Nikolai's body was caught in the underflow. Enclosed in a canvas golf bag, the body tumbled around before being dragged deeper into the depths. Spinning, tumbling, constantly rotating, the corpse then dropped silently to the depths as the current carried it in a southerly direction towards Fort Augustus.

Strolling casually into the Operations Centre, the Colonel nodded at a new man sitting at a computer console. A nearby independent server hummed away in the background and a new set of windows opened in the man's computer browser.

'You must be Dimitry?' asked the Colonel.

'I am, indeed,' replied the cryptologist. 'And you must be the legend that is Colonel Korobov. I am delighted to make your acquaintance and quite proud to be working for you.'

'Good! Thank you,' replied the Colonel as they shook hands. 'I am sure our mission will be a success since you have been recommended to me by Moscow.'

'I hope so,' replied Dimitry. 'Where is Nikolai?'

'Gone!' declared the Colonel firmly. 'Family illness, I believe. No need to concern yourself. Tell me where you are up to in respect of the operational manual.'

'Well advanced! New mail ready to go, new stories in the course of uploading to various websites, and the bank is my next target. It is proving harder than I expected.'

'How hard?' enquired the Colonel.

'Oh, I'll need another hour and no more,' explained Dimitry. 'Nikolai had already contacted me about the latest advances in respect of breaking the bank down. As a result, the firewalls are in the course of destruction, but it takes time for it all to ripple through to the bank website. Once I'm in, I will identify the relevant accounts, remove the target text, replace them with your annotations, tidy things up, and then egress the system rebuilding the firewalls as I leave. I must tell you, Colonel, that this cyber weapon is good, but it is not yet excellent. In my opinion, routine maintenance by the bank's IT staff may well identify the breach sometime in the next year or so.'

'The mission will be ended by then,' revealed the Colonel. 'Just one thing, Dimitry, are you telling me that Nikolai had already discussed this operation with you before you arrived at our Operations Centre?'

Smiling, self-assured, full of confidence, Dimitry replied, 'Of course, he did, Colonel. We work in the same field so why shouldn't he? Although to be fair, he did not divulge any information about the operation. He just asked me to update him on current methods we are using to attack certain systems.'

'I see,' frowned the Colonel gently. 'Why would he do that?'

'It seems you're not familiar with my work, Colonel. Nikolai is a level six cryptologist. I am a level seven cryptologist. The gap between the two is huge. Seven is the highest level. The computerised attack system we are using is similar to Stuxnet which is a malicious computer worm: a form of computer malware. If you remember, way back in 2010, we suspected that Stuxnet was an American and Israeli combat partnership designed to destroy the capability of Iran's nuclear program.'

'Neither country ever admitted participating in the attack, but silence is often an admission of guilt rather than an argumentative denial. Yes, Dimitry, I do recall the introduction of Stuxnet to the cyberwar,' replied the Colonel. 'It was a very successful attack syndrome which destroyed much of Iran's nuclear capability. Considering the Motherland is a silent partner in Iran's aspirations to obliterate Israel and the Jews, there is no doubt that Stuxnet gave us all a bloody nose. But you are not using Stuxnet, Dimitry. Tell me how this attack system works.'

'It's a SCADA attack system,' explained Dimitry. 'The worm targets the supervisory control and data acquisition system (SCADA) and searches for automated electronic processes, which underpin the input to the computerised financial system. Identical to Stuxnet, it targets the Microsoft Windows operating system and similar networks then seeks out specific software that we know certain banking concerns use. Our worm has three modules: one that penetrates the website, another that delivers the payload, and one that hides the previous two systems to prevent detection.'

'It's almost identical to Stuxnet,' suggested the Colonel.

'Correct!' replied Dimitry. 'It's based on that program. The difference, of course, is that our attack syndrome allows us to rewrite the text into a targeted account. Such texts are written in MS Word. We choose to alter that text, hide it, and deny its computerised existence.'

'Fascinating,' exclaimed the Colonel. 'Why didn't we use a level seven from the start?'

'No disrespect intended, Colonel, but whoever recommended a level six cryptologist for this operation was out of their depth. This is level seven work and I have done it for you.' Dimitry checked the time and added, 'Or to be precise, I will have within the hour.'

'Oh, I see,' replied the Colonel. 'Excellent work! I am truly delighted in your ability. Well done! We're ready to move forward as planned.'

'I believe that is the case, Colonel,' remarked Dimitry. 'Once I've finished with the bank, I will double-check the security system inside and outside this building and inform you of any discrepancies I find.'

'Thank you! Yes, see that you do,' ordered the Colonel.

A golf bag carrying a murdered Russian cryptologist neared part of the watercourse where the River Foyers joins Loch Ness. Here, north-east of Fort Augustus, the River Foyers evolves into the Falls of Foyers where, from a height of over 160 feet, the river plunges into Loch Ness from the waterfall to create yet another unmistakeable underflow.

The body would tumble, spin, and continue its enigmatic journey until it finally reached its unknown destination.

In Cumbria, someone was crying!

Meg broke down at the table in the kitchen of their home. Opening more letters, she read about the mounting debts and used a calculator to tot up the total. Dismayed, the tears welled, flowed, and ran down her cheeks,

The telephone rang. She took the call, listened, and then threw the calculator at the wall without offering any reply.

There was an unhealthy crash when the phone slammed onto the cradle.

Gathering her kit together, Meg set off for the gym.

On turning into the main highway, Viktor and Nadia followed Meg at a discreet distance guiding their black three litre BMW in and out of the traffic as they consulted Colonel Korobov on a mobile telephone.

Meanwhile, in the city, the slim and attractive Lucia Bortelli met Boyd in her office at the bank and opened the conversation with, 'I'm so pleased you've called to see us, Mister Boyd. I was getting worried about how your account was being handled. Would you like tea or coffee?'

'Coffee will be fine,' smiled Boyd accepting a drink.

'Milk and sugar?'

'Black will do,' replied Boyd. 'Yes, indeed! Things have gone haywire recently and I decided it was time I dropped in personally to sort matters out. I'm sure you'll be able to help me with this problem.'

'I'll do whatever I can,' replied Lucia.

'Good!' voiced Boyd. 'It's a joint account in the name of my wife and I.'

'Yes, I have it here on the screen,' replied Lucia. 'I've made myself aware of the situation. How on earth did it get that bad?'

'Precisely!' replied Boyd. 'That's what I've come to find out. The account is inaccurate and beyond belief. We need to rectify it as soon as possible. These things happen, but let's not make a fuss.'

'I like your attitude, Mister Boyd. What do you propose?'

'A complete overhaul of the account,' replied Boyd. 'Somewhere along the line, one of your bank staff has made an error and recorded someone else's transactions in our account. We just need to amend the mistakes, if you don't mind?'

'Really,' remarked Lucia. 'You amaze me, Mister Boyd. I've never met anyone quite like yourself.'

'That's what everyone says,' chuckled Boyd. 'Now be assured, Mrs Bortelli.'

'Miss!'

'Miss Bortelli,' corrected Boyd. 'I really don't want to point the finger at any particular person in the bank. I'm not advocating a witch hunt and I'm not asking for compensation, an apology, or anything like that. My wife and I would just like the corrections to be made and our account to be returned to its former state.'

'I bet you would,' smiled Lucia. 'How do you propose we do that, Mister Boyd?'

'Presumably, we go through the account, find things that are wrong, and report the matter to your IT department. Or can you make amendments here? I really don't know how such things can be accomplished but I'm sure you will know someone in the bank who can make things happen for us. I don't expect things will be rectified immediately, but if we can make a list of false entries that would make a good starting point.'

'I see,' replied Lucia. 'And that is the summary of your problem?'

'As I see it, yes,' contended Boyd.

'My problem is,' replied Lucia. 'I've looked at your account status and take a different view.'

'What do you mean?'

'When a transaction is made, the bank records the transaction in what we call an online ledger – namely your account.'

'Yes, I know that.'

'The recording of such transactions is made electronically as opposed to being handwritten.'

'Yes, I know that too.'

'This reduces the likelihood of human error,' suggested Lucia.

'Provided the electronic system is sacrosanct, unblemished, and beyond malpractice,' argued Boyd.

'Absolutely!' smiled Lucia.

'Good! We're getting somewhere now,' replied Boyd.

'If you apply for a loan, credit card, mortgage, overdraft, or payment holiday, then annotations - notes – are made on your account, as well as in your application. This is routine standard practice in the banking industry, Mister Boyd – the recording of relevant details on applications and accounts. Such matters may also be referred to credit reference companies.'

'Even better!' replied Boyd. 'That should make our examination so much easier.'

Lucia Bortelli continued, 'I just wish you had contacted us earlier and we could have perhaps helped with an increase on your overdraft or…'

'Excuse me,' interrupted Boyd. 'What overdraft?'

Lucia frowned, straightened her skirt, and said, 'Come, come! Mister Boyd. Let's not play games. You know as well as I do that you and your wife have an above-average overdraft facility based purely on your extensive incomes.'

'I don't understand,' remarked Boyd taking a sip of coffee. 'Look! Is Mister Nixon available? No disrespect intended, Mrs Bortelli but Brian Nixon has been our relationship manager for years and will have a much better understanding of our financial affairs than your good self.'

'It's Miss Bortelli actually,' revealed Lucia. 'I've told you that once already. Perhaps you will listen to me if it's not too much trouble?'

'My apologies,' offered Boyd.

'I take it you are not aware that Mister Nixon died from a heart attack some weeks ago?'

'No! No, I'm not,' replied a shocked Boyd. 'I had no idea. That is such bad news. He was such a good man.'

'Well, now you have a young Italian woman to contend with,' replied Lucia. 'I hope my accent is not putting you off.'

'Not at all. You speak good English. I thought you were new to the bank.'

'I've recently moved here from Rome,' replied Lucia. 'But I have examined your account at length. It is a joint account, as you know, and I can confirm that after due diligence and forthright examination, you are currently overdrawn to the amount of £50,000. If we add the recent loan you took out and add it to your credit card account, the actual sum is estimated at £100,000. The sum will continue to grow, will attract interest, and needs to be curtailed immediately.'

Stunned! Shocked beyond belief, Boyd was lost for words as he fumbled for pen and paper to make notes.

'How do you propose to deal with these debts?' challenged Lucia.

'Debts! Is that what you call them?' floundered a confused Boyd. 'I don't understand. I just don't understand at all.'

'It's money that you have spent, Mister Boyd,' explained Lucia. 'What more can I say?'

'On what?' probed Boyd. 'Where do you get those figures from?'

Turning to a computer screen, Lucia engaged the keyboard as her light brown hair flowed across her shoulders, enhanced her beauty, and briefly caught Boyd's attention when he moved closer to the table.

'Membership of a gambling club in Soho,' began Lucia. 'Two gentlemen's clubs in the Pall Mall area of London, a private striptease and lap dance club in the west end, membership of an international champagne circle, and…'

'Let me see,' demanded Boyd as he closed with the screen.

'A world cruise some months ago and a motor cruiser berthed in the Thames. Goodness, Mister Boyd, you have been busy but now it's time to make us an offer.'

'This isn't right,' declared Boyd emphatically. 'Look, I've told you once already. Your records are incorrect. You've debited our account with details of another person's expenditure. It's as simple as that.'

'I fear not,' scolded Lucia. 'The integrity of our systems is beyond criticism.'

'Get your IT department on the 'phone now,' demanded Boyd. 'There's a technical hitch somewhere and, with respect, Madam, I demand an investigation. The situation is preposterous.'

'It isn't,' contended Lucia. 'That is not the case at all. There's a note here that reveals the account was updated at nine o'clock this morning following an audit by our Head Office. Why don't you stop playing games, Commander Boyd?'

'Oh!' exclaimed Boyd. 'So, you know who I am and what I do?'

'Of course,' replied Lucia. 'But it's time you realised that your position in society is quite irrelevant when you owe the bank money. It's time to get wise, Mister Boyd. I had hoped you would stroll into my office, apologise for being a spendthrift, and make an offer of a monthly payment for the next – shall we say – five years?'

'Five years?' queried Boyd. 'This is not my account! There's been a gross error somewhere in the system. You still don't get it, do you?'

'Get it? Oh, rest assured, the bank will get it,' smiled Lucia in an abstract way. 'We could take the matter to court and seize your house, your cars, your motor cruiser. Everything! And we will do that fairly quickly if you don't come clean and make an offer of some kind. Are you able to repay at the sum of three thousand pounds per month?'

'What?' voiced a bewildered Boyd.

'That way we could consolidate your debts into a three-year loan commencing now.'

'You must be joking? Notes! Annotations about applications and suchlike,' argued Boyd. 'Are they there?'

'Of course,' replied Lucia. 'Clearly transparent.'

'That's my point,' argued Boyd. 'They don't refer to us.'

'I'm afraid they do,' replied Lucia.

'I'm not in the mood for jokes, Miss Bortelli,' revealed Boyd. 'Tell me you feel embarrassed on behalf of the bank and have decided to make a joke of it all?'

'No, I'm not at all embarrassed, but you appear to be. Do you need longer to pay?' suggested Lucia. 'I see your salary and that of your wife and I am aware of your standing in both the police and nursing communities. However, you should know that these things are really quite irrelevant, Mister Boyd. The bank is coming after you whether you like it or not.'

Crumpling his notes into his fist, Boyd said, 'I'm wasting my time here. I have other avenues I can use to investigate. Print my account off please.'

'Absolutely,' replied Lucia. She negotiated the keyboard again, heard the printer kickstart into life, and added, 'I can give you until tomorrow afternoon if you wish. By then I expect either an early financial resolution from you, the proposed sale of assets to meet your expenditure, or a discussion as to how much you can repay the bank every month at, shall we say, between three and five thousand pounds per month?'

Boyd took a drink of coffee, replaced his cup on the saucer, and said, 'Hacked!'

'Hacked?' queried Lucia. 'I'm still picking up parts of your language, Mister Boyd. Am I right in thinking that you mean hacked off? You know, angry, annoyed, something like that.'

'No,' replied Boyd shaking his head. 'I mean I've been hacked or, come to think of it, you've been hacked. In fact, it's more likely you've been hacked than me. Someone has hacked into your computer created some falsehoods and is now sitting back laughing at us. Except it's not funny anymore and something needs to be done pronto. They are trying to make fools of my wife and I. Get your manager in here now and then ring your IT department. I smell a rat.'

'Impossible!' chided Lucia. 'When will you learn that your status is irrelevant? You could be the Chief Constable or the Home Secretary for all I care. It would make no difference. The bank's computerised system cannot be broken, and I will not be bullied into calling my manager here to listen to you making stories up about being hacked. Your account was audited by Head Office at nine o'clock this morning. That means it was checked and double-checked, cross-referenced, and proven to satisfaction. How many times do I have to tell you, Mister Boyd, that you are at fault, not the bank?'

'I don't accept your explanation at all,' frowned Boyd. 'You haven't tried to address my concerns in any way.'

'In that case, it's time to leave if you don't mind. Or shall I call the police to have you ejected?'

Placing his cup and saucer on the table, Boyd replied, 'Okay! I'll go and do it my way. But before I leave, I want you to know that we've never held an overdraft on our account. Furthermore, we've never had a credit card, a loan, or a world cruise, and my wife and I are as close now as we ever were. There's no-one else. Do you understand?'

'So, you say,' replied Lucia. 'How are you to know if that is the truth? Tell me you trust your wife implicitly.'

'Look, I'm not getting any further into this at the moment,' declared Boyd. 'I can account for my movements over the last twelve months, longer if need be, and I can tell you we've never spent money like that. As for strip clubs, gambling clubs, champagne and boats on the Thames, then I'm at a loss to explain to you how they feature in the account. Those things did not happen. They've been concocted by someone else or, more likely, your staff have recorded the debits in the wrong account. I'll take legal advice before coming back to you.'

'That's what they all say, Mister Boyd,' replied Lucia. She stood up, offered him a printout of his account, opened the door, and said, 'It's your life. Just remember I gave you twenty-four hours to get to grips with things and you refused to accept my offer. The small print in your account contains annotations made by various staff members regarding your historic successful applications for credit cards and loans. The digital record is there for all to see, Mister Boyd. There'll be a paper trail too somewhere, I have no doubt.'

'Precisely,' argued Boyd. 'A digital record that has been altered so that if you print it out it will correspond to the digital record. Good day to you.'

Snatching the printout, Boyd strode from the bank, fuming, annoyed, and angry as hell as he voiced, 'Hacked! I've been hacked and the bank couldn't care less.'

Pausing for a moment, Boyd looked skyward and then took in the rooftops of the city streets. Shaking his head, he set off for the Coffee Shop wondering what to do to solve the problem before him.

A short time later, Boyd and Meg sat in a quiet corner of the Coffee Shop eating an all-day breakfast and drinking coffee.

'Did you enjoy your time at the gym?' asked Boyd.

'Yes, thanks,' replied Meg.

'Good! It will have done you good.;' ventured Boyd.

Meg propped the bank account papers up against a convenient cruet as she read the details and regularly shook her head.

Turning another page over, she glanced at Boyd and said, 'This isn't you and it certainly isn't me. It's fiction! Pure fiction! Can't they double-check their system?'

'I repeatedly asked that question,' replied Boyd. 'It was like talking to a wall. The bank has so much confidence in their computerised system that our relationship manager wouldn't even entertain the prospect that there was something wrong.'

'I wonder if they have another customer with the same name,' suggested Meg. 'Boyd isn't exactly unique. There will be a lot of people with that surname surely.'

'I didn't think to ask,' voiced Boyd. 'I should have done. That said, such a person would surely have a different bank account number. It's just so obvious that they've put someone else's transactions against our account. Are you happier now that you've seen the account?'

'Not really.'

'Meg!'

'No, I don't mean in that way, if that's what you are thinking. I'm happier that things between us are how they should be if that's what you mean. The problem is, Billy, we've no money in the bank, a car that might be repossessed at any time, and a gang of debt collectors who want paying about to knock on the door. That's not easy for me to accept. Is it right that if they get a warrant at court they can come and take anything they want out of the house if we've no money?'

'Not quite, but more or less,' confirmed Boyd.

'I thought so. Can we beat them by employing a local solicitor? Who do you recommend?'

'No-one in Carlisle, that's for sure,' replied Boyd tidying his knife and fork at the end of his meal, 'We'd need to look at Manchester, Birmingham or London for an expert in that field.'

'An expert in what field though, that is the question,' replied Meg.

'Expert!' remarked Boyd. 'Yes, Antonia, of course. She's got more contacts in the establishment than she'd ever admit to. I bet she knows someone in the banking world that can help us.'

'Then ring her as soon as possible,' ordered Meg. 'I'm slowly losing my mind over this situation. I need a break from it all. A weekend away somewhere.'

'I'll make a 'phone call, but…'

'But what?' queried Meg.

'Money! I've no money to pay for breakfast.'

'I have a twenty-pound note which was destined for school meals for the kids. I'll pay. Our debit cards have been cancelled. They're worthless.'

'I'll ring Antonia,' confirmed Boyd.

'Or Phillip,' suggested Meg. 'If the Director-General of the Security Service can't help us nobody can.'

'In that case, I'll catch you later. I'll need this though.'

Boyd reached over the table, collected the bank account papers, kissed Meg on the forehead, and made his way out of the building.

On arriving at the city police station, Boyd took the lift to the second floor and strode down the corridor into DI Stan Holland's office where he opened the conversation with, 'Stan! I need a secure 'phone. Is there one in the building?'

'This one,' revealed Stan pointing to a red telephone on his desk. 'I presume you need to ring London urgently?'

'Something like that,' replied Boyd reaching for the 'phone. 'Do you mind?'

'Of course not. I'll rustle up some coffee while you make your call.'

Boyd dialled Antonia in the Special Crime Unit in London whilst the DI went to the canteen.

'Hey!' suggested Stan as he stalled at the doorway. 'How about we invite you and Meg around for dinner one night? It's been a while since the four of us got together.'

'Brilliant, Stan. Yes! Let' do that.'

Moments later, Antonia answered, and Boyd pleaded, 'Antonia! I need your help. The world is collapsing on top of me and I don't know what to do.'

'What again?' chuckled Antonia. 'What is it this time? Tell me the car won't start or is that the lawnmower is playing up again?'

'I've been hacked!' declared Boyd. 'I need your help and I need it now.'

'What?' queried Antonia. 'Hacked! Home or office?'

'Home, I presume,' replied Boyd. 'That said, it could be the bank that's been hacked. I really don't know. I just know that the bank tells me I owe them money.'

'Oh! I see,' replied Antonia in a pragmatic manner. 'How much?'

'Between fifty and one hundred thousand pounds!'

A shocked Antonia countered, 'What?'

'You heard! Between fifty and one hundred thousand pounds.'

'I can't help you, Boyd. I don't have that kind of cash in my purse and you should know better than to ask me.'

'No! You've got it wrong. You're not listening to me. I don't want your money,' replied Boyd. 'I want your help.'

Antonia paused, allowed her mind to consider what had been said for a moment, and then ventured, 'Are you serious?'

'Yes!' bellowed Boyd in frustration. 'I've got a printout of my account from the bank to prove it. It's wrong. They've put someone else's expenditure into our joint account.'

'Joint account?' queried Antonia. 'Does Meg know?'

'You bet she does,' revealed Boyd. 'Life is not worth living at the moment. She doesn't believe a word I say.'

'Speak to the bank,' replied Antonia. 'It's the obvious thing to do.'

'I have. They've given me a printout. It's false. I owe them money and they are after me big time.'

'Just a moment,' replied Antonia. 'There's another call on the line.'

Antonia placed the 'phone on the desk and sat back. There was no other call to answer but she needed time to assess the situation. Her fingers drummed the table as she thought.

Eventually, she returned to Boyd and said, 'You just said to me that you owe them money. Is that the most honest thing you've told me today? Don't answer that, Boyd. Sorry, but I can't help you. No kidding but it sounds like that promotion has gone to your head and you've gone overboard with it. Do you really think we can help you out with debts like that?'

'It's what the bank states, Antonia. You're missing the point,' argued Boyd. 'There's no-one else I can think of that is better placed to help me. The bank tells me their systems are correct, but I know that we have not spent this money. I'm sending you the printout to have a look at. Please do what you can. Maybe you have a contact, or better still one of those uncles that you keep conjuring up who works in the banking industry. Kick some doors down for me, Antonia. Something is very wrong here.'

'Do you have any idea how busy I am with the investigation into the Mayor of London and the threat against him, Boyd? I'm up to my ears in meaningless intelligence that is leading me nowhere, but I still have to get on top of it until I find a useful lead that we can react to. No! Sorry, but no! I'm too busy.'

There was a long pause on the 'phone before Boyd replied, 'I thought I could rely on you. I was wrong. All I'm asking you to do is make a few calls to those in the finance system that we know. Tell them you're doing a vetting procedure or something. Just open some doors for me so that I can get the right people to sort this out for me. Can you do that for me?'

Growing angry now, Antonia replied, 'I can't do that, Boyd and well you know it. You're asking me to disregard the protocols and do you a favour without anything going on paper or without anyone knowing. Just use the old pal's act, is that what you want? Have you forgotten how long it took us to make such contacts? These discreet alliances are at the top of the tree and are based on trust, knowledge and honesty embedded in the legal system and a high degree of transparency between us. Now you want me to wander into someone's office and ask for the world because a friend is in need. What's next? Can they erase the debt for me? Sorry, Boyd, but that's a favour too many. It's not only against the grain, but it's also contrary to the service protocols. You know, as well as I do, that I would need to create a file authorising the investigation to cover ourselves. We need to be transparent in everything we do, even when things are classified to kingdom come. That's not going to happen with this lady. You picked the wrong horse, Boyd.'

'Listen to me for a moment,' begged Boyd. 'Open a file on me. Do whatever you need to do to investigate me, my wife, and our lifestyle. Whatever you need to do and wherever you need to go. I need to sort this out before the roof falls in on all of us.'

'Open a file on you!' snapped Antonia. 'Who do you think you are, Boyd? No way! I'm not risking my career to help you out. Pay the money back, you idiot.'

Boyd took a deep breath and replied, 'Antonia, I'm not an idiot. Either I or the bank has been hacked and well and truly hacked by a professional of some kind. I'm going to fax my bank printout to you. Read it and if you think that's me then get back to the Mayor's job and forget about yours truly. But if you read it and think otherwise, then do what you can for me. I'm counting on you.'

'If I find the time. Maybe next week,' offered Antonia sarcastically.

'If that's the best you can do then yes, do read it,' beseeched Boyd. 'Analyse it and think about the document and its contents as soon as you have time.'

'What do you really want?' probed Antonia. 'Me to raise an office collection and send you a couple of hundred quid because you've gone bust and it's your fault? Rescue Meg because she's gone and booked a world cruise and ruined your finances, or what? Come on, Boyd. What the hell is going on with you?'

'Exactly what I want to know,' delivered Boyd. 'I'm sending the printout now. Do me the biggest favour possible and open a file on the subject. I know you will. You are my only hope at the moment.'

Boyd replaced the handset.

'All done?' queried Stan on returning with two coffees.

'Yes, yes, thanks,' replied Boyd.

'What's the problem? Can I help at all?'

'Not at the moment, Stan,' said Boyd accepting one of the drinks. 'Hopefully, London will sort this one out for me. Fingers crossed!'

'London!' remarked Stan. 'Need to know and all that. I understand but just remember as you help us, there may be a time when we can help you.'

'Of course, thanks, I'll remember that,' nodded Boyd.

Simultaneously, a computer screen flashed in a house on the shores of Loch Ness.

CYCLOPS AUDIO ALERT appeared on the screen.

Colonel Korobov entered a password and listened to the latest conversation undertaken by Boyd and Antonia recorded by a tiny bugging device sewn into Boyd's suit jacket and transmitted to her by a satellite orbiting the planet.

Fidgeting with the end of her chin, the Colonel listened intently, sat back, and immediately engaged her mobile 'phone to enter the Satcom network. She hit the buttons and waited for a reply.

'Something wrong, Colonel?' enquired Dimitry.

'No, not really,' replied the Colonel. 'Except I appear to have misjudged my adversary.'

'Well, the British are famous for their determined resolve,' suggested Dimitry. 'But then they've no previous experience of tangling with a Russian spymaster. Can I get you some tea, Colonel? Or perhaps a large vodka?'

'No, thank you, Dimitry. I shall need a clear brain to accomplish the tasks ahead, defeat the British, and bring one particular individual to his knees.'

'I see,' replied Dimitry. 'I'd better get to my post then. I have things to tidy up.'

'Yes, why not indeed,' declared the Colonel holding onto her 'phone. 'I have a call to make and then I'll join you.'

Major Viktor Petrov and Senior Lieutenant Nadia Koshkin sat in a hired grey Skoda motor car on the outskirts of Carlisle. Their telephone rang as they watched Meg Boyd deliver James and Izzy to the village school for the afternoon.

The passenger answered with, 'Nadia!'

'Is everything going according to plan?' asked the Colonel.

'Yes, we are in position and ready,' replied Nadia.

'Hold back,' ordered the Colonel. 'It is time to move to the next stage. Two friends will join you later today to ensure a good night out. Understood?'

Nadia glanced at Viktor who nodded his understanding.

'Yes, we have that,' replied Nadia.

'Good luck!' offered the Colonel.

Closing her 'phone, the Colonel walked into the lounge area of their temporary Operations Centre room where she found Pavel and Talisha who were watching television.

'Sorry to interrupt,' remarked the Colonel. 'You're up next. Travel to the target and make contact with team one.'

'When?'

'Now! Take a couple of security guards with you just in case.'

'Is it on?'

'Yes! We're ready to go,' stated the Colonel. 'I may have underestimated the enemy. The subject might be on to us sooner than I had anticipated, but we're still well ahead in the game. It's time to expedite the next phase of the operation. Good luck!'

In the office of the Special Crime Unit in London, Antonia stared at her computer screen and read recent intelligence reports concerning the threat against Benjamin Epstein, the Mayor of London.

Unable to put Boyd's telephone call out of her mind, Antonia suddenly swivelled her chair towards the coffee pot. Clumsily, she knocked the coffee pot over, swore, and then stood up to clean the mess with a handful of tissues.

'Damn you, Boyd!' voiced Antonia. 'One coffee! That's all I asked. One coffee and you've upset my mind to the point that I couldn't even manage that without spilling it all over the desk. Damn you, Billy Boyd. Damn you.'

Mopping the mess up didn't take too long and Antonia soon found herself with a fresh mug of piping hot coffee and a computer that had gone into hibernation. Thumping the keyboard in frustration, Antonia brought the screen back to life.

'Two minutes, Boyd. I'll give you two minutes of my valuable time and no more.'

Negotiating the Ticker Intelligence system took Antonia straight into the supervisor's area where she tapped BISHOP into the keyboard. The system recognised Boyd's MI5 coded name and brought his personnel file to the screen.

Antonia studied the man's history from the date of his birth to the present day.

She noted that the last vetting procedure undertaken against Boyd had occurred only three months ago and had been personally supervised by Sir Phillip Nesbitt K.B.E. who was the Director-General of the Security Services, her fiancé, and the love of her life. It was no surprise to her given the extensive remit imprinted on the minds of those who were members of the Special Crime Unit.

Sipping her coffee, occasionally mopping a drip that she had missed from the table, Antonia shook her head and said to herself, 'Top Secret Omega Blue! An identifiable person under the Official Secrets Act! The highest level of security clearance going and a record that is second to none. Unless of course, you count all those complaints made against him for excessive use of force, inappropriate terminology, questionable use of firearms, and criticism of his leadership.'

Antonia drank more coffee and voiced aloud, 'Criticism? Well, that's a load of rubbish. I was with him most of those times. Well, some of those times then. Whatever! The reality is that an individual in his position is covertly examined by one of our branch officers every six months to make sure he remains fit for purpose. One to you, Boyd. You're in the lead, so far. But what else can I find in your file? I'll print it out and read it later. There's a lot of pages to scrutinise.'

Quietly, she manipulated the keyboard and a printout spewed from a nearby facility.

Tapping away on the keyboard took Antonia to Boyd's early years, from infant school to primary school, from secondary school to college and beyond.

A self-made man thought Antonia and a great personal friend.

There was a smooth passage of paper in the fax machine that alerted Antonia to the arrival of Boyd's promised bank account.

Antonia walked to the machine, removed the paper, and read the document. It was the account received by him that morning from the bank and forwarded to her for assessment.

Negotiating out of one window in the Ticker browser, Antonia opened another. She paused, said, 'What the hell. That's not what Boyd would spend his money on!' and entered the file authorisation system.

'Spooks, crooks or weirdos? That's what you once said, Boyd. So, if I choose to believe you then it's one of those three.'

'Spooks, crooks or weirdos,' she repeated. 'How about thimbles, thieves, or twisted minds instead?'

The redhead began opening a file on Boyd.

Case officer? That's me, thought Antonia. Title? I'll call it THIMBLES. Reason for investigation? A covert enquiry into BISHOP. Authorising officer? Well, now I have a problem because there isn't one and there's not enough evidence to persuade one following a plea from an idiot who looks like he's lost the plot. But I'll go with him for old time's sake. Only so far!

Tinkling with the keyboard, thinking things through, Antonia entered JUPITER and read the summary of the file relevant to Sir Phillip Nesbitt K.B.E. He was her fiancé, the love of her life, and the Director-General of the nation's Security Service.

Staring at the screen, a burst of inspiration penetrated her mind and she entered the Director-General's details into the THIMBLES FILE. The screen showed Sir Phillip as the authorising officer for a covert enquiry into William Miller Boyd.

If I'm found out. That's me finished, thought Antonia. Should I tell Phillip? No, not yet.

The door behind opened and in walked Sir Phillip Nesbitt.

Antonia pressed ENTER, falsely authorised the investigation, and then immediately withdrew from the Ticker system.

'What brings you here?' probed Antonia. 'Have you run out of coffee or biscuits in your neck of the woods? How can I help?'

'I wanted a word,' replied the Director-General.

'I see!' acknowledged Antonia. 'Are you looking for a new Miss Moneypenny?'

'I'm not but seeing as you mention it, would you like a job as my secretary?'

'No way!' chuckled Antonia playfully. 'Absolutely not! I'm a field officer, not an office canary.'

Sir Phillip Nesbitt K.B.E. was slightly older than Antonia, in his fifties, slightly overweight, and of medium height. Handsome, his looks centred around his light brown hair and brown eyes. Yet he was fairly nondescript otherwise. He did, however, carry an air of confidence that had the potential to beguile the unwary and unprepared. Those that knew him well would testify to his tenacity when chasing down a specific matter of importance. Others would tell you that he was a 'Jack of all Trades' and

'Master of None'. He was a fairly quiet and reserved individual who was seen by some as occasionally arrogant. The truth of the matter lay in his upbringing. Phillip's parents were doctors when they were alive and had both been senior partners in a General Practitioner's Surgery on the edge of Bournemouth. Upon their passing, they'd left a sizeable estate for their son to inherit. The size of the estate was such that Phillip would never actually have to work for a living in the future. But Phillip never intended to be a loafer and it wasn't the only thing he would remember his parents for. They'd provided a loving and caring environment for the youngster to find his feet and soon recognised the power of his memory. He had an uncanny ability to remember the slightest detail and took pleasure, as a youth, in learning the contents of the surgery's pharmacy products off by heart. He recited them 'parrot fashion'. It was a game he played with his parents, and he always won. Sadly, he relinquished such knowledge when the speed of development in the pharmaceutical industry reached such a rate that it became impossible to keep up with new products. Being a wealthy doctor's child had its problems both at school and in his teens. He found it difficult to mix with children of a similar age who were from totally different backgrounds. Grammar School preceded Cambridge University where he majored in Politics and Economics whilst flirting with courses and lectures relevant to Social Sciences and Overseas Development. With degrees under his arm, Phillip answered an advertisement in a national newspaper and began a lengthy application and recruitment program into the Security Service. Quietly proud of his achievements, Phillip would remind only his very closest friends that he had started on the factory floor before working his way to the top of the tree. He'd enjoyed a long career in the Service and specialised in both Irish and International Terrorism before rapid promotions followed in the realms of protective security and organisational administration. It was here that he gained a Knighthood and took the reins as head of the intelligence community. Surprisingly, to some degree, Phillip was not the most popular man in the Service. He'd deliberately chosen his friends carefully determined to do the best he could in his chosen profession. Charting his career brought with it some accolades and, eventually, it was generally accepted amongst the rank and file that Phillip Nesbitt fitted the seat of Director-General well.

Sir Phillip bent down and pecked Antonia on the cheek before saying, 'That's a pity. Maybe one day you'll take me up on my offer. Good secretaries are hard to find.'

'There's nothing wrong with the one you've got now,' proposed Antonia. 'What's wrong? It's not like you to leave your ivory tower and come and see me.'

Sir Phillip chuckled and then said, 'I wondered why you didn't call last night but then I remembered you had a meeting with Woodpecker. How did it go? Are we any nearer to considerations in respect of Sparrow Hawk?'

'Woodpecker?' queried Antonia quietly sliding Boyd's printouts into a drawer.

'Yes, Woodpecker,' replied Sir Phillip. 'Your source at the Russian Embassy.'

'Of course, yes. Sorry, Phillip, my mind was elsewhere working on the threat to the Mayor when you came in. The meeting went well other than Woodpecker insists that Sparrow Hawk must be brought here from Moscow before she tells all.'

'There's no change then?'

'None whatsoever.'

'And your thoughts?' probed Sir Phillip.

'To some degree, Woodpecker has us over a barrel,' proposed Antonia. 'My source has unquestionable access to the Russian Embassy and Sparrow Hawk has a long story to tell us about his years working in the Kremlin and his relationship with the President. I understand Sparrow Hawk has MI6 over the barrel too. He refuses to co-operate fully until he is reunited with Woodpecker.'

'Has it been suggested to Sparrow Hawk that he takes a flight out of Russia and ends up in our hands?'

'It has,' replied Antonia. 'Unfortunately, he only has papers that authorise movement in Russia itself. One of the problems is that his right to leave Russia is legally suspended because he has had access to classified documents while working for the State. The State ban such people from leaving Russia for up to five years after their employment ended. Since Sparrow Hawk has worked in the Kremlin all his life, he's prohibited from leaving Russia. Do you think they would grant him a long weekend's holiday break in London with a track record of working as close to the President as he has? Not a cat in hell's chance. It's as simple as that.'

'Yes, I'm aware of the restrictions the State imposes on Russian citizens,' replied Sir Phillip. 'I would have thought he might find it easy to acquire a false passport from the Moscow underworld. That would solve the problem.'

'I think Lucy in MI6 is using that guise at the moment, Phillip. She can turn her hand to anything. It's not as easy as it seems though. Sparrow Hawk is an elderly man who doesn't want to put himself in danger. His daughter, Woodpecker, won't divulge everything until she is reunited with her father.'

'Yes, I understand her concerns, Antonia, but in some ways, this is bordering on blackmail. Is it part of a sting operation? Is she trying to deceive us into a position where we commit some kind of crime that ostensibly appears to be beneficial to her and then we're caught out? Are we being pulled into a situation that resembles a false flag operation? Consider the dilemma we face in deciding whether or not to authorise continued resources to this operation. It could be a dangle: one of the oldest tactics in the intelligence game. Are they luring us into a situation where we trust them and then, when the time is right, they can either expose us or feed us false intelligence for years to come?'

'It's you that has the dilemma, Phillip,' replied Antonia. 'Ultimately, it's your decision as to whether we go on or stop now. You're Britain's spymaster. Tell me! I'm all ears.'

'To defeat the enemy, one often has to think outside the box, second guess events, and think in the broadest way possible,' suggested Sir Phillip. 'We have to analyse this scenario and make a decision based on the facts as they might be, not necessarily as we believe them to be. Let us presume Moscow has found out that we are running Woodpecker as an agent. They've turned Woodpecker into a double agent and told her to string us along since they know we have to extract Sparrow Hawk from Moscow before both sources come clean on everything they know. Simultaneously, they've also discovered that Sparrow Hawk is a British spy. You should never under-estimate your adversary.'

'To do so is to fail,' remarked Antonia.

Sir Phillip continued with, 'These two sources may well be double agents in waiting. Woodpecker can feed us false information provided to her by the Russians and designed to put us on the wrong track whilst Sparrow Hawk wants us to extract him from Moscow. In so doing, he will learn how our people in Moscow operate, meet and identify our officers working undercover, and potentially blow our counter-espionage capability in Russia into a thousand pieces.'

'It's potentially that bad?' probed Antonia.

'I'm not sure. Possibly!' responded Sir Phillip. 'If Moscow is aware of what we are doing they could be ahead of the game waiting for our next move. The problem is they may have already worked out our next move which would be to extract Sparrow Hawk.'

'Now I know why you sometimes seem preoccupied in thought,' remarked Antonia. 'I can't criticise you when you have decisions like that to make. The wrong decision is not worth thinking about. Potentially, hundreds of our people are at risk and the government will change its stance on a score of things dependent on the intelligence it receives from our spies. Governments have been formulating policy based on covert intelligence for centuries. The term 'rogue spies' comes to mind. I surely hope that is not the case. Phillip, can I help at all?'

'It's just a game, isn't it?' chuckled Sir Phillip. 'That's what they call it: The Spy Game.'

'It's not a game anymore,' declared Antonia.

Phillip nodded and replied, 'I need to consider this case carefully before making a decision. The Russians may be trying to make fools of us by using these two people to their best advantage.'

'I know,' argued Antonia. 'And I understand but I need to know if we are going to extract Sparrow Hawk from the Motherland or not?'

'Is it worth it, I ask myself,' replied Sir Phillip. 'Is Lucy ready?'

'Not yet,' voiced Antonia.

'In that case, the answer is no!' decided Sir Phillip. 'Not at the moment. Keep playing Woodpecker and update me as to the situation regarding Sparrow Hawk regularly, Antonia. We'd do well to keep our fingers on the pulse regarding this one.'

'Phillip! Are you ever afraid of the job that you do?'

'Why should I be afraid of the things that I don't yet understand? Things will evolve and develop, and then we will deal with them appropriately.'

'Yes, of course,' replied Antonia. 'Anything else you need to know?'

'No, why do you ask?'

'Boyd!'

'What about him?' probed Sir Phillip cautiously.

'Heard anything about him lately?'

'No!' an emphatic Sir Phillip declared.

'Phillip!' pleaded Antonia. 'You're not a good liar. What have you heard?'

'That he's in debt.'

'And? What else?'

'How do you know about, Boyd?' ventured Sir Phillip.

'He told me,' replied Antonia.

'When?'

'Recently! Boyd has been told that he owes more than fifty thousand pounds.'

'And the rest,' added the Director-General.

'Phillip! He and Meg are our closest friends. Can we help them?'

'You mean should we help them, and the answer is no,' replied Sir Phillip. 'If Boyd has got himself into trouble then he needs to dig himself out of it.'

'Is that where friendship begins and ends?' enquired Antonia. 'With a shovel?'

'No,' replied Sir Phillip. 'If he's been hacked then get the IT department on it and help him in any way you can in that respect, and only that respect, Antonia.'

'There are other ways we could help him,' proposed Antonia.

'If the bank has been hacked, then I presume he'll go to see them and complain his account has been interfered with.'

'He's been. They didn't help,' replied Antonia.

'I'm not a bank and neither are you,' declared Sir Phillip. 'If you give once, you'll be expected to bail them out regularly and completely. I'd cut my right arm off for Boyd but sadly I need the same arm to sign some authorities that are much more important than one individual. Sorry, but that's the way it is?'

'What if it's all a big mistake?' ventured Antonia.

'In what way?' probed Sir Phillip.

'The bank may have made a mistake.'

'I doubt it. No-one hacks a bank these days. Their protocols are very advanced and use state of the art technology. I think Boyd has just gone overboard and spent too much.

'Alternatively, he may have been hacked.'

'Boyd! Hacked?'

'Why not?' proposed Antonia. 'How about the bank being hacked instead?'

Frustrated, Sir Phillip replied, 'Right now, I have a lot of decisions to make, Antonia. Best friend or not, Boyd isn't a decision I'm involved with. There's no evidence to say he was hacked, or the bank was hacked. Sorry, I'm not falling out with you over this but it's down to Boyd and his family to sort themselves out. I'll see you for lunch as arranged.'

'Yes,' replied Antonia. 'Of course.'

Angrily, Sir Phillip slammed the door behind him causing Antonia to offer the unheard reply, 'Get you and your temper. Where did that come from? Lunch indeed! Maybe, maybe not.'

Antonia slid open the drawer, withdrew the printouts and scanned through them before saying to herself, 'Perhaps I'll look for some evidence after all. Someone needs to watch out for Boyd and Meg and Phillip doesn't have the time or the inclination at the moment.'

On the outskirts of Carlisle, Meg walked into the hall of her home and answered the ringing telephone unaware that a miniature microphone was covertly hidden inside the telephone base with the ability to transmit conversations to Colonel Korobov in Scotland.

Listening to the words of yet another individual representing a business that was owed money from her husband, Meg slammed the 'phone down, dropped to her knees, and began to sob.

'Enough!' she cried. 'Stop! Please! No more.'

The 'phone rang again. Reluctantly, she answered it and heard the words, 'Mrs. Boyd?'

'Yes! Who's that?'

'Chasers Debt Collection Agency, according to our records…'

Crashing the 'phone onto its cradle, a furious Meg stormed into the kitchen, found paper and pen, and wrote a note. When she had finished, Meg placed the message inside a white envelope and then propped the envelope up against the kettle.

There were two police stations in Carlisle. One was for city personnel where the uniform and CID branches were situated. The other was the Divisional Headquarters for North Cumbria where the Administration department was situated, along with the Rural section, the Traffic Department, and the Dog Section.

It was to the Divisional Headquarters that the paraffin man made his way. Dressed all in black and wearing an anorak with a hood that covered most of his face, he had stuffed a plastic fuel can inside his clothing, along with a box of matches and a mobile phone.

Making his way across an area of parkland, he eventually entered the housing estate that bordered part of his intended target. Fifteen minutes later he circumnavigated the housing estate, entered an industrial estate that also ran close to his destination, and then came to a standstill as he studied a palisade fence that encircled Divisional Police Headquarters.

A wooden building that was once the dog section kennels ran parallel to the palisade fence. No longer in use, since the restructuring of the department, the abandoned kennels backed onto the fence and looked inwards to a sports field, a helipad, and the police building.

Making his way cautiously along the fence line, the paraffin man reached the old police dog kennels. He could see them despite the darkness of the hour but couldn't find an entrance.

In the silence of the night, the paraffin man began throwing fuel through the gaps in the fence. The inflammable mixture landed on the roof of the kennels, soaked the wood, and then trickled down the sides to the ground. He moved further along the fence line repeating his actions, continuing his attack, making ready for the ultimate event of his day.

Finally, he set down the fuel can and rummaged in his pocket for a box of matches.

Chuckling to himself, he knew he would not be blown off his feet this time. All he had to do was make sure a lighted match landed on the roof of the building where he had doused it with his mixture. Only the fence stood between him, the old police dog kennels, and an unseen security guard that was patrolling the interior of the complex.

A match was struck.

The paraffin man cast it over the fence and watched it land on the roof.

There was an explosion of flame when the match hit its target and caused a chain reaction. The flames gathered pace, stretched out their tentacles of destruction, and began their journey of annihilation.

Stepping back, he took in the sight before him and adored the very essence of his latest experience. He began recording the fire on his mobile 'phone.

A dog barked.

The paraffin man stepped closer to the fence looking for the source.

Wood crackled noisily. Flames gathered pace. Smoke began to spiral into the sky.

The dog barked again.

Confused, the paraffin man narrowed his eyes and looked through the fence, but then quickly averted them so that he could take in the glory of his creation. His video rolled on.

The flames leapt into the sky. The unstable human who caused them felt his heartbeat surge with the excitement of it all.

'Who's there?' shouted a voice.

The paraffin man stepped back in shock, stumbled over his fuel can, and immediately looked to his left and right. There was no-one there and his shallow mind was in a state of flux.

A torchlight penetrated the fence line from inside the complex. Its beam flickered on its journey along the palisade structure where there were gaps. The beam of light fell on the ground, lit up the land, and finally found the paraffin man spellbound and steadfast on the other side of the fence.

'Stand right there,' shouted the security guard. 'Don't move.'

Galvanised into action, the paraffin man saw the torchlight, heard the voice, and ran along the fence line back towards the industrial estate, the housing estate, and the parkland that would afford him cover.

Lurching from left to right, he pocketed his 'phone, ran clumsily into the night, sought the streetlights ahead for guidance, and then crashed into the side of the fence.

A jagged piece of metal protruded from the fence, snagged his anorak sleeve, tore it, and held the residue of cloth in its structural grasp.

'Go on, boy,' shouted the security handler. 'Seek him out!'

The dog barked at the same time the paraffin man realised the security guard was accompanied by a guard dog. Panicking now, he threw himself forward as fast as he could, stumbled again, but eventually made the pavement and the industrial estate.

To the paraffin man's rear, the guard unlocked a gate in the fence, and rushed through in pursuit with his dog on a longer lead yapping and barking in its desire to bring down the fireraiser.

A wireless cackled. A transmission was made. The security guard gave chase with a radio held close to his ear and a dog straining at the leash.

The paraffin man was through the streets, down an alley, across another road, and into the housing estate with his hood blowing in the breeze, his hands trembling, and a heart rate nearing capacity as it pounded in his chest. His mind was blown now with no time to smell the smoke, feel the heat of the fire, sense the power it gave him, and no thought of reconciling his brain to capture.

Wanted!

For the first time in his sad, deplorable, lonely life he knew he was under the cosh, close to capture, and scared out of his wits. It was the dog!

Barking!

The dog was barking and snarling in its lust for his blood. And then there was another dog and more barking with the paraffin man stumbling from gatepost to gatepost, bumping into parked cars and trying his best to keep on the straight and narrow of the cracked uneven pavement.

Sirens!

The atmosphere was filled with the sound of sirens coming from all directions when they blotted out the sound of barking dogs, people running, and chasers shouting.

Then a strange new sound suddenly filled the air.

Glancing over his shoulder, the paraffin man took in the sight of the old police dog kennels now well alight. Flames reached into the sky and lit up a helicopter which was taking off from the helipad in the police complex.

Moments later, the streets were bathed with the helicopter's searchlight when the craft had gained height and begun its search. The searchlight scoured the ground from left to right as it penetrated every corner of the ground below.

Dogs barking! Sirens blaring! A torch flashing! Footsteps growing louder! And now a helicopter searchlight chasing the most wanted in the city.

Rolling around a corner, the paraffin man paused for breath and then bolted to the bottom of the street where paving ended, and the waste ground began.

The paraffin man lifted the lid of an industrial recycling bin and climbed in. There was a loud clatter when he pulled the metal lid down and gradually sunk into a collection of industrial, commercial and domestic waste. Up to his knees in muck and gunk, it wasn't long before he found himself dropping to the bottom of a stinking hell hole.

Gasping for air, he threw his arms upwards, found the handle and pulled himself into a safer position. Gradually, the crap around him surrendered and the paraffin man dropped his head to his chest and closed his eyes.

Frightened, perplexed, confused by the events of the night, he sobbed before a slice of his brain reminded him of his predicament.

Listening out, the only sound he could hear was the far away throb of a low flying helicopter.

Outside, the security guard's dog reached the bin, sniffed at one corner of the rusting receptacle, and then bounded away into another part of the estate.

Elsewhere in Cumbria, there was a knock on the door at the Boyd household.

Meg ran to the door shouting, 'Billy! About time too! Where the hell have you been?'

Pulling the door open, Meg stared directly into the eyes of Major Viktor Petrov who greeted her with, 'Mrs Boyd, I presume. We are so sorry but it's Mr Boyd. I'm afraid I have some bad news for you.'

'What?' crumbled Meg. 'Billy? Where is he? What's happened?'

'May we come in?' insisted Viktor.

'Yes! Yes, of course,' replied Meg. 'Has he been shot? Is it a road accident?'

Viktor took a step into the house. He was accompanied by Senior Lieutenant Nadia Koshkin who asked, 'The children, Mrs Boyd! Where are they?'

Retreating backwards into the house, Meg gasped, held her hands to her face, and then said, 'The children? You mentioned my husband. Where is he?'

'Let me explain,' remarked Viktor.

'Just a minute,' replied Meg. 'I don't think I know you. Who are you? Do you work with my husband?'

'Yes, of course, we do,' declared Viktor.

Stepping further away, Meg responded with, 'Where's Bannerman? Anthea? Antonia?'

There was no response.

Meg continued with, 'Your warrant cards! You must have your warrant cards with you.'

'Now!' yelled Viktor.

Two burly Russian guards - Igor and Oleg - burst through the doorway and pushed Meg hard against the wall as Pavel and Talisha followed through shouting, 'Where're the children?'

'Izzy! James!' screamed Meg.

Forcing a damp handkerchief into Meg's face, Igor chloroformed her with the colourless sweet-smelling liquid that was once used a general anaesthetic.

Nursing knowledge kicked in and Meg knew she was beaten by the first whiff of the substance despite a pitiful attempt to thump Igor's chest and resist his advances. Within seconds, she slumped towards the floor only to be caught by Oleg. Between them, the two men lifted Meg horizontally and made for the open doorway.

'Get the children!' ordered Viktor.

Standing with his back against the wall, the Major watched Pavel and Talisha rush down the corridor and into the children's bedroom.

Moments later, they were joined by Nadia who helped force Izzy and James into some clothes before lifting them bodily and carrying them towards the entrance.

Igor ignored the screaming, kicking children and merely waved his sodden handkerchief beneath their noses saying, 'Just a whiff. No more.'

'Let's go!' ordered Viktor.

Black rumbling clouds greeted the kidnap party as they bundled Meg, Izzy and James into the back of a van. Igor and Oleg turned Meg over onto her stomach and tied her hands behind her back with plastic handcuffs As she began to recover from the chloroform, they propped her up on a bench, pushed her back against the van wall, and then tied Izzy and James together with similar restraints.

Igor thumped the compartment wall behind the driver twice and the van set off.

A black BMW led the van followed by a dark blue Audi. They set off smoothly in full view of a dormant CCTV system that lined the avenue and ended at the junction of the main road. The convoy turned left and headed north.

Half an hour later, Boyd pulled into his driveway, closed the vehicle down for the night, and entered his home.

'Meg!' he called. 'Meg! I'm home.'

There was no reply and no sign of a recent disorder. There was only a faint smell of a mysterious substance that Boyd presumed was a product of Meg's home cooking.

Wandering into the kitchen, the off-duty detective removed an envelope propped against the kettle and began to make himself a coffee. Ripping the envelope open, he read Meg's words and shook his head in sorrow.

Why has she decided to take a break now? Boyd thought. How am I supposed to know where the hell she's gone? Where are you, Meg? Goddamit, woman! Where the hell are you? You only needed to add one line as to where you were going.

Quickly snatching his mobile 'phone, Boyd 'phoned Meg. There was no reply and he began texting their friends.

Where can she be? Is this the end? Too much for her? Or is she just pressuring me when she needn't? he thought.

Boyd's fingers continued to drive the texts as he prepared himself for a longer night than he had anticipated.

Glancing at the clock, he synchronised his wristwatch and thought, I'll have answers in the morning. She'll be back soon, of that I'm sure.

~

6

Carlisle
Early the next morning.

Boyd was up early.

Washing and shaving before devouring a couple of slices of toast, he eventually answered his mobile. Briefed on the telephone by DI Stan Holland, he promised to respond to the ongoing enquiry regarding the arson attack that had occurred during the night.

Astonished to hear the news, Boyd snatched the squad car keys from the kitchen table as he briefly checked messages on his mobile.

There were a few concerned replies, but no-one had heard from Meg.

Half an hour later he pulled into the car park at DHQ and joined PC John Dillon who met him at the entrance.

The police helicopter hovered here and there before moving on in a circular search pattern.

'Message from DI Holland, Mister Boyd,' explained Dillon. 'He's allocated enquiries and paired everyone doing various jobs. The DI has put us together and asks that we revisit the precise scene of the crime and work on possible escape routes. Think out of the box, sir. That's what the DI said because it looks like the offender got clean away.'

'Maybe!' replied Boyd. 'How long has that helicopter been searching?'

'Not long! It went up at the time the crime occurred, reported a negative search, and went back up about half an hour ago, just after daybreak. It had to refuel apparently.'

'And still nothing?'

'No!' revealed Dillon. 'They had cordons in place within five minutes of the alarm being raised. Every vehicle was checked going through the cordons with a negative result. They're still in place and the DI is pulling his hair out. A house to house team has been set up checking every building in the area searching outhouses and making sure the wanted man is not holding anyone against their will in their own homes.'

'So, the estate is in lockdown,' proposed Boyd.

'Pretty much,' replied Boyd. 'And the industrial estate?'

'The same! Surrounded!' replied Dillon.

'Any description of the offender?' probed Boyd.

'Not really,' replied Dillon. 'Male in dark clothing full stop.'

'That's a big help.'

'What do you want me to do?' enquired Dillon.

'Think like someone who has just tried to set fire to the old dog kennels and is now a wanted man. Come on. We've made a good team in the past. No reason why we can't work through this one together either. Are you ready?'

'Yes, I'm with you all the way.'

The two men made their way to the old dog kennels, studied the charred remains which were still smoking in the afterlife of the fire, and then opened the gate in the palisade fence.

'What's that?' enquired Boyd.

'A piece of cloth of some kind,' replied Dillon.

'Yeah, that's what I see,' frowned Boyd. 'The interesting thing is that it's on the other side of the fence.'

'Where the bolt is twisted outward,' noted Dillon.

'That's right,' replied Boyd. 'Have you got a forensic envelope?'

'Here,' responded Dillon rummaging in a pocket. 'I picked some up before we set off, just in case.'

Boyd gently removed the torn cloth from the outside bolt in the gate and dropped it into a clear plastic envelope saying, 'I wonder if we're looking for a man wearing a torn jacket of some kind?'

'If we are,' explained Dillon. 'Then that bolt is set at about my shoulder height.'

'You never know,' replied Boyd. 'Okay, he was last seen where?'

'At the beginning of the footpath,' explained Dillon.

'Oh good,' chuckled Boyd. 'He could be anywhere in the entire housing estate then.'

'Yes, or the industrial estate that borders it,' added Dillon.

'Come on, let's walk,' proposed Boyd.

Yard by yard the pair set off from the palisade fence as they tried to fathom out the direction which the offender may have taken.

'Industrial or residential?' queried Boyd.

'If I was the arsonist, I'd be hiding in a factory somewhere,' indicated Dillon.

'How would you do that?' probed Boyd.

'I'd find a side door and break-in.'

'Not a window?'

'No, too easy to spot. Alternatively, I'd shin up a drainpipe and either force a second-floor window or get onto the roof and lie as flat as a fluke.'

'In which case,' argued Boyd. 'The heat-seeking source from the helicopter would have found you had you been on the roof.'

'So, he's got in through a window on the second or third floor then,' replied Dillon.

'Maybe,' nodded Boyd as his mobile vibrated. He checked another negative reply about Meg on his mobile and then said, 'I don't think that's how our man would react.'

'Why's that?' asked Dillon.

'It's like I said at the morning conference the other day,' explained Boyd. 'A criminal would smash a window or climb a drainpipe to get into a building. He'd act just like a burglar and use his crooked mind to work out the best way to get into a property and hide from us at the same time. No, that's not how his mind works. He's a pyromaniac with a mental health problem. Our man is mentally unstable and a bit of a weirdo, I'd say.'

'Where does that leave us?' enquired Dillon.

'Running in a straight line as fast as he can,' replied Boyd.

'Then why didn't they find him last night?' probed Dillon.

'Because it was pitch black and they were too far behind,' answered Boyd.

A vibration in Boyd's jacket caused him to check a text message. It was a negative reply once more.

'Something troubling you, Mister Boyd?' enquired Dillon. 'Your 'phone hasn't stopped ringing since you arrived.'

Boyd replied, 'Just something else I'm dealing with, John. Sorry, if my mind seems elsewhere but keep walking in that straight line.'

'Near as I can,' nodded Dillon.

The two men strolled quietly along the streets noting row upon row of terraced housing, scores of parked cars and vans, and not much more. Here and there, people went about their business oblivious to the two plainclothes officers who merely acknowledged their presence with a nod, and then walked on.

'In a vehicle?' muttered Dillon.

'Possibly,' replied Boyd. 'Keep your eyes open because if he's hiding in a car or a van, it will be in the driver's seat or the passenger seat.'

'Or the back of an insecure van,' remarked Dillon.

Glancing at his partner, Boyd said, 'Yes! Something like that.'

Dozing in a rusting hulk of metal that was a commercial recycling bin, the paraffin man gradually opened his eyes, shook his head, and came to his senses. His heart rate was normal. The adrenalin had stopped flowing at speed, and his panic and nerves had disappeared. Cautiously, he pushed the lid of the bin skyward an inch or two.

The sun blinded him for a moment, and he dropped the lid with a loud bang.

'What was that?' enquired Dillon on the approaches.

'I don't know but it came from around the corner,' replied Boyd. 'Let's take a look.'

The two men took a left and entered another street of terraced house. At the end of the street, the highway swung to the left again and a patch of wasteland was apparent. The officers noticed three large industrial recycling bins set about ten yards away from footpath and on the wasteland.

'There!' pointed Boyd.

Smelling himself, the paraffin man held back the desire to vomit, dragged his feet from a pile of sludge lining the bottom of the bin, and pushed open the lid. A shaft of sunshine pierced his environment immediately causing him to raise his hands to shield his eyes.

The lid dropped again and there was a loud clang.

'Did you see that?' snapped Dillon.

'Yes,' replied Boyd. 'Let's get closer.'

'Do you want me to run down there?' asked Dillon.

'No,' responded Boyd. 'Take your foot off the pedal and let him make the moves.'

'Okay!'

The recycling bin lid eased upwards again as Boyd and Dillon gradually stepped out towards the paraffin man's hiding place.

Suddenly, the lid was up, tilted to the vertical, and then thrashing down fully open with the paraffin man climbing from the depths. His head and shoulders appeared first followed by a leg that was thrown over the side thereby escaping the clutches of the crap inside. Then he was waist-high, throwing himself over the edge, landing with a deep thud on his back, and rolling over in agony.

'That's our man,' voiced Boyd.

'I'll call it in,' replied Dillon.

'No,' ordered Boyd. 'This is no ordinary man and I don't want to panic him. Let's see what he does.'

Clambering to his feet, mud, crap, and black sludge trickled down the paraffin man's jeans, gathered on his trainers, and held him fast as he checked his surroundings.

Daylight!

Unaccustomed to the light, the paraffin man shielded his eyes once more as Boyd and Dillon approached.

Taking flight again, the paraffin man found little purchase in his trainers, skidded full length after a couple of yards, and looked up at an extended arm offered to him.

'Can I help you up?' offered Boyd softly.

There was no reply, but Boyd gently pulled the suspect to his feet and asked, 'How are you this morning? I bet that was an uncomfortable night in there.'

Bewildered, the paraffin man looked Boyd up and down and then focused on Dillon before asking, 'What time is it?'

'Early morning,' replied Boyd. 'About eight o'clock. It's breakfast time for some.'

The smell of a repugnant fuel mix, a ton of sludge and industrial waste dripping from the man's clothing, and a torn anorak near the shoulder area, merely inspired Boyd to continue with, 'Why did you get in that filthy bin in the first place?'

There was no immediate response from the paraffin man until he looked down at his trainers, appreciated the state his clothes were in, and eventually replied, 'Who are you?'

'We're policemen,' explained Boyd. 'Can we help you?'

'How? Why? What for?'

'Why did you hide in the bin?'

'The dog!'

'Are you afraid of dogs?' probed Boyd.

'They bit me once.'

'A long time ago or last night?'

'When I was a little boy,' revealed the paraffin man.

'Oh dear,' replied Boyd. 'Is that why you ran away from the dogs last night?'

'Yes! I had to run quickly.'

'Why?' asked Boyd.

'Don't know,' whispered the paraffin man gently.

'What did you do that was wrong?' asked Boyd softly.

There was no reply just a strangely nervous look from the suspect.

'My name is Billy,' offered Boyd. 'And this is my friend. He's called John. What's your name?'

'Don't know.'

'I bet you do,' smiled Boyd in a friendly manner. 'We'd like to help you, but I need to know your name so that I can talk to you properly.'

'Simon,' replied the paraffin man.

'How old are you, Simon?' asked Boyd.

'Don't know. Why?'

'I'm very old compared to you,' declared Boyd. 'I don't think you are a little boy anymore, not even a teenager. I'll guess you are in your mid-twenties. Am I right?'

'Don't know! Don't care.'

'I bet you do,' ventured Boyd.

'Don't care!' snapped Simon suddenly.

'Simon is a nice name,' offered Boyd changing tack as the atmosphere approached the possibility of unwanted hostility. 'And so are Billy and John. I think you are a man and not a child, Simon. So, I am going to ask you man questions and not child questions. Do you understand that?'

The paraffin man nodded as he shook more gunk from his trouser leg.

'What did you do last night, Simon?'

'A dog chased me.'

'What happened to make the dog chase you?'

The suspect's head dropped down.

'Were you at the old dog kennels?' probed Boyd.

Reluctantly at first, but then almost proudly the paraffin man replied loudly, 'Yes, I had fun.'

'What did you do?'

'There was a fire?' replied the paraffin man.

'How did the fire start, Simon?'

'I lit it,' laughed the paraffin man in glee. 'It was me. It was warm. It was fun. It was like being with girls.'

'Girls?' ventured an astonished Boyd. 'What was it like being with girls?'

The paraffin man looked down at his feet again.

'You can tell me,' suggested Boyd. 'I like girls too.'

'Girls make me hot. They are very sexy. Hot! Very hot!'

'Does the fire make you think of girls?'

'Hot ones,' replied Simon. 'Hot! Hot! Hot!'

'Were there any girls at the fire last night?' enquired Boyd.

'No, just dogs!'

'Dogs!' remarked Boyd. 'Where did they come from?'

'I don't know,' replied Simon. 'The dog chased me. It was a bad dog. All dogs are bad, but the girls are good. That's why I light the fires. The fire is my best friend, my girlfriend, my love. I fancy my girlfriend. She's hot, hot, hot!'

There was a sigh of relief from Dillon when Simon admitted setting the fire and Boyd continued with, 'How did you make the fire, Simon?'

'With paraffin and petrol and diesel and white spirit and firelighters and more petrol and…' gabbled the paraffin man.

'Wow!' intervened Boyd. 'Can you show us where you did this?'

'There!' pointed the suspect directing their attention towards the area of the Divisional Police Headquarters.

'Can you take us there?' asked Boyd gently.

'Why? What will happen when we get there?'

'Whatever happens, will be good for you,' replied Boyd. 'We are here to help you, Simon. Let's go back to where you set the fire and see what you did. Can you show us?'

'The fire is out now. I don't want to go.'

'Is that where you ripped your anorak?'

Simon, the paraffin man, checked his clothing, saw the torn area, and replied, 'I don't know. I don't remember doing that.'

Boyd removed a forensic envelope from his pocket, showed the torn piece of the anorak to Simon, and said, 'This looks like it came from your anorak. It's the same colour and seems to be the same cloth.'

Studying the piece of cloth through the transparent window, Simon replied, 'It does. Where did you find it?'

Boyd glanced at Dillon and then said, 'Simon! Take us to the last fire you made.'

'Can I make another fire there?' queried Simon.

'Just take us there, Simon,' pleaded Boyd with a slight smile on his face. 'We want to know where it is.'

Backtracking, the trio made their way to the old dog kennels at Divisional Police Headquarters. Simon led them with both Boyd and Dillon struggling to cope with the horrid smell emanating from the individual in their charge. A mixture of dirty smelly sludge from the depths of the recycling bin mixed toxically with the unsavoury odour of the paraffin man's complex mix of fuel which adorned his body

Simon took the two police officers through the housing estate and on a route that bordered the industrial estate. It was virtually a long straight line that they walked before reaching the scene of the fire.

'It's dead,' revealed Simon. 'I knew it would die. They always die when I leave.'

'How did you light this fire?' gestured Boyd.

'With stuff in that can,' explained Simon pointing to an abandoned fuel can.

Taking the can into his possession, Dillon said, 'This one, Simon?'

'That one, yes,' replied the suspect.

'The kennels are on the other side of the fence, Simon. How did you set fire to them?'

Almost proud, perhaps slightly arrogant, Simon explained, 'I splashed the fuel through the gaps in the fence. I covered the roof and it ran down the sides.'

'Then what?'

'I lit a match and threw it on the roof. Would you like me to show you how to do it?'

'No, that won't be necessary, Simon,' declared Boyd. 'Thank you for bringing us here. Now John is going to arrest you and we are going to take you to the police station and get you changed into some dry clothes. When did you last eat?'

Simon studied the two men and said, 'Eat?'

'Yes! Food!' remarked Boyd.

'Ah! Last week.'

Boyd nodded to Dillon and said, 'Do the honours quietly, John, please. We need to take Simon in.'

Dillon stepped forward and in a quiet, almost friendly voice formally arrested Simon on suspicion of arson.

Confused, perplexed, Simon stared into Boyd's face and said, 'I didn't hurt anyone, Billy. I didn't do anything wrong. I just have to do it because I love the flames. The flames help me. That's all. Why don't you like fire?'

'Because I've never been near enough to one to feel the flames like you, Simon,' replied Boyd. 'I'd like to hear why you feel you have to make a fire. Can you tell us?'

'Later, maybe!'

'That would be good of you, Simon,' ventured Boyd. 'Is that a promise?'

'Okay, Billy, I will,' replied Simon. 'It's a promise.'

'Thank you.'

'Do you like vodka, Billy?'

'I don't know,' replied Boyd. 'Why do you ask?'

'I like vodka when I'm at home watching the fires, that's all.'

'How do you do that?' probed Boyd.

'On my 'phone. I film the fires. Would you like to see them, Billy?'

'Yes! I think we should look at them, Simon.'

Beaming a huge smile, Simon produced his mobile 'phone and replied, 'Vodka! We'll need vodka!'

'Come on!' voiced Boyd taking possession of Simon's 'phone. 'I know a nice kind Sergeant who will help you into some clean clothes, feed you, and get you somewhere nice and warm to sleep tonight.'

As the early morning rush hour came to an end in Carlisle, the paraffin man was taken to the cell block at the city police station where he gave the name Simon Woods with an address in Denton Holme, Carlisle. He was incarcerated in a cell where he broke down in tears when the Sergeant closed the door behind him.

Boyd and Dillon strolled down the corridor with the echo of the closing cell door still ringing in their ears before Boyd asked, 'How are you feeling, John?'

'Strange! Odd! I don't really know how to describe the last hour,' explained Dillon.

'The pitiful individual has finally struck his last match,' declared Boyd. 'That weird creature has concocted his last mix and set his last fire. I'm never going to forget the smell of his clothes and that noxious odour that seemed to be all over him. We can rest easy now, but I know what you mean. Solving a serious crime usually gives you a good feeling inside, but when the villain of the piece turns out to be suffering from a mental health problem that is beyond my real understanding I feel like we've been talking to someone from another planet.'

'I thought you were for a while, replied Dillon. 'You sounded as if you were at times.'

'I guessed he might be lonely and childlike,' explained Boyd. 'Luckily, I was close enough and he responded to us. It could easily have gone the other way. Coffee?'

'Please,' nodded Dillon. 'And then we should let the DI know.'

'Absolutely,' agreed Boyd. 'But I've just remembered, my wallet is on the kitchen table at home. How are you fixed?'

'I'll buy them,' offered Dillon. 'You can get them next time.'

'Thanks,' replied Boyd.

'I've learnt something today,' ventured Dillon as they made their way to the canteen. 'Something that I had never even thought about.'

'Such as?' probed Boyd.

'That not all criminals are bad, and you don't have to fight them all when you arrest them. Some of them run away because they are frightened of something else, not just the police. Does that seem stupid?'

'No,' replied Boyd. 'His actions were bad. Simon will be interviewed, investigated, and charged with criminal offences arising from the fires. He's caused over five million pounds worth of damage in a city that can ill afford it, but he mentioned girls. Do you remember?'

'Yes,' voiced Dillon.

'I thought from the start that the type of person responsible for this string of fires was a pyromaniac and not a criminal in the sense of being some kind of thieving crook,' stated Boyd. 'I think I was wrong.'

'Why?'

'Simon mentioned that the fire was his girlfriend. I'm not a psychologist, John, but I think Simon has replaced sex with fire and his mention of hot girls makes me think he is possibly suffering from pyrophilia.'

'What on earth is that?' enquired John.

'An impulse-control disorder similar to pyromania,' explained Boyd. 'It's a very rare mental condition whereby the fire-raiser derives gratification from fire and starting fires. It's different from pyromania because the gratification is sexual. I'm sure we'll learn much more when we search his home, check his telephone, and get inside him. One day soon, we'll fully understand what turns him on sexually.'

'My God!' exclaimed Dillon. 'I had no idea policing was so complex.'

'It isn't,' replied Boyd. 'It's what you make it and how you investigate it. But the explanations for the various causes of crime are often very complex. Put this one in the back of your mind, John, and pray to God that you never come across another one like him. Such people are neither man nor beast and neither adult nor child.'

'Yes! Yes, I will,' declared Dillon. 'A great arrest but a very sad ending when the villain doesn't know right from wrong.'

'By now, an officer will have been withdrawn from other duties and will probably be sitting watching him in his cell and making sure he doesn't harm himself. We have nowhere to take such people, John,' explained Boyd. 'He's a danger to the public and a danger to himself so, right now, that's the best place for him.'

'Can anything be done for him?' enquired John.

'The Custody Sergeant will call out the police surgeon who will examine him and move on from there. The police are not qualified medical practitioners or experts in mental disorders. All we can do is present the result of our investigations to the authorities and, in due course, a decision as to how he should be dealt with will be made.'

'What do you think will happen?'

'On the presumption he is guilty of all charges, I'd say he will end up in a mental hospital of some kind.'

'Okay! Understood!' replied Dillon.

Come on, let's get something to eat with that coffee,' suggested Boyd.

'Yes! Oh, for a hot dog!' replied Dillon.

The hotdog stand outside the Churchill Arms on Kensington High Street was a favourite stopping off point for Sasha Mendoza on her way to work at the Russian Embassy.

Today was no exception as she shuffled along in the queue waiting to be served.

'How many?' asked the store holder eventually.

'One jumbo, please,' replied Sasha.

'Mustard?'

'Yes, please.'

'Onions?'

'Of course.'

'Chilli?'

'No thanks!'

A hot dog exchanged hands for a five-pound note. Sasha pocketed the change and stepped away into a bus shelter where she caught a glimpse of Antonia Harston-Browne.

Dressed in denim jeans, a roll-neck sweater, and a dark nondescript anorak, Antonia was also eating a hotdog. There was a glance between them, but it wasn't until the bus shelter was empty that Antonia opened up with, 'Morning, Sasha! I got your message. Is everything okay?'

Sasha took another bite of her hotdog, glanced casually around, and replied, 'Yes, fine! I have something for you.'

'What have you got?' enquired Antonia.

'I was hoovering through the offices last night. I had your tape recorder hidden inside the cloth bag as usual. When I finished duty, I downloaded it for you. I thought you might be interested in the content.'

'Where did you remove the tape?' probed Antonia. 'Inside the embassy?'

Handing the tape over, Sasha remarked, 'Fortunately, I'm not just the cleaner. I'm also the secondary keyholder for my particular floor. Last night, the primary keyholder was off sick so I ended up in charge of the embassy keypad for the floor I was working on. That includes the electronic keys for some of the rooms.'

'Are you telling me that each floor in the embassy has a separate security procedure relevant to both physical and electronic keys and that every floor has someone nominated to be responsible for the keys on that floor?'

'Of course,' revealed Sasha. 'You can't even change a lightbulb in the building unless you have a key for the room, office, storeroom or lift, and then security has to be with you when you change the light bulb.'

Shaking her head in astonishment, Antonia pursued the conversation with, 'Go on. What happened next?'

'I took the tape out of the vacuum bag while I was in the locked storeroom. No-one else saw me because I had the keys. I walked out of the embassy with the tape without being challenged. Security on the door is pretty lax at night. It's the day workers they stop and search, the main office workers.'

'Let's hope it stays that way,' ventured Antonia using a tissue.

151

'The security procedures change every month,' explained Sasha. 'Next month, workers like myself could be the prime target for stop and search. Who knows? I took a chance because I want my father back and thought this would be a good trade. My father! What news of him?'

Antonia pocketed the tissue she had used to wipe her hands and offered, 'Things are progressing well. I hope to have more for you very soon. It takes time but the matter is underway, and we are looking forward to a successful outcome.'

'Good! Are you sure you can get him out of Russia?'

'Yes,' replied Antonia as her heart skipped a beat in the hope that what she had said could be done.

'Anyway,' continued Sasha. 'Do you want to know why I thought you might want the tape today.'

'Yes! That would be helpful,' suggested Antonia.

'On the tape, I heard Alexei talking on the 'phone to the Head of Station. They were talking about the recent arrival of Cyclops.'

'I see,' replied Antonia wiping her fingers from the residue of the hotdog. A surge of adrenalin pulsed through her body when she repeated the word, 'Cyclops!'

'Do you know the name?' asked Sasha. 'It's a codename for an intelligence officer. Does it mean anything to you?'

'Yes, oh yes,' revealed Antonia. 'Very much!'

'I can tell you who it is,' ventured Sasha. 'The name is a legend in the embassy.'

'A man?' tested Antonia. 'Or a woman?'

'A Colonel in the GRU,' replied Sasha. 'You must know that. Please don't mess me with me at this stage of the game. Cyclops has been around for a long time. My father used to speak of her years ago when he knew her. She is a dangerous woman.'

'Colonel Anna Korobov,' suggested Antonia apologetically. 'That is the woman I know as Cyclops. She is well known to western intelligence agencies.'

'And occasionally spoken of in the embassy,' delivered Sasha. 'She is a formidable woman who fears no-one. One of the best, apparently.'

'Yes, I know,' voiced Antonia. 'How do you know that Cyclops is Colonel Korobov?'

'Because I read things that I find in their litter bins. They put things in the bins before they use the shredder at the end of the day. Some of them forget. It's just a habit that they get into. You told me to look for habits once. Others leave their computer screens turned on when they should be off. I can tell you lots of things that I find by chance.'

'Can you really?' reacted Antonia. 'Then tell me something interesting.'

Happier than usual, perhaps because she was in charge of the conversation, Sasha replied, 'If you listen to the tape, you'll hear that Alexei is worried. Cyclops is in Scotland. The Colonel is supposed to be doing an annual security review at Faslane nuclear submarine base at Gare Loch. Wherever that is. I've never heard of it before. Anyway, someone gets the job every year. They stay for about a week, count submarines, photograph personnel, do all kinds of things that I don't know about. You'll know more than me about it.'

'Yes, I know what you are driving at,' revealed Antonia. 'What else is on the tape?'

'Cyclops is acting on her own and without the authority of Moscow,' continued Sasha. 'She has told the team with her that she has orders from Moscow. She hasn't. No such orders exist. Cyclops has gone private. I'm not sure what that means but it's on the tape. Anyway, Alexei wants to take me out for dinner. What do you think? Should I say yes?'

'Is there anything else on the tape I should know now?' probed Antonia.

'That's the main gist of it all,' revealed Sasha. 'What should I do about Alexei? He's Deputy Head of the station and a bit of a whizz kid. He's very popular and I've heard them say he'll get his own residence one day.'

'Do you trust him?'

'I don't know. Why do you ask?'

'Because his interest in you may be more than having dinner,' suggested Antonia. 'Do you think he suspects you in any way?'

'I hope not,' replied Sasha. 'I just thought he has taken a liking to me and wants to find out more about me. You know, friendship.'

'During which time he will get to know more about you,' pronounced Antonia. 'That's what I'm getting at. What's his motive?'

Annoyed, Sasha suggested, 'Well, I do have a good figure; haven't you noticed?'

Antonia stepped back into the depths of the bus shelter when a bus appeared, disembarked passengers, and took off again.

'Okay,' remarked Antonia. 'Just dinner, and don't give too much away about your lifestyle. Don't mention your father and...'

'Okay! Okay!' barked Sasha. 'I understand. Look, I've got to go now, or I'll be late.'

'No problem,' replied Antonia. 'Thanks for the tape. I take it you replaced it with a fresh one?'

'Yes, of course,' revealed Sasha as she moved into the street and began her walk to the Russian Embassy.

Antonia sat for five minutes alone in the shelter, worded in mind the intelligence report she needed to submit to the organisation, and then took a tube to the office.

In the darkness of a cellar, Meg and the children were hunched up together with their backs against the wall trying to keep warm.

'Where are we?' sobbed Izzy.

'In the basement of a building somewhere,' suggested Meg.

'When's Dad coming for us?' asked Izzy.

'Soon!' snapped James. 'Dad will be along soon.'

'Where is he now?' asked Izzy.

'At work,' explained Meg. 'Now cuddle in closer, keep warm, and try and get some sleep.'

'What's that noise?' whispered Izzy suddenly.

Somewhere in the basement area, the sound of voices penetrated the walls of the cellar and reached the ears of Meg and her children. The voices were muffled at first but then grew louder as they approached their prison cell

'It's Dad,' suggested an excited James.

'Is it?' surged Meg. 'Are you sure?'

'Yes! Yes! Yes!' yelled James.

The sound of footsteps suddenly stopped. The rattle of keys was heard. A key was inserted into the lock and turned. The cell door opened.

Meg and her children found themselves pressed hard against the wall almost trying to bury themselves in the brickwork when a male voice barked, 'Food! Eat! Drink!'

A plate of corned beef, some porridge, and mugs of water was slid into the room. The door was pulled tight. A key turned and confirmed incarceration. The sound of footsteps receded along the corridor into a place not known to Meg or the children.

'Where's Dad?' asked James.

'Get something to eat,' suggested Meg. 'You too, Izzy. Dad will be here when he's ready and not before.'

As the children delved into the food, Meg relaxed slightly with her back against the wall and thought, 'If only he were here now. Where are you now, Billy? Where are you when we need you the most? Do you even know?'

Not far away, the Royal National Lifeboat Institution boasted a lifeboat station serving Loch Ness. The building is stationed at Drumnadrochit which is a village lying on the west shore of the loch at the foot of Glen Urquhart. The community grew up around a bridge over the River Enrick and the name Drumnadrochit is derived from the Scottish Gaelic **druim na drochaid**, which means the 'Ridge of the Bridge'. It's quite a well-established settlement with a village hall, the Glen Urquhart High School and library, a doctor's surgery, a pharmacy, a post office, a supermarket and various shops distributed evenly around the village. The village is popular with tourists and there are several hotels in the village and close by.

Visitors are attracted to the area, not just by the enigma of the Loch's alleged monster, but by the beautiful scenery and the history of nearby Urquhart Castle. In addition, the village is home to the Loch Ness Centre and Exhibition which feeds those who want to know more about the mystery of the monster.

The loch inspires the tourist industry in the area and is the location of many a local business set up to entertain holidaymakers.

One such business was a family-run cruise company that plied its trade from the harbour next to the RNLI station.

'Right, young Jack,' stated Roderick. 'You can take the boat out yourself today.'

'Wow!' replied young Jack. 'My first solo run, Dad. Great!'

'You know what to do,' suggested Roderick. 'Nice and easy out from the harbour. Run towards Urquhart Castle but then cut across to Inverfarigaig, then over to Lenie, tell them about John Cobb's fatal world water speed record attempt in 1952, and…'

'I know where the measured mile is, Dad,' interrupted Jack. 'It's a sad story about a great man and having listened to you telling the same tale over and over again, I know it backwards.'

'Good!' chuckled Roderick. 'Then a slow cruise passing Urquhart Castle, lots of photo opportunities, plus a circle in the bay and then back to the quay. An hour exactly, no more and no less.'

'I'll be fine,' proposed Jack. 'Look, here's the minibus. Can you escort them to the boat?'

'Of course,' replied Roderick. 'Good luck, son. I'm sure you'll be fine.'

A minibus from a local hotel arrived and discharged a dozen customers who lined up to board the cruiser. Roderick inspected their tickets, happily escorted them onto the boat, and showed them to their seats before regaining his feet at the quayside.

'You can cast off now, Dad,' shouted Jack from the cabin. 'Welcome aboard everyone. Take your seats and enjoy the tour. My name is Jack and I'll be giving you a running commentary once we set out across the loch.'

As Jack continued his spiel, Roderick slipped the boat from her moorings and waved his son away on his first solo voyage in charge of the tourists.

Almost immediately there was a loud thud, a surge of water, and the cruiser wobbled slightly.

'It's snagged,' yelled Jack. 'Dad! The line at the port side is snagged on something.'

Stepping forward, Roderick peered into the gap between the boat and the harbour wall to see what appeared to be a fairly large bundle which had caught on the line.

'Bring her back,' ordered Roderick. 'Don't worry folks. It's just a tree branch that's got caught in the moorings. We'll have you away in two minutes.'

Roderick walked along the quayside, took some steps down towards the water, and gasped, 'It's a golf bag! Pass that mooring hook, son.'

Taking the hook from Jack, Roderick reached across the water, caught the golf bag, and pulled it towards the steps. Letting go of the hook, he then dragged the bag to the steps and then up onto the quayside.

Jack secured the cruiser and watched as his father unzipped the golf bag.

There was a deluge of water from the bag followed by the shout of 'Jesus H Christ!' when a body rolled partially from the golf bag and beached itself on the quayside.

'What is it?' shouted Jack from the cabin. 'I can't see from here.'

Roderick knelt beside the bag, gradually pulled the body out, and said, 'You don't want to see, son. It's a body. Ring Angus. Tell him we've got a dead body in a golf bag down at the lifeboat station. I'd say he has a murder on his hands.'

Ten minutes later, the cruiser had been evacuated and Sergeant Angus Grant from Inverness police was at the scene. A resident of Drumnadrochit, Angus was a former member of the Black Watch Regiment who had served in Iraq under Operation Telic before his battalion became part of the Royal Regiment of Scotland and adopted Fort George, in Inverness, as its base. He was also the holder of the Conspicuous Gallantry Cross.

Pleasantries conducted, Angus ventured to the quayside, knelt by the body, and said, 'What have we here then?'

'Something very unpleasant, Angus,' suggested Roderick. 'But I'll tell you one thing though.'

'Such as?'

'He's not a member of the local golf club, that's for sure.'

'Not with a tattoo like that,' remarked Angus. 'Do you see his shoulder?'

'Where?' enquired Roderick.

'His shoulder! It's tattooed with the hammer and sickle.'

'He's nae from Glasgae then.'

'Russia, I would say,' surmised Angus. 'Or he has some connection with Russia.'

'Had,' proposed Roderick. 'The poor man is dead now.'

'But how did he die?' probed Angus. 'The only marks on his body seem to be from bashing the quayside and the boat. I can't see a bullet wound or a knife wound?'

'Not a gangland killing then?' remarked Roderick.

'Didn't know we had gangs in Drumnadrochit, Roderick,' posed Angus. 'Who is the head of the local mafia?'

'You, I suppose,' chuckled Roderick. 'I was thinking of the body being dumped by a gang in the loch, that's all.'

'Could be, Roderick. Could be,' suggested Angus. 'Thanks for the call. I'm going to have to ring this in and declare it a major crime scene. I need to call out the circus on this one.'

Roderick and his son shut up shop for the day. Angus secured the murder scene and began enquiries into how, why and where an unidentified male person had ended up dead in the loch at Drumnadrochit RNLI station.

Two hours later, the area was teeming with murder squad detectives and Sergeant Angus Grant was on the case.

Grant was a familiar name in the Loch Ness area since Clan Grant had owned land in Strathspey since 1316. The centre of activities for Angus, however, was the clan's stronghold in the valley of Stratherrick, to the east of Loch Ness. It was here, on the shores of Loch Mhor, to which he travelled. It was the home of his older brother, Duncan.

Parking his police van on the gravel car park outside his brother's licensed guest house, Angus strolled into the bar, removed his cap, and said, 'And how is Duncan today?'

'Your brother is fine,' came the reply. 'And it's good to see you, Angus. Have you time for a wee one?'

'That I have,' smiled Angus.

His brother, Duncan, poured one finger of malt whisky, slid it towards him, and asked, 'What brings you here, Angus. It's not Sunday and you're in uniform. What's the problem?'

'The problem is the body of an unidentified male person found in a golf bag that has been washed up at Drumnadrochit Bay, near the lifeboat station. A post-mortem will be conducted shortly but right now we've no idea who he is or how he ended up in a golf bag.'

'Are you on the case?' enquired Duncan.

'Of course!'

'How can I help?

'The body has the tattoo of a hammer and sickle on his shoulder,' revealed Angus. 'I just wondered if you'd had any visitors from Russia recently.'

'Not here, no!' replied Duncan. 'But then we're one of the biggest accommodation providers in the area so I can understand why you thought we might be able to help. I've over a hundred rentals that I look after up and down the loch and surrounding area. Do you want me to take a look?'

'I'd appreciate that,' replied Angus tasting the whisky with approval. 'A single malt. Here's to you, Duncan.'

Moving through into another room, Duncan returned some moments later with a ledger. Flicking through the pages he remarked, 'Should I go back three months or further? What do you think?'

'Three months for starters sounds good, Duncan.'

The pages turned as Angus sipped his whisky and Duncan perused his records.

'Are they all rented accommodation that you are responsible for?' enquired Angus. 'What do you manage if you don't mind me asking.'

'Generally speaking,' explained Duncan. 'I run the books, take the orders, make the bookings and do the admin. My wife manages the operational side of things and runs a team of cleaners and tradesmen that service the rentals in the area. We own half a dozen ourselves, but we do the bookings for individuals or companies who own property in the area. We have a couple of small hotels, lots of private villas, scores of lakeside lodges, and quite a few detached houses on the books. You know how these things work. We're essentially a property management company that takes a percentage of the booking fee every time a rental is taken.'

'I'd have thought you would have had everything on a computer,' ventured Angus.

'We use the computer to take bookings and payments, but we use the ledger like a diary,' explained Duncan. 'We can allocate different people specific rooms in the diary, along with mealtimes in hotels, cleansing times, times of arrival and departure, and any relevant notes or reminders that we need to be aware of. Anything from disabled people to dietary concerns to mobility to the type of room or accommodation requested. It's easier and cheaper than funding an expensive complex computer system to record what is essentially who is living where and when, and what they want. We try our best to make money, not spend it unnecessarily.'

'I see, thank you,' replied Angus.

'You're welcome, little brother.'

The pages continued to turn until Duncan said, 'No Russians anywhere. I've got Americans, Chinese, Japanese, English, French - in fact, a lot of Europeans – but not a Russian in sight. Have a look for yourself?'

Duncan swivelled the book around for Angus to view.

'I'll take your word for it,' replied Angus spinning it back. 'No Russians! Okay! How about couples, groups, anyone that gave you cause for concern over recent months.'

Pouring a whisky for himself, Duncan offered his brother another but found a hand covering the glass. Duncan took a drink and replied, 'I remember there was an Algerian company. Yes, that's right. That was a bit strange, come to think of it.'

'Algerian?'

Duncan flicked through the pages until he reached his destination and continued, 'Of course. A strange woman with an accent I didn't recognise rang and booked Pine Lodge for three months. Yes, she was a bit odd and when I asked her how many would be staying, she didn't seem to know or care.'

'Pine Lodge?' queried Angus.

'Yes,' confirmed Duncan. 'It's a large detached house on the east shore of the loch not far from Foyers. It was a hotel many years ago but when the owner died it was inherited by the rest of the family who live in Cornwall. They're quite wealthy and rather than up sticks and run the business at Pine Lodge, they asked us to include it in our portfolio for them. It's mainly used as a conference centre. You'd be surprised how many businesses organise seminars in the area. They come for a week, enjoy the break, and work at the same time.'

'Yes, Pine Lodge,' murmured Angus. 'I've got in now. Set in a couple of acres of land that border on the water's edge, if I remember correctly. Quite an old building with imposing Georgian pillars.'

'That's the one,' confirmed Duncan.

'Interesting,' proposed Angus. 'You said it was used as a conference centre and most businesses come for a week and then leave.'

'That's right. Absolutely! It's not cheap but then it fits the bill for a week of working in the Highlands.'

'Exactly!' submitted Angus. 'But your lady from the Algerian company booked it for three months, not a week?'

'Correct!'

'How did she pay?'

'By credit card, I think. Hey. That is odd come to think of it. Mind you, we often get villas taken that long but not Pine Lodge. I'll have a record of the payment somewhere in the office.'

'Can I trouble you?'

'I might even have to ring the bank to get the details for you, but I can fax you the details later if you want?'

'Yes, please,' replied Angus. 'I'll follow it up. It's not quite the lead I was hoping for, but it's worth looking into. Thank you.'

'My pleasure,' voiced Duncan. 'Did you see the vintage cars outside when you parked up?'

'No, where are they?'

'In the shed at the back of the house. Come with me and I'll show you the latest addition to our collection.'

'Another old motor to do up in your spare time, I presume,' ventured Angus.

'Yes, I've just bought an old bus from a circus owner who has just gone bust.'

'I'm not surprised if that was the main mode of transport,' suggested Angus as he followed his brother to the vehicle collection.

'Oh, I intend to do it up like the others and then sell it on when I'm ready,' replied Duncan. 'What do you think of it? It's a thirty-two-seater passenger coach that needs a massive paint job and overhaul. It will keep me busy on my days off.'

'It's a rust bucket,' observed Angus. 'It will take you ages just to get rid of the corrosion. Does the engine work?'

'Not sure, but I've got the know-how and the time.'

'You could try another hobby,' suggested Angus.

'Such as?'

'Golf!'

Back in London, Antonia was alone in the Special Crime Unit Ticker Intelligence cell.

She'd studied Boyd's bank account in detail, made notes, shook her head, and decided that it was time to assemble all the facts before her.

Her slender fingers trickled across the telephone pad and she convinced the Director-General to join her to discuss a matter of utmost secrecy. Antonia replaced the telephone before Sir Phillip could reply.

Five minutes later, as expected, Antonia glanced at the internal CCTV system, saw the Director-General approaching the cell, and promptly released the electronic lock for him.

'Antonia,' snapped Sir Phillip. 'A matter of the utmost secrecy, and then the 'phone goes dead! This had better be damn good because I've just broken up a meeting with Home Office officials to respond to your call. Please note, if I didn't love you so much, I'd have a damn sight more to say. You, young lady, would be well and truly on the carpet.'

'Why, Phillip,' remarked Antonia. 'I didn't realise you loved me that much. Thank you for stopping by. I want to tell you what I've discovered about Boyd.'

'Boyd?' queried a perplexed Sir Phillip. 'Boyd! We've been through this before. He owes money and although it grieves me to say it, he has to come to grips with it. Not me and certainly not you.'

'That's where you are wrong,' replied Antonia. 'Take a look at this.'

Antonia handed a file to the Director-General. It was marked TOP SECRET OMEGA BLUE – EYES ONLY - THIMBLES.

'Read it!' pleaded Antonia.

Reluctantly, Sir Phillip took a seat and began to scan the file whilst Antonia made a fresh pot of coffee. As she was pouring two mugs, Sir Phillip voiced, 'Who authorised this file?'

'You did,' replied the redhead. 'Don't say another word, Phillip. Just read it.'

In between sips of coffee, Sir Phillip frowned at Antonia, returned to the file, and then finally placed it on the table between them.

'And your summary is?' proposed Sir Phillip.

'My findings…'

'Which are unauthorised by the way,' intervened Sir Phillip.

'My findings suggest that Boyd owes a three-figure sum of money to an online gambling club,' continued Antonia ignoring the interruption. 'However, please note, there is no trace of the said club on the internet. Yes, the website may well have been taken down since the debt was incurred but I don't know if that is the case or not. Various other debts don't prove to satisfaction when you trawl the net for websites and companies that he is deemed to owe money to. Yet, on the strength of the online gambling club alone, his bank account plunged below zero. According to the papers that he sent me…'

'Which you are presuming are authentic,' interrupted Sir Phillip once more.

'Please don't interrupt me whilst I'm talking,' chided Antonia. 'According to the papers he sent me, namely his bank account, he was granted an overdraft facility despite never having asked for one before and irrespective of running up those debts from the gambling club. If you dig further back in his account, you'll come across a loan he took out for a world cruise. That money went down the drain too. Now before you say it, Phillip, we both know that neither Meg nor Boyd went on a world cruise, but the loan agreement says that is what the money was for. The family Porsche was also repossessed by the finance company and, within days, he's a broken man and his family collapse around him. It doesn't make sense.'

'The evidence is scant so far,' suggested Sir Phillip. 'You have nothing concrete and, as you say, the online gambling club might easily have closed itself down since the debt was incurred. You have no proof either way. Furthermore, it's fairly common for people to borrow money from the bank for one thing and then use it for another. Perhaps Boyd borrowed money under the pretext of the cruise but used it to pay off gambling debts?'

'The dates don't match,' ventured Antonia. 'The world cruise issue preceded the gambling club. If they ever existed?'

'Please continue to dig yourself deeper into the hole you are creating for yourself,' ventured Sir Phillip. 'Because you've not convinced me about anything so far. You're looking for excuses for Boyd as opposed to uncovering evidence to support him.'

'Oh, don't worry, I will,' revealed a confident Antonia who interrogated the Ticker computer and said, 'I invite you to follow these intelligence leads I've pruned from the system. I'll superimpose it on the big screen.'

Antonia engaged the computer keyboard and then joined Sir Phillip who was peering at a large touchscreen facility that dominated one corner of the room.

Triggering the onscreen technology, Antonia began speaking when a video presentation burst into life.

'This is from our arrivals system at Heathrow airport,' explained the redhead. 'Let me introduce you to Cyclops.'

'Colonel Anna Korobov of Russian Intelligence,' observed Sir Phillip. 'One of Russia's top spymasters and a legend in her lifetime. One might call the woman a worthy opponent although I would call her as tough as old boots considering her advancing years. She has a reputation which is second to none.'

'Formerly a chief instructor at the Red Banner Espionage Institute in Moscow,' explained Antonia. 'She is the mother of Mikhail Korobov, and husband of Sergei Korobov who is Head of the Second Chief Directorate in Moscow. Sergei is responsible for counter-intelligence.'

'And Mikhail was a spy once working out of the Russian Embassy in London,' added Sir Phillip.

'According to my source Woodpecker,' continued Antonia. 'The Colonel is believed to be in Scotland engaged on a review of the Faslane Submarine base on behalf of Moscow. My source informs me that is not the case. Moscow is quite livid because the Colonel has gone private. She's conducting a personal operation of some kind.'

'A rogue operation?' queried Sir Phillip. 'Yes, I read your report following your meeting with Woodpecker. The Russians must surely know we've previously targeted the Colonel when she's been in the UK.'

'I would think so,' replied Antonia. 'Most certainly. Why do you ask?'

'Because it's not usual for them to send such an operative to the same country twice. It's not how they work.'

'That's another reason to accept my argument that she is on a rogue mission,' contended Antonia.

'How interesting! Go on!' instructed Sir Phillip.

'During the same week the Colonel arrived at Heathrow,' continued Antonia. 'The following persons of interest also arrived. In dribs and drabs, they arrived from Lisbon, Paris, Berlin and Amsterdam. They didn't all fly directly from Moscow. I suggest that is a standard operational protocol used by intelligence agencies when they need to covertly insert a team into another country. Don't be surprised if my enquiries about their passports result in them being false, by the way.'

'Oh, I see,' replied Sir Phillip. 'You have been busy.'

A series of images appeared on the screen and Antonia pointed them out as, 'Nikolai Vasiliev, level six cryptologist, Major Viktor Petrov of the GRU, Lieutenant Nadia Koshkin of the GRU, Pavel Kuznetsev of the GRU, Talisha Lenedev of the GRU, and then interestingly, last but not least Dimitry Oblonsky, a level seven cryptologist also with the GRU.'

'How did you identify them?' quizzed Sir Phillip as he perused the screen with an interest not seen that day.

'It took me quite some time since they did not all fly in together,' explained Antonia. 'I just married them all up as arriving during the same

165

week. Some are identified from our registry system and some from our colleagues in MI6. Others with her might be soldiers or bodyguards, but we have little to go on in that respect at present. The cryptologists are amongst the best Moscow has to offer and Kuznetsev and Lenedev were recently suspected of spying on a United Nations official in Lisbon. The point is, Phillip, this is a covert team that deliberately arrived in the UK at different times on separate flights and they are all involved in an operation of some kind. The Colonel is the only one we know of with a previous history of visiting the UK. The others seem to be all first-time visitors. This is not one or two Russian spies popping across to test our systems and drag us out on a needless surveillance operation for weeks on end. This is a team sent to damage and destroy.'

Closing with the screen, Sir Phillip used his fingers to repeat the presentation and pause it at various points.

'Cryptology,' murmured Sir Phillip. 'Why is Moscow moving people from their desks in Russia to another desk over here? These level six and level seven people are crypto warriors. They are more likely to attack another country's website infrastructure than Boyd's bank account.'

'They aren't here to attack Boyd's bank account, Phillip. They've successfully targeted Boyd's bank, used an advanced worm of some kind, and broken into the banking system. Once in, they've added a program which has amended or altered that part of the banking system that relates to Boyd and Meg. That's how the bank ends up with a false digital record of Boyd's account.'

'Why did Moscow send them?'

'If my source, Woodpecker, in the Russian Embassy is correct, Moscow didn't send them. The Colonel arranged their attendance via her husband. It's a rogue operation aimed at Boyd. I'd say the operation was designed to inflict maximum damage in the shortest possible time. Such an attack is hugely successful but will eventually come to light when an audit is carried out. That could be weeks or months away, but by then the damage is done and Boyd is gone, irrelevant, no longer important in the scheme of things. Have you figured it out yet, Phillip?'

'You seem to have. There's more? I'm all ears.'

'I examined Boyd's file; his secure one coded BISHOP.'

'Go on.'

'Bishop was recommended for service to the Special Crime Unit by Commander Herbert.'

'Agreed!'

'We coded Commander Herbert as SHEPHERD because he became an endangered species when the other side wanted rid of him. I withdrew the Shepherd file from the registry. He'd put so many drug dealers, gun runners, blackmailers, terrorists and spies away that the underworld had a contract out on him. We changed his identity, rehoused him, and completely documented his new life because those who promote their various evil trades couldn't take any more. It's one of the reasons the Shepherd recruited Boyd into the team. He wanted the best to be there with him.'

'Understood!' offered Sir Phillip. 'I hadn't realised Boyd had reached those dizzy heights yet. Commander Herbert was the Special Crime Unit Commander for quite a few years before he retired. Yes, he made many enemies because of his position, but Boyd hasn't been in that job very long.'

'True,' admitted Antonia. 'Boyd's problem is that he gave evidence against the inquest into the death of Mikhail Korobov. He told the coroner that Mikhail Korobov was killed in a road accident on the M6 motorway whilst working for the Russian Embassy.'

'He was. I remember,' declared Sir Phillip. There was a sudden gasp of breath, 'Good God! Korobov! That's the link. It's right there in front of us. Mikhail's mother, Colonel Anna Korobov doesn't believe it was an accident. She's come to revenge her son.'

'Exactly!' voiced Antonia. 'The Colonel's private operation is a personal vendetta she has mounted against Boyd. Her husband, Sergei, has provided her with the manpower. Don't you see, Phillip? Woodpecker has given us some real information we can act on and the enquires I've made prove we are onto something. We need to mount an operation to find the Colonel and destroy her before she annihilates Boyd and his family.'

Deep in thought, Sir Phillip double-checked the images, shook his head, and replied, 'Right there in front of us the whole time and I didn't see it.'

'Why would you?' soothed Antonia. 'It took me long enough. When you're investigating the threats against the Mayor, serious crime, routine spying and terrorist operations, I don't suppose people expect you to catch everything that's thrown at you.'

'You caught this one.'

'I'm so glad you authorised the opening of the Thimbles file, Phillip.'

'Yes, well, we'll talk about that another time,' proposed Sir Phillip. 'Right now, I'm going to ring Reg in Canterbury and ask him to check some lines for me. Who has been ringing the Russian Embassy from Scotland? That might lead us to the exact location of Cyclops. Meanwhile, brief Anthea at length and bring Boyd's old wing of the Special Crime Unit onboard. I'm not sure they know anything about Boyd's predicament at the moment other than rumours. And if they've heard any rumours, then we've got a mole to contend with as well.'

'Phillip!' pleaded Antonia. 'One thing at a time, please. You must stop seeing spies in every nook and cranny.'

'That's where we usually find them,' argued Sir Phillip. 'And it's my job to find them. Note to self – Must do better. There's one more thing that persuades me with regards to what you have said.'

'What?' queried Antonia.

'Despite being a serving police officer, Boyd approached you for help, not the police. Is that because he's embarrassed or believes in you?'

'No, he believes in us and the service,' replied Antonia. 'That's why.'

'I believe so,' declared Sir Phillip. 'I want you to get onto MI6 and activate Lucy. Let's get Sparrow Hawk out of Moscow. If we've just turned a corner, then these two birds of yours have a lot of good singing to do, and, personally speaking, I'm going to put the possibility that they might be double agents onto the back burner. If I were Moscow, I'd want a lot from an operation if I was offering up Cyclops to the other side in a stupidly complex false flag operation. No! I see the way ahead. It's clear now. Activate Lucy! Expedite Anthea. I want the team fully briefed and ready to go at a moment's notice. I have a growing feeling that we are about to unsettle a nest of wasps and if we do, I want the Special Crime Unit in the frontline.'

'Not ours?'

'No! Boyd would never forgive us and it's a job for either the police or the military. I'll go with Boyd's team for now.'

'Anything else?'

'You can get Reg on the 'phone for me and give me that Thimbles file. I'll sign it now before I forget.'

With renewed vigour, Sir Phillip was quickly talking to Reg in the Operations Centre: an underground facility near Canterbury, in Kent. This was the centre of operations relevant to electronic communications in the UK. It was at this location that the nation's intelligence services covertly monitored landline telephones, mobile 'phones, internet use, and the highly sophisticated technical penetration of selected targets. Enjoying a close relationship with GCHQ in Cheltenham, the centre executed electronic operations authorised under warrants issued by the Home Office following case presentation and application from the intelligence services. Unsurprisingly, its location was underground, secret, and known only to those who 'needed to know'.

'Reg! How are you today?'

'Fine, Phil! How can I help?'

'I need to know if there have been any particular calls from Scotland to the Russian Embassy in London during the past four weeks. It's urgent.'

'Standby,' from Reg.

A new window opened in a browser. Reg rattled the keyboard as a man possessed. The image of an egg timer dominated the centre of his computer screen and a short time later, Reg replied, 'Glasgow! Edinburgh! Dundee! Aberdeen! Just the usual, Phil. Nothing new that stands out.'

'Are they all previously known points of contact?'

'Stand by! Confirmed! Yes! If you're looking for new points of contact, the answer is nil. The positives are the usual suspects. Do you want me to send you a list on Ticker? These are landline only!'

'How about mobiles?' enquired Sir Phillip.

'Wait!' replied Reg repeating the process. 'No! That's a negative return, but I have an interesting one from a satellite 'phone.'

'Satcom!' murmured Sir Phillip. 'Where from?'

'Wait one!' responded Reg.

A cursor moved across Reg's computer screen, clicked on an icon, and then revealed the tiny image of a satellite with a number next to it.

'I can tell you that a satellite owned by an Algerian media company has communicated with a couple of satellite telephones in Scotland. The satellite in question was recently launched from the Ernst Krenkel Observatory which was once a former Soviet rocket launching site. It's located on Heiss Island, on the Franz Josef archipelago, in the Arctic Ocean. The launch site was established in 1957 and closed in 2001.' Reg paused and then said, 'What did I just say?'

'That it was closed in 2001,' voiced Sir Phillip. 'Define recently! 2001?'

'No, 2020 and within the last few weeks. Phil, it's so recent that there's not much initial information on the system. The Space Sector team will no doubt be updating it soon. But it's an oddball,' chuckled Reg. 'And it's new to us. So new that such a satellite would last between five and fifteen years at the most then it would run out of fuel, lose orbit, and burn up on re-entry. There's your bad apple, Phil. It certainly wasn't launched in 2001. Let me put a team on it and make some calls. I'll get back to you.'

'If the satellite is bouncing signals from the phones, where are the calls being made from, Reg?'

'Imagine a box drawn between Inverness and Aberdeen down to Dundee and across to Glasgow then back up to Inverness. Your Satcom user is in that square somewhere.'

'Can you narrow that down?' probed Sir Phillip.

'We'll try but the angle of the earthbound signal is determined by the satellite itself. I'll put a team on the satellite and monitor it. By the way, it's in a geostationary orbit about two hundred and twenty miles above the planet. It might seem like it's hovering in the exact place but it's really just in orbit and moving at the same time as the planet. I'll get back to you.'

'Soon as you can please,' replied Sir Phillip.

The phone line closed. Reg spun in his chair, plugged into an internal wireless channel and ordered, 'Emergency Response Team! Activate target procedures and report activity. Your target is Alpha One Nine Zulu Four, zone two coverage. It's new, fresh and probably hostile. Expedite.'

Operators acknowledged Reg as a dedicated team focused on the satellite launched from the Russian part of the Arctic Ocean.

In the Ticker Cell, in London, Sir Phillip remarked, 'Interesting! Why have the Algerians launched a media satellite from a Russian base no longer in use?'

'It must be a falsehood designed to deceive,' suggested Antonia.

'Absolutely,' replied Sir Phillip. 'There's something not quite right there.'

'Boyd!' remarked Antonia. 'Is there anything else we need to do?'

'Yes! Let me give it some thought, Antonia. If we accept Boyd has been subjected to a technical attack, then we need some carefully selected words to switch him on.'

'Words!' remarked the redhead. 'I was going to telephone him but perhaps not. Not just at the moment.'

At Boyd's home, the Commander of the Special Crime Unit was in despair. There was still no sign of Meg and there was no positive information emanating from his telephone calls.

Reading Meg's note again, Boyd drummed his fingers on the table in frustration and thought, what is she doing? Where has she gone? Yes! Have a short break if you must but where and what with? We've no money and no car. They've repossessed the Porsche Cayenne! If it wasn't for the borrowed squad car, I'd be stuck. You haven't left for good, have you, Meg? No! You said a break. No!

The telephone in the hall rang and Boyd responded like an Olympic sprinter.

Snatching the 'phone from its cradle, he shouted, 'Meg!'

'No! Would you like it to be?' came the reply.

'Meg! Is that you?' ventured Boyd. 'Where are you?'

'Now wouldn't you like to know, Mister Boyd?'

171

Pushing the 'phone away slightly for a moment, Boyd look at the mouthpiece, considered that the voice on the other end was a female with an accent he did not recognise, and eventually replied, 'Hello! Who is this?'

'The person who kidnapped your wife and children. That's who.'

With a vice-like grip on the telephone, Boyd's temper flared when he yelled, 'Who is this? Who are you? Where are you? If you touch my family, I'll tear you to pieces with my bare hands.'

There was a long pause before the female voice replied, 'Have you settled down yet? I need you alive not with a heart attack. Do you want your family back or not?'

'Of course, I do,' snapped Boyd. 'Where are they?'

'Right here! Would you like to speak to Meg?'

'Yes! Yes!' ventured Boyd.

'Billy! Billy! Are you there!'

Recognising his wife's voice, Boyd responded with, 'Meg! Where are you? Who's got you?'

There was no reply just the sound of an inaudible muffled reply and a thud that suggested someone might have been thumped.

'Don't touch her,' screamed Boyd.

'I wouldn't dare,' said the voice. 'She's part of the trade.'

'What trade? What are you talking about?'

'Commander Boyd, you are in charge of the Special Crime Unit. You will deliver the Ticker Intelligence Computer system to me together with all relevant codes, passwords, and ancillary software. If you do not, you will never see your wife and children again. Do you understand?'

'Who are you?'

'A voice on the other end of the 'phone holding a gun to your wife's head, that's who. Ticker, Mister Boyd. Your wife for Ticker. It's as simple as that.'

'It's not that easy,' suggested Boyd.

'Can you hear this, Commander?'

The sound of the trigger mechanism cocking on a revolver rushed down the telephone wire and into Boyd's ear.

'No! Don't you dare!' screamed Boyd.

'It's your choice!'

'When? Where? How?' pleaded Boyd. 'I can't just make that happen. I need time.'

'Oh good, your hearing is fine,' said the voice. 'You have twenty-four hours to make the arrangements. The next time I contact you will be by mobile 'phone. Make sure you have it with you at all times otherwise, if you miss the call, the trade is off, and your family will be disposed of.'

'No! Not long enough. Nowhere near long enough!'

'Twenty-four hours, Mister Boyd. It's your problem. Don't make it mine.'

The telephone line went dead.

'Hello! Hello!' shouted Boyd. 'Don't go!'

In the lounge of Pine Lodge, on the shores of Loch Ness, Colonel Anna Korobov closed her satellite 'phone, holstered a revolver, and removed a photograph from her purse.

Holding the image of her son close to her, the Colonel touched her lips and then transferred her kiss to the photograph saying, 'Soon, Mikhail. Soon! This man and his family will soon be history. Just for you.'

The Colonel pocketed the photograph and removed a partially completed quilt from her bag. Selecting her favourite porcelain thimble and a broad-eyed threaded needle, she relaxed as she drove the needle into the quilt in a determined and cold-blooded manner.

In the Operations Centre in an underground secret facility near Canterbury, an intelligence officer trained in high-end electronics shouted, 'I have a call from the box to the satellite. Monitoring! Closing! Engaging! Stand by!'

Incessantly rattling his keyboard, the intelligence operator shouted to Reg, 'Narrowing! The satellite is narrowing the angle. Stand by!'

Reg rushed to his colleague's side, looked over his shoulder, and said, 'Good work! Fingers crossed!'

'The box reduces in size,' revealed the operative. 'The target is now in a box from Inverness to the Cairngorms. The Cairngorms to Perth. Perth to the Trossachs. The Trossachs to Inverness.'

'Getting smaller,' remarked an excited Reg.

'Call ended!'

'Keep on it,' ordered Reg. 'We'll get there. Keep on it! If it's the Russians, let's show them what we can do. They're not the only ones with cyber weapons.'

It was a dark and cloudy evening when the black Mercedes saloon car cruised alongside Loch Ness.

At a point midway between Fort Augustus and Drumnadrochit, the driver reduced speed until a turnoff appeared which took the vehicle a short distance down a track towards a deserted building.

Parking at the side of the holiday let, the driver locked the vehicle and strolled casually to the water's edge. With wet gravel from the loch beneath the driver's feet and an outstanding view of the loch at night, the driver returned to the car, unlocked the boot, and removed a suitcase. A short time later, the upstairs light in a bedroom overlooking the loch came on when the driver of the Mercedes decided to settle down for the night.

~

7

Meanwhile in Moscow
That day

The couple leaving the British Embassy at 10 Smolenskaya Naberezhnaya in Central Moscow expected to be followed by the Federal Security Service whenever they left the embassy. The Federal Security Service (FSB: Federalnaya Sluzhba Bezopasnosti) had replaced the KGB in 1991 when the Soviet Union had collapsed. Now the FSB was the formidable opponent of western intelligence agencies.

Equipped with flats for the staff, shops, leisure facilities for children and adults alike, a swimming pool, and a large car park, the British Embassy complex was separate from the Kremlin by the Moskva river upon which the city stood.

Ironically, a sculpture of Sherlock Holmes and Doctor Watson was situated on the Smolenskaya embankment that bordered the embassy and looked out across the Moskva to the Kremlin. The popularity of the Sherlock Holmes stories in Russia had followed the Soviet adaption of the works of Arthur Conan Doyle. However, the couple from the British Embassy often wondered if their Russian opponents, in the Kremlin, had any regard for the two most famous fictional investigators in the UK standing so close to the embassy. If sarcasm is the use of irony to mock or convey contempt, then Holmes and Watson were well placed to represent the British attitude of the day.

The Kremlin is a fortified complex in the middle of Moscow, overlooking the Moskva River to the south, Saint Basil's Cathedral and Red Square to the east, and the Alexander Garden to the west. The complex includes five palaces, four cathedrals, the Kremlin Wall and the world-renown Kremlin towers. It is steeped in fascinating history dating back to the second century BC. Similar to the White House in America or 10 Downing Street in England, the Kremlin is the seat of political power.

Within this complex is the Grand Kremlin Palace that was formerly the Tsar's Moscow residence. The complex also serves as the official residence of the President of the Russian Federation and has a museum with about three million annual visitors.

The Kremlin and its activities were the central focus of MI6 in Moscow and the reason why Leonid Morozova: code name SPARROW HAWK, father of Sasha, was the subject of an intensive enquiry commanded by intelligence operative Lucy Henderson, a native of Gravesend, in Kent, who had left school with a modicum of intelligence and a ton of common sense.

It wasn't unusual for embassy staff to be placed under surveillance by the FSB. It was looked upon as part of the job, and a game to be played with the opposition.

Travelling in a Russian made Lada Xray crossover, the two booked out of the building, were stopped, as usual by the Russian police, and allowed to proceed once their papers had been checked.

Within minutes, Gerrard, the driver, was into the city and checking his mirror.

Glancing at his passenger, Lucy, he said, 'They're with us. One high-powered black GAZ 24 Volga. Where're the others.'

The younger Lucy nodded and replied, 'Another joining from the nearside junction.'

They drove on, negotiated traffic lights, and crossed the Moskva at Bolshoy Bridge before heading north. The first car following them carried straight on, but another car took its place.

'Another black one. It's their favourite colour. That makes three, Lucy.'

'As usual,' she replied. 'Nice and easy does it. Keep to the speed limit otherwise they won't hesitate.'

'My foot is prohibited, limited, and locked on,' chuckled Gerrard.

They drove on for half an hour touring the city streets with no particular place to go. The half-hour grew to an hour and then moved steadily towards two hours still under the watchful eye of the FSB. Eventually, they turned back towards the river but then turned down a side street and pulled up close to the pavement.

Lucy remained in her seat, checked her wristwatch, and looked across at a block of Russian apartments that climbed to four floors.

'This is where it all started eighteen months ago,' remarked Lucy.

'Well, that time has certainly flown,' replied Gerrard. 'It was around about the time I moved here from Oslo, wasn't it?'

'That's right,' responded Lucy. 'Those apartments are state-owned and occupied by people who work at the Kremlin. It's common for the Russians to provide such accommodation. They get perks with everything, even better food than others. It dates back to the days of Communism and is still deemed essential if you happen to be the dictatorial President of the Federation. They've got all their important people under one roof. Easier to bug, easier to watch, easier to govern.'

'How did you recruit Sparrow Hawk?' enquired Gerrard.

'I didn't,' chuckled Lucy. 'I occasionally just sit here in one of our embassy cars. They're all fitted with diplomatic number plates, unlike this one which is privately owned. These people know the registration numbers of diplomatic cars. I like to know their faces. They can tell who is British, American, French or whatever by the car you're driving. One day Sparrow Hawk sauntered past my car and surreptitiously dropped a note through the open window and walked away. It was a shock to the system when that first happened, I can tell you. I wondered what the hell he was doing. Anyway, I drove away half an hour later, got back to the embassy, and then read his note. He wanted out and promised another mail drop the following week at the same time and same place.'

'Did you believe it was an honest approach or just a dangle the FSB had laid down so that they could entice you into a well-organised trap?'

'How would I know so soon?' replied Lucy. 'A week later, I returned on cue, received another note, and we moved on from there?'

'Why does he want to come over to our side, and what has he to offer?' enquired Gerrard.

'Basically, he tells me that he hates Russia because it has become a brutal dictatorship that he no longer supports. I get the impression he was happier with communism, accepted glasnost and perestroika under President Mikhail Gorbachev, but has had enough of the present regime.'

'Glasnost and perestroika,' chuckled Gerrard. 'Now that takes me back to the period of openness, transparency and the restructure of the communist state. I presume our man has a few years about him now?'

'Oh yes!' revealed Lucy. 'He wants to be with his daughter in London. Fortunately, for us, he's one of the curators at the Kremlin museum. He knows the President intimately.'

'Hence our interest?'

'Indeed,' replied Lucy, 'He has shared many a day talking to the President about motorbikes. They've even been biking together apparently. They share a common love of motorbikes and he was more or less given the job of curator because of his friendship with the President. He's positioned to know a lot about the present regime, its main players, its aspirations, and the individuals that are likely to follow the present leader.'

Gerrard nodded and replied, 'I thought that was the case. Let's hope he's a valid entity and not an unwanted plant. Are you ready?'

'Whenever you are,' suggested Lucy.

Tall and well built, Gerrard swept a hand across the blond hair that dominated his good looks before getting out of the driver's seat and closing the door behind him.

In her late twenties, the younger Lucy had light brown frizzy hair that complemented a beige blouson and brown denim jeans. Casually, she altered the angle of the interior mirror to enable a better view of events to her rear.

Gerrard popped the bonnet, checked the oil and water levels, and then looked through a narrow gap to the windscreen where he could see Lucy: the lady he had been detailed to look after during the operation that had now commenced.

A black GAZ 24 Volga drove by containing two males in dark suits.

Gerrard did not respond to their presence but stood up, stretched his back, and then moved around to check the front offside tyre. From that position, he caught sight of two other black Volgas. One had pulled into a parking space about twenty yards away whilst another held back about one hundred yards away. It was obvious to the experienced Gerrard that the Russian operation represented more of an intimidating presence than covert surveillance. It was what he had come to expect during his time as an apparent low-level driver for embassy officials. It was also what he had been taught as an MI6 officer attached to Moscow station.

Motionless, Lucy eyed one particular apartment on the fourth floor and noticed the curtains were open. A shadowy figure seemed to be present, stepped back, and disappeared from view.

Gerrard, fiddled with the car fan belt, checked the oil again and waited.

Lucy checked the time.

On the fourth floor of a Moscow apartment block, a set of curtains were pulled tight.

Placing her handbag on the dashboard, Lucy opened it and rummaged for her lipstick.

Looking through the gap between the car bonnet and the windscreen, Gerrard noticed Lucy's handbag, recognised the signal, and closed down the bonnet. He returned to the car and got into the driver's seat.

Once in the driver's seat, the MI6 officer fired the engine and asked, 'All good?'

'Sparrow Hawk has the message,' remarked Lucy. 'Let's go.'

Selecting first gear, Gerrard pulled away from the kerb, checked the mirrors, and noticed the FSB gradually fall into convoy once more.

As the first FSB Volga reached the place where Lucy and Gerrard had stopped, the passenger leaned forward and briefly studied the apartment block that had been of interest to Lucy.

Inside the apartment, Leonid Morozova, watched the progression of the vehicle through a chink in the curtains as he thought to himself, The signal is down. It's time for me to go. At last, I'm going to see my daughter.

Elated, but still vigilant, Leonid sought to gather the possessions he needed fully aware that if he was suspected of being a British spy then it was likely his apartment would be bugged and a hidden camera would be watching his every move.

'Work!' he said. 'Time to go to work.'

Leonid strolled to his office in the Kremlin. It was only a short walk from his residence.

Four hours later, Leonid, in his late sixties, balding, overweight, and limping slightly, walked out of his office in the Kremlin Museum and hobbled down the staircase and into the fresh air of Red Square.

Out of breath, he paused for a moment, glanced over his shoulder to the edifice where he had worked most of his adult life, and then turned his back on history and walked into the future. The future was in a white plastic bag that contained an internal passport that allowed him to travel within Russia but no further, a cold meat sandwich, a bar of chocolate, toiletries, and not much more.

The future was also an underground Metro station close to Red Square and a tube train that would take him north to another station.

He caught the train, took a seat, and looked around. There was an older couple seated nearby, plus quite a few solitary commuters, and a noisy pair of teenagers who insisted on playing loud music from a transistor radio. There was no sign of Lucy.

The train set off with Leonid peering out of the window checking the platform for any sight of the fizzy-haired girl who had promised to reunite him with his daughter, Sasha.

Half an hour later, worried about what might lie ahead, Leonid disembarked from the train and sauntered to the destination board. Studying the display, he sought the right platform for Sheremetyevo airport. It was the busiest of the four international airports in Moscow.

Two uniformed police officers came into view. Stationary, they both watched Leonid, exchanged words that he did not hear, and then approached him.

'Papers!'

Heart thundering, Leonid tried to control his anxiety as he handed his internal passport over.

'Where are you travelling to?'

'Sheremetyevo airport,' replied Leonid, hurriedly adding, 'To meet my daughter.'

'You are on the wrong platform,' revealed one of the officers. Turning, he pointed to a hallway and said, 'That way! Through the tunnel and turn left. The metro is every fifteen minutes. You should get one soon.'

His passport was returned. They walked away.

'Yes! Yes! Thank you,' replied Leonid. 'That way! Of course.'

Leonid followed the police directions, found the correct platform, and boarded the train seconds before it set off. He found a seat next to the window and returned his passport to the plastic bag. Glancing around, there was still no sign of Lucy and he began to worry about what he should do when they arrived at the airport.

No passport out of the country, he thought. No ticket! I've done what she told me but where are they?

The train eventually pulled into the station. Deliberately, Leonid allowed everyone else in the carriage to leave first. Finally, he stepped into the queue, shuffled along the centre aisle, and stepped onto the platform.

Sheremetyevo airport was a hub of activity that threatened to destabilise the elderly, and Leonid was no exception.

Still carrying his white plastic bag, Leonid strolled along the platform and onto the concourse before a lady wearing a long black coat came into view. Lucy was standing beneath a destination board and was no doubt guided to Leonid by the brightness of the bag he was carrying. Or had she followed him from Moscow? Leonid did not know.

Lucy held her ground for a moment, glanced casually at the elderly man carrying a white plastic bag, and then slowly walked away.

At last, sighed Leonid. I have found Lucy.

Falling in behind his guide, Leonid allowed plenty of room between them as he followed her out of the metro station, through the airport complex, and towards the exit.

The hub was packed with people all rushing here and there with one hand on their luggage and their mind occupied with the route they needed to take.

There were police everywhere. The hub was swarming with both uniformed and some obvious plainclothes officers. Russia's surveillance state was alive and well.

Lucy made for the exit, slowed down when a yellow Lada taxi came into view, and then turned to greet her follower as if he had been there all the time.

'Oh, there you are. I thought I'd lost you. Well, here's our taxi. Climb aboard.'

'Taxi!' muttered Leonid.

181

'Get in,' suggested Lucy holding the car door open for him. 'We haven't much time.'

Climbing into the rear passenger compartment, Leonid shuffled across the seat when Lucy moved in beside him with, 'Settle down. It's one of ours. Just relax. We're going to see your daughter. Okay?'

'Sasha!' exclaimed Leonid. 'Yes, Sasha. I'm so tired of walking and then the train.'

'Sleep!' suggested Lucy. 'We have a long journey ahead. Put your head down and have a nap. Everything is going just fine.'

The taxi driver set off, checked his mirror, and said, 'Still clean! No problems.'

'Well done, Gerrard,' replied Lucy. 'Leonid is clean too. Now get us out of here before my friend here as a heart attack.'

'Consider it done,' replied Gerrard working through the gears as he joined the traffic flow.

'Aren't we going by aeroplane?' enquired Leonid.

'No, but if there's anyone following you then we've lost them for now and they'll spend the next hour running around the airport looking for you,' explained Lucy. 'Get some sleep while you can.'

They skirted the airport terminals with a flow of regular aircraft flying above them before turning back towards Moscow and then cutting west towards the Baltic Highway. They headed out of the capital at a steady but casual speed, made good progress towards Latvia, and then, after about an hour's drive, pulled into an isolated layby in front of a Transit van.

'Leonid,' said Lucy. 'We're changing vehicles. Quickly now, out of the taxi and into the van.'

The elderly man found a burst of speed, clambered from the taxi, and made his way towards the passenger side of the van.

'Do you remember me telling you there was a hard part?'

Nodding, Leonid replied, 'I thought we'd just done that bit.'

'No, but it's time now,' explained Lucy guiding Leonid to the rear of the van where she opened the twin rear doors. Helping the man into the back of the van, she slid a false compartment open in the floor and said, 'This is where you'll be for the rest of the journey. There's not much room but you'll find food and water down there. If we stop, don't make a sound until I come for you. Meanwhile, you'll be as safe as houses. In you get.'

'Have you done this before?'

'You don't need to know,' replied Lucy. 'There's lots of police on the road ahead and the Border Guard will stop us at the Checkpoint when we reach Latvia. There's a check by Passport Control and then one by Customs. It could take us an hour to get through. Let me do the worrying. We have all the right papers. My advice is to take a little food, a sip or two of water, then lie low. You'll be fine.'

'Do I have a choice?'

'No!'

Leonid did as he was told, slipped into the false compartment, and stretched out full length. Above his head, he found a small pillow and a plastic box which contained an energy bar, some chocolate, and a small bottle of water.

'Ready?' queried Lucy.

'Yes,' replied Leonid.

Lucy closed the compartment, locked the rear doors, and jumped into the passenger seat just as the black Volga drove by.

'FSB?' she queried.

'Probably,' remarked Gerrard. 'But they don't seem to be interested in us. It's the Baltic Highway and usually a busy one but we've had a nice smooth ride so far. Buckle up and off we go.'

Abandoning the yellow Lada taxi, the occupants of the grey Transit van entered the highway and motored casually towards the border where they were held in a queue for half an hour before they were questioned.

'Papers?'

'Of course!' replied Gerrard handing his passport over.

Another guard approached the passenger side where Lucy handed her passport over. The passport was made out in the name Helen Verezova and indicated she was Latvian by birth. Gerrard's revealed he was her husband.

'You are man and wife?'

'We are,' replied Gerrard.

'Come with me.'

Gerrard and Lucy were escorted into the passport control office where both documents were checked for validity via an electronic screening process.

Curt as ever, the guard continued with, 'Reason for travel?'

'Delivering electrical parts to a customer in Russia. We're on our way home now.'

'You may continue,' voiced the officer.

Gerrard drove the van a short distance to the Customs Office where they waited for another fifteen minutes before being processed.

One of the Customs Officers had made his way to the rear of the Transit. He tried the doors and found them locked.

'Open,' he ordered.

Lucy attended, smiled at the guard, and unlocked the doors.

Stepping closer, the guard looked inside, allowed the tip of his rifle to rest on the floor next to the opening of the false compartment and eventually remarked, 'Empty!'

The guard retreated. Lucy locked the door with her heart thundering and about to explode.

Seconds ticked by before Customs declared, 'Proceed!'

Gerrard fired the engine and said, 'Thank you! Have a good day!'

Moments later, they entered the European Union at the town of Terehova, in Latvia. Leonid Morozova had been successfully exfiltrated from Russia and was now in Europe.

~

8

The Russian Embassy
Kensington Palace Gardens
London
The Following Day

The vacuum cleaner was abandoned, plugged in, but not in use. It had been in the same place since the embassy had opened earlier that morning.

With a smile and nod to all, Sasha unplugged the machine, pushed it out into the corridor, and then into the storeroom where she kept her cleaning utensils. Switching the light on, she closed the door behind her, unzipped the hoover bag, and removed a tape from the device inside. Quite proficient at such things now, Sasha linked the tape to a recorder in her handbag, fitted an earpiece, and activated the tape.

Scanning through the content, she settled on a conversation between Alexei and the 'rezident', Russia's Head Spy in the UK. In the United States of America, such a person was known as the 'Station Chief.' He was Alexei's boss.

'Out of town for a couple of days,' whispered Sasha to herself. 'A new security protocol coming into play and the rest.'

Checking her wristwatch, Sasha removed the tape from the device, ripped it into a dozen pieces, cut it again with a pair of scissors, and then flushed the proceeds repeatedly down the toilet. There was a box of matches lying on a shelf which she touched and then remembered the fire alarm system.

A fire might activate the sprinklers, she thought.

She abandoned the matches, buckled and then broke the plastic tape recorder with her bare hands, destroyed it as best she could, and then deposited it in the waste bin.

'That's the last one,' she voiced. 'It's getting far too dangerous for me.'

Now aware of a new security system in place, Sasha wondered what it entailed, who it would affect, and whether it was because they suspected

185

there was a leak from the embassy. One thing was for sure, she decided, she couldn't run the risk of being exposed as a British spy working inside the Russian Embassy, and not knowing how a new set of security procedures would work was an obvious danger to her.

Will they search us all every day? she wondered. Will we be searched entering and leaving the embassy every day? Will they increase internal CCTV coverage? Will they search my storeroom? Will they uncover the vacuum cleaner? What will happen to me if I'm caught?

Tidying up, Sasha tried to control the emotions rising within her and stepped back from the vacuum cleaner that had become her accomplice over so many recent months. It was like saying goodbye to an old friend.

She locked the storeroom and headed towards the exit in the basement.

Boyd's mobile sounded.

'Boyd!' he answered.

'Inverness!' came the reply.

'What? Where?' yelled an astonished Boyd.

'You do still want to see your wife and family safe and well, don't you?' spoke the female voice.

'Of course,' replied Boyd suddenly aware he was talking to the kidnapper.

'Do you have the Ticker system?'

'Yes, I do,' lied Boyd.

'All of it?'

'All you'll ever need,' suggested Boyd. 'Yes! It is complete and in good working order.'

'Good! Take it to the golf course at Inverness.'

'Inverness!' posed Boyd. 'That's hundreds of miles away.'

'Not that far if you want your life back, and your family. Mister Boyd, you have all the time in the world,' suggested the voice. 'Hire a car and set off in good time. The exchange will take place at noon tomorrow. You will be alone, unarmed, and will have left the Ticker system on the back seat of the hire car. The car doors will be unlocked and the key in the ignition. The exchange is simple and the trade worth your while if you want to see your family alive again. You have plenty of time to make the rendezvous so don't even think about making excuses.'

'Okay! Okay! I'll get there,' declared Boyd.

'When you arrive at the golf course, travel to the clubhouse, and park your vehicle near the flagpole. Stand clearly beneath the flagpole for at least three minutes and then walk towards the sea, find the beach, and stroll along the beach.'

'Beach?'

'Yes! Beach! You can't miss it. There's lots of sand there. You will be notified when it is safe to return.'

'Meg! How will I get Meg?'

'On returning to the vehicle the Ticker system will be gone and your wife and children will be in their place.'

'How can I trust you?'

'You can't, but you will.'

'Do I have a choice?'

'No!'

In the Operations Centre at Canterbury, things had reached fever pitch.

'Active call taking place.'

'Where to?'

'The satellite is sending a signal to the target box!'

'Close in!' from Reg. 'Narrow the angles if you can. It's all about the angle from the satellite.'

'Engaging! Stand by! It's all about the maths involved from here and how quickly the computer works it all out'

'Narrow it down!' from an excited Reg.

'Box is reducing in size.'

A map of Scotland appeared on the screen. A shaded box representing the satellite's target area concerning the location its signal was reaching appeared and covered the whole of the country. Gradually, the box reduced in size and the target area began to focus on the Highlands of Scotland.

Get the Director-General on the 'phone,' voiced Reg. 'Keep talking, Boyd. Keep talking and we'll find the caller.'

'It might not be Boyd,' from an operative.

'What?' demanded Reg.

'We've locked onto the download signal from the satellite not the upload signal from Boyd's 'phone. The signal strength depends on the angle of the signal from the satellite and the hope that the sky is clear, and the weather is good.'

'Damn it, man. Technology!'

With the 'phone in one hand and his eyes on the screen, Reg watched the situation develop.

Moments later, Sir Phillip thanked Reg for his call, replaced the receiver, turned to Antonia and said, 'Make the call to Boyd now. Use the agreed form of words and, when you get through to him, put the call on speaker.'

'Will do! Fingers crossed!'

'We'll need more than fingers crossed,' replied Sir Phillip. 'I want Boyd's mind on the job, working, and back in tune. Ring him.'

In the hallway of his home, Boyd felt terrorised and alone, but he needed time on his own. Engaging his mobile, Boyd rang DI Stan Holland who answered immediately.

'Stan, it's Boyd. I'm sorry, but I'll have to take a few days off. I've got things to do.'

'You might be the Commander of a half hitch lazy mob in London, Boyd,' chuckled Stan. 'But you've got work here that you volunteered for.'

'I know. I can't make it,' replied Boyd.

'What's wrong. Billy?' enquired a concerned Stan. 'You've not looked your usual best since you joined us recently? Can I help at all? We've been friends for a long time, Billy. Is the new job taking its toll on you?'

'No! No, of course not,' snapped Boyd. 'Look, I'm sorry for shouting but there are lots of things I need to sort out.'

'Take a day or two off,' suggested Stan. 'Have a gentle walk with Meg, open a bottle of wine, try a relaxing evening watching television.'

'Television?' remarked a puzzled Boyd.

'Yes!' laughed Stan. 'That box in the corner of the living room that brings you the news every day. Or do you just use it to monitor your CCTV?'

'CCTV!' voiced Boyd. 'Yes! Yes! Thanks, Stan. You've just reminded me. It's not working and needs fixing.'

'What? The television?'

'No, the CCTV system!'

Boyd closed his 'phone, hurriedly switched the television on, and activated his computer. Minutes later, his fingers rattled across the keyboard as he scanned recent images stored on his CCTV system. All the still images were linked to his television screen. There was no working video system in play.

Suddenly, Boyd felt as cold as ice when he thought to himself, I'm stupid. I forgot about our CCTV system because I know the video isn't working. It hasn't worked for months and I couldn't be bothered to repair it. Too busy catching crooks and not enough sense to look after my own home. I need to get my mind in focus. That's the truth of the matter. I've been stupid, forgetful, and on the wrong track completely. Detective Chief Superintendent William Miller Boyd is no more than a first-class idiot ill-equipped to look after his own family, never mind a CCTV system. And that policeman in Carlisle told me his youngsters hero-worshipped me. If only they knew the truth.

Boyd's fingers froze before his mind went into meltdown when he arrived at the images of three vehicles parked outside their house. Studying the images, he saw several men and a couple of women entering the building by the front door. Finally, he realised he was looking at still photographs that had been captured by the CCTV system during the kidnap of Meg and the children.

'Where are they?' he sobbed. 'What on earth are they going through right now?' Boyd sank to the floor in despair murmuring, 'What's wrong with me? My mind is broken. I can't think straight.'

Thumping his fists on the floor, Boyd's world collapsed on top of him when he tried to think rationally.

It all began with the Torchlight Parade! What happened there then? Candy floss! Ice-cream! Marching bands and then a downward spiral into total mayhem. Why did I get involved? I didn't need to! The burglar in Carlisle. Estonia! John Dillon! Jewellery! The circus and everything in between. Why me?

His fists hammered the carpet, moved up to the wall, and then clung to the wallpaper as his mind fought the demons dancing in his brain and he mulled over the misspent days of recent times.

What's it got to do with me? thought Boyd. Why did I have to get involved? Simon whatshisname and the smell of paraffin! Arson! Pyromania! Fire! And the Mayor of London! Still on my mind and still not sorted. Will it ever be? Is it for me to worry about in the scheme of things? They're all building up inside me and I still haven't put pen to paper. Statements to do, reports to write, people to see, enquiries to do. What the hell am I chasing crooks and weirdos around for when someone somewhere is destroying my life? Not just my life. Meg's, Izzy's, James's! All of us! Where is she? What have they done to her? And my answer has been to chase the circus, douse the paraffin, and get lost in a quagmire of crime investigations that I shouldn't have touched with a barge pole. Not when the world is collapsing around me.

Gradually, Boyd pulled himself to his feet and thought, Get a grip, man! Focus! Focus on what you know you can do to sort this problem out. Not crimes that others can sort. Focus, you idiot! Otherwise, you won't just lose Meg. You'll lose your mind as well. Billy Boyd, you're on the verge of a nervous breakdown.

On two feet, Boyd took a deep breath, looked at himself in the mirror and wondered if he should punch himself in the face to get his mind back on the right track.

My eyes, he thought. There's no life in them anymore. I need a shave and my hair needs cut. Am I growing a beard and if so why? Where have I been and why did I go there? It's all so confusing. All that work when I should have been elsewhere. Do you know something? I forgot. I forgot how precious the real things that matter in life are. Well, Billy Boyd. Not anymore. Get back to where you know you should be.

The 'phone in the hall rang again.

Boyd rushed to answer it and yelled, 'Put Meg on now.'

'Steady on, Boyd. It's Antonia. I said I'd ring when I had some news. Now I want you to listen carefully because the shepherd was asking after you today. You do remember the shepherd, don't you?'

Mesmerised, more confused than ever, Boyd, shook his head free of the onslaught going on inside his brain and replied, 'The shepherd! What are you talking about?'

'The shepherd, Boyd. Phillip and I were only talking about him this morning. He's a good friend of the bishop if you remember?'

Ignoring the remarks, Boyd blurted out, 'Not that shepherd. No, do you mean…'

'Get a grip,' cried Antonia. 'Yes! That shepherd and that bishop. They worked together for a long time but, amazingly, events separated them into two different schools. One bishop and one shepherd. It's an amazing story and they'd like to meet up again soon. Phillip is arranging everything as we speak. A reunion even. Okay so far?'

'Yes,' mumbled Boyd trying to make sense of the strange conversation. 'Go on!'

'By the way, Phillip is planning a reunion. He insists on bringing us all together for dinner and we must wear our best bib and tucker to the event. What do you think of that?'

Silence! No reply! Wandering through turmoil.

Boyd wanted to scream down the telephone and tell Antonia that he had proof his wife and children had been abducted by a gang.

A gang of what? He wondered. A gang of who? Should I tell the police, or should I tell Antonia?

Yet his mind wandered back through the years to a Commander Herbert, codename Shepherd, and himself, codename Bishop, and how Commander Herbert had been the subject of an attack on his very being. The Security Service had re-housed him, arranged a new identity, and ensured his safety thereafter. And it wasn't that long ago that he remembered Commander James Herbert was coded by the Security Service as Shepherd and he was coded as Bishop. This stilted conversation was beginning to make sense.

The Shepherd! thought Boyd. That's it. No! Not me too! Am I a target too?

'Boyd!' continued Antonia. 'Phillip insists you turn yourself out as smart as possible for the reunion. You know what he's like for protocols, procedures and stuff like that.'

'Yes, I do,' replied a more enlightened Boyd. 'What does he suggest?'

'That you dry clean your best suit,' insisted Antonia. Then, chuckling conspiratorially, she added, 'Now that means you'll have to take all your clothes off, stand naked in the shower, and then get dressed up in the best you have. He wants you clean and posh. Understood?'

'Lounge or evening wear?'

'Both! Dry clean both. Phillip wants you as smart as a new pin and ready to go at the drop of a hat. He has all kinds of surprises planned over the next few days.'

The penny dropped, Boyd stood up, walked around and realised what Antonia meant by dry cleaning. Eventually, he replied, 'I'll take my evening suit to the cleaners unless Phillip can pick it up for me on his way?'

Standing behind Antonia, Sir Phillip smiled and nodded in agreement as he whispered, 'Boyd's back. He's worked it all out. Now reel him in quickly.'

'Picking your evening suit up? Yes, I think that can be arranged,' revealed Antonia. 'Phillip will be in the area shortly I'll tell him to collect it. Just wait there.'

'My family have been kidnapped,' blurted Boyd to the astonishment of Antonia and Sir Phillip. 'It's all on my CCTV system. I'll send you the product.'

'What?' cried Antonia. 'Kidnapped! When?'

'The time and date are on the images. I'm sending you them now. The kidnappers want an exchange.'

'How much?' enquired Antonia as she glanced warily at Sir Phillip.

'There's no mention of money,' stated Boyd. 'They want the Ticker Intelligence system, software, hardware, passwords, the works in exchange for Meg and the kids.'

Sir Phillip immediately bent towards Antonia and whispered, 'Express surprise but agree with him. Wind it up quickly. The Colonel might be listening.'

'Really, Boyd?' queried Antonia buying a little time for herself.

An icon appeared on the computer screen. It was a set of images sent by Boyd. Antonia downloaded the images and waited. When they appeared on screen, Sir Phillip whispered, 'Kidnap confirmed. Some of those are on the Heathrow video from when they entered the UK. The Colonel hasn't just destroyed Boyd, she's kidnapped his family too.'

Antonia nodded in agreement.

'Yes, I'm going to swop Ticker for my family, and I don't care what you think,' continued Boyd. 'Some things are more important than computer systems. Listen to me, Antonia. I've worked it all out. My family and things I love are more important than Ticker.'

'I agree with you,' replied Antonia. 'It's only a computer system.' As an aside to Sir Phillip, Antonia whispered, 'Did you hear that? Boyd said he'd worked it all out.'

The Director-General nodded in agreement and whispered back, 'Yes, but does he understand the code?'

'The computer system is the best in the world,' proposed Boyd.

'Do you understand what is happening?' enquired Antonia.

'No! Do you? I've got access to the Ticker system in my office at Divisional Headquarters in Carlisle,' revealed Boyd. 'And I don't want you to get involved. Keep out of my way.'

'I can't keep out of your way, Boyd,' argued Antonia. 'If the other side gets their hands on the Ticker system you will jeopardise security right across the board. It will be a catastrophe.'

'Not my problem anymore,' replied Boyd.

'Right! Okay!' murmured Antonia. 'If that's how you feel.'

Boyd cut the connection.

Sat at a computer in Scotland, Colonel Korobov read the words CYCLOPS AUDIO ALERT appearing on the screen and downloaded the latest product from the hidden devices in Boyd's home.

'Problem?' enquired Dimitry.

'The Colonel smiled a replied, 'No! Nothing we need to get overly worried about at the moment. We are going ahead as planned.'

In London, Sir Phillip lifted another 'phone, dialled a number, and said, 'Anthea! Deploy the team immediately. As discussed, if you please.'

Following an acknowledgement, Sir Phillip replaced the 'phone and said to Antonia, 'On the presumption, Boyd has been hacked with some form of advanced technology, then the Colonel heard that conversation. Interestingly, Boyd didn't mention where or when they want to do the exchange. I think that was deliberate on his part. He didn't ring the police. He rang us and in so doing got his message across. If he'd rang the police in Carlisle to report the kidnapping, the conversation would have been different.'

'How are you going to play this one out, Phillip?' probed Antonia. 'Are you going to allow the Russians to get hold of the Ticker system so that Boyd's family will be liberated at last?'

'Not a chance,' voiced Sir Phillip loudly. 'There's no chance whatsoever that we will give up the Ticker Intelligence System. It's the most advanced computerised intelligence system in the world, worth a couple of billion, never mind millions, and has covert links to every major spy network in the western world including our allies in Australia, Canada, and elsewhere. The codes, passwords, levels of security access and clearance protocols alone are priceless.'

'I thought as much,' agreed Antonia. 'I know the rules. We don't give in to people who try and blackmail us but when it's your best friends that have been kidnapped a hundred and one scenarios go through my mind.'

'The real conversation wasn't you talking to Boyd. It was you talking and the Colonel listening,' explained Sir Phillip.

'What if it were me, Phillip? If the enemy had kidnapped me would you give up the Ticker system to get me back?'

There was no hesitation in Sir Phillip's voice when he snapped, 'No!'

'Do you love me, Phillip?'

'Antonia! This is no time to discuss love and our relationship! Give it a rest!'

'Do you love me?' persisted Antonia.

'You know I do,' voiced Sir Phillip.

'Unequivocally?' demanded Antonia.

'Yes! Replied Sir Phillip.

'That's quite hard for me to believe when you tell me that a computer system is more important than your love for me,' challenged Antonia.

'You called me a spymaster recently, Antonia,' explained Sir Phillip. 'Why?'

'Because you are,' replied Antonia. 'You are the boss, the Director-General: the top decision-maker in the nation's intelligence system. Colonel Korobov is one of Russia's spymasters. Well, Phillip, you are our spymaster whether you like that description or not.'

'If you put it that way then yes,' responded Sir Phillip. 'My job is to preserve the integrity of the nation, defend the State, and keep our secrets secret from those with prying eyes.'

'Is the defence of the realm more important than our love?'

'Yes! It's what I do,' explained Sir Phillip. 'It's what you do too, or have you forgotten? I'm sorry, Antonia but complete love is restricted by barriers that can never be breached.'

A red icon flashed continually from the Ticker screen.

'Incoming alert message,' declared Antonia who picked up a red telephone on the desk and listened to the message before returning the device to its cradle.

Turning to Sir Phillip, she remarked, 'That was Lucy speaking from Latvia. Sparrow Hawk has been delivered into our hands safely. He will be with us in the UK within the next twelve hours and I have a meeting with Woodpecker shortly.'

'Excellent!' replied Sir Phillip. 'By the way, you do realise Boyd was telling lies, don't you?'

'What do you mean?' probed an intrigued Antonia.

'He told us he would collect the Ticker system from his office in Divisional Police Headquarters. There's no Ticker system there. His office is in the city police station where he can access less secure parts of Ticker via a stand-alone secure loop, but he wanted us to know he was playing along with the enemy. Boyd's worked it all out. That was deliberate on his part. He's back with us.'

'Oh my God! So, he did,' realised an astonished Antonia. 'Do you think he knows who the enemy is?'

'It's possible but I doubt it,' proposed Sir Phillip. 'I think it will be the most puzzling thing on his mind at the moment.'

'Apart from where his wife and children are,' remarked Antonia.

'I'll put the coffee on,' stated Sir Phillip. 'I love you that much.'

'Perhaps!' chided Antonia. 'But second place is always first loser.'

Checking his wristwatch, Sir Phillip replied, 'In that case, you will always be first loser. Look at the time. Anthea will be there soon.'

The sound of Charlie Tango Charlie circling in the skies above quickly reminded Boyd that the team's eight-seater Agusta 109 immediate response helicopter had arrived and was in the process of landing opposite his house.

Opening the front door, Boyd's heart missed a beat when he encountered the unmistakeable vision of the unit's second in command: Anthea Adams. She was waving from one of the windows at the front of the helicopter gesturing to him to stay exactly where he was. As the helicopter began to descend, Anthea held her right index finger to her lips and indicated Boyd should not speak.

Elated to some degree, a surge of wellness rippled through Boyd's body when he reconciled himself with the knowledge that Antonia had at last turned up trumps and his colleagues were coming to rescue him from the horrors of recent times. Furthermore, that latest telephone call with Antonia had alerted him to the possibility that there was something amiss. Dry cleaning to Boyd could only mean two things: Being followed or being bugged. Or perhaps both?

The helicopter landed and Anthea led the team out of the Agusta towards Boyd. Five metres from the Commander, she stopped in her tracks and gestured that he should remain silent and not come any closer.

Boyd smiled, complied, and remained motionless as newly promoted DS Ricky French approached and handed a note to him.

The note read, 'Dry Cleaning in Progress. Stand Still. Remain Silent. You have been bugged.'

Boyd nodded in agreement.

The Glaswegian, DS Janice Burns, approached, quickly erected a pop-up paper tent and then pointed to the inside of the makeshift construction.

Boyd stepped inside. Once undercover, he stripped off until he was naked.

Ricky handed Boyd underclothes, a coverall suit, socks, and trainers, and waited for him to dress whilst he gathered the discarded clothes in a bundle on the floor. Activating an electronic sweeping device over the clothing, Ricky studied the LED display on the handle and realised it had recorded a positive reading. Separating the clothes, Ricky repeated the sweep and focused on a pair of Boyd's trousers. Recording a positive trace on the trousers, Ricky smoothed the device over the trouser hem and saw the LED display reach its peak. He angled the device towards Boyd so that the two men could both see the result of the sweep.

Boyd replied with a thumbs up and conformed to Ricky's gesture to leave the tent.

Once Boyd was in the open air, Janice moved inside and covered his trousers with some sheets of aluminium foil before securing them in a canvas holdall.

Anthea approached and voiced, 'We can talk now. How are you?'

'The better for seeing you all today,' replied Boyd. 'You'll never realise how glad I am to see you. Looks like my trousers have been bugged. Who did that? When? Why? And how?'

'It wisnae me,' delivered Janice in a stronger than normal Scottish accent. 'If you wanna ask me mare questions, I want a solicitor present. De ye ken that?'

'Nor me!' added Ricky. 'I was off yesterday. You don't need to know where I was the day before, you know where I am now, and I've nothing to add to my earlier statement.'

'Jeez!' replied Boyd. 'You lot never change then. Where do we go from here?'

'To do the business,' replied Janice. 'I'll need extra slugs for the side by side. Touch one of us and they touch all of us.'

Ricky added, 'We're all with you, Guvnor. We just need the where and when.'

'Start with the who?' suggested Boyd.

'The Director-General sends his regards, Guvnor,' voiced Anthea. 'The rest of the team will be joining us in due course. For your information, the main suspect is Colonel Anna Korobov: Mother of one Mikhail Korobov. I'm sure you remember he was a spy attached to the Russian Embassy some time ago. It's not known at this stage if the Colonel is working for the Russian State or is acting on her own. I think she's acting out a personal vendetta. Her history might go some way to suggesting that she is on her way to becoming something of a megalomaniac.'

'Where's Meg?'

'We're working on that,' replied Anthea. 'I have a full briefing package for you onboard Charlie Tango Charlie. The briefing is extensive and has been personally put together by the Director-General of the Security Services: Codename JUPITER. He's in personal charge of this operation, Guvnor.'

'Well, that has to be a first,' replied Boyd. 'But to be fair, he carries the can for everything MI5 do, and I know he has some really tough decisions to make every day of his working life. By the way, who are those people?'

Boyd pointed at three men dressed in white forensic-styled suits who walked past the gathering towards the house. Each man carried a white briefcase and walked with purpose and determination.

'The MI5 technical team,' revealed Anthea. 'Jupiter authorised their attendance. I am required to report directly to him as to the results of the initial search. I always thought he was a fairly quiet man. He's highly committed and doesn't seem to have much time for fools, vagabonds, and the unwary.'

'No! He's a formidable individual who seldom courts public opinion or support. He's one hell of a guy, the like of which few would strive to understand or recognise.'

'Special?' queried Anthea.

'Yes! What are his team doing?'

'Checking your house for bugs.'

'But you found one in my trousers.'

'Guvnor,' suggested Anthea. 'You're not quite with us yet, are you?'

'What do you mean?'

'I'm told you've temporarily lost your mind,' ventured Anthea. 'There could be more than one active bugging device in play.'

'Oh, yes! I never thought.'

'We know all about your financial destruction,' revealed Anthea. 'I think it is directly linked to your current mental disposition. It's as simple as this, Guvnor, you need to come back to us. We need you to be fit, switched on, mentally alert, and ready to go. We understand what has happened to you and your family. We're here to help, not to criticise. In all the years I've known you - we've known you - you have been in front of us leading the way. Come with me to the helicopter and I'll show you the briefing video. Jupiter wants you to lead the operation on the ground whilst he will retain overall control.'

'I see,' replied Boyd. 'Jupiter is ahead of the game. He's covering all the bases in case the opponent turns out to be the Russian State and not one individual. Ground control and political control seldom make good partners.'

'He's also asked me to determine whether or not your current mental and physical status is suitable. What do you think? With us yet?'

Boyd looked into Anthea's eyes but did not respond.

'It's as simple as this, Guvnor,' continued Anthea. 'The opposition wants to destroy you, and your family, because of your impact on the Korobov family. I understand they are a family of spies and something of living legends in the corridors of the Kremlin. They want to discredit the unit, you, and a nation who put their trust in men like you, us, the British Police Service, and the intelligence services. Historians may perceive these events to be an attack on yourself, but such events may also be construed as a unique and daunting attack on the very fabric of our nation's status in the global scheme of things. Because if they can do this to you, they can do it to all of us. Are you with us or would you prefer to take a back seat and get your mind back? We're with you any which way you choose. It's called loyalty and you'll only ever find it on a two-way street.'

Nodding, Boyd replied, 'I'll get there eventually. Have you any idea where they've got Meg and the kids?'

'Not really, but we have our suspicions. If you want my personal opinion, Guvnor, I'd say they are locked up somewhere safe. The Colonel is trading Meg and the kids for the Ticker system, so she surely has to keep her side of the bargain.'

'I hope so. Take me to the helicopter, Anthea,' proposed Boyd. 'Run this briefing past me.'

Ricky approached with his mobile 'phone and intervened with, 'I'm in touch with the technical team inside the house. They've conducted a brief preliminary search. Most of your wardrobe appears to be fitted with some kind of advanced listening device. They've also recorded positive traces on the landline telephone and most of the doors inside. It will take them an hour or more to do a proper sweep and cover everything but right now the decision is unanimous. You've been well and truly bugged, Guvnor. The enemy has known your every move since the beginning, and probably everything you've said since the operation began.'

'In that case, keep those trousers close to me,' suggested Boyd. 'Let's not switch anything off or destroy whatever device is hidden in there. We can take them with us and feed some information to the enemy when we've decided how we're going to play this one.'

Anthea glanced at Janice and then Ricky before declaring, 'He's on his way back! Come on. Time for the briefing update.'

Kensington Central Library was a short stroll from the Russian Embassy and the location chosen by Antonia for her next meeting with Sasha Morozova.

Browsing the romance section, Antonia selected a book from the shelf and began reading as various customers mingled in the fiction area and potentially looked like they may cause a problem. Deliberately, Antonia assessed the people around her as she ostensibly leafed through the book.

Bad decision! Too many people, thought Antonia, who replaced the book and strolled towards the philosophy section where she encountered Sasha sat at a table reading a book entitled *War and Peace* by Leo Tolstoy.

'A good choice if I may say so,' remarked Antonia in a casual fashion, 'Have you read Tolstoy before?'

Another library customer strolled down the aisle and began browsing the shelves.

'I prefer Anton Chekov actually,' replied Sasha. 'We have a lot in common.'

'Russia, for example,' remarked Antonia. 'My favourite is one of his plays: The Cherry Orchard. I recommend it.'

'Yes, I've heard of it before today,' replied Sasha.

The library customer replaced a book on the shelf and walked on.

The two were alone when Antonia sat down close to Sasha and said, 'I've not much time and there are more people than normal around today. The longer we are together, the more risk we face. I'm sorry to sound rushed, but what have you got for me?'

'My father?' queried Sasha. 'Any news?'

'Yes, it's progressing well,' nodded Antonia.

Sasha stood up as if to go and immediately said, 'Progressing well? In that case, I have nothing for you. You know how important he is to me, but you haven't understood a word I've been saying. Why is it, you are always progressing well but never have a result? Time and again you tell me, it's progressing well. If that's all you can tell me then I have nothing for you until my father is safe.'

'Sit down,' advised Antonia. 'I wasn't going to divulge anything to you until later but as things are moving a little faster now, I'll tell you what I know so far.'

Reluctantly, Sasha sank back into her seat and listened to the redhead.

'Yesterday your father was successfully taken by our people from Moscow to Latvia where they crossed the border into Europe and safety.'

There was a gush of relief from Sasha.

'At this moment he is airborne into the United Kingdom from Latvia posing as an ordinary customer on a commercial flight. He's travelling on a false passport which we've arranged for him. We're not expecting any problems whatsoever and we're pretty sure the Russians haven't yet realised he's jumped over the side. Our people are with him all the way and will take him to a safe place in the countryside. The site is secret, guarded by armed personnel, and I am not at liberty to tell you where it is located. However, I can tell you that when he arrives, he will be given fresh clothing, a hot meal, and good clean accommodation. Tomorrow, I want you to go to your local gym as usual. Stay there all day and wait for me to arrive. As soon as you see me, follow me out, get into the front passenger seat of my car, and we'll drive away. Don't take anything with you to the gym other than a change of clothing. Leave everything behind you. I mean everything. It's time to close you down now that your father is on his way. You've been in danger long enough. A new life awaits, Sasha. Leave the old one behind. It's time to walk out of the door and not look back. You will have the opportunity to spend some time with your father. If all goes well, our people will be talking to you both for quite a while. Possibly for quite a few days, probably weeks. We are very anxious to listen to what you have to tell us about the Russian Embassy as well as the Kremlin. The plan is to rehouse you somewhere out of London, but that is for the future.'

Stunned, Sasha looked directly into Antonia's eyes and said, 'It's just like you said. You told me that's the way it might go when we started this conversation eighteen months ago.'

'I've kept my word,' voiced Antonia. 'Can you keep yours?'

Considering her position, perhaps thinking of her father, Sasha eventually replied, 'Yes! It's time I think.'

'Sasha,' explained Antonia. 'Your father is safe, but I can't produce him to you now because his safety is paramount and his location secure.'

A library customer strolled down the aisle checking books out, appeared not to find what she wanted, and moved elsewhere.

'Cyclops is in the Loch Ness area. She's causing a problem in the embassy,' revealed Sasha. 'She's gone rogue. They are all upset and arguing about what should be done.'

'Who is upset?' probed Antonia.

'Alexei isn't happy, and neither is the Head of Station.'

'Do you have the latest tape?'

'No!' voiced Sasha. 'I downloaded the last one and listened to it. That's how I know about Cyclops being somewhere in the Loch Ness area. She's supposed to be covering the Faslane area for the latest astute class submarine that was launched from Barrow in Furness, wherever that is. I've never heard of it before. But I do know they are worried about another attack submarine being launched. Anyway, I also heard them talking about a new security system coming into play anytime now. I destroyed the tape. It's too dangerous for me now that they are changing procedures. Maybe, they're on to me. I don't know. I'm not going back. I'll get caught eventually. I want out and I want to see my father as soon as possible.'

'The gym tomorrow, Sasha,' replied Antonia. 'Let's not upset the applecart by rushing into things. Your father is safe and so are you. If we change the game plan, we just might cause someone to ask questions. Thanks, but the gym tomorrow. Okay?'

'It's all about trust now, isn't it?' suggested Sasha.

'It always has been. Trust me! I'll be there for you at the gym tomorrow.'

'In that case,' revealed Sasha. 'I'd better tell you the rest. Cyclops is with a team of others that have been specially selected to do whatever it is she is doing. I don't know what she is up to, but I can tell you they are all staying in a place called Pine Lodge on the east side of the loch.'

'Pine Lodge! Are you sure you that's what you heard?' probed Antonia.

'As sure as I heard you tell me that I was to be at the gym tomorrow.'

'I'll see you there,' responded Antonia. 'That's for sure.'

Armed with a pair of trousers resting on the seat beside him, Boyd set off as planned. Fully dressed, he gunned the hire car north into Scotland, found the M74, reached Glasgow, and cruised along the side of Loch Lomond singing badly to a bugging device he knew was in the hem of a pair of trousers. He switched the car radio on in the hope that if the Colonel was listening in, she would be well aware that he was alone and heading towards Inverness.

What the Colonel didn't know was that Boyd was headed for Fort George, on the outskirts of Inverness, where he would bunker down for the night and contact London for an update as to the state of the enquiry.

Back in the Special Crime Unit offices, Antonia and Sir Phillip were discussing the latest intelligence she had received from Sasha Morozova: Codename Woodpecker.

'Pity she has destroyed the tape,' remarked Sir Phillip. 'Producing it would have added credence to her information.'

'It's become too dangerous for her.'

'I understand that. Such operations are always very risky. Do you think Woodpecker told you the truth or is she reeling you in and looking forward to meeting her father and co-conspirator tomorrow? Potentially, they could wreck us if they threw a ton of false information at us.'

'I understand your concerns,' replied Antonia. 'But to some degree, it's about the relationship I have with my agent and I believe her when she tells me the Colonel and her team are at Pine Lodge. My problem is that there are dozens of places called Pine Lodge in the Loch Ness area. It could be any one of them.'

'Something to do with trees in the area perhaps?' chuckled Sir Phillip.

'Absolutely,' replied Antonia. 'I will find the right one eventually. I promise. Even if I have to ring the local police.'

'Good!' nodded Sir Phillip. 'I hope you are right about Woodpecker because we're running with what she's told us. What are you researching at the moment?'

'Loch Ness,' replied Antonia gliding her fingers across the Ticker keyboard. 'Or to be precise, I'm on the Police Scotland website researching anything and everything they have to offer about places called Pine Lodge as well as Loch Ness in the last three months.'

'A monstrous task,' frowned Sir Phillip before breaking into a smile. 'Let me see.'

Based on the Stock Exchange ticker system, which is a listing of the ticker symbols of the stocks trading on that particular exchange, and their price, a constant flow of intelligence reports, crime reports, suspicious occurrences and various intelligence-related events, appeared in constant and gradual succession at the bottom of the Ticker Intelligence computer screen.

'There's a lot to consider,' remarked Sir Phillip. 'No source reports! No intelligence reports! I take it you're on the basic level.'

'Yes, I'm on one of the lower levels,' revealed Antonia. 'I've entered a search pattern for the two items I'm interested in. It should search for crime reports and incident logs for the Scottish Highlands. It will bring the results shortly. It's a good place to start.'

'It certainly is,' agreed Sir Phillip. 'Let's hope you get lucky.'

'It's Ticker. If it's happened and been reported to the police, it will be on this part of the Ticker Intelligence system.'

Minutes later, Antonia clicked on the Ticker flow and opened a report concerning a body found in the loch at Drumnadrochit.

'For example,' explained Antonia glancing at Sir Phillip.

'Can you access the full report?'

'Hopefully,' replied Antonia. 'Drilling down.'

An egg timer appeared in the middle of the screen but seconds later a report written by a Sergeant Angus Grant from Inverness came into view.

The spymaster and his fiancée read the report.

'Move to a higher security level and superimpose the photograph of the cryptologists who arrived from those Heathrow flights,' ordered Sir Phillip.

'I'm on it,' replied Antonia. 'There's a tattoo of the hammer and sickle on the body's shoulder. Coincidence?'

'Let's see,' suggested Sir Phillip. 'We both know the hammer and sickle appeared on the flag of the former Soviet Union.'

'But not the flag of the current Russian Federation,' added Antonia. 'Watch the big screen, Phillip.'

The two moved from the computer desk station and stepped towards the larger standalone transparent screen in the corner.

Side by side images appeared of a photograph of the body of a drowned man recovered from the loch near Drumnadrochit and the image of Nikolai Vasiliev: a known cryptologist attached to Russian intelligence and a suspected member of Colonel Korobov's team.'

'That's the man,' proposed Antonia. 'Yes, the body is bloated but there's enough resemblance to convince me.'

'I agree,' declared Sir Phillip. 'The chances of a Glaswegian having the hammer and sickle tattooed on their shoulder is virtually nil. Who is the author of the report?'

'A Sergeant Angus Grant from Inverness.'

'His file?'

More computer interrogation resulted in records appearing on screen before Antonia replied, 'Angus Grant is a serving officer in Police Scotland stationed at Inverness. He has ten years of police service and resides in Drumnadrochit. He's a former member of the Black Watch Regiment and he served in Iraq during Operation Telic. He is the holder of the Conspicuous Gallantry Cross - one level down from the Victoria Cross - It was awarded for gallantry in Iraq. Do you need more?'

'Stop right there. Potentially, he's the local you wanted to help find Pine Lodge. He lives slap bang in the middle of the target area and may be able to pinpoint the building for you. Or at least rule out a few. We need feet on the ground, and he sounds like the kind of man we could use. I want to know everything he knows about that body,' replied Sir Phillip. 'Get him on the 'phone. I'll ring his Chief Constable.'

'Looks like Woodpecker was right all along,' stated Antonia.

'Yes,' admitted Sir Phillip sarcastically. 'We are making steady progress. Isn't that your favourite saying to the lady in question?'

'I'll get the 'phone,' scolded Antonia. 'Interesting though!'

'What is?' probed Sir Phillip.

'Colonel Korobov has her eyes set on Ticker yet it's Ticker, and its allies, that are contributing to her downfall.'

'And a couple of birds plus the entire resources we have at our disposal,' contended Sir Phillip. 'But yes, there's an irony in there somewhere.'

In the underground facility near Canterbury, Reg was busy studying computerised actions relevant to the target satellite and its downward angled trajectory. Lifting the 'phone, he rang a secure number and spoke to Sir Phillip.

'What you got Reg?'

'My best guess is a building of some kind on the banks of Loch Ness between Inverness and Fort Augustus. It's a goodly distance but I'm afraid we can't be more precise due to the nature of the signal.'

'That coincides with similar intelligence we have,' admitted Sir Phillip. 'Thank you! The puzzle is gradually coming together.'

'By the way, we have something new for you from GCHQ. The Algerian company that owns the target satellite is no longer in business. It's now a state-owned subsidiary. The target is no longer private, Phil. It's a federation satellite, not a private concern anymore.'

'Just what I needed,' chuckled Sir Phillip. 'The plot thins then thickens and gets more complicated every day. Anything else?'

'There's a lot of activity on the satellite. It's as if someone has been making contact regularly but then, as suddenly as it started, it stopped.'

Sir Phillip replied, 'Hold on a moment,' and then held the 'phone to his chest as he considered the information. He then proposed, 'Could they be calls to or from someone in the Russian Embassy?'

'Just a moment,' replied Reg. 'The satellite is focused on one area of Scotland but, hey, that was when it was owned by the Algerian company. Hang on!'

Sir Phillip listened to the faint tapping on a keyboard before Reg came back to him with, 'But since the Russian Federation took possession of the satellite, the orbital path has changed slightly and that means the downward angle of trajectory has changed by less than one degree.'

'Oh, well, it was just an idea,' replied Sir Phillip.

'Phil,' suggested Reg. 'Less than one degree! Think about it! Sometimes we can't hack into everything going because the technical expertise employed by the enemy is akin to making us run a mismanaged Olympic four hundred metre hurdle final. There's a fence to jump every ten yards! But we can monitor traffic to and from targets. The increase in the angle of trajectory is less than one degree but it's enough to capture both London and the Orkney Islands. I'll put people on it, but you could well be right. If so, the embassy has been talking to your target and then suddenly stopped. Does that make sense to you?'

'It does,' replied Sir Phillip with an inner smile. 'From what you've told me, I think the Russian Federation may now be supporting our adversary. They've changed sides by the look of it. Stay in touch, Reg. We need you.'

'As ever, you can rely on my unit,' replied Reg ending the call.

Immediately, Sir Phillip dialled a direct number to the Chief Constable of Police Scotland and agreed with the constabulary's leader that a temporary secondment to the Special Crime Unit, concerning Sergeant Angus Grant, would be mutually beneficial.

Thereafter, Sir Phillip made one secure and direct video call to the Prime Minister, the Foreign Secretary, and the Home Secretary. The highly encrypted secure video conference informed the recipients of historic events relevant to the Boyd family, a recap of the historic attack on Commander Herbert, and how such activities were part of a systematic assault on UK society, its freedoms, its democracy, and its very being. An attack on one of us is an attack on all of us. Sir Phillip also appraised his audience of matters under immediate investigation and the likely outcomes that might impact on the UK and their relationship with elements of the Russian Federation. The Director-General made it clear that he intended to tackle the situation head-on and deal with the incursion by physical intervention if necessary. Everything was discussed from the breakdown of international relationships to the closure of embassies and consulates to the removal of staff in both countries, and elsewhere, in a tit for tat reprisal scenario. They also spoke about the possibility of trade embargos that would deny the UK access to Russia's all-important gas reserves. If an argument escalated out of control, it was said, there was even a risk of conventional warfare or at worst a nuclear strike. Such was the nature of global power politics when one nation chose to stand against another. Experienced in such political protocols and necessary procedures, Sir Phillip was succinct in his interpretation and rendering of such events, did not seek assurances of any kind, and spoke bluntly as to his intentions. Listening keenly to the advice given, he expressed gratitude to his contacts and ended the call intent on progressing his plans to satisfaction. He was that kind of leader.

On the western banks of Loch Ness, a solitary figure stood in a second-floor bedroom and looked out across the water in the general direction of Foyers, Easter Boleskine, and Stratherrick.

Removing a handheld night vision monocular from his suitcase, using military precision, he began to scan the opposing side of the loch. Gradually, he took in the land between Foyers and Easter Boleskine, revisited a specific area, and then engaged the laser rangefinder that comprised part of the device. Dedicated, and highly trained, he continually adjusted the focus on the telescopic device, and the laser range finder, and mentally recorded the various distances involved.

Finally, he studied the shadowy enigmatic waters, the unique serenity of the valley, and row upon row of darkened trees that looked down upon area and hid Loch Mohr and Stratherrick from his sight.

A wave from the wake of a passing cruiser gently made its way to the opposing side of the loch. The cruiser moved on and out of sight. Eventually, the wave kissed the bank and then curled gradually back towards the middle of the water. It was one of the falsehoods that persisted in stories about the loch. It was often said that a monster lurked beneath the waters and caused such a ripple just below the surface line. After all, the cruiser had long gone and was no longer in sight.

The wave flattened out and joined the black mirror sheen of the loch.

Drinking black tea from a flask, the stranger allowed his eyes to become accustomed to the darkness before he set the alarm clock and turned in for the night.

~

9

Fort George.
The Shire of Inverness
The Following Day

Dawn broke over the Moray Firth.

Leaving his accommodation in Fort George, Boyd decided to stroll around the fortress before attending the administration block where a briefing by Sir Phillip would shortly take place. His hire car was locked in a hotel car park in Inverness and the pair of trousers he had brought with him from his home in Cumbria was lying on the front passenger seat. He had promised to be at Inverness Golf Club later that day and hand over the Ticker computer system in exchange for his wife and children. Since he now knew that a slender listening and location device had been sewn into the trouser hem, he chose to believe that someone somewhere was following his every move and listening to every word spoken in his presence, provided of course, he was wearing them.

Standing on the ramparts, Boyd admired the old cannons from long ago and then looked out across the Moray Firth. It was an awesome and inspiring sight that all who had served in the castle had enjoyed in years gone by.

Fort George is a large eighteenth-century fortress near Ardersier which lies about twelve miles north-east of Inverness and sits on a promontory jutting into the Moray Firth where it controls the sea approach to Inverness. This allows the fort to be supplied by sea in the event of a siege taking place and was a useful tactic, and part of a defensive strategy, during more troubled times. Indeed, the star designed fortification was built to control the Scottish Highlands following the Jacobite rising of 1745. It has never been attacked and has remained in continuous use as a garrison despite the presence of tourists who are now granted access to visit certain areas of the complex. With its harbour below the walls, the fort is a formidable site with a history to match.

The first commanding officer of the original Fort George was Sir Robert Munro, 6th Baronet, Colonel of the 42nd Royal Highlanders

(Black Watch) and Chief of the Highland Clan Munro. The barracks became the home of the Black Watch, 3rd Battalion, Royal Regiment of Scotland in 2007. In November 2016 the Ministry of Defence announced that the site would close in 2032.

For Boyd and Sir Phillip, it was a secure location to hold a top-secret briefing since the barracks were devoid of tourists and the military area was in a restricted zone.

Boyd walked past three passenger-carrying helicopters and noticed that one of them was Charlie Tango Charlie: The unit's emergency response Agusta 109 helicopter. Parked next to the Agusta, Boyd saw a black Dauphin 2 helicopter and knew that Sir Phillip had called in the Joint Special Forces Airwing.

Armed with hot drinks, bacon sandwiches, and various chocolate and energy bars, the gathering settled down as Boyd and Sir Phillip took to the stage.

'Firstly,' began Boyd. 'I'd like to introduce you all to Sergeant Angus Grant of Inverness Police. Angus was the first officer at the scene when the body of a Russian cryptologist was recovered from the loch at Drumnadrochit and has been working on the case ever since. Check out the video screen behind me.'

There was a brief round of applause for Angus before an onscreen presentation appeared on the stage behind Boyd who continued, 'This is the deceased Nikolai Vasiliev. A full toxicology report is expected soon but we believe an initial examination of his body shows that the cause of death is quite possibly poisoning. The mark of a needle or similar sharp instrument is found on the deceased's neck. Whilst, for obvious reasons, formal identification has not yet been made, we are certain this man is the same individual who entered the country via Heathrow airport with a gang of Russian intelligence officers who appear in the video shortly. One thing is for sure, he certainly didn't curl up into a golf bag and commit suicide by throwing himself into the loch. Our suspect for his murder is Colonel Anna Korobov. Why? Because she is the leader of this gang, that's why.'

A flow of images appeared on the screen including one of the Colonel.

'As such, she is the most likely person to have committed the crime,' added Boyd. 'Alternatively, the Colonel ordered one of her cohorts to execute the cryptologist. It's one of the things we need to find out during our enquiry. Sergeant Grant is an ex-military man and has been looking into this matter for some time now. Intelligence reveals Nikolai was a level six cryptologist. Intelligence also points to a level seven cryptologist who arrived some days later on his own and not with the gang previously referred to. Angus and I have chewed the cud over this and we both wonder if our level six man was replaced by the level seven officer because something went wrong. You have to consider, at times, if people fall out and why? The Colonel, I understand, is a legend with a reputation for having things done her way, and no other way. I wonder if they argued about something they did not agree on. We don't know and may never find out, but such things drive us in our endeavours and make us think the way we do. Anyway, if you refer to the files you have been issued with, I'd like to make you aware of the following.'

The gathering leafed through their handouts.

'You'll see the plan drawing of a building called Pine Lodge,' continued Boyd. 'This is where the targets are laid up. Commit these plans to your memory and know them inside out because that's where we're going later this morning. Room by room! Sergeant Grant and I have made some preliminary visits to the immediate area of Pine Lodge through the night. Together with an MI5 technical team, we can tell you that the approach to Pine Lodge, and its surroundings, are protected by a passive infrared detection system. PIDS for short. Fortunately for us, it was confirmation that Pine Lodge is the correct target. Do you know of any holidaymakers or tourists who wander around their rentals populating three acres of land with PIDS? No, you don't and neither do I and this is the type of security system professionals use. You can't see the system unless you are standing on top of it and by which time it will be too late. It's a computerised electronic alarm system which links together a series of devices that are all shaped like a tent spike. The spikes have been plunged into the ground and linked electronically to form a shield. If you break the circuit or penetrate the shield, the alarm goes off silently and the host is prepared for your arrival. One more thing, ladies and gentlemen, the technical team also used a thermographic camera to examine the building. Thermal imaging reveals that there are well over one dozen people in the building. They are situated in the front lounge area of your plans as well as the rear kitchen area, various bedrooms on the second floor and in the basement. The PIDS and the thermal imaging situations have caused us to change our planned attack somewhat. But more of that later.'

There was a shuffle of feet and a scrape of a chair as the briefing continued.

'If the primary reason we are raiding these premises is to arrest a murderer,' argued Boyd, 'the secondary reason is to ascertain if my wife and family are in these premises having been kidnapped by the same gang. These are the CCTV images of the kidnap taking place. Before the kidnap, my house was covertly entered and my possessions, including clothing, were bugged. It's important to point these things out to you as this is a trigger operation and we will all be armed. One or more of their number is suspected of murder, kidnap, conspiracy, and the rest. We know they originate from a hostile enemy state. I expect them to be armed too, hence the authorisation. There's almost certainly going to be an internal enquiry once this matter is concluded so the files you are reading, and the video presentation you are watching will be part of any inquiry or proceedings that take place in the future. It's our reasoning and explains our motives for mounting the operation. Make sure your body-worn video cameras are fully charged, operational, and up to speed because there will be a host of journalists, self-appointed home-based solicitors, keyboard warriors, police procedure investigators, and holier than thou politicians queuing to view them in the coming weeks if the Russians make trouble. Take care. Stay safe. You are the best of the best. Be the best.'

Janice glanced at Anthea and pulled a face before revealing, 'I should have been a piper but I've nae enough wind in ma Glaswegian lungs to be filling the pipe bag.'

'And ya canna play the pipes for a wee bawbee, you once told me,' replied Anthea with a cumbersome rendition of a failing Scottish accent.

More images flashed across the screen.

'Note the basement area in the Pine Lodge plans. That may well be the location where we will find them. My callsign for this operation is Bishop. Now Sir Phillip – callsign Jupiter – will say a few words before we get stuck into the how and when.'

Sir Phillip took over and said, 'Commander Boyd has successfully demonstrated the crimes committed by this group but managed to get them in the wrong order. I thank him, and you all, for undertaking this operation. It is fraught with difficulty and unique in its execution and has my full support since, between you and I, we've been up half the night planning it. Realistically, we are here to save the lives of Meg, Izzy and James, and rectify the Boyd family to their rightful place in society. Boyd has operational control on the ground but be assured that I have complete control over this operation for political reasons. Why? Because the people we are going after are all Russian Intelligence officers on a rogue mission on behalf of their misaligned Colonel Korobov who wants revenge because of her son's death some time ago. Alternatively, my other concern is that the Russian State has discovered what the Colonel is up to and has taken over the management of that operation to secure our intelligence system. If the Russians were successful, it would be akin to them securing the firing codes for a nuclear attack by one of our Trident submarines, and they are classified ultra-top secret. The Colonel is either conducting a personal vendetta or has been assigned by the Russian State to do their bidding and acquire the Ticker system. We don't know at the moment but its's my intention to find out which in due course. I'll be with Antonia, callsign Juno, covering any possibility of a waterside escape from Pine Lodge. You also need to know that I have called in the Joint Special Services Aviation Wing to provide aerial cover if needed. 658 Squadron Army Air Corps using callsign Eagle One will be watching over you – quite literally. You will recall they landed one of their helicopters on Westminster Bridge during a recent terrorist attack at that location. Accordingly, if I call 'Aces High' please break off all armed conflict as soon as possible. Operationally, you need arrests, evidence, and convictions. Consequently, I have drafted in military support which may provide mutual assistance to both parties concerned, namely the Police and the Security Service.'

'And he can silence the military,' whispered Janice. 'But not the police who are the more likely to end up in court with this carry-on.'

'Politically,' continued Sir Phillip. 'I need to read a situation that renders us some success whilst simultaneously making sure that we don't create more problems for the government in the relationship we have with the Russian Federation.'

Anthea queried, 'So we are armed to protect ourselves; we are being monitored constantly, and you don't want us to shoot anyone?'

'Standard operating procedures apply,' interrupted Boyd. 'That's the way it is these days. Use the minimum degree of force necessary to make an arrest, but if that means you have to use your firearm, then do so. Legally, your judgement must be such that you may use such force as is reasonable in the circumstances in the effecting or assisting in the lawful arrest of an offender. I think we all know that off by heart now.'

'Agreed,' replied Sir Phillip. 'Hence the taped briefing we are having. Protect life, defend yourselves, and stick to the rules of engagement. I'm sure there will be a huge political row between the Russian Federation and the UK if firearms are discharged and anyone is hurt. Hence the reminder on the use of force. Okay, later this morning, one of my officers is going to set off and drive Boyd's hire car towards Inverness golf course just before we mount the raid. His trousers are on the passenger seat and they are bugged. On the presumption the bug is still working, Colonel Korobov should know that Boyd is on his way to the golf club to keep the rendezvous for noon. That's our ace in the hole. Local enquiries at Inverness airport reveal there is an inbound flight from Moscow arriving at noon and departing two hours later. It's a quick turn round. It's also a regular daily flight and I believe its arrival coincides with the intended departure of Colonel Korobov and her team. Now you may understand why she picked this neck of the woods to set up her operation. It's safer for her here, and quicker than in Heathrow. It took me a while to figure out why Scotland. But now I see why. Inverness is an easier way out in comparison with other places. Commander Boyd will now explain how and when.'

There was another shuffle of seats, the scrawl of a pen, the scratch of a pencil, and the muttered questionings and remarks of an eager team as the briefing wore on and the hands on the clock moved slowly towards ten-thirty.

Meanwhile, two children woke their mother when the sound of footsteps were heard in the basement of Pine Lodge.

'What's the matter?' queried Meg. 'Are you okay?'

Izzy snuggled up to her mum and whispered, 'Someone is coming. I can hear them.'

The basement cell in which they had survived for the last few days was damp and smelly. There was no window, no board games to play, no books to read, no crayons to draw with. Nothing, not even fresh air. Just walls that were damp to the touch, felt cold and offered no comfort to the abandoned trio.

'It's Dad,' offered James. 'I knew he would come. I told you so.'

'Shh!' whispered Meg. 'Cuddle in and keep warm. They might be feeding us again.'

The footsteps grew louder, stopped, and then stood their ground as a key was turned in the lock. The door opened and a plastic tray was slid across the floor towards them. Upon the tray sat three enamel mugs containing water, some bread, butter, slices of cheese, a splodge of jam, and three biscuits.

A deeply accented voice boomed, 'Eat! Drink!'

'What time is it?' cried Meg.

'Time to eat! Drink!' came the negative reply.

'How long will we here?' shouted Meg.

'Forever!' laughed the male voice.

'The children!' proposed Meg. 'Please can the children be set free and returned to their father?'

The guard began to pull the door closed but replied, 'You're going nowhere, woman.'

'Please! Help us!' pleaded Meg.

The door scraped on the floor and then banged shut. The key turned in the lock. Footsteps padded along the basement corridor and up the staircase into the body of the building.

'That wasn't Daddy,' yelled Izzy. 'He's never coming for us, James. Never! Never! Never!'

'Oh yes, he is,' shouted James. 'He'll be here soon. You'll see! And then I'll say I told you so!'

'Quieten down,' pleaded Meg. Get some of that food into you. It's good. You like cheese and jam.'

'No, we don't,' replied James. 'It's horrible and the bread is stale.'

'Have some water first and then try some bread,' urged Meg.

'I want out,' screamed James.

'Me too!' yelled Izzy. 'Mum! Mum!'

Gathering the children into her arms, Meg held them close to her chest and hoped that there was enough heat in her body to keep the children warm.

Staring at the door, straining her ears to listen to the outside world, a feeling of total despair enveloped the trio as the timeless day wore on from morning to afternoon or was it evening? They had no idea what time of day it was, or what day it was and had lost all understanding of normality.

At ten-thirty that morning, an MI5 operative drove Boyd's hire car out of a hotel car park in Inverness and made towards the golf club which was situated slightly over twelve miles away. Boyd's trousers, carrying an active listening and location device in the hem, sat unworn on the passenger seat.

Moments later, a secure and encrypted audio alert was sent by the target satellite to Colonel Anna Korobov's computer. On opening the message, she smiled in the sure and certain knowledge that her instructions were being obeyed and Boyd was travelling to the golf club at Inverness with the Ticker computerised intelligence system firmly secured in his hire car. She had no reason to doubt him and every reason to distrust him, but her strength lay in the basement of Pine Lodge in the form of one woman and two children. Yet her weakness lay in her arrogant attitude, her carefree disposition to planning an operation that she now took for granted, and delusions of grandeur that bordered on megalomania.

The time had come to deliver the final blow to Boyd, to seize the Ticker system, destroy him, his wife and family, and escape to the Motherland in an aeroplane piloted by her husband Sergei.

Soon! she thought whilst removing the photograph of her son from a purse inside her handbag. Soon the family name will be restored to its former glory. I shall walk the corridors of the Kremlin with my husband, Sergei and place the framed full-length photograph of our dearly beloved son Mikhail on the wall approaching the President's office. It is the hero's wall. He will be forever revered as a hero of the Motherland and I shall rejoice in the fact that I am once more deemed to be all-knowing, all-powerful, and formidable. It is true. By this time tomorrow, I shall be the heroine of the Russian Federation and truly revered as Russia's greatest ever spymaster.

The Colonel put away her photograph and laid down her thimbles and quilts before instructing her team to make ready for a movement to Inverness Golf Club. In so doing, she instructed three armed guards by the names of Igor, Oleg and Max to prepare to execute the three prisoners once she had the multi-million-pound Ticker system.

In her mind, there had never been any intention to liberate the prisoners. Their lives were irrelevant once she had Ticker in her hands.

Sir Phillip Nesbitt KBE, the Director-General of the nation's Security Service, stood with Antonia Harston-Browne at the bow of a motor cruiser as it ploughed the waters of Loch Ness south from Lochend towards Foyers on the east bank. A posse of armed plain-clothed detectives hastily assembled from Inverness crewed the vessel and studied plans of the landing area as the waters churned, bobbed and bounced, on the journey they undertook.

Simultaneously, a convoy of vehicles led by Boyd made their way south along the A82, reached Fort Augustus, and then travelled north up the B852 on the east side of the loch. The road was known locally as General Wade's Military Road.

On schedule, Boyd pulled into the Upper Foyers car park close to a shop and café. Here, the team abandoned their squad cars and climbed into Boyd's newly acquired brainwave. It was an ageing thirty-two-seater coach that was best described as a rust bucket. The vehicle had been borrowed for the day from Duncan Grant: the brother of Sergeant Angus Grant. For Boyd, it had all the essentials. Namely good signage plus two luggage compartments fitted to the lower part of the vehicle both of which were in good working order.

All aboard, covert radio checks completed, and everyone properly kitted out for the raid, Boyd instructed onward progression and hung on as Angus awkwardly crunched first gear and the vehicle lurched off.

'Angus,' remarked Boyd. 'It has an engine, a radio, and a gearbox. What more could we want?'

'Music!' came the reply as Angus held up a bottle of whisky. 'And a wee dram or two?'

'Give me strength,' chuckled Boyd. 'Just drive, Angus.'

Ten minutes later, Pine Lodge came into view, Angus braked and brought the vehicle to a standstill causing Boyd to transmit, 'Jupiter! We are in position and ready to go!'

'This is Jupiter. I have control. Understood! Stand by! We are withdrawing our technical team. There is no change to the original information. Stand by. Withdrawal taking place.'

'How are they doing that?' asked Angus.

'They're in the woods with their gizmos. They'll retreat from cover and let us know when they are safe. By the way, they probably saved our lives. We're doing it this way because they warned us about the PIDS. We'll just have to wait a short time.'

'We're making ground,' spoken on the radio.

Boyd waited patiently.

'Jupiter is in position. We are all clear. Wait! Wait! Wait!'

A few seconds later a Eurocopter SA 365 Dauphin 2 helicopter, in civilian livery, came into view flying over the Drumnadrochit area. One pilot flew the craft and was accompanied by one officer who worked the thermal imagery camera as well as other cameras and devices on the helicopter. The vessel descended slightly before the pilot radioed, 'Eagle One on plot and standing by.'

Sir Phillip nodded and radioed, 'This is Jupiter! Eagle One, I have that. Bishop, you have control. Execute!' ordered Sir Phillip.

Angus selected first gear and the battered old coach wobbled forward again, accelerated around a bend, and arrived at the entrance to Pine Lodge. Enclosed in three acres of woodland, with occasional clearings, the main building lay at the end of a winding gravel lane situated about half a mile from the main highway. The gravel encircled the Georgian styled dwelling and gave way to a sizeable lush lawn which led gently downhill to the edge of the loch

'Bishop,' radioed Boyd as he checked his wristwatch. 'I have control. Teams one and two, stand by. Two minutes to launch. Team three, take closer order.'

Out on the loch, Jupiter's cruiser turned inland towards Pine Lodge.

Ducking out of sight, Boyd radioed, 'If music is the food of love…'

'Play on!' chuckled Angus activating a tape recorder attached to a loudspeaker on the roof of the coach.

The vehicle careered from side to side as it made its unsteady way into the estate bobbing and bouncing at every bump and pothole in its pathway.

'Holding at twenty miles an hour,' declared Angus.

The faint sound of music emanated from the loudspeakers mounted on the roof.

In the Operations Room of Pine Lodge, the intruder alarm system sounded indicating the electronic shield had been breached.

'PIDS breached,' shouted Dimitry. 'Colonel, we have unauthorised access.'

Startled, Colonel Korobov immediately abandoned her quilting, stood up, and rushed to the window shouting, 'What the hell is that?'

Floundering from nearside to offside, a multi-coloured rusting old coach appeared travelling slowly down the tarmac approach towards the house. The vehicle sported a battered old loudspeaker mounted on the roof and the logo 'CIRCUS' emblazoned on a roof panel above the windscreen. The same logo appeared on both sides of the coach where various shades of corrosion competed with faded images of circus animals for the attention of prospective customers.

'I think they call it a wrap advertisement,' explained Dimitry.

'It's an old wreck but what's it doing here?' queried the Colonel.

'It's a mobile billboard,' chuckled Dimitry. 'The circus is coming to town and any moment now that loudspeaker on the roof is going to announce the next performance and the sale of tickets.'

'Circus?' queried the Colonel.

'Yes, the circus,' giggled Dimitry. 'It's one of those advertisement coaches. They travel around the area just before the circus arrives, advertise themselves, and put posters up everywhere. We've got them in Russia too, you know.'

'Yes, I know,' replied the Colonel. 'It's just what we need. Wait a second, Dimitry. Where's the target?'

Dimitry engaged a computer keyboard, studied the image of a map that filled the screen, and replied, 'Doing as he's been told, Colonel. The subject is approaching Inverness Golf Club.'

'Good!' replied the Colonel. 'What's that I see?' Raising binoculars to her eyes, she continued, 'The coach is empty. Just the driver who is drinking whisky from a bottle. Just what we need – a drunken yob from a stupid circus. Settle down, everyone! I think we've got one of those drunken Scottish morons to contend with. Guards!'

Timofey, Adrian and Dima appeared in the doorway. They were all of military extraction, sported crew cuts and dark suits, and resembled a team of bouncers securing a Glasgow night club.

'Out there on the drive, you'll find a circus coach!' announced Colonel Korobov. 'Be nice. Be firm. But get rid of that drunken idiot and make sure he doesn't come back.'

'Consider it done,' replied Timofey.

In the coach, Angus remarked, 'When are you letting the monkeys out of their cage?'.

Boyd remained on his haunches out of sight but replied, 'Soon!' and then radioed, 'Bishop, I have control. Eagle One activate! Teams One and Two, one minute to launch. Stand by.'

The coach neared the building. The sound of drums beating softly suddenly rent the air when the loudspeakers came into play.

In a display of drunken driving, Angus momentarily steered the coach onto the grass before quickly returning to the tarmac and honking the horn loudly.

Eagle One flew gradually down the length of the loch towards the scene of the impending raid. The observer activated his cameras and zoomed in on proceedings below as he radioed, 'Eagle One! Cameras rolling!'

Timofey, Adrian and Dima, moved along the corridor, into the porch area, and then out onto the gravel frontage. With his hands on his hips, Timofey burst out laughing at the quite ridiculous site he beheld before him.

'This man is a joke!' he said to his colleagues. 'But we will send him packing.'

'Bishop I have control,' radioed Boyd. 'All teams! Mask! Mask! Mask! Stand by for deployment.'

Adrian eased his right hand inside his suit as Timofey and Dima stepped forward with their hands up beckoning the coach to stop.

'Put the gun away,' ordered Timofey. 'It's a drunken clown in an old broken-down rust bucket. We just need to turn him around and point him elsewhere.'

'Volume!' remarked Boyd to Angus as the coach motored onwards.

A finger pushed the volume control to its maximum reach. The sound of music penetrated the atmosphere to the point where the guards suddenly lifted their hands to their ears.

'What are you playing?' voiced Boyd as he bobbed up in full view of the three guards.

'The pipes and drums of the Black Watch, of course,' declared Angus. 'Scotland the Brave!'

'Nice one,' replied Boyd.

'My way of saying welcome to Scotland,' ventured Angus.

'Now!' ordered Boyd.

Angus began to swing the coach feverishly to the offside as he tugged on the steering wheel and Boyd radioed, 'Team One! Strike! Strike! Strike!'

Boyd threw three CS gas canisters from the open nearside window towards the building. One after another, they flew towards their target.

Angus swung the coach to its offside. The nearside luggage compartment burst open allowing Janice Burns and her team of five to roll from the belly of the vehicle and rush the three guards. Janice, Martin Duffy, Mick Turner, Geoffrey Fish, Phil Charlton and Terry Anwhari all wore gas masks and carried firearms.

There was the crunch of a boot on the loose gravel followed by a throaty roar from the team as they connected with the three muscular guards and pushed them to the ground.

Simultaneously, Boyd's gas grenades burst through the windows of the ground floor of the building and exploded into huge clouds of an incapacitating agent.

Inside the building, Dimitry delved into a drawer and removed a handgun. He checked it was fully loaded, pushed it into his belt, and shouted to the Colonel, 'Some circus. We're the clowns! They're the monkeys!'

Eagle One flew in circles above the scene as the observer captured proceedings below and the pilot kept Pine Lodge in his view.

Beneath the Georgian pillars that dominated the front of the building Timofey, Dima and Adrian were putting up a tremendous fight. Having regained their feet, they backed into the porch area with Terry Anwhari throwing his entire body weight into the pack.

Behind the struggling mass, a cloud of CS gas billowed into the rooms, the corridor, and the porch area as it began to slowly invade every inch of the target area.

Struggling violently, Adrian broke free, reached for his pistol, and fired three shots wildly into the air when Terry Anwhari luckily grasped his hand, diverted the shot, and banged the gun hard against a stone support pillar.

Dropping the gun, Adrian headbutted Terry as the two men fought for supremacy.

Timofey screamed, 'Viktor! Dimitry! Colonel!'

'They're armed,' yelled Dima. 'Assistance required!'

There was no response other than a growing balloon of CS gas and the sound of uncontrollable coughing from within.

Wrestling with the steering wheel, Angus heaved to the offside and then swung the circus coach around the nearside corner of the building as it approached the rear kitchen area.

With 'Scotland the Brave' blaring full blast from the loudspeakers, Boyd engaged the internal wireless system and radioed, 'Team Two! Strike! Strike! Strike!'

Boyd threw more gas canisters at the rear of the building. Two canisters crashed through the windows whilst another exploded on the gravel. The side luggage compartment of the coach burst open allowing Anthea Adams and her team to join the fray.

Ricky French, Joe Harkness, Harry Nugent, Tom Richardson, and Hazel Scott were right behind Anthea when she slammed hard against the rear wall, heard gunfire coming from the front of the building, and pushed the safety catch to the off position on her weapon.

The pipes and drums of the Black Watch were at full pelt now with Angus slamming his foot onto the accelerator and hitting the floorboards as the rear tyres spat gravel from the rubber and the back end of the coach swung around on its second approach to the front porch area.

'Team Three! Strike! Strike! Strike!' voiced Boyd.

The cruiser on the loch increased speed and headed towards the east bank and the Pine Lodge landing area.

'Spread out,' shouted Jupiter.

The bow of the cruiser beached on the east bank of Loch Ness

Antonia led the group onto dry land with Sir Phillip moving to occupy the bow of the vessel and use his binoculars to watch proceedings unfold.

'Hold the ground,' screamed Antonia.

At the front of the premises, Timofey had retreated inside the building and was firing indiscriminately at the intruders.

Disarming Adrian, Terry Anwhari tried desperately to completely overpower the Russian guard. Kicking, punching, and struggling, Adrian was on the point of escaping when Martin Duffy delivered a fierce blow to the guard's head.

Adrian's eyes rolled, his heads dropped backwards, and Martin withdrew a set of handcuffs from his trouser belt. Turning the guard over, a set of plastic handcuffs were hastily applied to Adrian with Martin radioing, 'One tango arrested in the porch.'

'Got that!' acknowledged Jupiter.

Nearby, Dima had winded Mick Turner with his knee and then sideswiped Phil Charlton with his handgun. Once free, the muscular Dima stepped inside the building and pointed his handgun at the intruders shouting, 'Get back! Get back!' Then, reaching inside his jacket, he withdrew a hand grenade and threatened, 'I mean it. I'll take you all with me'

Meanwhile, panic ruled every fibre of those in the Colonel's Operations Room.

'Destroy the computer hard drives,' ordered the Colonel. 'They must not get the program.'

Nadia began to destroy the computers and servers that filled one wall of the room whilst Viktor rushed to a gun cabinet, withdrew a Kalashnikov assault rifle, and made for the corridor shouting, 'Enter WORM ESCAPE into the keyboard, Nadia.'

'Worm escape?' queried Nadia.

'Yes,' replied Viktor. 'That's the emergency code. The system will self-destruct once you type that into the keyboard.'

'Oh!' replied Nadia. 'Dimitry! Where are you?'

The Colonel and Dimitry were nowhere to be seen. Neither were Pavel and Talisha. Only the faint glimpse of four figures disappearing into a CS cloud was visible from the computer station.

Unsure, Nadia tapped in the destruction code and stared at the computer screen. Confused, distressed, she didn't know how to respond to the raid taking place.

In the basement of Pine Lodge, Meg and the children were deafened by the noise of gunfire and destruction taking place above them.

'Daddy!' shouted James. 'Daddy is coming for us. I knew he would.'

The noise of repeated gunfire penetrated the walls as Meg clung to her children and said, 'If that is Daddy, pray he's alright.'

225

Izzy broke free, ran to the door, and began battering it with her hands shouting, 'We're here! We're here!'

James joined her and before too long, Meg and the children were making as much noise as they could.

Picking up two enamel drinking mugs, James clattered them together whilst yelling, 'Down here! Down here, Dad! We're in the basement!'

Outside, Angus stamped his foot hard down on the accelerator and headed for the front of the building once more. The tyres gouged the gravel, spirited fragments of broken rock into a flurry of vengeance, and then failed to find purchase on the ground when Angus applied the brakes and the coach skidded. Tragically, the brakes had seen better days, half-heartedly did their job, and failed to stop the front of the coach from climbing the first few steps into the porch and colliding with one of the pillars that dominated the front of the Georgian façade.

There was a rumble then a tumble when the pillar crumbled. Lying at an angle of forty-five degrees, the stone support miraculously wedged itself in a precarious position above the bodies of those below.

There was a rush inside when the attackers and the defenders realised the front of Pine Lodge might collapse at any minute. They were met by a man with a Kalashnikov rifle who stood in the corridor next to another individual holding a grenade in his right hand and threatening to pop the pin with his thumb.

The Kalashnikov moved forward. The grenade shook and was held higher.

Unaware and undisturbed, Boyd was out of the vehicle, through the porch area, and running down the corridor as fast as his legs would carry him with Janice at his side sporting a double-barrelled shotgun every step of the way.

The level of the Kalashnikov dropped to waist height. Viktor's finger curled around the trigger. A thumb unclipped a grenade pin. Adrenalin hit an all-time high.

Two slugs flew from Janice's side by side shotgun and took Viktor out when they thudded brutally into the Russian's chest and blew him into a dozen pieces.

Simultaneously, holding his Gloch 19 at ninety degrees to the horizontal, Boyd let off a salvo of shots that hit Dima who took bullets to the head, chest and shoulder. He was dead before he hit the floor.

'Shots fired!' radioed Boyd from his throat mic. 'Entry made! We are engaging!'

'Welcome to Scotland,' remarked Janice running alongside the Commander.

'Better late than never,' replied Boyd.

'Got that!' from Jupiter out on the loch.

'That's a gamechanger,' observed Antonia standing nearby.

'It certainly is,' proposed Sir Phillip.

Still running flat out, Boyd kicked the grenade as hard as he could into a room used as a library.

Screaming, 'Take cover!' Boyd ran on passing the open doorway.

Janice paused, broke her gun, wiped her gas mask clear, reloaded, and followed Boyd.

Behind her, the clouds of CS gas finally rendered the Russian defence incapable when Nadia stumbled into the corridor, collapsed coughing into a heap, and sat helpless as those around her surrendered. Beaten by the gas and the element of surprise, Russians hands reached skywards as their weapons hit the floor.

A grenade exploded in the library doing untold damage to a thousand novels from yesteryear. The glass windows splintered into as many shards, a chandelier in the centre of the ceiling collapsed to the floor, and a mahogany table flew through the air and smashed into a glass cocktail cabinet. Simultaneously, the computer system finally reacted to Nadia's WORM ESCAPE by finally kickstarting an electronic pulse that travelled around the motherboard and into the servers. One there, it diverted into a secure electronic compartment and ignited a chain reaction which caused the system to explode and catch fire. The explosion merely added to the grenade's blast wave and rippled through the building until it reached the severely damaged column at the porch. Seconds later, the structure dropped a foot towards the ground as gravity fought to win the day and the angle of descent denied calamity due to its wedged position.

Sitting in the driving seat of the coach, Angus gazed at the front of Pine Lodge, unscrewed the bottle of whisky for the first time that day, took a slug, and muttered, 'Duncan! What the hell do I tell him now? He'll never forgive me.'

In the aftermath of the exploding grenade, the remnants of a broken bottle of fifteen years old Scottish whisky dripped carelessly from the cabinet and stained the carpet below.

'Team One taking prisoners at the front,' radioed Phil Charlton. 'Medics required!'

Sir Phillip replied, 'Jupiter has that. Medics One and Two move to the outer marker and wait.'

Back at the Foyers Falls car park, there was an acknowledgement before two army ambulances from the Royal Army Medical Corps fired up and began their short journey to the Pine Lodge entrance. They wouldn't enter the battle zone until told to do so.

At the rear, Anthea and Ricky French were held at the entrance to the kitchen by Igor, Oleg and Max. All three guards were former Russian soldiers recruited into the team for a dangerous and secret operation on foreign soil. Well paid for their ability as well their silence, the trio constantly changed positions as one fired, one reloaded, and the other watched their backs.

Anthea pressed her back hard into the exterior's brickwork, whispered instructions to the team close by and then said, 'On three!'

When Anthea began the count down with 'One!', Igor grew in confidence, stepped forward, and emptied his firearm at the intruders.

'Two!' voiced Anthea.

As Igor retreated into the kitchen to reload, Anthea shouted, 'Three!' and rolled on the ground from one side of the rear door to the other firing a salvo of shots that penetrated the room and hit the woodwork, pots, pans, lightbulbs, and an electric kettle.

In tandem, Ricky French and Terry Anwhari stood away from the brickwork and both fired into the opening.

The result of three individuals all shooting into a narrow gap at the same time resulted in a cacophony of noise, a veritable machine gun like response, and a succession of bullets that struck Oleg in the chest and blew him backwards into the kitchen sink.

His body twisted in its final throes and then slumped to the floor as Igor and Max retreated into the depths of the building reloading on route.

Anthea's team were in and she radioed, 'Team Two! Shots fired at the rear. One tango down. We are engaging. Entrance made.'

Anthea led her team into the rear of the building, fanned out, and pursued Igor and Max.

In an old part of the basement, the Colonel said, 'Count ten bricks along from the doorway and ten bricks up from the floor.'

'What then?' queried Dimitry.

'Push!' replied the Colonel.

Dimitry complied and, to his amazement, realised this part of the basement wall was a secret door leading to a hidden tunnel.

The Colonel led Pavel, Talisha and Dimitry into the secret passageway saying, 'Close it behind you, Dimitry and stay close.'

'Where does it take us?' enquired Pavel.

'To freedom,' replied Colonel Korobov. 'And a mooring where a speedboat is covered with a camouflage tarpaulin.'

'She thinks of everything,' remarked Talisha.

'Except circuses,' ventured Dimitry. 'Come on! We haven't much time.'

'What about the others?' enquired Talisha.

'What about the others?' replied Dimitry. 'Forget them! Just follow the Colonel. She knows what she's doing.'

The four stooped low as the tunnel narrowed and led them away from Pine Lodge towards the east bank of Loch Ness.

At the rear, Anthea's team made good progress hampered only by the need to search and secure each room as they cleared that part of the building. Eerily, there was no sign of the two remaining Russian guards. Igor and Max were nowhere to be seen.

Room by room, the team progressed through the building unaware that Igor and Max had encroached upon the basement where Meg and the children were held captive.

At the front, Boyd reached the entrance to the basement, kicked the door open, and peered down the staircase into a black void.

'Meg! Are you there?'

'Daddy!' came the faint reply from the far end of the basement.

A shot rang out at the precise moment Boyd stepped back to check his Gloch.

The bullet zipped between Boyd and Janice and slammed into the woodwork behind them.

'Get back or the kids get it first,' shouted Igor.

'Can you see him?' asked Janice.

'No!' whispered Boyd. 'It's just a black passage. Have you got a torch?'

'Somewhere on the back of this kit belt,' replied Janice.

'I have a deal for you,' shouted Igor.

'Such as?' probed Boyd.

'My freedom in exchange for your family.'

'I've heard that before,' replied Boyd. 'You can't be trusted.'

Janice stepped away from the top of the staircase and showed the torch to Boyd.

'You can trust me,' shouted Igor.

'How bright?' whispered Boyd of Janice.

'You have to trust me. You don't have a choice,' shouted Igor.

'How many of you are there down there?' shouted Boyd.

A door scraped open and a woman's voice shouted, 'Billy!'

It was followed by the riposte, 'Shut up, woman!'

'Different voice, Janice,' whispered Boyd. 'There's a least two. One in the basement corridor and the other has just opened the door of a room.'

'That's where Meg is,' suggested Janice.

Unclipping his belt torch, Boyd handed it to Janice and whispered instructions before gesturing her to step well back from the doorway.

Simultaneously, Boyd shouted to Igor, 'Okay! I'll take a chance on you. I'm coming down slowly.'

'Throw your weapons down first,' ordered Igor.

Boyd stepped further back, nodded three times to Janice and then sprinted along the corridor and launched himself into the basement area at a truly awesome speed. At the same time, Janice almost collided with Boyd in flight when she stepped into the middle of the corridor above the staircase and shone two brilliant torches into the black chasm.

For a second, Igor was blinded by the light, automatically lifted his hands to his eyes, and felt the butt of Boyd's Gloch smash down on his nose and render him unconscious.

There was a clatter on the staircase behind Boyd when Janice ran down the treads and shoulder-charged the Russian guard to completely close him down.

Kicking a door open, Boyd was faced with Max huddled over the children with a gun skewering into Meg's head near the temple.

'Not an inch,' voiced Max. 'Don't come any closer or she gets it first.'

'Whoa!' replied Boyd standing with his legs wide apart.

'Drop your weapons,' ordered Max. 'The woman out there as well. Both of you. Drop those weapons.'

In the split second that followed, Detective Inspector Anthea Adams rolled into the basement from the kitchen area, came to rest directly beneath Boyd's crotch, and double-tapped two shots into Max's forehead from the prone position.

Max initially fell backwards but then slowly, gradually, almost in slow motion, the Russian soldier turned undercover guard fell flat on his face with two clearly defined bullet holes in his forehead.

'What kept you?' asked Boyd.

'I had to reload,' replied Anthea.

Immediately, Boyd rushed forward to gather his family into his arms as the children went wild with delight and Meg broke down in a fit of tears.

Anthea entered the room, gathered up Max's firearm, and then gestured to Janice saying, 'Give them space and get the medics in. It's over.'

It wasn't over outside when the Colonel and her people began to walk slightly uphill when the light at the end of the tunnel appeared and the Colonel knew they were only yards from the east bank of Loch Ness and ground level.

Reaching the end of the trail, the Colonel pushed her fingers into a gap and pushed a paving stone up an inch or two. On tiptoe, she peered towards the loch, looked around as best she could, and then turned to say, 'Come on! We're safe. Quickly now. Dimitry, I need your help.'

Dimitry stepped forward, holstered his weapon, and heaved both shoulders hard against the paving stone.

Moments later, a shaft of sunlight invited the company above ground. They clambered out of the tunnel onto dry land and waited for the Colonel's orders.

'Where to now?' enquired Dimitry.

'Freeze,' yelled Antonia. 'Stand right where you are and don't move an inch.'

Caught unawares, Dimitry unholstered his weapon, thought better of it when he realised Antonia was not alone and held his hands high. They were surrounded by a team who had been tipped off about the secret tunnel by Duncan Grant: Angus's brother.

Pavel, Talisha and the Colonel set off running in different directions.

On the other side of Loch Ness, on the west bank, approximately two-thirds of a mile from Pine Lodge, a stranger occupying a second-floor bedroom in short term rental accommodation set down his laser range finder and climbed onto a table. The furniture had been deliberately manoeuvred next to a window which offered a good view of the loch and the opposing bank. Securing himself comfortably behind a Chukavin sniper rifle, which boasted a lethal range of sixteen hundred yards, he opened the tripod, steadied the weapon, and took one last view through the telescopic sights. The shooter tugged the short stock into his shoulder, selected his target, and gently squeezed the trigger of the most accurate sniper rifle in the world.

The bullet travelled at a speed in excess of one thousand yards per second across the loch, penetrated the skull of Colonel Korobov, and then smashed into the brickwork of Pine Lodge.

The marksman then patiently used a handheld monocular to view the scene of devastation before closing the tripod, folding his sniper rifle, and sliding the monocular into a leather case in his possession. He made for the car park and his executive styled vehicle.

Moments later, the killer fired the engine and drove leisurely south along the A82 towards Glasgow.

Pavel and Talisha froze at the sound of the unusual weapon and surrendered immediately. They had little choice when the armed squad moved in closer and adopted firing positions. Dimitry shuddered, dropped to his knees, and surrendered his firearm.

The three were taken to the ground and handcuffed.

The virtually headless body of Colonel Anna Korobov lay motionless on the blood-soaked earth. Only her quilts and her thimbles rolled from her bag and threatened the blood seeping from her body.

The helicopter overhead radioed, 'Eagle One to Jupiter. Did you see that?'

'Yes!' replied Sir Phillip. 'Do you have a sighting?'

'Eagle One to Jupiter, we are recording a male individual who has driven south away from the scene in a motor vehicle bearing diplomatic plates, registration number….'

Sir Phillip jumped from the bow of the police cruiser, surveyed the scene, and radioed, 'Ace High! Aces High! I say again Aces High!'

'Including us, Jupiter?' queried Eagle One.

'Yes! Yes!' radioed Sir Phillip. 'Break off the contact. All units break off contact. I have control. All units! Aces High! Aces High!'

'Eagle One copied. Aces High! We're going to touch down at the scene.'

'Eagle One, I have that,' from Jupiter. 'All medics! Attend the scene! Prisoner vans to the scene! Acknowledge, please! Jupiter over.'

Eagle One turned north, swooped low over Pine Lodge, and selected a safe landing pad about a hundred yards from the building.

233

A succession of vehicles journeyed to Pine Lodge from the Foyers car park, joined the ambulances, and travelled to the scene. Some took prisoners into custody. Others took injured parties into their care. Together, they rendered first aid, provided emergency medical procedures, and arranged to take Meg, Izzy and James to Fort George for recovery procedures and appropriate healthcare.

Soldiers attached to another vehicle tended to the dead as Eagle One touched down. Her blades drooped when the engine was switched off and the crew got out of the aircraft to stretch their legs.

Kissing Meg and the children, Boyd said, 'Have you any injuries at all?'

'None!' replied Meg. 'But we are cold, damp, hungry, and probably in shock. And I need a bath and my hair combed.'

Boyd smiled and said, 'That makes two of us. They'll take you to Fort George where they'll check you over and make sure everything is alright. You're in good hands. I'm going to say thank you to some people and then I'll follow the ambulance and see you in Inverness. Okay?'

Reaching for Boyd's hand, Meg replied, 'Yes! Of course! Thank you. We'll see you soon. Is it over? I mean, is everything over?'

'Yes!' replied Boyd. 'I think so. We'll need to sort things out with the bank because right now we're penniless. It will take time, but we'll get back to normal soon. Trust me!'

'I didn't for a while,' ventured Meg. 'I thought you'd gone completely off the rails.'

'And I thought the same of you,' revealed Boyd.

'By the way, Billy,' ventured Meg. 'We're not penniless. There's much more to life than money.'

'How right you are. Do you remember Commander Herbert?'

'Of course,' nodded Meg. 'We named James after him.'

'Well, the easy way to explain what has happened is to tell you that an individual tried to do the same to us as they did to the Commander.'

'Oh, I see,' gasped Meg. 'I remember what happened to the Commander. It was terrible. Now it all makes sense.'

'I'll tell you the full story later,' proposed Boyd.

'Tell everyone 'thank you', Billy.'

'I will.'

As the rear doors of the army ambulance closed, Boyd stepped back and waved the vehicle away before turning his attention to those who had taken part in the operation and given the Boyd family their life back.

Smiling, shaking hands, pausing to offer gratitude and comfort to those who were injured, Boyd finally arrived at the water's edge where Sir Phillip stood with Antonia, Dimitry, Pavel and Talisha.

The headless body of Colonel Korobov lay at their feet.

'Ah! There you are,' remarked Sir Phillip.

'The porch, the building, and the coach,' ventured Boyd. 'I see we have a problem or to be precise, Angus and his brother have. There's a question of damage to be considered.'

'Tell Angus to send you the repair bill and then forward it to me. We'll cover the costs,' replied Sir Phillip. 'It's pennies in the scheme of things. By the way, we saved these three for you, Bishop. They have yet to be formally arrested by a police officer. Would you care to do the honours?'

Suddenly brought back to reality, and not wanting to give Sir Phillip's identity away, Boyd replied, 'I certainly will, Jupiter. Thank you.' Turning to Dimitry, he probed, 'And what was your part in all of this?'

Dimitry held his tongue but Pavel answered, 'Tell him, Dimitry. It's all over for us.'

'Name, rank and number,' replied Dimitry. 'And nothing else.'

'He's the cryptologist who hacked into the bank and changed your account,' revealed Pavel. 'Talisha and I were part of the kidnapping team, but we didn't hurt anyone.'

'You fool!' screeched Dimitry lunging forward.

Boyd held the cryptologist back and said, 'Is that right, Talisha?'

'Yes!' she replied. 'Dimitry, you might as well tell the truth. We'll be out in twelve months once the State arranges a swap: Theirs for ours.'

'Who do you think you are working for?' probed Boyd.

'You know that,' scowled Dimitry. 'We are all Russian intelligence officers. Who do you think we are working for? The Motherland of course!'

Boyd glanced at Sir Phillip and ventured, 'Jupiter!'

Stepping forward, Sir Phillip enquired, 'Who killed the Colonel?'

There was a sudden silence as the three Russians gradually realised what had happened, looked down at the Colonel's body, and then peered across the loch to the other side.

'You, I presume,' replied Dimitry sheepishly.

'Don't be stupid,' intervened Pavel. 'They attacked us in a bus with military precision yet do you really think they used a sniper to kill the Colonel from about a mile away?'

'You killed the Colonel,' declared Sir Phillip. 'Listening to you I get the impression you were all working for the Russian Federation and that Colonel Korobov was in charge of the operation.'

'Correct!' replied Pavel.

'Absolutely,' confirmed Dimitry. 'That's why you'll get only my name, rank and number.'

'We know them already,' declared Sir Philip. 'And I'm afraid you are all wrong. Colonel Korobov brought you all to the UK so that she could exact revenge on one of our number. Because of her rank, her reputation, and her standing in the intelligence community, she fooled you all into thinking it was an operation authorised by Moscow. She even managed to hoodwink your embassy into believing she had the President's blessing. The truth is the operation she led was a private affair. You undertook a rogue operation that did not enjoy the backing of Moscow.'

'But the embassy was in touch with her,' declared Dimitry. 'I was there, I heard her talking. I set up the satellite link for her and heard what was said. The embassy was told to support her. The orders came from Moscow.'

'I know,' replied Sir Phillip. 'She convinced everyone that her kidnap-blackmail operation would be a success. Eventually, Moscow gave her full backing.'

'Then why did they kill her?' enquired Dimitry.

'Because the operation failed when we took you down. You didn't know we were on the case until it was too late. Moscow doesn't want to be part of a failed operation. They don't want problems with the British people, and they don't want to be held to account, internationally, for a failed espionage operation that they can now say was nothing to do with them. Had you been successful and spirited the Ticker system out of the country, you would have been hailed heroes upon your return to the Motherland. The Colonel would have been awarded more medals and then revered by all. Russia would have revelled in the success and stood arrogantly on the world stage shouting, 'Prove it!' Well, we can prove all kinds of things now and a lot of it has been captured on videotape from CCTV systems and helicopters in the skies above. The bad news for you is that once your people realised the game was up, they sent one of their number to dispose of the Colonel. As far as they are concerned now, Moscow didn't know anything about the operation. It was a rogue operation by a gang of Russian intelligence officers in the pay of Colonel Anna Korobov. What happened here today, and in Cumbria recently, has had nothing to do with the Russian Federation. They've covered themselves by removing the Colonel from the equation. After all, she is the only one who knows the truth. Your colleagues played the game both ways until the final dice was thrown and then they used a sniper to rub away the main link to themselves. They've effectively traded you and the Colonel for a potentially trouble-free solution that they are now able to say has nothing to do with them.'

Boyd nodded, glanced at Antonia, and proposed, 'It's time to go. You're all under arrest for being accessories to murder, conspiracy to kidnap, blackmail, hacking into computers, unauthorised possession of firearms, and... Well, I'm not finished yet.'

'Okay,' replied Dimitry. 'Just a minute while I think this through. You mentioned murder. No-one was killed by anyone here.'

'Perhaps not,' replied Boyd. 'I understand from my colleagues that you are called Dimitry and that you are a level seven cryptologist.'

'Perhaps!'

'I'm also aware that a level six cryptologist came before you. Where is he?'

'The Colonel told me he had returned to Russia because of family illness.'

'And if I told you that one of your number murdered him and dumped his body in the loch would you believe me?'

'It wasn't me,' ventured Dimitry. 'It wasn't any of us here.'

'Who do you think it was that murdered your predecessor?' probed Boyd. 'His name was Nikolai, by the way. He sported a tattoo of the hammer and sickle on his shoulder.'

Dimitry looked into Boyd's eyes, sought the truth of the man, glanced at the body of the Colonel, and then replied with the words, 'I think we know who killed him and why.'

'And I think we've just solved a murder for the local police,' suggested Boyd. 'You are all party to that offence in various ways. From a conspiracy of silence to an active coverup. Who knows? A criminal court might be asked to decide. It's not my problem. We can make it yours. Why didn't any of you ask questions of the Colonel? Sorry, but a prosecution barrister might make your life hell and press charges that will not be easy to defend. Silence is not always golden.'

Waiting, studying the faces of those before him, Boyd offered, 'Of course, there's always a way out.'

'We all thought we were working for our country,' stated Dimitry.

'Then you all thought wrong,' replied Boyd who continued. 'They've abandoned you. Do you hear me? You'll be treated as common criminals here in the UK. You won't be treated like prisoners of war engaged in counter-espionage duties for your country. Your countrymen have abandoned you.'

There was a mutter of disapproval and shared glances of incredulity amongst the trio of captured spies.

'Does anyone want to talk to my friends from British Intelligence?' probed Boyd in a matter of fact manner.

'I will,' replied Pavel. 'In fact, we all will. I don't want to spend years in a British jail. What do you want to know?'

'Me?' queried Boyd. 'Nothing! But the lady here is a good listener.'

The red-headed Antonia smiled and replied, 'You three will have to go through the arrest and prosecution procedure with the police and take it from there initially, but I can tell you this.'

'Go on,' suggested Dimitry.

'We can work things out,' replied Antonia. 'You know as well as I do that you can tell us a lot about Russia and its intelligence community. That's your bargaining chip. Your problem is that we have the keys to your locked cells. If you want out, it just takes time, but we can turn the key and unlock the cell for the right person and the right intelligence.'

The three Russians exchanged looks before Dimitry said, 'Okay! Start the clock!'

Boyd turned to Sir Phillip and enquired, 'Jupiter! Anything else?'

'Welcome back,' ventured Sir Phillip with a wry smile. 'Now take them away.'

'Detective Chief Inspector Adams,' shouted Boyd.

'Me!' replied Anthea. 'I'm the DI, not the DCI. You don't have a DCI'

'I do now,' revealed Boyd. 'By the time we get back to London, you'll have that promotion. Janice will be the new DI and Ricky will have his stripes. Now do me a favour.'

'Such as?'

'Process the prisoners and put an evidence file together.'

Shaking her head, Anthea replied, 'I might have guessed. Janice! Ricky!'

The clear-up operation continued as the prisoners were conveyed to Inverness police station. Meanwhile, Antonia and Sir Phillip returned to Fort George via Lochend and a leisurely ride in a cruiser whilst Anthea took responsibility for case preparation.

Cheekily, Boyd hitched a ride in Eagle One to Fort George and Angus McIntosh wondered when and how he should break the news of a damaged Pine Lodge and a decrepit coach to his brother, Duncan.

As night fell, there was a mysterious upheaval in the loch near Pine Lodge. The waters suddenly heaved onto the beach, rushed back into the centre of the loch, and contributed to the continuing enigma that was Loch Ness.

For some, it was the end.

For others, a new dawn was breaking, but the operation was still alive and running.

~

10

The Tate Gallery
Bankside, London
Ten days later.

Andrey Petrov was a Russian by birth having been born in the town of Golokhvastovo a few miles south-west of Moscow. Like many in his business before him, he had attended the Yuri Andropov Red Banner Institute in Moscow where he had learnt the delicate skills of being a spy.

Years later, he was posted to the Russian Embassy, ostensibly as a military attaché, but factually as Head of Station, London. In Russian parlance, he was the 'rezident'. As such, Andrey Petrov, the Head Russian spy in the UK, was responsible for all espionage activities undertaken by his intelligence officers in the United Kingdom.

Dressed in a dark suit and black overcoat, and in his fifties, Andrey sauntered through the corridors and hallways of the Tate Gallery with the air of a confident businessman on his way to meet a client. He stopped here and there to admire the exhibits but, at the appointed place and time, took a seat next to a similarly dressed man who was eyeing a sculpture which dominated the room in which they met.

'Phillip,' remarked Andrey.

'Andrey,' replied the Director-General of MI5.

'Thank you for accepting my invitation to lunch,' ventured Andrey. 'I did not expect you to select an art gallery but here we are now.'

Sir Phillip offered a slight smile and revealed, 'There's a restaurant within the building. It has a wonderful view of the River Thames that I thought you might enjoy. Furthermore, Andrey, we must be seen in public together as opposed to being unseen and in private.'

'Perhaps,' ventured Andrey. 'But the press in the UK are not governed in the same way as they are in Russia. They have much more freedom. I'm sure some of your journalists would love a photograph of us together. It would surely be front-page news.'

'They may know who I am, Andrey, but it's doubtful they will know who you are. Indeed, my friend, I don't think I'm supposed to know who you are.'

Andrey chuckled and asked, 'How are you these days?'

'Well,' offered Sir Phillip. 'What do you want to talk about?'

'Scotland!' replied Andrey.

'I'd recommend it for a holiday,' delivered Sir Phillip. 'Glasgow and Edinburgh are both worth visiting as are Dundee, Perth and Aberdeen.'

'The Highlands?'

'Very hilly,' suggested Sir Phillip.

Andrey looked the other way for a moment, glanced around, and then continued, 'We need to stop playing games. We want our people back.'

'Your people?' probed Sir Phillip. 'I understood they were in the employment of Colonel Anna Korobov or was that merely a device for you to switch on and off as you required.'

'Phillip!'

'Let's get this straight, Andrey,' contended Sir Phillip suddenly. 'You didn't care about Boyd and his family. They were just pawns in a game of chess that you played. You took the Colonel to task for going off the rails but when you heard from her that a state-of-the-art computerised intelligence system was on the table you went from opposing her to supporting her.'

'You are not a stupid man, Phillip, but without access to our people, I have been tasked by my political masters to find out if you can prove what you have just told me. They are trying to work out a response to the UK government. As it is, I decided to abandon normal protocols and approach you directly.'

Sir Phillip removed an envelope from his pocket and passed it to Andrey saying, 'The Colonel was shot by a sniper who drove away in a car bearing a diplomatic number plate. The number is written on the envelope. Keep it. We know who he is and so do you. He has full diplomatic immunity which means that neither he nor the vehicle he was driving at the time can be searched. He cannot be arrested or detained. You asked me to stop playing games so I will ask you to do the same. We have the entire incident captured on video. Do you want me to tell you who the driver of that vehicle is? The British name equivalent is Alex, but then I suspect you know that because you're not a stupid man either. You know what, Andrey, I call checkmate.'

Andrey did not answer. He studied the envelope, recognised the number, and eventually replied, 'Is the cold war dead and buried, Phillip?'

'So, they tell me,' ventured Sir Phillip. 'But power-based politics and competing ideologies persist in a world of ever-changing cultures and beliefs. When nations fall out, who knows what might happen in the scheme of things. Some politicians thrive on emotion, others on fact. They are often uncomfortable bedfellows.'

'Only when the sheets are crumpled,' remarked Andrey.

'You killed the Colonel, Andrey. Thank you! You solved us both a problem that we do not need.'

'I can neither confirm nor deny your accusation,' replied Andrey.

'Do you recall Exercise Mainbrace?' enquired Sir Phillip.

'From way back when?'

'Yes! That's the one,' replied Sir Phillip. 'It was the first large-scale naval exercise undertaken by NATO and was part of a series of exercises that took place during the Cold War. 1952, if memory serves.'

'Correct! Why?' probed Andrey.

'Mainbrace was conducted in September 1952, and involved nine navies from America, Britain, France, Canada, Denmark, Norway, Portugal, Holland, and Belgium,' explained Sir Phillip. 'Its objective was to convince Denmark and Norway that they could be defended against attack from the Soviet Union. The exercise involved simulated airstrikes against the Russian target in the region. Eighty thousand men took part along with two hundred ships and about one thousand aircraft.'

'It almost kickstarted the third world war,' remarked Andrey.

'I'm told the Soviets figured it was the beginning of a pre-emptive strike against them.'

'I believe that was the case,' replied Andrey.

'I know that was the case,' declared Sir Phillip. 'Your nation moved to a war footing.'

'I believe that was the case too,' admitted Andrey. 'What are you driving at Phillip?'

'Russian intelligence officers of the day could covertly decipher NATO transmissions without NATO knowing.'

'Did they really?' frowned Andrey.

'You know they did,' suggested Sir Phillip. 'The cyberwar is not today's latest weapon. It has a history as well you know. Fortunately, your officers concluded that the operation was no more than an exercise and convinced your leaders to withdraw forces and return to normality. The Americans led the move towards war planning through the exercise, but we are grateful that the Soviets reacted by taking a move that took us along the path of peace.'

'Not spoken of much in the west,' remarked Andrey.

'But known of in certain circles of importance,' replied Sir Phillip. 'It is not the kind of news that NATO would wish the west to know of. It would reveal a weakness in the security system that they would find hard to share with their people.'

Andrey hid a smile about to creep across his face, glanced around, and then replied, 'You are well informed.'

'It is my job to be well informed as it is yours.'

Nodding quietly, Andrey replied, 'Sometimes I think it is people like you and me who keep the world at peace. Our political masters make rash decisions. Sometimes the rogues that live amongst us do the same thing and lose the plot altogether. They don't always take into account the problems that may need to be taken care of by people at our level of the game. Most countries have intelligence agencies to covertly investigate potential enemies and prepare for the eventuality of war. Sometimes it is the intelligence agencies that prevent wars by making decisions outside the sphere of politicians and the Statesmen of the world. And that, my friend, is a fact.'

'As you did recently,' added Sir Phillip.

A silence passed between the two men before Andrey asked, 'There's something else I need to ask.'

'Such as?'

'One of our cleaners at the embassy in Kensington has gone missing. I wondered if you knew anything?'

'A cleaner? I'm sorry, Andrey, I can't help you there. Perhaps your cleaner is ill and just taken a few days off work. Mind you, if she is nowhere to be found, you could report her to the police as a missing person. They would investigate her disappearance if it came to that.'

'Really?' posed Andrey.

'Really,' replied Sir Phillip.

'It's just that her father has gone missing from his home in Moscow at the same time.'

'My goodness,' declared Sir Phillip. 'I can't help you there either, I'm afraid, Andrey. Presumably, they are together?'

'I thought you might know,' suggested Andrey.

'Me?' queried Sir Phillip. 'No, not at all. I've no idea what you are talking about, Andrey.'

Silent, the Russian spy chief held his tongue, studied the face of his adversary, and then looked away.

A short time later, Andrey ventured, 'Phillip! What is it that you are looking at?'

'The sculpture?' queried Sir Phillip.

'Yes, the sculpture on the stand in front of us,' replied Andrey.

'Orpheus by a sculptor named Hepworth. It's what they call an abstract sculpture.'

'Yes, I can see that,' declared Andrey. 'What is it trying to tell us?'

'Orpheus features three things, Andrey. By the way, Hepworth spent her career carving in the 1950s.'

'Ah! How interesting,' observed Andrey. 'They say the Cold War began in 1947 and ended in 1991. This Hepworth lady must have been a sculptor all that time.'

'She started to use sheet metal and string, as well as wood,' explained Sir Phillip. 'She called this one Orpheus after the ancient Greek musician and poet of the same name. The sculpture brings together ideas of harmony between modern technology, musical composition and Greek myth. They are represented by the components of the sculpture namely copper alloy, cotton string, and a wooden base.'

'Harmony?' queried Andrey. 'Peace!'

'Not quite!' replied Sir Phillip. 'The Greek musician would have told you that it's a combination of simultaneously sounded musical notes that produce a pleasing effect.'

'I see,' nodded Andrey. 'So, to achieve harmony, the notes have to work together to makes things work correctly?'

'Close enough for me,' declared Sir Phillip.

'Our people,' probed Andrey. 'They are alive and well?'

'Mostly,' revealed Sir Phillip. 'Casualties were taken on both sides. Your side took a couple of fatalities, I'm sorry to say. But it's a game, isn't it? That's what you called it.'

'We call it a game, but it's not,' ventured Andrey. 'I take it you have talked to our people: the ones who were not killed?'

'Yes!'

'Then we can never use them as intelligence officers again,' noted Andrey.

'It's not for me to make decisions for you,' replied Sir Phillip.

'They have family, friends, and homes to go to,' suggested Andrey. 'They were duped by a megalomaniac.'

'And you would like us to repatriate them?'

'Is it possible, my friend?'

'Achievable in time,' revealed Sir Phillip. 'But it will depend on the politics in play and when our leaders decide to make such decisions.'

'Unless we can create harmony, and all reach a pleasing effect?'

'I take it you like the sculpture?' proposed Sir Phillip.

'It's why you brought me here, isn't it?'

'Yes,' replied Sir Phillip. 'I wanted you to understand Orpheus.'

Andrey studied the sculpture for a moment and then enquired, 'Would you join me in moving towards the repatriation of our people?'

'Only if you could guarantee their safety,' contended Sir Phillip. 'It would be the wrong step to take if any of them had an accident of some kind and disappeared from the radar for no apparent reason.'

'It might bring about a sense of harmony between our two countries,' suggested Andrey.

'I'd support that movement,' revealed Sir Phillip. 'Before I forget, I have something for you.'

'For me?'

'Yes, for you. I found it on the shores of Loch Ness. I think it may have fallen out of someone's bag.'

Sir Phillip handed over a porcelain thimble which Andrey took hold of, examined with affection, and replied, 'Thank you, Phillip. This one brings back so many good memories of someone when they were much younger. It was her favourite thimble. Harmony? Yes, I can certainly see why you picked Orpheus and an art gallery for our meeting. It is something we both need to work for.'

'Agreed!' declared Sir Phillip. 'Lunch?'

'Only if I can try some British roast beef and Yorkshire pudding.'

'Then I will try that good old Russian favourite of mine: Salmon and parsley sauce.'

'With a slug of vodka?'

'Just this once,' chuckled Sir Phillip. 'And in the interests of harmony.'

As the two men made their way to the restaurant, Boyd was driving his family to Newcastle airport and a date with a beach somewhere in the sunshine.

He had a full tank of fuel in a newly acquired dark blue Porsche Cayenne, money in his pocket, money in the bank, his wife by his side, and his children in the back of the car. A world that had been turned upside down for the Boyd family had been rectified and was gradually nearing normality as a result of friendship, comradeship, leadership, luck, enduring love that knew no boundaries, and – at the request of the Director-General - the direct involvement of Her Majesty's Treasury.

The Boyd family were no longer torn apart.

Driving, Boyd glanced in the rear-view mirror and realised that Izzy and James had fallen asleep. Even Meg had dropped off, slumped down the passenger seat, and was far away in the land of dreams.

Boyd thought back to his younger days and allowed his mind to take him to those first steps in his chosen career.

Dillon, he thought. Police Constable John Dillon! I was just like him when I started years ago. I wanted everything to happen immediately. Well, somewhere that young man is walking the beat with his Sergeant. He's no longer on dead-end street. Young Dillon has made some great arrests, found a fire in his belly, and now has the confidence to look the job in the face and get on with it. He'll do well, will the boy.

Pulling out to overtake a wagon, Boyd realised how so many people had been part of the last few months of his life. Each one had played their part. Some had contributed to his mental downfall, his forgetfulness, and his lack of common sense. He'd dealt with the paraffin man and recognised a severe and unique mental health problem in that individual. Yet he had failed to recognise failings in himself, declined to diagnose his shortcomings, and plunged into an abyss that he had never visited before and had no wish to visit again. Others had risen to his rescue and a few – those special ones – had always been there for him.

He wondered if the characters he had met had, directly and indirectly, influenced his decisions, twisted his mental health, weakened him, or strengthened him. How would he ever know because one thing was for certain, he didn't want to take that journey again.

'Eduardo Menzies!' remarked Boyd. 'Arrested in possession of stolen jewellery from various burglaries in the north of England. Wanted on a European arrest warrant because it was known he was part of a gang responsible for smuggling diamonds. Now to appear in a Dutch court charged with theft of diamonds and smuggling before appearing in a UK court to face British offences. And Dubois, the circus owner? Well, he was found to be innocent in all respects. Just misled by those he had employed. And the Carlisle victim – the owner of the jewellery shop in Botchergate – had been charged with attempted fraud. John Dillon's suspicions had proved correct.

Why did I get involved? thought Boyd. I should have left it to Stan Holland and his team. But that's me, I suppose. I knew my mind was going, didn't know how to get out of the predicament I had been trapped in, and reverted to the thing I knew best because it was the easy way out for me. Catching the criminals I could see before me and not those online somewhere in the shadows.

Driving on Boyd, turned off the main road and headed towards the airport as he chuckled to himself saying, 'Here am I thinking of my mental health. What do I know about mental health problems?'

Boyd turned left, reduced speed, and took a ticket for the long stay car park.

I'm back, thought Boyd. According to my saviour: one Phillip Nesbitt, I'm back. How can I ever repay the people who brought me back?

'We're here,' shouted Boyd. 'It's holiday time. Come on Izzy. James, can you help me with the suitcases? Meg!'

Meg stirred, stretched her arms and chuckled, 'You mean we're at the airport ready for the flight. We're not there yet.'

'I know,' professed Boyd. But there's one thing you need to know.'

'What's that, Billy?'

'I'm back! Come on. We need a holiday. Let's go!'

The End…. Nearly…

~

You are invited to join Paul Anthony as he looks back on some of his real-life experiences as a detective in Cumbria and elsewhere. They are consolidated in 'Author's Notes' and indicate how some of these 'notes and memories' have inspired Paul Anthony thrillers over the years. The author recalls some true events that he experienced. They are particularly relevant to thimbles, pyromania and a case of pyrophilia that he dealt with in the dim and distant past.

~

Author's Notes

~

Thimbles, Pyromania and Pyrophilia.

~

The Thimble

Some years ago, as a detective working in the Regional Crime Squad, I attended a course on antique identification at Exeter University from which I travelled to various locations in the south-west to enjoy 'hands-on' learning. In the years that followed, as the 'RCS antique man', I became deeply embroiled in various antique enquiries throughout the UK and recall dealing with a 'theft of antique thimbles' case. In later years, thimbles took on the meaning of which you may now be aware.

I remember studying and then writing a paper about a 'Meissen Thimble' that I had encountered on my journey. Meissen is a town of approximately 30,000 people and is situated on the banks of the River Elbe, in Dresden, Saxony, Germany. The town is the home of Meissen porcelain which was first manufactured in 1710. It is derived from extensive local deposits of china clay (kaolin) and potter's clay (potter's earth) and was the first high-quality porcelain to be produced outside of the Orient.

In today's antique world you might easily find yourself paying between £3,000 and £5,000 for a top-quality Meissen porcelain thimble.

Yet what on earth has a thimble to do with the book you have just read. I'm sure you've already worked it out but let me explain 'thimbles' to you.

Intelligence work is seldom discussed 'outside the office' but on rare occasions when it is, codewords may well be used to describe people, events or places. I decided 'The Thimble' would be a good euphemism to describe an individual who would push, persuade, and drive a needle to do a job. In the world of covert intelligence gathering, where codewords are part of a hilarious secret language, a thimble surely supervises a needle when one is engaged in making something – sewing for instance. Getting the job done properly by a show of strength when that finger pushes the needle through is exactly what a thimble is primarily used for.

If a needle is the code word for a spy, then the thimble is the supervisor who inspires and drives their operative - the needle - to complete the job.

But there's much more to thimbles than meets the eye as my research suggests.

In China, a single steel needle from the time of the Han Dynasty (206BC – 202AD) was found in a tomb in Jiangling. There were no needles with it so one wonders if the thimble recovered was used in sewing, or did it have another use that we are not aware of? It's likely, however, that thimbles were in common use at this time. The earliest known thimble, in the form of a simple ring which also dates back to the Han Dynasty, was discovered fairly recently during the Cultural Revolution of the People's Republic of China. The item was recovered from a commoner's grave and this suggests widespread use of the thimble as opposed to use by the elite or wealthy nobility only.

It seems that neither the Romans nor the Greeks used metal thimbles, so I rather suspect they used strong leather finger guards, or gloves, for sewing, making, and repairing their illustrious collection of clothing. It's interesting to note that there is no archaeological data linking metal thimbles to any Roman site.

According to the United Kingdom Detector Finds Database, thimbles dating to the 10th century have been found in England, and they were in widespread use in this country by the 14th century. Aligning 'thimbles' with spies leads me to the revelation that Queen Elizabeth 1 (1533-1603) had her own 'watchers'. It was a network of agents (spies) who intercepted letters, cracked codes, and captured possible dissenters to protect the crown in secret. The network formed the original surveillance state in the United Kingdom. I wonder if they used 'thimbles' and 'needles' when discussing their work privately?

Queen Elizabeth I is said to have given one of her ladies-in-waiting a thimble set with precious stones. This would indicate the esteem in which such a person was held by the Queen since metal thimbles were usually made of brass. The first centres of thimble production were those places known for brassworking, such as Nuremberg in the 15th century, followed by Holland two hundred years later.

Thimbles are usually made from metal, leather, rubber, and wood, and even glass or china. Early thimbles were sometimes made from whalebone, horn, or ivory. Natural sources were also utilised such as marble, bog oak, or mother of pearl. Rarer works from thimble makers utilised diamonds, sapphires, or rubies. Advanced thimble makers enhanced thimbles with semi-precious stones to adorn the apex or along the outer rim. Adornments are sometimes made of cinnabar, agate, moonstone, or amber. Thimbles soon became collectables.

From the 16th century onwards, silver thimbles were regarded as an ideal gift for ladies.

Early Meissen porcelain and elaborate, decorated gold thimbles were also given as 'keepsakes' and were usually quite unsuitable for sewing. This tradition has continued to the present day. In the early modern period, thimbles were used to measure spirits, and gunpowder, which brought rise to the phrase 'just a thimbleful'.

Prostitutes used them in the practice of thimble-knocking where they would tap on a window to announce their presence. Thimble-knocking also refers to the practice of Victorian schoolmistresses who would tap on the heads of unruly pupils with a thimble.

Before the 18th century, the small dimples on the outside of a thimble were made by hand punching, but in the middle of that century, a machine was invented to do the job. If one finds a thimble with an irregular pattern of dimples, it was likely made before the 1850s. Another consequence of the mechanisation of thimble production is that the shape and the thickness of the metal changed. Early thimbles tend to be quite thick and to have a pronounced dome on the top. The metal on later ones is thinner and the top is flatter.

Collecting thimbles became popular in the UK when many companies made special thimbles to commemorate the Great Exhibition held in the Crystal Palace in Hyde Park, London. In the 19th century, many thimbles were made from silver; however, it was found that silver is too soft a metal and can be easily punctured by most needles. Charles Horner solved the problem by creating thimbles consisting of a steel core covered inside and out by silver so that they retained their aesthetics but were now more practical and durable. He called his thimble the Dorcas, and these are now popular with collectors. There is a small display of his work in Bankfield Museum, Halifax, England.

During the First World War, silver thimbles were collected from 'those who had nothing to give' by the British government and melted down to buy hospital equipment.

People who collect thimbles are known as digitabulists. I think, for a little while, in creating the book cover, I became a digitabulist.

One superstition about thimbles says that if you have three thimbles given to you, you will never be married.

Thimblettes (also known as rubber finger, rubber thimbles and finger cones) are soft thimbles, made predominately of rubber, used primarily for leafing through or counting documents, banknotes, tickets, or forms. They also protect against paper cuts as a secondary function. Unlike thimbles, the softer thimblettes become worn over time. They are considered disposable and sold in boxes. The surface is dimpled with the dimples inverted to provide better grip.

On 13 June 1995, Sotheby's sold a Meissen thimble adorned with two pugs for £10,350.

The thimble is a unique piece of kit.... In many of its various forms. But they all have one thing in common. If you remove the needle you don't need the thimble.

~

Pyromania

~

The term pyromania comes from the Greek word pyr (fire).

Pyromania is an impulse control disorder in which individuals repeatedly fail to resist impulses to deliberately start fires to relieve tension or for instant gratification. It is similar to, but distinct from, arson, which is the deliberate setting of fires for personal, monetary or political gain. Pyromania is perhaps closer to an element of mental health as opposed to an act of blatant criminality.

Pyromaniacs start fires to induce euphoria and often fixate on institutions of fire control like fire stations and firemen. It is actually a type of impulse control disorder, along with kleptomania, intermittent explosive disorder, and others. Pyromania is also known as 'Jomeri's Syndrome', named after a psychologist who studied and developed the first forms of treatment for the disorder.

There are specific symptoms that separate pyromaniacs from those who start fires for criminal purposes or due to emotional motivations not specifically related to fire. Someone suffering from this disorder deliberately and purposely sets fires on more than one occasion, and before the act of lighting the fire the person usually experiences tension and an emotional build-up. When around fires, a person suffering from pyromania gains intense interest or fascination and may also experience pleasure, gratification or relief. Another long-term contributor often linked with pyromania is the build-up of stress. When studying the lifestyle of someone with pyromania, a build-up of stress and emotion is often evident, and this is seen in teenagers' attitudes towards friends and family. At times it is difficult to distinguish the difference between pyromania and experimentation in childhood because both involve pleasure from the fire.

Most studied cases of pyromania occur in children and teenagers. There is a range of causes, but an understanding of the different motives and actions of fire-setters can provide a platform for prevention. Common causes of pyromania can be broken down into two main groups: individual and environmental. This includes a complex understanding of factors such as individual temperament, parental psychopathology, and possible neurochemical predispositions. Many studies have shown that patients with pyromanias were in households without a father figure present.

The appropriate treatment for pyromania varies with the age of the patient and the seriousness of the condition. For children and adolescents, treatment usually is cognitive behavioural therapy sessions in which the patient's situation is diagnosed to find out what may have caused this impulsive behaviour. Once the situation is diagnosed, repeated therapy sessions usually help continue to a recovery. Other important steps must be taken as well with the interventions and the cause of impulsive behaviour. Some other treatments measures include parenting training, over-correction/satiation/negative practice with corrective consequences, behaviour contracting/token reinforcement, special problem-solving skills training, relaxation training, covert sensitisation, fire safety and prevention education, individual and family therapy, and medication. The prognosis for recovery in adolescents and children who suffer from pyromania depends on the environmental or individual factors in play but is generally positive. Pyromania is generally harder to treat in adults, often due to lack of cooperation by the patient. Treatment usually consists of more medication to prevent stress or emotional outbursts in addition to long-term psychotherapy. In adults, however, the recovery rate is generally poor and if an adult does recover it usually takes a longer time.

A 1979 study by the Law Enforcement Assistance Administration found that only 14% of fires were started by pyromaniacs and others with mental illness. A 1951 study found that 39% of those who had intentionally set fires had been diagnosed with pyromania.

~

Pyrophilia

~

As a Detective Constable in Penrith CID, many years ago, I recall carrying several 'arson crime reports' relative to a long-term arsonist who was difficult to catch. In the end, he was caught via a process of illumination, or was it elimination? All sightings, witness interviews, enquiries about people, and suspicions eventually pointed to one man. The all-important gut feeling grew and put the suspect in the frame. Like the fictional character, Simon Woods – the paraffin man – the offender had a child's mind in an adult's body. That does not define a person suffering from Pyrophilia because every case is different, just like every offender is different. That said, I know now he probably suffered from Pyrophilia, which was a condition not known of in the time to which I refer. It is the only time I ever came across a case of Pyrophilia.

Pyrophilia is a relatively uncommon mental condition in which the subject derives gratification from fire and fire-starting activity. It is distinguished from pyromania by the gratification being of a sexual nature. Participating in the aftermath of fires might be sexual or even contain a sexual arousal component.

Some described cases of Pyrophilia include fantasies or talk of setting a fire. In other instances, the patient may derive arousal primarily from setting or watching their fire.

Pyrophilia has been diagnosed in very few instances and is not fully accepted by the general psychological community.

In the case outlined in this book, I've tried to get as near to my experience of Pyrophilia as possible to develop a normal criminal tale of 'fire' into something more academic and interesting for the reader. I vividly recall the day I arrested the offender described. I reckoned him to be childlike and interviewed him on the street in a similar manner to that which is described in the pages you have just turned. The experience was unique and has never been experienced since.

Sources: Personal experience, Wikipedia, Black's Health Journal, and Aberdeen University.

~

Paul Anthony Reviews

~

'One of the best thriller and mystery writers in the United Kingdom today'....

Caleb Pirtle 111, International Bestselling Author of over 60 novels, journalist, travel writer, screenplay writer, and Founder and Editorial Director at Venture Galleries.

~

'Paul Anthony is one of the best Thriller Mystery Writers of our times!'...

Dennis Sheehan, International Bestselling Author of 'Purchased Power', former United States Marine Corps.

~

'When it comes to fiction and poetry you will want to check out this outstanding author. Paul has travelled the journey of publication and is now a proud writer who is well worth discovering.' ... Janet Beasley, Epic Fantasy Author, theatre producer and director - Scenic Nature Photographer, JLB Creatives. Also Founder/co-author at Journey to Publication

~

'Paul Anthony is a brilliant writer and an outstanding gentleman who goes out of his way to help and look out for others. In his writing, Paul does a wonderful job of portraying the era in which we live with its known and unknown fears. I highly recommend this intelligent and kind gentleman to all.' ...

Jeannie Walker, author of the True Crime Story 'Fighting the Devil', 2011 National Indie Excellence Awards (True Crime Finalist) and 2010 winner of the Silver Medal for Book of the Year True Crime Awards.

~

'To put it simply, Paul tells a bloody good tale. I have all his works and particularly enjoy his narrative style. His characters are believable and draw you in. Read. Enjoy'....

John White, Reader and Director at Baldwins Restructuring and Insolvency.

~

'Paul Anthony's skills as a writer are paramount. His novels are well-balanced throughout, all of which hold the reader with both dynamic and creative plots and edge-of-your-seat action alike.

His ability to create realistic and true-to-life characters are a strength lacking in many novelists that pen stories based on true events or real-life experience. He is a fantastic novelist that will have you craving for more! Get his books now...a must-have for all serious readers!'

Nicolas Gordon, Screenwriter - 'Hunted: The enemy within'.

~

'Paul Anthony has been working with the Dyslexia Foundation to develop a digital audio Library, he has been very generous in giving his time and expertise for free. As a long-time fan of Paul's work, it was very altruistic of Paul to allow us to use one of his excellent books. We have recently turned 'The Fragile Peace' into our first audiobook, to be used in an exciting project to engage non-readers into the world of literacy. The foundation has an audiobook club that will be running in Liverpool and Manchester and Paul again has been very generous with his time in agreeing to come and talk to the audiobook club about his book The Fragile Peace. The Foundation and clients are very appreciative of the support of the author Paul Anthony.

Steve O'Brien, C.E.O. Dyslexia Foundation,

~

This guy not only walks the talk, but he also writes it as well. Thrillers don't get any better than this...

Paul Tobin, Author, novelist and poet.

~

The UK ANTI-TERRORIST HOTLINE
~

If you see or hear something that doesn't sound quite right, don't hesitate. You may feel it's nothing to get excited about but trust your instincts and let the police know.

~

Remember, no piece of information is considered too small or insignificant.

~

If you see something suspicious – tell the police.

~

'Suspicious activity could include someone:
Who has bought or stored large amounts of chemicals, fertilisers or gas cylinders for no obvious reason…?
Who has bought or hired a vehicle in suspicious circumstances…?
Who holds passports or other documents in different names for no obvious reason…?
Who travels for long periods, but is vague about where they're going…?

~

It's probably nothing, but if you see or hear anything that could be terrorist-related trust your instincts and call the Anti-Terrorist Hotline on 0800 789 321.

~

The UK Anti-Terrorist Hotline
0800 789 321

~

THE END…

Until the next time….

Printed in Great Britain
by Amazon